# Bitter for Sweet

*A NOVEL*

# DARYL POTTER

Paper Stone Press
Oakville, ON, Canada
www.paperstonepress.com
Published 2022



Paperback: 978-1-990388-02-6  eBook: 978-1-990388-05-7
Hardcover: 978-1-990388-03-3  Audiobook: 978-1-990388-06-4
Large Print: 978-1-990388-04-0

*Bitter for Sweet* was first published in Canada. Canadian spelling conventions are maintained throughout.

The novel's epigraph is by Stephen Crane. I first read this poem in the *Concise Anthology of American Literature*, 2nd edition, edited by George McMichael (New York: Macmillan Publishing Company, 1985). Crane's original work is now in the public domain. The Poetry Foundation refreshed my memory of this work with the following online resource: *https://www.poetryfoundation.org/poems/46457/in-the-desert-56d2265793693*, accessed on July 14, 2021.

Edited by Amelia Wiens of Amelia Wiens Editing
Proofread by S. Robin Larin of Robin Editorial
Map designed by Daryl Potter and Jackson Potter
Cover and typeset by Damonza

*For Mackenzie,*

*who taught me*
*about the muscle kind.*

*In the desert*
*I saw a creature, naked, bestial,*
*Who, squatting upon the ground,*
*Held his heart in his hands,*
*And ate of it.*
*I said, "Is it good, friend?"*
*"It is bitter—bitter," he answered;*

*"But I like it*
*"Because it is bitter,*
*"And because it is my heart."*
*Stephen Crane, "In the Desert"*

ERETZ-ISRAEL
1st Century BCE
The Great Sea
Sidon
Damascus
Tyre
Ituraea
Akko
GALILEE
Dora
Strato's Tower
SAMARIA
Jordan River
NABATAEA
Joppa
JUDEA
Jerusalem
Jericho
Ashkelon
Dead Sea
Gaza
IDUMEA
Ein Gedi
Beersheba
ZIN VALLEY
ARABAH
NABATAEA
NABATAEA
Petra/Raqmu
N
LEGEND
REGION
River, Lake, or Sea
City/Village

# 1
## 77 BCE

THE GIRL FLED across the desert.

The sand and wind erased all sound but the rasp of air in her throat. She ran and did not stop. A Moabite followed.

The girl's throat burned and her legs burned and still she ran. Where the desert was hard, she ran faster. Where the ground grew soft, she stumbled, recovered, and then ran again. Whatever the ground, the man did not stop his pursuit.

In addition to the Moabite, her people were far behind her, along with the other Moabite raiders. Her people were not dead yet. She was too far gone to hear their cries now, but she did not believe that they could all be dead so soon. Not yet.

She ran, and all she could hear was the desert wind in

her throat and the slap of her feet when the ground turned to stone. Her heart also turned to stone, and still she ran.

❧

A great creature mounted the sky on black wings that stretched a span of nine feet and more. It rode the high desert heat with terminal feathers stiff like burnt fingers, feeling the sky for rising updrafts to carry it higher and higher. Its yellow-rimmed eyes stared from a featherless head as though it were the victim of some scourge or had been scarred by close views of horror.

The bird and its kin claimed this treeless waste as home. The Nabataeans also knew this land. They knew its sand and rock like the birds knew its columns of heated air.

There was a place of burning in the desert, and tendrils of smoke entered the sky. The birds passed over and on from that place.

From that place of burning, there stretched a trail and signs of pursuit that led to a place of slaughter. Death lay fresh. Eight satisfied men in blood-stained clothing rested with their spoils. The raiders' hunched postures suggested some form of dissolute alliance with the yellow-eyed birds passing overhead.

A second, thin trail led in a different direction. This was the off-trail of a child and the one raider who pursued her. The track of this pair angled towards the desert's worst quarter.

In the late afternoon, the birds passed over the carnage again. The eight men below had burned their victims. The smoke was another column of heat entering the sky. This manner of men was unknowable to the birds. To mate then murder, turning the meat to ash, uneaten, a banquet ruined, none satiated, was abhorrent.

The birds swept on and found the one man and the child, the man still pursuing, the child still running. A great distance lay between this pair. It was not yet the time for birds.

Later that day, the birds returned once again in hopes of finding fresh tragedy without fire. They found the eight killers on foot, tracking the trail of their companion.

The birds floated on and found that the two who charted their own route across the desert were now together. At the pace of humans, the two—man and child— were hours ahead of the eight. The lone raider had finally caught the girl.

The birds circled to study this strange new scene. Low rock outthrust from the heart of the earth and broke the smooth regularity of the ground. The rock barely breached the sea of sand. Stone looked in its various places like the overturned hulls of half-sunken ships. The rose-coloured rock signalled a beginning to the mountains that stood squat in the heat-shimmering distance.

In this place of overturned stone hulls lay a gully where the wind had scooped out sand down to the desert's hard base. This place so created was not a place for hiding, not from the birds, not from the sun, not from the eyes of the eight that would arrive by nightfall. The shallow hollow lay exposed, revealing the pair within.

❧

From low ground, the girl rose, released now from the man who had pursued her. Her legs trembled, and her eyes shone in bright slanting sunlight. They shone with fear and something else. Her head covering was in disarray and trailed about her. A long tear in her robe exposed one shoulder. One side of her face began to swell. Her hands shook even more than her legs. From wrists to fingertips, she glistened with blood. Long fingers stretched out as though each wet tip was loath to touch the other.

The girl, Cypros, climbed up to the flat place and stood looking back the way she had come. She stood with her hands outstretched like a priest of al-Qaum before a rising or setting sun, feeling what little wind the desert had to offer. Her eyes were large and dark. Even in fear, they bore a translucent quality. Blood filled one eye, but it would heal. She started to wipe her eyes, then saw the blood and stopped. She stood as before, hands and fingers outstretched, tears tracking cheeks unchecked.

She saw no sign yet of her assailant's companions. The pathless desert recorded only two sets of footprints. She knew the others would come. They would finish with the caravan and her family and then find her trail. They would come.

The girl bottled what rose within. She used each shoulder to dry her cheeks. She studied the back trail. Then she looked down on the one raider who had pursued her to this place.

In the shallow trench below, he rocked up on one hip and made as though to rise. He held the two halves of his throat closed with slippery hands studded by a layer of coarse sand and kicked his legs against the sides of this unexpected grave. His eyes strained in his head as though seeking an exit. Each time he gasped, bloody foam breached his nose and lips and a weak sound like a cry came not from his mouth but the wound in his throat, and then he lost his grip on the unnatural liquid opening. Each resealing of the wound with clumsy fingers was less successful than the last. The wound grew more slippery, and his kicks became weaker as he lost the battle to gain air and retain blood. He could only do one. The need for air overcame that for blood, and he gasped from both his mouth and the new opening. He did so a second time, a strange new mouth obscenely gaping at hot, dry air and countering the arid with a wet welcome. His legs kicked fiercely, then less so, then not at all. He lay back down and stared at the falling sun as though to match its relentless gaze, and the girl watched him the while.

Once sure, Cypros returned to the hollow and retrieved her small blade. She wiped it clean on the man's tunic and returned it to its place, bound up in her hair.

She rewrapped her head covering, unmindful now of her hands. She took the man's remaining water. She did not drink it but emptied it on the ground before him. She pierced the water skin, then cast his blade and the skin out into the desert.

She climbed back onto level ground a second time. She looked again at her back trail, then turned in the opposite direction and began to walk. There was a hitch in her breathing, but her eyes, now dried, stayed dry. She charted a course farther into the sand. Some miles deeper into the desert, the hitch in her breathing settled into a barely voiced union between a cry and hiss that no one heard but her.

She was thirteen years old and alone. She intended to marry a Jewish governor's son next year. Eight raiders pursued her.

# 2

## 77 BCE

THE GREAT BLACK birds of the desert landed on prehistoric feet near the dead raider's body. They trailed now cumbersome wings as they stepped about, uncertain and cautious. Tilted and nodding heads inspected the body from a distance. Slowly, they put their wings away.

Next, there came a time of hissing and posturing—a rehearsal of dominance. They moved on stick-like limbs as though unfamiliar with the awkward procedure of walking.

In time, the birds resolved the formalities between them. Then came other sounds, sounds of clicking and softer notes yet.

⌘

As the sun rose the following day, the girl's wilting shape stumbled through an empty land. She had walked all through the night. Her hands clenched and unclenched. A quiver passed over her throat, but she made no sound.

Cypros looked ahead and noticed a long shadow that stretched across the desert towards her. At the shadow's base stood a wide, squat pillar of stone—a natural tower that dominated the surrounding desert. The peak of this tower lay flat-topped and bare—a place for the worship of al-Qaum.

The sun continued to rise as she walked, and the shadow retreated as though drawing her to al-Qaum's platform.

She bowed her head as she approached the tower. She came alone in the desert before the Nabataean god of war, of night, of nomads and caravans.

"Al-Qaum is our god," her father had told her many times, "and his name means *the people*." The divine and mortal duality of al-Qaum was fundamental to his identity.

Cypros came to the base of the tower and sat down in its shadow. Her elbows rested on her knees, and her arms extended in front of her.

*Al-Qaum does not change.*

She might have said it out loud.

Her family had changed, in Damascus, before this long journey south, through the desert.

*Why did you change?*

Again, she might have spoken aloud, but there was no one to hear her. A sob seized her throat and burst out, and then she stifled further emotion. She wiped her cheeks on her shoulders again. She swallowed down the pain that tormented her. Sorrow swamped the fear that had driven her all through the previous night.

She tried not to think about the bodies in the desert,

their caravan raided, the murders, and other atrocities. She knew that those who had raised her and loved her were gone. She did not need to witness the Moabites' actions to know. Everyone knew the reputation of that foul nation. She also knew that the other raiders would follow their companion. They would continue after her when they found his body.

She turned her mind to what her people had done—how the Nabataeans had changed.

Her people were the people of the vast and secret caravan routes through the world's Great Desert. Theirs was the Empty Quarter. Theirs was the mastery of moving from sea to sea where others became lost and died in dry places.

"We are the people of al-Qaum," she said out loud. She felt the rasp of dry air in her throat. "And al-Qaum guides us."

After a short rest, the girl stood again and circled the tall pillar of rock. It was a mountain in miniature with a flat platform at its top. She did not have the priests' ladders, so she studied the formation to decide on her best approach. Once she had chosen a route, she stood on the balls of her feet in thin sandals, and her hands reached up for a hold. For a moment, she paused, and then she stepped up and found a crevice the thickness of a finger. It was enough.

Cypros took a deep breath and then straightened her leg, lunging upwards and reaching as high as she could. She searched for a handhold, found one, and hung there for a moment. Then she kicked about until she found another ledge for her dangling foot. She lunged upwards again, and so in this haphazard manner, she climbed the rock until she had both arms over the platform's edge. Her feet dangled below.

The top of the platform was smooth. The girl did not know how she could pull her feet up with nothing to hold. She laid her palms flat on the rock, but she had no grip, and her hands were wet with sweat. The raider's dried blood melted, and she left dark streaks on the platform.

Cypros pressed her arms against the stone and lifted herself onto her elbows. The top of her hips rocked on the platform's hard edge, and her feet hung out in space. She bent her leg but could not get her foot back to the cliff's edge without going backwards and falling. There was nothing to do but go forwards. She rolled towards one shoulder and then shifted the opposite elbow forwards, then did it again on the other side until she could finally lift one knee over the rock's sharp edge.

She rolled onto her back then and lay there for a time, looking up at the day's new sun. Her sandalled feet hung out over the edge of the platform. Her eyes were heavy. She had not slept since the previous morning. She put an arm over her eyes to shield them from the sun and fell asleep.

Lying on the platform, she dreamed of her people. The Nabataeans maintained their secret routes through the Great Desert. These routes supplied spice and other trade goods from mysterious places in the east to the Greeks and Romans and Egyptians in the west. Besides caravans, the Nabataeans now held cities like the other people of the world. Damascus in the north was now Nabataean. Raqmu in the south as well. Recently, the Jews had stolen territory from her people. Lands lost on the eastern side of the Jordan River included Ragaba, Medeba, Zoar, and others. Some took the loss of these cities as a warning from al-Qaum. Few did anything to heed the warning.

Many of her people had begun to rely on other gods. Memories of this unfaithfulness entered her dream. She moaned out loud, louder than she had even during the raider's assault. One hand reached up as though to grasp something or find someone, then settled back down at her side. The other arm still covered her eyes.

Her family had been among the apostates from al-Qaum. They had been en route from Damascus to Raqmu without the protection of the god of caravans, war, and night. As a result, they had died in al-Qaum's desert. Unprotected by him. In her dream, she saw the great hand of al-Qaum mark her family with black soot. She felt that same hand lift her and carry her to this place.

Cypros awoke stiff on hard stone.

*I have always loved al-Qaum above all.* She might have said it out loud. *I love the caravans. I love the night. I love al-Qaum.*

Her destination, Raqmu, was unlike any other city in the world. The city rested forever undisturbed, never threatened. No man had built Raqmu's buildings and aqueducts. Instead, men had carved and continued to carve the city into the living mountain, the way the Greeks might cut stone for a column. Raqmu's columns were not brought to the mountain but revealed within it. Greeks made objects to build with. Raqmu's architects did not make things—they made space. They did not add to the mountain but removed material from it. It was a city carved into solid rock.

The Nabataeans had been a people of caravans since the dawn of time. But when they settled, they did so with a permanence that humbled all the other nations of the world.

The Greeks called the city Petra. The Stone. Raqmu was the city of al-Qaum, the inviolable stone city, the Mountain.

Cypros marked where the sun had risen. She estimated where she expected it to set. She paid her respects as her father had taught her in the early days before he had forsaken al-Qaum for Dushara.

That break from al-Qaum to Dushara had been many years ago when her uncle had conquered Damascus. Nabataeans did not call him King Aretas. That was a term other nations used. Her uncle was just Aretas. Nabataeans were the people, and so was al-Qaum, so Aretas was not king; he was just Aretas.

Many took to the new gods, to Dushara and the others, but the girl did not. Only al-Qaum was the people. Aretas was the nation's leader. Aretas was her uncle. Al-Qaum was her god.

The climb down would be more dangerous than the climb up. Her legs felt weak. Her mouth dry. She drank the last of her water and then studied the surface of the platform. Only the Nabataeans knew how to read the marks left in places like this. Her people kept no paper records like other nations. They wrote little, as they built little, but like their buildings, what they wrote lasted forever.

*Like the way we kill,* she said to strengthen herself.

The girl peered at the markings on the stone platform and found what she sought. She checked the markings a second time and noted the landmarks. Then she studied her back trail. From this high place, she could see the eight raiders now. They were in a group. They were faint, little more than shadows wavering in the far wasteland. She did not see any camels. The Moabite raiders from the eastern mountains and high rocky plains preferred horses. Horses would suffer in this land. The ground here was soft. Those that followed were not Nabataeans. They were people of hot and arid lands, but not true people of the desert. The Moabites were not Nabataeans.

"I cannot fight you," she whispered through cracked lips, "and you cannot fight al-Qaum. This is his land. Come, follow me. Let me take you to meet him."

To get off the platform, the girl lay on the rock with her feet stretched out into space as before. Lying down, she eased herself over the edge of the platform and then made her way down to the desert floor.

Back on the flat ground, the girl searched for the landmarks she had seen from the platform and then began to walk. As she walked, she counted her steps out loud. When she reached the right number, she stopped, her voice a dry whisper. Her water skin was limp at her waist. She rechecked the guide peaks and confirmed the alignment. She turned then to the east and counted the remaining steps until she came to the final number.

Cypros stood in that place like a human tree, the edges of her headscarf moving lightly about her like leaves in the air. After a few moments, she knelt and began to move the sand. She dug and searched for what al-Qaum's tower markings promised. She cleared a large area until she found a stone lid, like a cap on the earth itself.

The girl struggled to pry the massive lid open. Once it was open, she looked inside the earth, and the smell of wet rock met her face. The markings on al-Qaum's high place did not record this cistern's size. She could see that it was many times deeper than her height and the width of five men in diameter. The air inside was cool and clean.

Cypros felt inside the opening, careful not to fall in, and found the rope coiled and hung. She lowered it and the attached jar into the water. When the jar reached the water below, it floated. She joggled it until it tipped over and began to fill.

The girl quickly raised the stone jar before it became too heavy for her. Once the jar was in her hands, she broke custom and drank straight from it. She was alone and more parched than she had ever been before. She put the jug down and stared at the flat horizon as though daring anyone to correct her. The horizon wavered before her. No one came. There was no one to help her, no one to rebuke her, no one to tell her right from wrong or provide comfort. There was only the desert, the wobbly horizon, the heat, and al-Qaum.

After a short time, the pressure in her head eased, and she could see clearly again. She filled her water skin, drank from the jar again, then poured the rest back into the cistern. As the water impacted below, the cistern sang a deep bass note that was alien in this place. She put the rope away on its secret hook. She left the jar to hang and await the next of her people who might come.

She wrestled the lid back into place, drew sand back over it, and then unwrapped her head covering. She scooped sand into the great cloth and returned the way she had come, dragging the sand-filled cloth behind to obscure her passage. At a hard place that left no track, she shook the sand from her cloth and retied her head covering.

She had come some distance back towards her pursuers, and that made her afraid, but she had no choice. She could not outrun them forever, and so she could not let them find the cistern. She honoured the rule to protect the secrets of her people. Thirst was her only weapon against eight.

Cypros looked hard and eventually saw the men following her. They had abandoned their animals. Even camels would have difficulty in this place. Men as well, but the girl knew that she was smaller and sank less in soft ground. She did not know if they could see her. She saw them as a group. Individuals were hard to discern.

She found her original trail on the far side of the hard place and extended it, skirting the edge of rock, making sure her feet left clear markings. She dropped a bit of bright cloth, something of her mother's. There was only heat now, no wind, and the cloth lay where she dropped it.

She came again to softer ground and continued. Here the raiders would follow her trail easily but curse their slow arid progress.

The girl led them on.

They would have no water.

The girl walked that entire day. She was mad with exhaustion, but she still had a third of her water by the end of that day. The men were far behind her. They were distant wraiths in the wilderness. They continued to come but could not close the gap.

Cypros smiled as the sun dipped below the horizon. She wiped an escaped strand of hair from her eyes. She had another drink from her water skin, then continued to walk.

She did not stop through that second night. In the dark, she followed the stars and came to understand things known only to those who starve, those consumed by fever or possessed by a witch's potion.

In that empty silence, she saw herself as a furious raptor

on the land. She imagined herself able to fly but choosing to leave this trail instead. She would kill the killers of her family, with al-Qaum's desert. When hunger began to gnaw at her, she imagined consuming her pursuers as the great black birds of the desert consumed their victims.

This merciless land belonged to the Nabataeans, the people of al-Qaum. She worshipped al-Qaum, and al-Qaum guarded her as he did all his people.

She was thirteen years old. Even though her legs shook, she walked. Her mind roared with pain multiplied. Still, she did not stop walking.

The raiders had no water.

# 3

## 76 BCE

Two Jewish children perched on a broken stone wall in the shade of an old olive tree in Jerusalem. Their resting place overlooked the passing of hundreds in and out of the city gate below. The two were both ten years old. The girl, Pninah, was small, thin boned and bird-like. She was pretty but looked frail. The boy, Gavriel, was a miniature ruffian. His dishevelled hair, face traced with dirt, and rough clothing all spoke to his aloneness in the world. He slept where he found a place. He hustled for stolen coins as a thin boy could, with more technique than force, and did better than most. He did not speak of his parents and claimed to have little memory of them. Pninah had known Gavriel as a street boy for as long as she had memory. By contrast, she was clean. Her clothing was not ragged. She had a home, but in practice, she was as much an urchin as her friend.

She looked at him but turned away again before he caught her eye.

"They'll not let us be like this much longer," Gavriel said. "We're getting older."

"Mother doesn't care," Pninah said.

"She will."

Pninah shrugged and focused on the crowds below. She squinted, pretending to study someone in the throng. "She knows I'm safe with you." She wiped whisps of hair from her eyes.

"I've got some almonds," Gavriel said. He dug into one pocket and came up with a handful of nuts and two small bright stones. He put the stones back in his pocket and offered up the snack in a dirty hand.

Pninah picked out three nuts. Gavriel ate the rest. There was silence then except for the work of their teeth. She broke the silence finally with, "I don't see why getting older makes any difference."

She stole a look at him and saw a smudge mark across the top of one ear. She wanted to lick her thumb and wipe the dirt away.

"You don't think your mother and father will stop us from spending our days together?" Gavriel asked. "You know, when you get to be that—" He made a rude gesture then, trying to provoke her in the way that was his habit. "You know. That age."

Pninah felt her face flush, as much from her ignorance about what exactly he meant as anything else. "I don't see why it should make any difference to them or anyone else. No one pays attention now; why start later? We don't cause any harm."

"Not usually," he said.

She giggled at that. She heard her own quiet way of giggling and wondered why she did not laugh like other people. She was never loud.

"The farm by the low road," she said, still laughing in her own way. She took her hand away from her mouth, forcing it down to her lap. She tried to study the crowd again.

"I wasn't even that hungry for eggs," Gavriel said. "You ran out of there so fast."

"Good thing he didn't get a good look at you."

"Or you. Either of us."

"Fistfuls of broken eggs."

Gavriel frowned. "I don't know why running made us clench our hands like that. You don't run with your hands."

Pninah giggled again. Shorter this time. "Now Eli ben Lazareth," she said, "his wife would stab you in the throat if you got near her eggs. She'd hunt you down."

Gavriel grunted. "Remember jumping off the Galilean's cart, off the bridge, into the Jordan?"

She smiled. "We were gone three days that time."

"I thought your mother would put you in chains afterwards."

"She knew I was with you. She doesn't care. She was drunk. I don't think she knew for sure I was gone."

"Hey, listen, I got this yesterday." Gavriel pulled back his tunic and showed a welt along his side, above his hip.

The line of muscle above his hip distracted her attention from the scrape. Her interest in a muscle was new to her, and strange. "How did it happen?"

He covered himself again. "The fellows from the east market were chasing me. I went over the wall by the baskets, you know, near the—"

"I know."

"I came down too fast. I didn't want to land too heavy on my feet, so I slid and got the scrape."

"You're the fastest boy I know. Faster than any of the men or even the runners in the army. You could get a job there—when you're older."

Gavriel was quiet for a moment. It seemed like he wanted to become angry. Then he said, "I'd rather work with the horses and donkeys."

An old conversation.

"You don't know anything about horses or donkeys."

"I'd still rather do that. Work in the stables. I'd like to learn."

"Nobody is going to give you a job in the king's stables. Or any stables." Her words felt mean. She did not intend to be mean. "You don't know anything about horses. It's too late to learn now."

"I've got to come up with something. I can't be stealing and scrounging forever."

"So you can marry me?"

"Of course. Or they'll separate us. You know, when you—"

Pninah waved his gesture away. It did not bother her this time. She did not flush.

"Come on," Gavriel said. "Let's go. Watch the thorns there. Bring your water."

He slid off the wall, and once she joined him, they entered the crowd leaving Jerusalem.

"Where do you want to go?" she asked.

"Along the wall. Go in the other gate, I guess, if we don't find anything better along the way."

"Pick pockets?"

"Not today. I did enough running yesterday."

They passed through the gate. His arm brushed hers as he steered her onto the path that followed the outside of the wall.

"That blind man might still be there," she said.

"We won't bother him today. He'll know the sound of our feet."

"You think so?"

"He won't fall for that again. His hearing is good."

"You said you found a way to get from the wall to the market along the rooftops," Pninah said.

"Yeah, we could do that." Gavriel paused to get his bearings. Then he pointed. "We'll go in the next gate and get up from there, and I'll show you. Just don't have a seizure up there."

"Miriam said I have a demon," Pninah said.

"I asked Anna at the Temple," Gavriel said.

"You didn't!"

"Why not?"

They walked in silence then. A stream of travellers moved away from the city. Another stream of travellers met them approaching it. The two children left the crowds behind and followed the curve of the city.

"What did Anna say?" Pninah asked.

"I told her it was just your muscles going crazy sometimes, and she said that was true."

"Just my muscles?"

"She said I was right."

"Why can't I remember it then?" Pninah asked. "And why does my mind go all fuzzy before and after if it's just my muscles? And why do I want to sleep for a long time afterwards?"

Gavriel shrugged. "Yesterday, when I stopped running through the market, I threw up. I hadn't even had too much to eat. I was all dizzy, but not from heat or thirst—just from running too hard. I couldn't think or even see well for a few minutes."

"That's different."

"It's similar," Gavriel said. "Maybe it's like that. Whatever it is, your seizures are not a demon. Anna said so."

"My mother isn't so sure."

"Your mother is a drunk." Gavriel pointed at the next gate they were approaching. "All I know is that it's just a good thing you're so small, so I can carry you when I have to. Just don't have a seizure up there and fall off a roof."

"You don't carry me. You half lift, half drag me."

"I carry you," Gavriel protested.

"You do not."

"I do. How would you know? You're sleeping and seizing at the same time and can't remember anything."

"If you're carrying me, then I get awfully scratched up on my knees and ankles from it. Do you take a detour through a bramble forest before bringing me home? I had drag marks the last time. Did you look for a mud puddle on purpose?"

Gavriel grinned. "Just don't do anything on the wall. I don't want to have to drop you over the edge to get you down."

She wanted to take his hand, but she did not. They were getting older. Older people did not hold hands like children.

# 4

## 77-76 BCE

IN THE DESERT outside Raqmu, the late, low sun illuminated a small whirlwind formed by bands of rose and tan sand and dust. It spun as the light dimmed, and the colours drifted from yellow to orange to red. Glints refracted in the swirling wonder like tiny works of magic.

This entrancing display welcomed the haggard girl home. The disappearing sun was to her right. Ahead lay Raqmu. Petra. Between her and Raqmu stood the miraculous whirlwind and, beyond it, a rider on a camel. Perhaps two. She saw them through the whirlwind and had trouble understanding what she saw.

The men approached, then stopped, and waited for the small twister to pass.

The girl sank to her knees. She could go no farther. She had been alone in the desert for more than a week and had eaten only what little she could find. She had drunk from five of her people's cisterns. She had found a sixth but had been unable to remove its cover.

The scouts took care unwinding the cloth from her face. "Cypros," one said to the other. They gave her water and then lifted her onto one camel and bore her away to the City of Stone.

❧

Several months later, naked heads and bulging eyes jutted ahead of dark wings. The great black birds mounted invisible stairways of sky and flew east over the heartless desert. Across the far side of the Dead Sea, they turned and travelled to its northernmost tip. South of Jericho and Dagon, they turned and came back down along the western coast of the inland Dead Sea.

After a time, they drifted westwards and passed over the fortress Hyrcania. On highways of rising heat, they floated soundlessly over a company of one hundred men—pilgrims in search of blood. This was a formation the birds recognized. Spear points held aloft made a promise, but not for this day. It was too early in this march of men for meat.

The birds returned to the Dead Sea, passed down to its southern tip, and then left the dead water behind. They slid along the border of Jewish Idumea and Nabataea and came upon two converging camps, one with a company of camels and the other with horses. Men dressed in Nabataean robes of cream and beige, fringed with grey and yellow borders, stood with the camels. Those with the horses wore the longer Jewish robes in white and green with blue or green tassels dangling. Between the two groups, temporary tents surrounded a grand pavilion of carved pillars that encircled a solitary stone platform. Upon this platform lay a rug, and upon that rug sat two men. Though these two wore finer clothes of warm, thick wool, one still resembled the horsemen with his green robe and tight turban, while the other resembled the camel riders with his flowing beige robe and looser head covering. The men of both parties wore their beards untrimmed. To the birds, their eyes were faded, leather lined, and lifeless. They were not like the camels or the horses whose eyes bulged with moisture and rolling life.

This the birds saw from a distance, studying this meeting of men and spying beneath the pavilion roof while skimming over the desert floor. The seated had before them a meal. It was a meal for two. There was no feast here. There would be no waste scattered about for the birds to pick through later.

With a sullen slapping of the air, the great black birds lifted higher and higher, seeking rising columns of heat. From this meeting of men the birds passed into the more reliable table of the Hopeless Lands.

Cypros stood some distance away from the two men, barely within the pavilion's shade. Her uncle, Aretas, sat with the Jew. The Jews used the term king when they referred to Aretas. The King of Petra. King of the Nabataeans. The Jews did not understand that he was just Aretas.

The Jewish man's name was Antipas. He was the governor of Idumea, the region of Eretz-Israel south of Jerusalem. Idumea lay between Raqmu and the Great Western Sea.

The Nabataean traders had good relations with Antipas. The traders used Gaza's port to ship their treasures on to Rome and Egypt. To get to the sea, the plodding camel caravans passed through Idumean territory. The terms for this transit involved a Jewish tax on Nabataean goods in exchange for freedom of movement and an assurance of security. Idumea allowed no bandits within its borders.

While peace between Nabataea and the Idumean region of Eretz-Israel reigned in the south, Jerusalem's policy was different in the north. Jerusalem's queen had claimed Nabataean land east of the Jordan River. The entire area north of the Dead Sea was now part of Eretz-Israel. The lost territory extended almost all the way to Damascus.

*I should despise you.* Cypros said nothing as she studied Antipas.

The Jew would be her father-in-law soon. Her mother had designed this marriage, aiming to increase goodwill between Idumea and Nabataea and to spark a broader conversation about Jewish conquests. Her mother had arranged matters through her brother, Aretas.

"The Jews are led by a woman," her mother had told her. "As the future governess of Idumea, you will have access to the queen in a way that neither Aretas nor any other man can hope to. I never influenced anything in your father's household, but through you and my brother, I can give you power I never had."

Cypros had watched her mother's face as she had said those words. She had never suspected before that her mother had ever wanted anything. Certainly not power. Women did not rule men. But the Jews had a queen. And no king.

After the talk with her mother, Cypros had consulted her brother's teachers, quizzing them on Jewish lore. They had told her about Esther, Deborah, and Delilah. She learned that Jewish women could change Jewish men. She learned through Delilah's story that even gentile women could change Jewish men.

When her time of womanhood had come, the family had left Damascus for Raqmu to begin Cypros's year of preparation. This had been the reason for their journey. This was what they had died for.

*I should despise you.* She was careful not to stare at her future father-in-law, but she felt a darkness settle on her each time she looked at him. *Instead, through your son and your queen, I will change you. I serve al-Qaum. Your Yahweh is no match for al-Qaum.*

Antipas sat with her uncle on the shared rug and contemplated the lone cup of wine before him. Aretas contemplated the same cup, for Nabataeans did not drink wine. Her people did not drink any strong drink at all.

Another point of weakness.

"It will be a strange wedding without wine," Antipas finally said.

Cypros studied him closely. She had never seen him before. She had yet to meet his son. She wanted to know which of the father's traits she might find in the son. The governor was tall. He was lean, but not in the way that old men tended to be lean. He looked like he had always been thin, even when young.

"You made a contract of marriage for my niece," Aretas said. "For your son. For a wedding without wine. And now my sister is dead." Aretas reached for his tea and drank slowly. He looked at Cypros without saying anything. He had yet to introduce her to his guest.

Cypros looked down while he regarded her.

"What does that change?" Antipas asked.

"She is my child now," Aretas said. "I have taken her into my house."

Cypros looked up again, took in her uncle, and then turned to Antipas and saw the governor frown.

"She was alone in the desert with the raiders," the Jewish governor said. "We have concerns—" He did not finish.

Aretas's complexion darkened. "There were *nine* in the desert," he said.

The emphasis on *nine* startled Cypros, and she wanted to protest. She stayed silent. What Antipas meant took another moment to register, and then she felt her own face darken.

She understood then all the Jewish conversations that had preceded this meeting. Heat blazed in her face. Her teeth met in secret, betrayed only by a faint hollowing of her cheeks.

"We followed the back trail," Aretas continued. "We found the last to the first. There was little left of the first."

Antipas pursed his lips as though he had bitten into something soft and discovered rot. He held his mouth in that shape for a long time. He looked like he wanted to spit. Watching him, Cypros knew she would never see her too-skinny husband now. This meeting in the desert would be her final encounter with Jews. She would wear an unwarranted shame forever. She wanted to lick her teeth. She wanted to say something.

Aretas was talking. He was describing how they had retraced Cypros's desert trail and reconstructed the chase, adding bits about revenge. Cypros did not listen closely. She absorbed little after the emphasis on nine and the Jew's frozen face. A sourness crept into her throat. Everything her mother had planned would come to nothing because of nine raiders, because of a slander. She would be nothing—a barren and unclaimed stain within Aretas's house. Her family was dead. Her uncle would provide for her. She would become lower than a fifth wife. An unwanted cousin. She would be dead weight among a nomadic people who did not carry profitless weight.

Her eyes focused hard and direct, and she dared to look boldly at the two men, daring them to meet her gaze. They continued talking between themselves. She calmed herself. She thought of the first raider and the intimate price he had paid, the blossoming of that wound in his throat. She tasted bitterness on her tongue. Something from deep inside crept up and gave notice and then sank back down within her.

She had not been paying attention to the two men and tried to focus again on their conversation. It seemed that the Jew had not been listening either. "I don't understand," he said.

"The first came closest," Aretas said. He held Antipas's gaze. "She put a blade in his throat. A blade for her family. A blade for threatening her."

"A blade?"

"She carries one in her hair. Something from her mother."

Antipas blinked. "She's fourteen years old. She was thirteen then."

"And beautiful."

"He did not touch her?"

"He did not."

"The others?"

Aretas frowned. Antipas reshaped his expression. It seemed to Cypros that he was trying to recover a lost narrative without sacrificing his dignity. "Tell me again. I didn't understand the first time. The desert. You people always become imprecise when talking about the desert."

"We keep our secrets," her uncle said.

"About the men. Tell me about the men."

"She led them into the desert."

"Led?"

"They pursued her. She travelled where their horses could not travel. She found water where our people hide it and did not let her pursuers find it. She led them until they were lost and had no choice but to keep following. She led them through the worst places. She did not lead them home to Raqmu." Aretas leaned in, still holding Antipas's gaze. "Do you understand?"

Her uncle held his fingers pinched together the way a woman might pinch up a bit of flour—a pinch in both hands. He held the fingers up before Antipas as though they held something the governor should see and understand, like invisible flies, one in each hand, held only by their legs.

"She did not come straight to Raqmu where the men could have escaped in another direction. She did not lead them to green places where they would have found relief. She did not cross trading routes where other caravans might have found and rescued her or them. She led them where there was nothing and no one, and they did not know where they were, and they had no choice but to follow."

He still held his pinched fingers up in the air before Antipas.

"For how long?"

"Seven days."

"How far back were they?"

"Sometimes an hour. They could not track her in the night. She made ground in the night. They recovered it during the day." Aretas continued still with his fingers pinched up in the air before the governor. High. At eye level. "Then gone," Aretas said, and he opened his fingers suddenly, hands wide, palms to the sky. "The desert took each man, and the only one left in that wilderness was the daughter of my people."

"Why didn't she go straight to Petra?"

Aretas smiled. Cypros knew her uncle. He was like her mother. That smile told her that he had spoken everything prior for the sole reason of soliciting this question. The Jew had asked correctly.

"Honour."

He said it like he had said the word *beautiful*. The widening of the Jew's eyes told her that the governor did not miss the connection, even if the answer still eluded him. "I don't understand," he said.

"You wouldn't. But she will teach your grandsons."

"None of them touched her in the desert?"

"I'm not talking about *her* honour." Aretas leaned in again. He seemed to be frowning at the Jew's inability to understand. "Her honour was never in question. I am talking about the honour of her father. He did not defend his family. He did not save my sister or her children. Cypros saved herself. And then she managed to kill all nine of the raiders. She restored her father's honour by killing nine men. Only then did she return to us."

Aretas leaned in towards the Idumean governor, almost rising onto his knees. "Now you tell me—is your son worthy of this girl?"

# 5

## 76 BCE

THE WEDDING OF the Nabataean princess to the Idumean governor's son was a sunlit and colourful affair. Banners of Idumean blue and rare purple complemented those in Nabataean yellow, black, and red. It seemed that white, silver, and gold were the only common colours between them. Both parties wore linen of the same Egyptian weave and quality. The Nabataeans also had silk, brought from some mysterious place across the Great Desert.

That evening, music filled Raqmu's canyons. The sound of voices and instruments flowed out to the desert like a stream of scented air. It announced celebration, the union of two nations, and the commencement of a First Day's Feast. Moonlight and torchlight held darkness at bay. The dances in great circles were of both kinds: Jewish and Nabataean. Laughter and applause intermingled.

The next day brought games with camels. Nabataean men in shorter, rougher clothing rode racing camels and loosed arrows at frail targets and vied for prizes and attention until the dust they created drove onlookers out of the desert and back into Raqmu's enclosed canyon grounds.

As the golden light of evening faded, torches sprang back to life along with music and more dancing. The differences between the Nabataean dances and those of the Idumeans were the continual source of bright-eyed entertainment and gossip and yet more laughter.

The third day was much the same. And the fourth.

On the fifth night, the second last before the couple departed from Raqmu, the new bride and her husband slept in their own tent. It stood apart from the crowds, but not far.

It was late in the night, after even the servants had retired and the fires had gone out. All memory of merriment and music had faded into sleep's dark silence. Only the rustle of sand stirred outside. Jewish ghosts, Nabataean spirits of the dead, or a night breeze lifted a fine layer of sharp grains and chased them across the desert's skin. The motion raised a soft hiss as though the sand itself was alive. Everything else lay silent and still. The breeze, if there was one, did not touch the tents.

Cypros awoke in the dark with a start. Her mouth opened wide and air rushed from her, but no voice issued from her throat. It was a scream without sound. Her hands balled into fists full of Egyptian bed linen, and she panted, sweat soaked in the cavernous Nabataean tent. She imagined vultures in the dark. She heard the footsteps of men break through crusts of salt formed over hard, hard sand.

She heard the beat of great wings. She could taste the tang of blood and thirst and feel the ache in her hips from endless walking.

"Again?" her husband said as he came awake.

"It's nothing," Cypros said.

"Your voice is breathy."

"You've worn me out."

"I was sleeping," Antipater said.

"Earlier, you wore me out."

"You're still panting?"

She turned towards him, conscious of her nakedness, the sweat that ran from her, the deliberate adjustment in her breathing. "Maybe I'm just tired of waiting for you to wake up."

⁓

On the last day, the flat land before Raqmu's steep cliffs formed a staging ground for pack animals, wagons, and supplies. Jewish horses stood in polite rows. Some distance away, Nabataean camels sat on the ground or stood and bawled at their handlers.

Cypros walked among the Jewish wagons to the consternation of the Idumean attendants. After a while, she returned to the sidelines. She looked at Antipater and said, "No" and continued towards the Nabataean side of their escort. She found the old leather maker and his apprentice and took them over to one of the Jewish supervisors. Antipater followed her at a distance. He seemed to listen to her arrangements, but he did not say anything. She saw him later with his father. She did not go to him but let her Nabataean relatives claim her attention. They wanted to say their farewells. They also wanted to stop her from meddling any further with the caravan planning.

When the time came for them to leave, the leather-maker and his apprentice had completed her request.

"Two people do not ride one camel," Aretas said to Cypros. His voice betrayed a rare humour, not disapproval. Cypros was going to Idumea to become a Jew, but her insistence on leaving Nabataea on a camel seemed to please him. She sensed that forcing her husband to ride a camel as well pleased him even more.

Instead of the usual packs strapped to the upper sides of the camel, the beast wore two shallow baskets reinforced with leather-wrapped wooden braces. From the wooden braces, a canopy extended on flimsy poles. The canopy would fail in a strong wind, but in this calm weather it would provide welcome shade.

"You two won't balance the load," he added.

Cypros pointed at the jugs of water and other supplies. She did not say anything. Her voice would have betrayed her emotion.

*These are my people.*

She did not let herself decide which people she meant. The pressure she held deep inside threatened tears. The feeling could mean many things. She did not want anyone to draw their own conclusions about something she had sealed off.

When she put the plan to Antipater, she saw a look of amusement cross his face. It was the same expression that he had worn a few nights before when the Nabataean men had tried to teach him to dance properly.

"He doesn't take himself too seriously," one of Cypros's aunts had commented.

While the camel was still hunched and sitting on the ground, Cypros settled into her basket-saddle with Antipater's help, and then he climbed into his own. The imbalance was immediately obvious. Nabataean men added water jugs and other supplies to her basket until the load on her side matched the one on Antipater's.

"A bit crowded?" he asked her.

She looked at him across the camel's back. "Snug. So I won't fall out."

Antipater smirked as though this were a joke, and then the camel lunged up and straightened its hind legs only, its front legs still bent and pressing into the sand. It grunted and wheezed, and the sudden motion combined with the equally sudden stop at this strange angle nearly threw Antipater from his basket. His outer hand grabbed onto the wooden frame while the other tried to grip camel hair. He tilted farther and farther forwards as the flexible leather straps steadily twisted and bent the basket deeper into the dangerous angle. Then the camel's front legs engaged and the beast was suddenly standing on all four legs and the couple's seats were level once more.

Cypros watched as her husband let out a deep breath and then settled back in his seat.

"Do you need some supplies to wedge you in better?" she asked.

Calm and normal colour returned to his face. "You might have warned me," he said with a weak smile.

"You've never been on a camel before," she said. It was not a question.

He shook his head.

She leaned towards him and waited until she had his attention. Around them, Nabataeans on foot were starting to return to Raqmu. Those going with the caravan remained on their camels and in their designated places before and behind the royal couple. The Jews with their horses and wagons were at the front of the procession.

Aretas had already said his goodbyes and stood some distance away. If he said anything further, it would be to Antipas or the head of the Nabataean contingent of this caravan guard.

Antipater leaned towards Cypros and gave her his full attention.

"My aunts taught me something for brides," she said.

He watched her and waited and did not say anything. They would certainly not kiss in public, and their faces could not reach each other had they wanted to. They were close enough, however, to talk without others overhearing them.

The camel below them stepped forwards as the whole caravan began to move.

"It's the camel-bride posture," she said.

Antipater looked at her without understanding.

"I'll show you tonight."

His face coloured and he looked around quickly. She turned away then, knowing he would come back to her. When he did, he would find her waving to her aunts as though she had not said anything to him at all.

❧

Late in the afternoon, Cypros looked at Antipater. "What else was different about Nabataea?"

"The bowls," he said.

"Bowls?"

"The cups. For drinking."

He was eating a yellow-orange fruit that she did not recognize. The flesh of the fruit seemed to adhere stubbornly to a central pit. It smelled good. She did not ask him what it was—she did not want to admit her ignorance.

"What about the cups?" she asked.

"They fall over."

"Not when they're full," she said. For fourteen years, her world had been Damascus and Raqmu. It had never occurred to her that people made cups any other way. "They only fall over when they're empty."

"Or half empty."

"Why would a cup ever be half empty?"

Antipater stared at her, holding the last of the fleshy fruit in one hand. He wore a look of puzzlement on his face. He was clearly waiting for her to admit that this was a joke. She waited him out. He was older and more experienced than she—but he was not that much older. He was seventeen. Cups were a minor topic. Still, it occurred to her that she could not bow to every Jewish difference right from the beginning, or she would be bowing for the rest of her life. She was a Nabataean princess—even if no Nabataean would ever use that term. Antipater was just a governor's son.

"You design your cups so that when you take a drink, you have to keep holding it until you drink it all?" Antipater asked. "Or you drink it all at once to begin with? Otherwise, they fall over?"

"Of course."

He took one last bite and was about to toss the fleshy seed out into the desert when her eyes stopped him. "How do you not get drunk?" he asked.

She took the slimy remains from him, the sweet flesh clinging to its hard pit. "We don't drink wine." She tasted the seed and tore off stringy fibres that remained and ate them. Then she handed the seed back to him.

"Right. That. This was probably the first Jewish wedding ever with no wine." He tossed the pit into the desert.

She did not say anything but waited until he turned towards her again. When he did, she found his eyes, held his gaze, arched one eyebrow, and let slip a small smile. "Was it so bad as that?"

He flushed, grinned, and said nothing.

The caravan of Jewish and Nabataean riders crossed into Idumea. "Tell me something good now about Nabataea," Cypros said. The camel below them groaned at his fellows or the desert or the wind. She could never tell with camels.

"We agreed to discuss Idumea now," Antipater said.

"One more thing about my place. Tell me something good—the best thing about Nabataea."

He looked at her.

"Not about me," she said. "About Nabataea."

"How about the Siq?"

She nodded and closed her eyes. "Tell me what you remember. I want to see it through your eyes."

Antipater started speaking about the tent city that stood

before Raqmu's cliffs. He said nothing about the narrow canyon that cut a route into the heart of the mountain.

"The Siq," she reminded him, her eyes still closed. She tilted her head up to the light that filtered through the swaying shade cloth above. He did not respond right away. After a few moments, she looked over at him. He was staring out at the wasteland border between their two countries—everything around lay dry and rock-strewn as it had since the beginning of time.

"The Siq is like a fold in the cliffs," Antipater finally said, still staring out at the wasteland. "The mountains are normal craggy mountains. Like the ones at Qumran."

Cypros closed her eyes and leaned back again. "Poetry," she said. "Tell me like it's poetry. Make it like Solomon's Song."

"Solomon's Song isn't about cliffs or canyons."

"It talks about hills, but we'll get to that later. Tell me about the Siq. Put something beautiful in it, or your Nabataean wife will mourn the loss of her country and die of sorrow in Ashkelon."

She felt him shift around in his basket. When he moved, she had to balance in reaction until he settled himself again.

"The Siq is a narrow canyon, but it starts as a vertical shadow in the cliff," he said. "Then it becomes a cleft as you get closer, then it opens and only shows itself in full when you get right up to it. It's not a fold at all but an entrance."

She opened her eyes and looked at him.

He smiled and shrugged. "You said poetry."

"Do better."

"Close your eyes. I can't concentrate with you looking at me."

She smiled and acquiesced.

"Inside the canyon, the right side is stiff and straight, but the left ripples and bends back from the opening. The right is like a man. The left, a woman."

She started to open her eyes again in protest, then did not. She let him talk.

"At the opening of the canyon, there is a bridge that brings the two sides together. No, not a bridge—it's an archway. Beyond the archway, the Siq is a hallway of stone, maybe fifteen horses wide. It must be over two hundred feet high."

"Poetry," she said.

"The size of it *is* poetry. It's miraculous and beautiful. Once you're past the opening and into the Siq, there is a belly of stone on the right. Vertical bands like the ribs of a leviathan curve along its bulge. It looks like bone. Bone in stone."

In her mind's eye, she could see what he saw, and it made her think of al-Qaum.

Al-Qaum was not like the foolish gods of other nations. The world's gods amused her. They were the imaginations of children, full of talking animals, flying horses, and other nonsense. The Jews were better, but only marginally so. The Jews believed that their god was the only god—that she could go along with. They also thought that their god had made the world and everything in it. That was nonsense on a par with the gods of the Greeks and Romans. Not even al-Qaum had made the world. The world simply was and always had been.

However, the giant rib-like stones within the Siq did raise a question about al-Qaum and the world's uncreated permanence. The canyon looked made. As Cypros listened to Antipater describe the beautiful canyon trail through the Siq, it occurred to her that perhaps that was what her husband believed—that someone had fashioned the Siq the same way a potter shaped clay. Perhaps the Jewish god had made the canyon and then abandoned it to a people who did not even recognize him.

She wanted to snort at the thought, but it would have distracted Antipater. She had no desire to explain the foolishness of the Jewish religion to him. She smiled again and kept her eyes closed, face up to the filtered light.

"Past the ribbed stone belly," Antipater continued, "the path curves to the left and opens up to a much wider space before narrowing again. It goes down to maybe three horses wide. It winds through the mountain, left and right, narrower and wider. It's a magical kind of passageway. In some places, both sides of the canyon are male—tall and straight. Nothing sensuous. In other places, one side or both are curved."

She opened her eyes and looked at him again, but he did not see her. He was staring now into the distance. She brushed hair from her eyes that was not there.

"I remember you brushed up against me in one of the narrow sections," Antipater said. "It was the first time we touched. Your aunt got between us then. You leaned around her and told me to look up. The sky above was a thin channel of blue. You could block it out with one hand. It was an upside-down river winding through a dry desert. A river in the sky."

"Yes," she said.

"In other places, where the passage is wide, the sky opens up into ponds and pools and eddies."

She kept her eyes closed and wondered if there might be hope yet for her Jewish man.

"The air is cooler in the canyon, the light dimmer. It adds to the effect. It's like you're underwater."

"What colour is it?" she asked.

"The stone," he said. Not a question. "White and gold with dark sections of brown and shades of grey. Reds and roses too. Even patches that seem blue. Also, there is a section where the horizontal grooves and colours are not straight. They branch away from each other like veins in the mountain, as though the mountain were a sleeping monster."

She imagined the mountain breathing and bleeding beneath its facade of stone. It would explain the redness of the place. She decided that if Raqmu's mountain was in fact a monster, then it was female. She had never considered the sex of a monster before.

"The narrowest place in the canyon is towards the end," Antipater said. "Vertical and horizontal bands are everywhere. Deep accents. Contrasting colours. The sky is a narrow creek overhead, curving to the left as the stone road continues. I remember the echo of footsteps there and the muffled sound of the water in the channel. Then the way opens, you turn the corner, and you're inside Petra."

"Raqmu," she said. "We call her Raqmu."

"Yes. An amazing place. How did I do?"

She looked at him without speaking.

"I did good," he said, smiling back at her.

"I hope I like Ashkelon."

"You'll like the sea."

# 6

## 76 BCE

Well into Idumea, in a place of smooth rock and sand, the caravan slowed to a stop. Wagons, horses, and camels congested and the Nabataeans in the escort gathered around Antipas.

"Lean back," Cypros warned.

Antipater gave her a wry smile, and then their camel dropped to its front knees as though it had been clubbed in the head. The sudden movement nearly threw her husband from his basket. She laughed as he grabbed for any kind of handhold, and then the camel knelt its rear legs as well and Antipater exhaled.

Once on the ground, he went off to join the conversation with his father and the Nabataeans. Cypros helped herself out of her basket. Some of the Jewish women approached her then and took her to a place with some privacy where she could attend to her needs. None of the women spoke Nabataean, but like Antipater, they all spoke the common Aramaic.

Cypros spent some time among the women. This group was not composed of Antipater's relatives but appeared to be various levels of palace staff. Antipater's female aunts and cousins had done little to engage with her at Raqmu. Their distance was even more noticeable on this trip with no other Nabataean women around.

When Cypros re-emerged with her attendants, the camels were gone. All of them. The Nabataeans had begun their return to Raqmu. None had said farewell to her.

Cypros adjusted her clothing, brushing non-existent sand from her front. She looked at the horses and donkeys. They did not have dual side saddles, and none looked strong enough to carry one. She had never ridden a horse before. She looked at the smaller mules and thought they might be safer, but they looked silly.

"No," Hanne said. The Jewish girl was not much older than Cypros. She was part of the governor's household staff in Ashkelon and, from what Cypros had gleaned, was now reassigned to Cypros. "You're with us now." The girl pointed at one of the larger wagons. Her mouth shaped into a half smile, and Cypros sensed kindness behind the Jewish accent.

"The wagons are loud," Cypros said. "Rattling and squeaking."

Hanne made a slight laugh, a hand covering her mouth. "The camels," the girl started and waved a hand across her nose before laughing and covering her mouth again. "And they complain when the men try to get them to do things. I've never seen such animals."

Cypros nodded and smiled in return and followed the girl to the designated wagon. She walked with a hand covering her stomach and the other open at her side.

Antipater did not join her or explain anything to her. He was already on one of the horses with the other men. She considered calling to him to get his attention but held her peace. This was Eretz-Israel now. She was not the governess. She was the governor's son's wife. She was a gentile among Jews. Antipater's relatives had not even warmly welcomed her. She would ride with the lower ranked women. Hanne was the only unmarried girl to join her in the wagon. The other unmarried girls travelled separately.

As the caravan set out again, it quickly became apparent that there was an established hierarchy among these women. The older ones spoke forcefully and loudly. The younger ones spoke quietly and less often. Hanne spoke hardly at all. One woman, who seemed to be the oldest of the group, dominated all the others. She spoke as though she had Antipas's ear directly, though that seemed unlikely. The Jews segregated their women as diligently as the Nabataeans.

Hanne tried to enter the women's discussion at one point with a gentle but slightly contrary remark and the senior woman silenced her with just a look.

Cypros did not try to participate in the Aramaic discussions. She wondered where she would fit in Ashkelon as the future governess, this most recent wedding's bride. She wanted the camel flirtations with Antipater. Or a conversation with real peers in Nabataean.

With a shout from the head of Antipas's guard, the caravan began to move again. The women gestured to a spot against the wagon wall where she could sit on a folded-up blanket. They gave her more space than the others, whether due to rank or her gentile blood, she did not know. Other than the space left around her, she was just another one of the women—the household staff—seated in a row, facing a similar row of women on the opposite side of the wagon. Some of the women's feet intertwined across the aisle. The woman across from Cypros kept hers tucked beneath her.

The squeak and rattle of the wagon was even louder inside than out. The hot air beneath the shade canopy was stifling. Either the afternoon had grown hotter or the air inside the wagon simply did not move. The front and back of the wagon were open, but still, there was none of the swirling breeze and movement of the camel ride.

They travelled for what seemed like half the afternoon this way. The women talked among themselves, mostly in Aramaic. Then a commotion arose outside the wagon towards the front of the caravan. Voices were raised, but Cypros could not make out the words. Both Antipater and his father had joined an apparently urgent discussion. The caravan did not stop, but it did slow. The centre of controversy seemed to be at the very front. She could not properly see or hear what it was about.

Cypros stood up. She hung on to one of the shade poles and tried to understand what was going on. Hands grabbed at the clothing near her knees, and they momentarily distracted her. Cypros stepped away from the clutching hands. She reached over the women as she moved from one shade pole to the next, getting closer to the front of the wagon. The view did not improve and she could not hear any better either.

"You shouldn't be standing," the senior woman said.

Antipas's wife had died some years prior. None here were second wives nor, as far as Cypros knew, concubines.

The men at the front of the caravan were consulting in quieter tones now. They talked across the width of several horses as they rode alongside one another. After a few moments, the caravan slowed further, though it still did not stop. Five riders rode on ahead at a quicker pace. Cypros stood up as tall as she could, trying to see where they were going. In the distance, a band of riders approached.

"You must sit down," the senior woman said again. Her voice was insistent and firm. She spoke with an edge to her tone, as though Cypros had exceeded the allotment of patience this woman was prepared to extend. She looked to be about forty years of age. A mole hung like a black insect over thin lips. They did not look like the kind of lips that had ever kissed anyone, man or baby. She wore a severe, unchanging expression, like she was used to being obeyed.

The woman was seated along the opposite wall of the wagon. The blanket she sat on was the most colourful thing in the wagon and was placed over several other thicker, folded blankets. Cypros looked at Hanne and noticed for the first time that the girl had no blanket to sit on at all. She had only the floorboards of the wagon below her.

Cypros looked back at the senior woman and saw a stern expression that brooked no argument. The woman pointed to Cypros's seat and raised her eyebrows, and then stabbed the air with her extended finger.

Cypros stood up on the balls of her feet once more, straining to see the two groups of riders approaching one another. She noticed the subtle signs in the caravan of men preparing for trouble. Eyes confirmed the location of weapons. Hands tucked loose clothing or knotted it out of the way.

"Sit," the woman said.

Cypros was fourteen years old. The woman was forty, or maybe older. Cypros tried to remember what she had seen of the approaching riders, and she considered the last two hours with these insufferable women. She looked over at Hanne, who Cypros decided she liked. Now, the girl looked strained. Hanne's eyebrows were raised unevenly, as though trying to communicate something sympathetic.

For a moment, Cypros stood very still. Then she stepped into the middle of the wagon, not holding on to anything, and so came directly in front of the demanding woman. Cypros crouched before her. She did not go down to her knees but balanced on the balls of her feet. When she had the woman's full attention, her hand shot out like a punch. She went below the woman's head covering, grabbed a fistful of hair above her ear, yanked her head forwards, and then tilted it back harshly while, with her other hand, Cypros removed the knife from her hair. The blade's sudden appearance spurred gasps around her, but Cypros kept her eyes on the demanding woman.

She set the point of the blade against the woman's throat. The wagon was still moving, and as the wagon lurched and swayed, Cypros was constantly, rhythmically rebalancing herself on the balls of her feet, the tip of the blade moving away from the woman's throat and then back, gracefully touching and retreating and touching again. The whole wagonload of women held their breath. In this perilous posture, any sudden jerk of the wagon, any unfortunate rock on the road, would be murder.

Cypros began talking in Nabataean. She was confident that no one understood what she said, but she sensed their rapt attention. She spoke eight long sentences, each one distinct. The women would not need to understand Nabataean to hear that Cypros was telling them eight separate things. Then she spoke in Aramaic. "You will not speak to me ever again," Cypros said. She said it with the same tone as the Nabataean pronouncements. "If you ever want to speak to me again, you speak to her." Cypros pointed her blade at Hanne. She continued to look at Hanne as she put the knife back where it had been at the woman's throat, and she could see the tension build in the faces around her at this blind manoeuvre. Very slowly, she turned to look again at the older woman. It was hard to gauge the woman's expression. The pulling of her hair clearly hurt, but the arching of her neck created a strange wrinkling around her eyes and mouth, and what she wanted to communicate was unknowable. The woman said nothing. Perhaps she could not say anything. The blade at her throat and the movement of the wagon was its own power.

"And your breath stinks," Cypros said. "I don't ever want you in my presence again or in the presence of any of these women, with that stench coming out of you. Do you understand?"

The wagon stopped. The whole caravan had halted. Attention outside the wagon remained focused on the action ahead, but the stage inside the wagon was its own world.

"Do you understand?"

"Yes," the woman croaked.

"Good. Now get out of this wagon. Find one of the others to ride in or walk back to Ashkelon. I don't care which. I will not put up with your presence for the rest of this journey. And leave your blankets here."

Cypros put her blade away and returned to the front of the wagon, holding on to the foremost shade pole. The riders, both her riders and the new group of men, were now making their way towards the caravan at a leisurely pace. She listened to the sound of the older woman getting out of the wagon behind her. She did not turn to watch. She watched the men.

When the caravan started moving again, no one sat where the demanding woman had been. Cypros took her own blanket, and the two extra blankets the banished woman had used and gave them all to Hanne to sit on. Cypros took the one colourful blanket for herself.

There was little conversation for the rest of that journey, but the words that were said were lighter. At one point, two of the women laughed. They were quiet laughs, but laughter all the same. The freedom of a joke between friends was a new addition to that journey.

Cypros listened and gradually learned all of the women's names.

When they arrived at Ashkelon, Hanne took charge of orienting Cypros to the palace. Later in the evening, Hanne ate a late meal with Cypros. Just the two of them. Then Hanne prepared a bath for Cypros with the help of other palace servants. Finally, Antipater reappeared, and they were alone together. She put a hand on his chest as soon as he entered the room.

"What was that about?" she asked.

"I was going to ask you the same thing. The servants are talking."

"You go first."

Antipater sighed. "You're not in Nabataea anymore," he said.

"This room," she said, "is Nabataea. This body is Nabataea. If you're talking to me, you're talking to Nabataea."

His expression creased, like he was making a decision. Once his features settled, the decision made, he still did not speak or move but just studied her. "You're only fourteen," he said.

"Get used to it," she said.

"No," he said. "No, I won't get used to it. I want it to be always fresh."

They came together then and forgot about words for quite some time. Night quieted everything within and without, and only two small lamps still lit the room when he finally spoke again.

"You go first," he said. "Why did you make Efrat walk half the day? She's in charge of all the women on my father's staff, and her humiliation could not be more profound."

"I didn't make her walk. I made her get out of the wagon. She could have found another place to ride."

"She was assigned to your wagon by my father. She walked behind it in the dust for the rest of the day."

Cypros considered that.

"And I heard something about a knife."

Seated in the bed, Cypros let slip her sheet. His immediate distraction was evident. "You'll have to take my word for it," she said. "The offence warranted the punishment. I'm not a lamb subject to Nabataeans or Jews."

"That message was sent."

"Now your turn. What happened on the road?"

"That was more my father's business," Antipater said and moved towards her.

Cypros pulled the blanket up, tucking it under her arms. "No. Tell."

Antipater sighed and frowned. "A company from Jerusalem came through Idumea while we were in Petra."

"Jews?"

"Yes, from the queen."

"From the queen? Into Idumea?"

"Yes. Into Ashkelon. They raided the Temple of Ashtaroth and destroyed it and everyone in it."

"I thought your father was governor of Idumea."

"He is, but Jerusalem still rules all. He is only the governor at their pleasure."

"They killed Idumeans?"

Antipater nodded. "They released most of the worshippers but rounded up all the priestesses. There were eighty of them. They knew how many they were looking for, when and where to find them." He shook his head. "They overwhelmed the grounds before the locals understood what was happening."

"They killed eighty women?"

"Priestesses."

"How?"

"Why does that matter?"

"How?" she asked again.

Antipater lay back down on the bed. "Crucified them. They started three days after we left for Petra. Hung them there for four days until the last of them died."

Cypros stayed as she was, seated, with the blanket wrapped about her. "Jews killed Jews."

"Idumeans. We're not really Jews."

"You said that before. You need to explain it now."

"My father was four years old when Idumea became Jewish. We used to be called Edom. A long time ago. Edomites and Jews did not get along. Then we changed our name to Idumea. It sounds more like Judea, so it's friendlier. We had a common enemy then in the Seleucids, and so we agreed to get along. We let the past fade. Then the Jews decided that we needed to fully become Jews if we wanted to stay friends. It was the sword or conversion. Judea was a lot more powerful than Idumea then, so Idumea converted. Now we're Jews."

"Except when Jerusalem decides to slaughter eighty women in Ashkelon."

"To be fair, if the Ashtaroth temple had been in Jerusalem, the Jews would have dealt with the priestesses a lot sooner. They lasted this long by being so far from the centre. They weren't Jews like the rest of us are. They worshipped the goddess after all."

"So now you're a Jew?"

Antipater frowned and did not answer.

"I worship al-Qaum," Cypros said. "Marrying you isn't going to change that. Do you need me to tell the queen?"

"No. I'd rather you didn't."

# 7

## 76 BCE

Vultures above Jerusalem do not land within the city's walls. In this place of stone and brick, instigators of Death's great act disavow any form of remorse. Men collect the bodies. The streets offer no memory. Within a day, the place of murder becomes just a doorway, an alley, a thoroughfare for the city's regular traffic.

Gavriel conducted Pninah's tour of the new rooftop route to the market area with little drama. He scraped a knee. He did not even notice it until Pninah pointed it out. She knelt before him and wiped the trickle of blood clean.

He stayed seated afterwards and she settled herself beside him. The market area bustled with people and noise below them. Off to the side she could see the valley that cut across the city's streets and encircled the city's heart: the Temple.

"I've got to go now," Gavriel said.

"Where?"

"I have someone to meet. The way down is over there." He pointed towards the slope of the roof and the stack of stones below it. He put a hand on her shoulder and stood up, then crouch-walked down the slope and hopped from stone to stone to the ground. He waved behind him as he left. He did not look back.

Pninah stayed where she was. The view was like that on the walls or the rare posts over the gate she and Gavriel could access. It was a commanding view. She liked it here.

Some time later, she followed Gavriel's route to the roof's edge. She was less sure of herself hopping down.

Once, when not drunk, her mother had said to her, "That boy assumes you are always healthy."

"It's what I like about him," Pninah had said. She had only been about eight years old then.

"He'll get you killed."

Pninah navigated down the uneven edges of the stone pile without incident. She passed a street of shops that she vaguely recognized. Then she came to a stall her mother frequented. From there, her route home was circuitous but familiar.

After rounding a corner, she saw a crowd ahead. She kept on making her way towards the crowd. After Salome had taken over the throne almost a year ago, Jerusalem had become a fractious city.

Jannaeus, the queen's deceased husband, had ruled the nation with great order. Sometime around Pninah's birth, the Pharisaic sect had made trouble for Jerusalem. Trouble had led to more trouble and then to a civil war. It took some doing, but Jannaeus had snuffed that out. In those days, the Pharisees had been executed or had gone into hiding. Dissension had come to an end. Peace had prevailed.

"He is even expanding Israel's borders," her father had once said, "taking back all the land across the Jordan." He had nodded with a lopsided and rare smile on his face. "The royal family may call themselves Hasmoneans now, but Jannaeus is a true Maccabee."

Since Jannaeus had died and his queen had taken the throne, Jerusalem stopped being a place of peace. It turned out that the queen had been a secret Pharisee all along.

Her father had huffed at that as well. "Not much of a secret," he had complained. "Jannaeus just wouldn't do anything about it. His wife was his one flaw."

With Salome's ascension to the throne, her Pharisaic allies had come out of hiding, and the nation had split apart. "She's not even a Maccabee," her father had complained. "She only married one."

As Pninah approached the crowd blocking the street, voices were becoming louder. Shouting cut across wailing.

Pninah looked behind her and could see more people coming. Riots were not common, but they happened more often now. Sometimes it was a Sadducee under assault. That religious sect, once so favoured by Jannaeus, was no longer popular with Salome on the throne. When found alone in the streets, they were often beset by commoners with old grievances. Sometimes the victim was a gentile who had committed some offence against Pharisaic sensibilities. Sometimes it was just murder for reasons not immediately clear.

This time, it was the latter. Pninah felt a sense of relief. She passed through the crowd unmolested. She caught a quick glimpse of the body, a man. Red obscured his face and soaked his chest, a trickle running between paving stones. The already dead did not trouble her. There appeared to be no assailant present. The victim was voiceless and the killer gone. There was no one to spark further trouble.

As she passed the body and the crowd, she thought of her father. He had done his share of work to maintain order as part of Jerusalem's guard. He had arrested Pharisees and their supporters in those days. Some had died. She wondered if now he would become a target for the Pharisees' assassins.

When Pninah returned home, there was no talk of roof running or murder, not even any casual inquiries about the day. She set about the chores assigned and stayed quiet. The evening meal passed with little conversation. She sensed tension in the air, but that was not unusual. Her mother would need some time for drink later. Her father might stay or go out. Whatever caused the tension, it had nothing to do with Pninah. Her parents hardly noticed her.

After the silent meal, Pninah cleaned up in the dimly lit room. Her parents stayed seated and said nothing. After cleaning up, Pninah retreated to a darkened corner where she knew they would forget her. After a while, they began to talk.

"It's just like before," her mother said.

"No. It's not the same," her father said.

"They were women."

"Gentiles. Priestesses of Ashkelon's temple. Not normal women."

"They were women. Somebody's daughter. You crucified eighty women."

"Enough."

"Under Jannaeus, you crucified eight hundred Pharisees and their families."

"Serach."

"Haven't you had enough of slow killing?"

"I had enough killing eleven years ago. Some things just need doing. Crucifixions stopped the Galilean war, back then. I may not like this queen, but on this, well. . . " Her father was quiet for a moment. "On this, she was probably right. The Ashkelon temple needed to be destroyed."

"Diogenes, you said you'd never do anything like that again. You stayed in bed for days after the eight hundred. Now they offered you a price, and you've gone and done it again."

Her father said nothing. After a while, he got up and went out into the street.

Her mother, Serach, went to the doorway. She stood there, half lit, half in gloom. "When do you start killing Jews again?" she said into the street.

"Serach!" he whispered fiercely. Both parents came back into the house, her father pushing her mother into the dim interior. He closed the door behind them.

"Do you think the Pharisees will only target Ashkelonites?" Serach put her right hand on her husband's shoulder and turned him towards her. She was not a small woman. Her right arm was thicker than her left, and her legs bore the same imbalance—the result of decades spent shaping the turning jars of her trade. When she turned a man, he turned. Nothing was muted with Pninah's mother.

"My brother's foreman died," she said. "They need someone new at Joppa."

Diogenes looked at her.

"You," she said.

"Me? I'm not a boatbuilder."

"He doesn't need a boatbuilder. He needs someone along the shore. Someone to run the men who load and unload. Someone who can take directions and count and organize and command men. You can do those things."

"I'm a soldier."

"Not a common soldier. You're a captain of mercenaries, who happen to be a lot like dock labour. You'll still be in charge of men, and likely no one will need to die. You certainly won't crucify anyone again."

Pninah's father moved towards the door again and then stopped. Her mother had invented many alternatives to soldiering over the years. Still, her father had always taken the next commission. Pninah watched him turn back. She watched, unseen, waiting to see the shape of his latest refusal. "You would come with me?" He waved a hand at the shop they lived in. "Move everything to Joppa?"

"We'll need two wagons. I've arranged it already."

Pninah felt her eyes widen. She kept her lips together and stayed silent.

"No, that isn't an option," her father said.

"This time, there's no other option," her mother said. "The Pharisees won't stop shedding blood now that they've started. They're killing people in the streets now. We need to move. They'll keep hiring you to do this evil, or someone will remember what you once did and for who. One day, you'll be the target of a commission instead of its executioner. It's time to go."

❧

In the following days, news circulated through Jerusalem that the Betrayer of Arbel, a famous enemy of the Pharisees, had been found hiding out in a ruin near Dora. A boy had tracked him down and run him through with a spear. It was all Gavriel wanted to talk about. It took her three tries to cut through his enthusiasm for revenge and murder to deliver her news.

"Oh, that's not good," he said. "You can't leave. Shouldn't leave."

"Maybe it's better," she said.

"How can it be better? You with your mother all day? No one to run with? No one who knows things? Who will help you?"

"What else can I do?"

"You can stay with me."

Pninah laughed at him. "You don't even have anywhere for you to stay. How can I join you nowhere?"

Gavriel made no immediate response. The two sat on their perch and studied the people moving below.

"That one," Gavriel said. He nodded. Did not point. "With the brown fringe." This was a recent macabre game—his way of bridging silence.

"The man with the donkey and cart and three children besides?" Pninah asked.

Gavriel shrugged. "Somebody is the next killer. It could be him. Maybe he already murdered his wife."

"She was a Sadducee?"

"Maybe."

"Not maybe. Women can't be Sadducees."

"You don't know that. Maybe her husband was a Sadducee."

"So why'd he kill her then?"

"Right." He rubbed his neck. "Maybe he converted from being a Sadducee to a Pharisee, but his wife didn't like it, and so, oh, forget it."

"You're just hungry."

"Yeah."

She dug into her bag and handed him the heel of a grainy loaf. Berries and honey had been pressed into a pocket in the soft interior.

He took it absently, then recognized it and turned to her with a look of pure joy. "Where'd you get it?"

"Mother. She's packing up her shop. People are coming by and making last purchases, and so she has money now. More than usual. She knows I don't want to leave." She shrugged. "She's more generous than usual. For now." She handed Gavriel a small water skin. "It's a bit dry."

The boy ate contentedly. "That one." He pointed with his remaining lunch, already half gone.

"You're not going to find the next killer," Pninah said. "Just chew and swallow. That's all you need to worry about."

✺

A visitor came late to see Pninah's mother and father that evening. Two lamps burned. The hearth's light augmented the lamps' and the door stood open to let in cooler air. "I'm not carrying the wood to Joppa," her father had said when her mother complained about the heat. "And I'm not leaving it here for the neighbours."

Their visitor left a long, dark object leaning against the exterior of the house. Once he seemed satisfied that the object would not topple, he came through the door wearing a long mantle that was wrong for the season.

"It's hot in here," he said.

Her father shrugged and gestured towards Serach, who was packing another jar into a wooden crate.

"Oh, you're packing up the shop," the man said.

"Looking for something?" her father asked. "It's all hers. She does good work."

"Something like that. You've sold the place already?"

"Yes."

"Then your stock will have to do. I'll take it all."

Pninah squinted through the dim light at their visitor. To sell all the remaining stock would be a miracle.

"What will you—" her father started. "How will you? When?"

Serach started to speak as well when the man turned and waved for Diogenes to follow him. "It's too hot in here," he said. He left the house, and the doorway stood empty.

Both her parents stood still. They looked at one another, then Serach stepped forwards and hissed at her husband. She shooed him out the door with two hands. He quickly followed the stranger outside.

Her mother looked over into the far, dim corner where Pninah sat, her knees tucked under her chin. She wondered if the woman could even see her this far into the shadows. Perhaps just her eyes.

The woman said nothing and continued with her packing. Then she stopped and looked towards the open door where the men outside were talking. The voices were muffled. She tried to listen, then shook her head and went back to packing a third time.

The men outside started loading a wagon or some similar task. There was a grunt of noise, something pushed or lifted and then settling heavily. The stranger had not bought anything yet. Outside was darkness, and the stock was inside, not already in the street. Perhaps he was unloading something to trade. Pninah was disappointed. They wanted money, not trade goods.

The doorway filled again, and the stranger came in. He went straight for her mother, one arm raised.

Serach was lifting another jar to pack. She looked up and reacted fast, throwing one arm up and spinning sideways. The stranger threw his javelin and what should have run through the centre of her mother's chest instead slid beneath her upraised arm, striking her ribs, and running her through from side to side.

Her mother staggered back into jars, crashed through them, and fell with her head on the edge of the unseasonably hot hearth. She did not die quickly. She stared at her killer with wide eyes. When he advanced, she bucked and almost managed to sit up, but the javelin caught against the floor, then against a table leg, and she gasped. She did not shout or scream.

"Did you think he'd crucify Jews for the Sadducees and, by switching allegiances on the Ashkelon job, escape punishment? And you as well?" The man knelt over her mother as he said this. He spoke low and then laughed. He stood up and took one of the lamps into the back room. He came out a moment later. "No babies," he said. He set the lamp back down. "Deformed body and no babies." He shook his head and began sifting through a box near the fire, the contents of which he seemed to know already. The stranger found the money from recent sales and the deposit advanced for the house, emptying the two small bags into his larger purse. He uncorked a bottle and sniffed the wine inside. Then he tossed the bottle onto the floor beside Serach. Its contents leaked and mixed with her blood. "Cheap vinegar," he said. "No taste in women. No taste in wine. Not fit to live."

He left with the money. The javelin remained where it had lodged, and Serach gasped around it.

Pninah wanted to get up and go to her then. Her mother was violent and often drunk, but she was also a skilled potter and the only mother Pninah had ever known. Pninah did not move from her dark corner. She could not move. The arching, the stiffness, and the shaking had not yet come. She never felt the reality of those things—others told her tales later. The demon, though, was on its way. She could feel the narrowing of her vision, the pain in her head, the agitation compounded by a weakness that spread through her limbs and eyes. This weakness was the opposite of what others reported after the demon struck. She only knew the beginning agitation and dislocation and weakness. The violence she never witnessed herself. She could not move. Then she could not see. Then she was not.

❧

Night is an impersonal companion. It embraces its sojourners sometimes with heat, sometimes with cold, sometimes with rain, but never with light except for the dim flicker of stars or the pale glow of an inconstant moon. Clouds remain invisible except for the light they take away. The air feels its way through secret and dark places with shameless fingers, like a blind man groping without intention. Blameless. Night sounds no alarms, makes no judgments, and knows nothing of comfort. It is a ghost with an unfinished and unspoken mission.

❧

Pninah came back into life, not like a waking sleeper but like a swimmer surfacing in a pool at night to uncertain light. A weight lifted that left every part of her exhausted and in pain. Arms, legs, stomach, and back—everything hurt and everything trembled. It was not the trembling of a seizure, which others assured her was not trembling at all but violence unleashed from her very centre. This trembling was the conscious aftermath of an attack, like the trembling after running too long with Gavriel. Her body could take no more.

As she became aware again, she forced herself to understand her surroundings. She lay in the dark, on stone. No one was with her. Her parents were not angry. Gavriel was not holding her head while strangers crowded around and gawked at the entertainment and horror of her existence.

One hand hurt. She must have beaten the stone floor with it. She flexed the hand and determined that she had not broken it. Then she remembered the visitor and lay still. Her hurting head listened, and it seemed that the night listened with her. No sound offered insight. There was a slight rustle nearby, near her mother, a small tumbling of settling coals in the remains of the low fire. By those remains, she measured the time that had passed. She hurt more than usual, and not just her hand.

She sat up. By the dim light of the dying fire, she could see her mother lying where the stranger had left her. The stark outline of the javelin stood proudly in the room. The lamps had guttered out on their own.

Standing was a fragile experiment. Her body and head wanted to sleep. Pninah felt her way across the room without adding light. Near her mother's body, she could make out the black shine of pooled blood. She would not step in her mother's blood. Her hand reached out and touched the woman's foot. The skin was cool. She touched the other foot and felt the hardness of ankle bone beneath skin. She wondered at the strange familiarity of this skin against her hand. She could barely make out her mother's face in the light. She could, however, make out the gleam of her final grimace.

Pninah found her father outside. He had been rolled up against the side of the house and wrapped in a blanket which lifted in the evening breeze and exposed his face

She covered him back up and left the front door open to invite inspection. Without looking back, she left and made her way along familiar streets made foreign by the darkness of the night and her mind. Her body trembled, but this was not the shaking of seizures, and it was more than the weakness afterwards. Nothing escaped her throat. She did not cry out, but she shook, and tears streamed as she walked.

Some time into her search, she felt the familiar queasiness and narrowing vision creep up on her again, and she knelt on the stone street and prayed to Anna's god for it to pass. She waited. The crisis did not come. The demon passed. Perhaps Anna's god had listened.

She stood again on legs that trembled more than before, and she knew she could not go on much farther. Not tonight. There was a blockage inside, something large lodged in her chest that would not come out. Her face was dry now. Her skin felt cold in the late hot season, but she was overheated within and had chills all over. Her head ached. Her knees touched the ground without her conscious awareness that she had started to kneel. She forced herself to stand again and continue. Tiny hands tucked up to her chest stayed clenched.

She did not always know where Gavriel stayed. Lately, however, he had developed a routine. She came to what she thought was the place, the broken arch between buildings partially framing an old alley. It was darker in the alley than night justified. Something in the place was antithetical to light, and she did not dare to go in.

"Gavriel!" she whispered.

From the darkness came a yawning silence. The alley swelled. She felt it enlarge but could not see anything inside.

"Gavriel!"

There was a sound, the suggestion of movement.

"Gavriel?"

"Pninah?"

The dark was overwhelming. Aloneness came upon her then like a new form of demon. Her cheeks were already wet before she knew she had started to cry again. Her voice broke, but no words came out. She tried again and forced out a whisper: "Something happened." Then tears came hard and the great knot inside loosened and tears came harder. She began to shake violently, and she felt terror at the loss of control, and then she felt his hands on her, felt him lead her through the dark.

He brought her deep into the alley and sat her down. He held her in his sleeping place the way she knew he held her when she had her seizures. Grief roared into her and through her and out again. From head to toe, she shook, sobbed finally, then muffled herself when the echo came back on them. He continued to hold her. It was like a seizure she was awake for, and while it rushed through her whole self, a part of her stood back and observed the scene. It watched how he was, what he did, the firmness of his grip, one hand always at the back of her head. It watched how he waited and waited and murmured. She only gradually became aware of the murmuring, the ritual words from some prayer she did not know, something Anna had taught him. He said it over and over, barely audible, just a boy. She tried to control herself, tried to talk, but could not, and he demanded nothing but continued to hold her. She sensed then that what he did for her this night he had done for her many times. She had never been aware to witness it before.

Houses, likewise, preclude the scavenging attention of the great black birds of the desert. A body may dry before a fire or go days beneath a covering before senses other than sight alert passers-by. Here too, men are called to deal with the dead. There is no procedure, and no one predesignated to perform the required tasks, but they get done. The labourer broods later over the injustice of unpaid work.

# 8

## 75 BCE

NOTHER HOUSE IN Jerusalem displayed death within and without. This house stood tall and proud, dressed in gold, white, and silver. Crowds came to this house, the Temple on Zion's mount, to watch the daily rituals of sacrifice and burning. The smoke of those ceremonies hung above the city as an ever-present pall.

In the year following the murder of Pninah's parents, when late spring had blossomed in the land and almond trees had surrendered their colour, a large group passed through the Temple's Court of Gentiles. They came to a wall as tall as Cypros, with protruding pillars that rose even higher above it. Inscriptions in Hebrew and Aramaic and Greek graced the pillars. Cypros could read the Greek. It warned all non-Jews not to proceed any farther upon penalty of death. As they passed the pillars and its trilingual warning, she suppressed a sneer. She wondered if the Jews had crosses already prepared for trespassers. Nabataeans did not post unenforced warnings—or any warnings at all. There was little that warranted the imposition of human-administered death in the desert. The things that did required no advertisement.

As they made their way through the Court of Women, even sour Efrat counted Cypros a Jew. Cypros considered again the warning sign. She kept her failure to convert to the Jewish religion as a secret known only to herself. And Antipater. He believed what he wished. She pretended as he wished but she would always be al-Qaum's and of the desert. The Jewish Temple of bleating and bleeding animals and death held no attraction to her.

For her apparent conversion, Antipater had arranged the proper sacrifice in Jerusalem while she stayed in Ashkelon and ignored the event. Two other ceremonies applied to gentile converts. The second rite, circumcision, did not apply to her as a woman. She had allowed it for the baby boy. The third and final ritual was immersion in one of the Temple's pools. The Pharisees were undoing the former Sadducean standards within the Temple. From what she could gather, not only did the Pharisees and Sadducees disagree, but both camps had internal disagreements as well. Could the regional holy sites perform this conversion ritual, or was it only valid in one of the Temple's pools? Could a local scholar conduct the ceremony or only a priest? In a case like hers, could a sponsoring Jewish husband baptize his converting wife? There was no consensus except the one she held within herself: she had not been cleansed by any party, in any form, whatever appearances might have implied when she went down and into and back out of the water. Likewise, she made no commitment to Judaism other than her marriage to Antipater. She supposed that this implied some direction for her children, but no one had explicitly discussed it with her. The Jews assumed a great deal about her. She allowed them their false assumptions. In her secret self, she remained al-Qaum's. The warning between courtyards applied to her, but no one cared or dared to question Antipater's wife. The warning had no power of its own.

In the Court of Women, Hanne led the way to the place for baby Phasael's offering. It had been more than a month since his birth, and the Jews required a firstborn redemption offering. For this, Cypros deposited money. It was a simple process. Priests would buy an appropriate animal on her behalf and perform the ceremony in one courtyard while she stood in another. It was more efficient than even the trader's market, since the Temple fixed the prices and delivered the goods, or in this case, executed the goods. Everything proceeded based on an honour system. Cypros didn't need to do anything significant herself to become a Jew. She simply needed to show up, deposit the coins, and leave.

When she had asked about the ritual's deeper logic, Antipater had shrugged. "Our part is to give. The priests look after the rest."

Cypros stayed with Hanne, Efrat, and the other women while Antipater went with his father one layer farther into the Court of Israel. Only men were permitted into the court closest to the sacrificing arena to see up close what they presumed was their son's redemption ceremony. No names were used. There might have been half a dozen such sacrifices paid for today, but if only two lambs were put down who was to know the difference? Cypros wanted to laugh out loud and mock the solemn and serious women around her. She held her peace.

Once Antipater was gone, Hanne regained Cypros's attention and led her up to the upper level of the court. Efrat followed but did not seem pleased by the extra stairs. From this level, Cypros could see into the men's court and beyond it to the one reserved for the priests and the altar.

A woman came then and spoke to Hanne. They spoke in the old Hebrew, which Cypros did not understand. They seemed to be friends, though the stranger was much older. Hanne did not introduce them, and after a few minutes, the woman moved off through the crowd.

"A relative of yours?" Cypros asked.

"A friend. Her name is Anna."

"Rather old for a friend. I thought she'd be an aunt."

"No, she has no family. Her husband died the year you were born."

"Oh." Cypros considered the woman as she moved across the courtyard. "A bit young then, to be a widow. Her husband was a lot older?"

"No. It was a violent time then, under Jannaeus." Hanne said the name quietly.

"The late king."

"And high priest." She said it in a lower tone yet, and with force but still quiet in the Temple crowd.

Cypros tried to read Hanne's demeanour. "Jannaeus killed her husband?"

"Not directly. His mad government killed many during the civil war. Anna's husband was one of many." Hanne looked at Cypros with an unusual openness in her expression. "Her family was of Asher. Their hereditary territory is up the coast, from Acco through Tyre. She lived with her husband in Galilee. Jannaeus hated Galileans."

"What tribe are you from?"

Hanne shrugged. "Mixed. I was born in Galilee, but I'm partly Judean."

"Now working for an Idumean."

"It's starting," Efrat said and gestured towards the courtyard below.

The music swelled, provoking a wave of prayers. The smell of burning incense filtered through the courtyard. Cypros watched, appalled, as the priests began the activities of ritual sacrifice. This was not common butchery for a meal, but a destruction and burning of flesh for the satisfaction of the Jewish god. Music arose as the animals died and then were burned and then one of the priests stepped forward to recite a prayer or incantation in a loud voice. Cypros could barely make out, and in any event could not understand, his old Hebrew and could not tell how many in the crowd understood it either. As he finished, prayers from some of the women around her arose in what seemed to be a spontaneous response. She observed the scene around her with puzzlement and a half-smile. The women then began to murmur together, as though reciting similar verses in semi-unison, and then they all began to sing.

Everyone but Cypros seemed to know and understand what was going on.

*They're all mad.*

That was the best she could come up with. No parts of what she observed connected to the other parts, though the crowd seemed to know each component and anticipate the movement of the ceremony.

When the official ceremonies finished, the women began to talk among themselves. None of the conversations touched on religious matters. It turned out that this unshaded public ground was for social respite. The ceremony of death and burnt hair and flesh was merely their excuse for gathering. She thought she understood it better now, though it seemed to be an overly elaborate setup merely to facilitate gossip.

The smell of burnt hair and flesh drifted through. The changing flow of the sun reflected off silver and gold and tapestries. The upper level was roofless and hot. Late-day brightness shone with a stark, colourless light and introduced a sombre mood to the scene around her. It seemed that the Jewish god had shone this light on the crowd and would not cease his inspection. The voices of the women faded, but the crowd did not thin. It was the only part of her time in the Temple that made sense to Cypros.

Antipater returned and found the women. He led them out past the pillars with their death warnings, past the Court of Gentiles, through the gates, and onto Jerusalem's streets. Her firstborn son, Phasael, was now officially redeemed. She had no idea what that meant.

She wanted to tell somebody.

The day after her first Temple visit, Cypros walked on Phalion's rooftop, the home of her husband's brother. Her view overlooked the stonework of Jerusalem. The area beyond the city's wall showed scattered trees, rocky slopes, and small groves. She was alone, and she wanted to tell someone what had happened. All of it. The desert, the Ashkelon temple massacre, the ongoing, petty household war with Efrat, the birth of Phasael. Especially the desert.

"I am of al-Qaum," she said in the late evening light. She said it quietly, so no one would hear.

Ashkelon had been her home for over a year now, and she wanted to go to other places in Judea and see Samaria and Galilee, which she had heard were greener and full of rivers, but she could not. She was the wife of the Idumean governor's son. They had no business anywhere but in Idumea and Jerusalem and the road between. She could travel to Raqmu, but Antipater frowned on it. In a nation led by Pharisees, he did not like to draw attention to his son's Arabic roots. Damascus, Cypros's birth town north of Galilee, was out of the question. She feared that she would never see its straight streets or beautiful gates again. Now the wares of the Damascus vendors, the smells, the colours, the sounds only existed for her as memories. No Jews offered news about Damascus to feed her hunger for that place.

The memory of her parents and her sisters came into focus then, her last memories of them in the caravan, in the desert, and the smoke she had seen rising late on that day of slaughter. She had known then, as she fled, what the smoke meant. That sacrifice had been as senseless as the Jewish slaughter of lambs and goats, except it had been her family slaughtered in that barren place. The raiders too had socialized to the scent of burnt fat and hair. There was much in common between her experience of the Temple and her time in the desert.

She felt another wave of that post-delivery heat and

emotion surge through her. Phasael was more than a month old now. This should have passed. She imagined her family and then forcibly turned her mind from the image.

She wanted someone who knew Damascus, someone known in Raqmu, someone with whom she could speak plainly, in Nabataean. No one knew about the desert. Not deeply. Not all of it.

Cypros thought about Galilee, the stories that Hanne had told her of that place, and she wanted to walk alone among the buildings there, in the private courtyards and gardens and orchards, with her hand out like a child, like she saw boys outside the Ashkelon palace do, touching everything. It seemed they never saw anything properly until they had touched it.

She saw two children then: a boy and a girl. They were running along the rooftops near Phalion's house, between it and the market. They came to a gap between buildings, and the boy leaped across the gap. The girl hesitated, backed up, ran, and jumped across as well. Then they were off again, just the two of them. At one point, the boy stuck out his hand, and the girl took it, and he pulled her up a ledge. Shortly after, they passed out of sight behind taller buildings.

Before the pair were gone, the girl turned and looked behind her. It seemed that she had heard something or wanted a last glimpse of evening light. Cypros saw her face. The girl was young, the age Cypros herself had been when she had been alone in the desert.

She saw the boy and the girl still, after they were out of sight, the two of them racing though no one followed. They were in pursuit of pure fun on Jerusalem's rooftops, travelling above the traffic below, exploiting a shortcut to a destination known only to them. What struck Cypros most was how natural they seemed to be together. Just children. They were too far away for her to hear, but she imagined that they laughed.

Cypros turned away from her view of the city and looked over the city walls towards the desert. It made her think again of her long and silent flight through the dry-lands. No one had taken her hand then. She had been alone, chased by Terror. Her uncle had made a great speech once about that flight. He had boasted about the deaths of those nine men. But he had never asked her to tell him the details. He surmised. She had not told him everything. Never told anyone. No one asked.

She wiped her face and then dried her hands on her dress. She looked around again, looking for watching eyes, but no one watched, no one saw. She straightened up, lifted her head, and returned to the stairway. Down below, she could hear Phasael starting to awake and cry—an Arabic boy in a Jewish city led by Pharisees.

# 9

## 75-73 BCE

PNINAH AND GAVRIEL lived Gavriel's way, running the streets, stealing, and working odd jobs. They slept in disused alleys and sometimes outside the city. She often awoke with her head pressed up against his shoulder. They contemplated mornings bleary eyed and hungry. They never had extra food. Everything they had they carried with them. Even basic matters like bathing were difficult. To wash, they used public pools and walked about in wet clothes afterwards. It was a practice that became harder to support in the winter months.

When winter turned to spring, they both turned eleven years old. Neither of them acknowledged the days.

Deep into spring, news of a new peace spread across Jerusalem. After two years of Pharisees hunting down Sadducees, Aristobulus had intervened. He was the queen's second son and took up the cause of his late father's beleaguered party. The queen listened to her son. She handed over Jericho, Ragaba, and several other Judean fortresses to the Sadducees as refuge cities.

"She's allowing the Sadducees to guard the cities with their own armed men," Gavriel said.

Pninah held her head in her hands, trying to rub away a dull headache. "We should go to one." They were on a wall overlooking travellers going in and out of the city.

"No one knows your father now," Gavriel said. "You're just a girl, here or there. And there, we'd have to start over with finding places to stay."

"We would do worse than this?"

Gavriel crouched beside her, arms over his knees, thighs against his chest. His chin rested on his arms. "I can find us something better. We need to get regular jobs. I can find something for us."

Gavriel made good on his promise. They did not find long-term work, but they found regular small jobs. They saved up some money and began renting a small ramshackle room that leaned against the back wall of a shop in the Lower City. When they could not find suitable work, they picked pockets again in the Upper City.

"Did you hear about Ptolemaeus?" Gavriel asked one night. A small candle lit their small room.

"Who is Ptolemaeus?" Pninah asked.

"The king of Chalcis."

"Oh. Him. What about him?"

"He has decided to take Damascus away from the Nabataeans."

"The governor at Ashkelon—his son married a Nabataean," Pninah said. "She's from Damascus."

"I don't think so," Gavriel answered. "Jews don't marry Nabataeans."

Pninah kept quiet the rest of the evening. Gavriel did not like to be corrected.

A few months later, as the summer heat began to intensify, Pninah and Gavriel walked through Jerusalem's Upper City streets looking for new ways to earn money. Despite the queen's creation of refuge cities, some Sadducees still chose to live in Jerusalem, but only in the Upper City. Those that remained maintained rich houses here. Unlike the Lower City's brickwork and rough stone, the stonework here was largely concealed beneath a layer of smooth white plaster. Some of the buildings had Greek-style fluted columns and walls covered with geometric friezes or mosaics. Even the outer courtyards were tiled with elaborate mosaics. If those were the outer courtyards, she wondered what the interiors would look like. It was strange that after years of Greek oppression, their architecture was now in fashion. Among the Sadducees at least.

Buildings with exposed stone walls boasted a more expensive style of masonry. The stone for these buildings was cut in precise rectangles like giant bricks, the edges of which were polished to create a frame for the rougher centre of the stoneface. One could see the stone's veins in these edges exposed like artwork for all to see.

Some of the finest towers had rooftop corner decorations of copperwork or polished white stone. These grand buildings and towers shone in the early light. Pninah wondered at the expense of their construction. She wondered how she and Gavriel could enter that world of people who had the money to build such things. People who owned buildings. She tried to imagine what that would be like.

She was about to pose a question about money and property when Gavriel pushed her off the road. She stumbled, surprised, and collided with the side of a rising staircase.

She turned to complain and then noticed an approaching group of men on horses and carts led by a small chariot. This company of riders looked like men with their minds set on something cold. There was not one smile among them.

The leader of the company stopped before Pninah and Gavriel. His closest chariot wheel was within Gavriel's reach. The man in the chariot wore his beard wild beneath strong cheekbones. His gaze passed over the children and the rest of the crowd in that narrow place. His men with their horses and wagons and supplies filled the street. There were hundreds of men and animals waiting, ready to be off again.

The man in the chariot finished his survey and barked orders. The company surged ahead, through the gate, and soon were gone.

"Aristobulus," Gavriel said.

"The prince." Pninah pushed away from the wall. "Do you know what that was about?"

"The queen is sending him to Damascus," Gavriel said.

"She's starting a war with Damascus?"

"To protect it. That's what I heard. Protect it from the king of Chalcis. I don't remember his name."

"Why would we protect a Nabataean city from—"

"Ptolemaeus. That's his name."

"So why—"

"I don't know. I guess we are against the Nabataeans except in the case of Damascus."

"Why?"

"I don't know. Maybe we're always against Nabataeans, but we're more against Chalcis than Nabataea, so that's why we're defending Damascus."

Pninah thought again about the Nabataean woman in Ashkelon. There was an obvious connection, but she did not feel like starting an argument. He still did not believe her story about the governor's son marrying a Nabataean.

"Listen," Gavriel said. "I know a place we can get some work—they have lots of weeds. If we dig it all out, they'll pay us. We have to haul all the waste away as well."

"Do they have a wagon we can use?"

"I don't know. We might have to carry it. Lots of trips. We can do it together. It will take about one day, I think."

"Okay. My hands are better now."

He took her hands in his own and looked at the cuts there, mostly healed. "We won't take another job like that one," he said.

"Your hands didn't get it as bad."

"I'm more used to it. If there are thistles at this place, I'll get them. You do the other stuff."

Occasionally, news broke about some Pharisaic revenge or a rare Sadducean counter-attack. Both Gavriel and Pninah avoided discussing these events. Neither of them knew what to do with the anxiety they created for Pninah.

The defence of Damascus raised the profile of the Idumean governor's daughter-in-law. Gossips speculated that she had inspired Jerusalem's decision to defend the Nabataean city.

As Gavriel and Pninah finished their small evening meal one night, Pninah finally brought up the Damascus and Nabataean topic again. "I never said he didn't marry a Nabataean," Gavriel protested. "She's just the daughter-in-law, though. A nobody. A gentile."

Near the end of Pninah and Gavriel's third year together, the Idumean governor, Antipas, died. The queen attended the funeral and appointed Antipater to replace his father.

"Now the Nabataean princess is no longer the governor's daughter-in-law," Pninah said. "She's the governor's wife. I'm sure she talks to the queen."

Gavriel shrugged and continued his efforts to get their fire going again.

"What else did you hear in the market?" he finally asked.

"She had another baby."

Gavriel looked up in surprise, and Pninah caught his expression. There was a pause, and then she burst out laughing. "Not the queen! The governor's wife—the Nabataean. She had another baby. They called him Herod."

# 10

## 72-70 BCE

AFTER HEROD CAME another child. When Cypros was at full term, the child, a daughter, came in blood and in silence but for a mother's cries. Antipater took the body from her, and she never saw the still girl again. The Jews had no ritual for such a birth. There was no trip to the Temple, no sacrifice, no cleansing, no closure. The stillborn did not exist. No one made a record of the girl.

Cypros's breasts became heavy. There was no child to ease her pain.

Phasael was old enough to ask questions about the baby, and he did, twice, until his father silenced him.

⤜

On the morning of the fourth day, Cypros woke late. Antipater had just come back into the room. She sat up, expecting Hanne, but it was just her husband. He looked as though he had been dealing with his records keepers and was distracted with numbers and administrative worries. This visit was merely to check in on her.

He sat down on the edge of the bed. Cypros rubbed wakefulness into her face. She looked at him finally with an expression that she hoped was neutral.

"It's day four," Antipater said. "You have done enough mourning. This is not proper. I want you to go down by the sea today with Hanne and the boys."

Cypros felt heat rise within her. This was not the grief of the last four days but a new and sudden anger. She found her hands in hair but there was no knife there. Her hair was loose and fell about her in disarray. She did not know what she would have done with a knife had she found it. She looked over at the small table where some of her personal things lay, including the sheathed blade. When she turned back to her husband to see what he had made of this instinct for assault, she saw that he was not watching her at all. His gaze was out the window on something distant. She combed out her hair with her fingers to finish the gesture for an audience of no one.

"We waited thirty days before we went to the Temple for each of the boys," she said. Her voice came out as a raspy whisper. It was a voice of exhaustion and sorrow and hate.

He turned and looked at her.

"Now I know why," she continued. "You wait to make sure they live. If they don't live, you act like they never existed."

Antipater smiled at her. It was a smile reserved for people beneath him—people he needed to be patient with.

"Go down to the sea with Hanne and the boys," Antipater said and stood. "Get back out into sunshine."

Weeks passed, and then a month. Then two months. Finally, Cypros and Antipater resumed intimacy, but in their time together, Cypros held something back. The experience was unfamiliar. She took less pleasure from him. Something wrapped her and guarded her as though she wore a veil between herself and emotion, between herself and her husband.

The winter came and went, and then another blow struck her sorrowful heart: Damascus fell. Aristobulus, sent to protect the city from Ptolemaeus of Chalcis, had failed. Everything about the man's northern quest had been a failure.

Cypros got the news in bits and pieces from servants. Finally, she stopped her husband in a passageway. She put a hand on his arm to detain him and asked not with words but a stare.

"A third party showed up and threw everyone's plans off course," Antipater said. He looked at her hand on his arm but did not move his arm away from her. Nor did he take her hand in return. He ignored it. "Tigranes of Armenia decided that he wants Damascus. Neither Aristobulus nor Ptolemaeus was strong enough to stop him. And the Nabataeans were, as usual, useless at defending themselves."

She ignored the insult. "What about Jerusalem's army?"

"What about it?"

"They could reinforce Aristobulus's band. Drive out the Armenians."

Antipater snorted. "You're interested in directing the generals now, are you?" He smiled at her. It was that condescending smile again. "Aristobulus is no longer there to reinforce. He retreated into Chalcis with Ptolemaeus."

He said this last bit as though it meant something. Cypros waited.

"He's married his eldest daughter off to Ptolemaeus's son, Philippion."

This change of plans was enough to jar Cypros from her focus on Damascus. "You say that as though you mean something deeper."

"For me to marry you," Antipater said, "well, we Idumeans are not real Jews to begin with. But for a Judean—a Hasmonean at that—to marry his daughter off to a gentile, and not just any gentile, but the one he was sent off to go to war against—I hear the queen is enraged. Enraged as a grandmother *and* as a queen. And as a Jew for that matter."

The bizarre marriage explained some of the gossip she had picked up from the female staff. Focus had never been a Hasmonean strength. They were forever marching out to do one thing and accomplishing its opposite within a matter of months. Sometimes weeks. Cypros let go of Antipater's arm. She did not notice him leave.

At some point later she roused herself from deep thought. She was sitting on a bench in an inner courtyard of the palace. She did not remember having walked there.

Later that spring, Cypros's monthly blood stopped again, and her belly grew. Antipater kissed her so firmly their teeth clicked, and they laughed into one another. He could have made her lip bleed and she would not have let him go.

With spring and her new pregnancy, lightness returned to their union.

The boy was born in the coldest part of winter. When he was seventeen days old, Cypros rose one afternoon feeling cold. The boy was warm, well wrapped near the fire. Hanne was on an errand beyond the Ashkelon palace wall. Antipater was due back from Jerusalem that afternoon. Phasael and Herod had been through the room a few hours before. Phasael had asked about the baby and Herod had mimicked his older brother's speech in a tangle of fractured syllables. Then the boys had crashed out of the room. They were napping now.

Cypros went to the baby and looked down on the miracle of him. He slept very still. His small lips were parted and dry. She touched them, then his cheek. He remained still. She smiled and picked him up to kiss him and found his only movement to be the sagging of head and limbs. He did not even breathe.

Cypros suppressed a scream. She looked about the room, but no one was present; the other servants were in other parts of the house. She swallowed and did not cry out.

They would take him. Seventeen days was not enough.

He was not alive to the Jews. He was not a person, had not achieved thirty days.

She unwrapped the body and slipped the naked child under her clothes, against her breasts. She pressed a nipple to him as though that would make him wake. She bobbed up and down, cried, looked about with blurry eyes, looked down into her clothes at the child who would not move, would not suck, would not breathe.

A trickle of milk ran from her and across the boy's

cheek. She smelled it and him. She sank to her knees before the fire. Antipater found her there later.

"Cypros," he said. There was a crack in his voice, but then he reached for the child, and she pulled roughly back from him.

"Don't," she said.

"It is done," he said.

"It is not done."

"It is."

His hands slid around the child, between her and the baby. He took the body from her. She watched him rewrap it in its blankets. Then he left the room.

She would never see the baby again. No record would be made. It had not lived thirty days.

The fire was the only witness to what happened afterwards. No one came to dry her tears or hold her. She was alone for the rest of the afternoon. Officially, the boy had never happened.

Months passed, and then again, there was a pregnancy, the third after Herod. Cypros did not make it the natural full term when she began to feel contractions signalling the birth to come.

"It's too early," she cried out to Hanne, to the midwife, to the doctor. She thought of the knife, but the knife would do her no good. She thought of running out of the palace. She could run south to where there was desert like Nabataea. As though she could outrun death. She could barely move. Blood seeped from her long before the baby came.

When the child was born, it was only partially recognizable as human. Hanne said something under her breath that she would not repeat. They took the abomination away.

Cypros was aware that stories would begin to circulate about the governor's wife and her Nabataean womb. The Jews were more superstitious than even the Nabataeans.

"Why is this happening?" she asked.

Antipater shook his head.

"Why were you somewhere else?"

"There's a problem at Gaza," he said. "Two ships have caught fire this year already. It's just a coincidence, but people like to speculate. Stories take a life of their own. One of the docks is being repaired at our expense to calm the rumours."

"You're thinking about the docks at Gaza?"

"Somebody has to," he said. He did not look at her. "There will be other children."

She stared at the side of his head. She wanted to hurt him with her eyes, but he would not turn to look at her. He left the room. He did not touch her or look back but left without another word.

After Herod, there were the three lost little ones, and then a fourth was born, another boy. They called him Joseph. On the twenty-ninth day following the boy's birth, Cypros got up at dawn, as she had the previous twenty-eight days. She offered prayers to al-Qaum, and then at nightfall, she begged for the boy's survival again. Antipater knew and did nothing to stop her. As long as she was discrete, he gave her no trouble about al-Qaum. On the thirtieth day, they left for Jerusalem. She had never been eager for the Jewish rituals before. Now, she wanted the Temple, its extravagant *tryphé* decorations and macabre warnings, smoke and sacrifices, chants and public prayers, the sound of money ringing in jars and women gossiping as the ash of burnt fat and hair fell around them.

They went to Jerusalem. They filtered through the Court of Gentiles and passed the trilingual warning signs and into the Court of Women. Antipater left her with Hanne and the baby. The ceremonies proceeded as they had before, but this time the smoke seemed thicker and heavier. It did not rise as on other occasions but washed through the open air Temple at ground level.

In that dry and dark haze, Cypros bent close to Joseph's sleeping cheek. She had not intended to speak, but as her lips brushed his face, she whispered to the baby. "You will rule this city one day."

The child murmured back to her in his sleep.

"You and your brothers—one day," she added.

She had her knife in her hair as she spoke to her son in the gloom of the smoky Temple. A woman was not permitted weapons at all, but she had her knife with her, here. Had any tried to harm the child, she would have flashed on them with the power of a desert leopard.

She recognized that the image, the imagined scene, was out of place. This was a time of worship and reflection and praise. The women around her were finishing up their prayers. The Temple was not a place to imagine a fresh murder.

She thought about her own mother then—the fierce Nabataean woman who had been equal to her kingly brother. Her mother designed Cypros's union with Antipater to shore up an alliance with Idumea and keep the Gaza port open. She was a woman with ideas. A woman who led.

Cypros thought of her mother's plans. Then she thought of her knife, hidden away in her hair, and in her mind she played it out again, her imagined defence of Joseph. Her mother's plans were too small. Her hidden knife was not enough. As ash fell around her, the seed of something else entered her. She looked at the baby in her arms.

*You and your brothers will be my knives.*

She looked around, but she had not spoken out loud. The time for prayers had completed. Hanne was talking with a friend. The other women were talking about things that did not matter.

*I won't hide you in my hair. I've taken you out of my body, but you are still me. And I won't hide you.*

She looked towards the inner courtyard where Antipater was with the other men and the priests and the crackling, smoking fire. She looked down again at Joseph and saw something powerful. She saw the beginning of an oak tree— one that walked. She saw all three boys, walking together, as fearsome men.

*I will no longer be the girl in the desert. I will stride, in you, anywhere. Everywhere.*

She looked around at the crowd in the Court of Women. They were all Jews who she knew secretly despised her. She was the Nabataean—the gentile—whatever the state of her conversion.

*Go ahead. Hide me away in despised Idumea. Accept me as good only for breeding. Among the ghosts of eighty witches, I will give birth to terrors who will rule you all.*

She bent her lips to Joseph again. "The ones that died were not strong enough," she whispered. Her breath stirred a piece of ash that had settled on the boy's forehead. It lifted and swirled and drifted away.

⁂

A few months later, outside the Ashkelon palace, smoke rose straight from lamps and two fires. The thin columns were invisible in the night. The light painted hematite shades across the courtyard's pillars. The colours reminded her of Raqmu's oranges and reds. Faces in firelight shone. Cypros's uncle, Aretas, had come to visit.

The night transformed Aretas's cream and yellow robes and turban and his flowing grey beard. He stretched out on his mat, reclining, one leg crossed over the other, one foot the highest part of him, and he looked the most drunk, though he drank nothing strong—because Nabataeans did not drink.

Hyrcanus, the queen's eldest son and, for nearly seven years now, Jerusalem's high priest, sat cross-legged, tilting, well past drunk. He was a regular at the Ashkelon palace. It was a strange friendship. Getting a Jewish high priest and his family to befriend an Idumean and Nabataean couple took some doing. The doing was all Cypros's effort. They were now Hyrcanus's closest friends.

On this night, Hyrcanus had brought something special—some mysterious Galilean drink that involved fermented quince, something not made anymore. It was a relic from the time of his namesake grandfather, before Jannaeus's civil war. The crops and all memory of the technique to make this liqueur had been destroyed in the war. The bottle alone was beautiful, a rare collector's item from craftsmen as long forgotten as its contents soon would be, the golden liquid slowly disappearing through this night of agreement and humidity. The quince liqueur was considered a prize, and the docile high priest had brought it to share.

Antipater's younger brother Phalion was also present. He favoured the Idumean wine more than Hyrcanus's exotic distillation. He made up for in volume what his wine lacked in strength and so approached the high priest's state of intoxication.

Antipater closely followed his brother and the priest. He propped himself up on one elbow, a sleeve pulled back and tangled at one shoulder, which he failed to notice. He favoured Hyrcanus's exotic quince offering, and the two of them worked on the bottle as though it were a duty to drain it.

Joseph slept in Cypros's arms. She had fed him by the miracle of her own body and knew nothing of alcohol, for she drank a cassia and cinnamon tea. Her Uncle Aretas had brought the ingredients for the tea to honour Joseph's birth. This tea was the gift of kings, a present from a Nabataean king to Antipater, now Idumea's governor. Hyrcanus tried the tea, then returned to his Galilean liqueur.

The night sky was without clouds and awash with stars. The ocean of light overhead was pocked with holes at regular intervals that were the black silhouettes of palm trees. They stood like motionless sentinels about the Ashkelon complex.

After much conversation and drinking, there came the sound of slack-mouthed breathing followed by sub-dued laughter. Hyrcanus had slipped into sleep, sitting up cross-legged, tilting over but not yet falling.

"These are the feared Hasmoneans," Aretas said in Nabataean, "who took my cities along the Jordan."

"He's the weak one," Cypros replied, also in Nabataean, "and his brother failed as well when he tried to protect Damascus."

Antipater did not ask them to translate. He stared into one of the two fires. His eyelids were heavy and half closed. Cypros had never seen him pass out from drink. He would not pass out tonight either but keeping up with Hyrcanus and his brother was going to cost him. It would not take him until morning to begin to pay. He would suffer even during the night.

Hanne came to take the baby, but Cypros refused her and sent her for the rest of the tea. The other boys were already asleep inside.

A breeze came from the sea then, and she smelled the warmth and the salt of it. Something green had piled up along the shore and spoiled. The smell was a faint but pungent odour that had bothered her with each pregnancy. Her disgust faded and did not cause her trouble after the babies came. It was just a part of the Great Sea.

The endless blue of the sea in daylight, as seen from their rooms in the palace, was a wonder. When the storms pounded waves into the shoreline, she loved to sit and watch and listen. It made her sons sleep. She learned to time her thoughts to the rhythm, and in this way, she could think when everything around her was busy. The effect that the sea had on her seemed to be what Antipater wanted when he drank. Her ocean solution was better.

Antipater stirred, sat up straighter, and discovered his sleeve. He adjusted it, and when Hanne brought the remains of the tea, he accepted some along with Cypros and Aretas. Phalion stayed with his wine.

Aretas sat up then as well, his head close to Antipater. They sipped at hot tea, holding their cups in two hands. They both drank from Idumean cups, not Nabataean. These cups could be set down, but Aretas did not—because they do not.

Cypros watched the two men as she tasted tea. Their postures made it look like they were conferring, but they said nothing. They were both strong men, but she knew them to be vulnerable in ways they would not acknowledge. Age made Aretas less vulnerable. She looked over at the listless and slack-jawed Hyrcanus. He was vulnerable in the same way but not strong to begin with. His state was just weakness now mixed with drunken sleep.

Hanne came back again. She hesitated at the edge of their gathering, but Cypros gave no sign. She kept the boy tucked into her robe. Finally, Hanne took a chance and stepped forwards and reached for the baby. Cypros let him go. He would awake again later and need her. For now, she let him go. Her arms felt empty, her chest heavy, her back sore.

They were alone then, the four of them, five with the sleeping high priest.

With the baby gone, her centre expanded, and she realized she could hear the sea again. Antipater had been right. She loved the sea.

⁘

Cypros had a dream that night. The baby woke her, and she fed him. Antipater woke her again later, heaving in an adjacent room. She judged that she must have slept through the first of his attacks. He would be fine again come morning. Their guests, Hyrcanus and Phalion, would sleep until midday. Hyrcanus, the high priest, had been the subject of her dream. That was all she could recall.

She went back to sleep then, and the dream returned. She recognized it as a returning vision, even in the dream. It was last night's scene, but with the conference held in daylight and not by firelight. There were just the five of them. She supposed that servants came in and out, like last night. The slice of time captured in her dream, however, was without anyone but the five. Even the baby was elsewhere.

In her dream, she circled the seated Hyrcanus. The logic of this dream did not provide a reason for this odd stroll. She supposed later that he was sleeping seated, as last night, though the dream revealed no reasons. Everything just was. As she circled behind the high priest, she saw that he had nothing on his head. Even his hair was missing. There were holes in his skin and his skull. She could see inside the back of his head. These were great holes that were large enough to put a hand through into that forbidden place. There was empty space within the skull. Farther down lay the meat that one would expect, but it had shrunken away from the top of the skull and its large openings. Down there, in the meat, there was a large green worm-like insect moving very slowly. It was as fat as three thumbs together and half again as long. The worm-like body of the creature had a separate articulate head. It might have been a smooth bulbous caterpillar, but she could not tell if there were legs. She saw it curling over the meat in the same curving posture that whales held after they breached offshore and then returned into the sea head first.

Similarly, the creature was already at the apex of its

movement, its head curving down, and slowly it slid back into hidden places. She could have reached for it and plucked it out. It was not small. It seemed to her in the dream that she should take it out of the man's head. She would have done the high priest a great favour with the operation. He would be upset to discover the gaping opening in his skull and the creature that resided there, but his distress would be less than if she left the thing to feed or breed or whatever its mission. She hesitated in her dream. The scene and the creature repulsed her. She did not know if the thing was safe to touch. She held her peace, and the worm's articulate head disappeared into head-meat, and then the dream passed into a deeper sleep.

She awoke suddenly. It was not the baby this time. Antipater slept loudly beside her. He slept this way when recovering from drink. The governor's residence was otherwise quiet. She could not hear the sea. She lay down again and let go of the image of the green worm and the awful head.

In the morning, she walked the gardens with her uncle. They spoke in Nabataean and privately agreed about Damascus.

# 11

## 70 BCE

ARISTOBULUS WAS NAMED after a tyrant uncle who both family and nation had hated. His namesake uncle had claimed Jerusalem's throne for less than a year. In that year, he had managed to murder his mother by starvation before he himself had been stricken with disease, upstaged by a younger brother, and then murdered by his wife.

The failed tyrant's nephew, Aristobulus, now sat with his young sons in their Jerusalem home before a gloomy fire. He sat in silence and weighed his stained name and the burden of carrying it an entire lifetime.

His oldest son sat nearest to him. The boy's name was Alexander. He had been named for another hated king: the Greek conqueror Alexander the Great. Naming the boy after a despised Greek was an act of perversion that was traditional within the family.

Aristobulus was content with having named his son Alexander. It was now a traditional name for kings. He planned to be king one day and pass the throne to his son after him.

He stayed silent as he thought these things. He brooded and contemplated the fire. His twelve-year-old son sat before him as he formulated a response to Aristobulus's question.

His younger son also sat with them, witness to these proceedings. His name was Antigonus, another Greek name.

Aristobulus sat with his perversely named sons in the dimly lit room, which was empty but for them and his words. He sat and he waited. Together the three formed a triumvirate united by blood and ugly names. He was waiting to hear how his boys would respond.

The nation did not think much of Aristobulus. He knew that. He was deemed a holdover from the Sadducean era, loyal to a dead cause. The gossips exaggerated and even exulted in his failure at Damascus.

When Tigranes had finished conquering Damascus, the Armenians had gone on from there to lay siege to Acco. That should have been Aristobulus's opportunity for redemption. His father had originally conquered that city. As his father's son, he should have recovered it, but Salome had not allowed it.

Queen Salome had not said so, but she had implied that her second son would fail again. She herself had gone to Acco. Upon her return to Jerusalem, Tigranes quit his siege of Acco and left the country. The Armenians had even given up Damascus to Salome. Aristobulus could not comprehend how that had come about. She could have done enough in her brief visit to scare off the Armenians, and yet she had gone and then the Armenians had left.

After the queen's return to Jerusalem, she had announced that she would gift Damascus back to the Nabataeans. He wanted to know what his young sons would say about this development.

"Everyone says—" Alexander started.

"I don't care about everyone," Aristobulus interrupted. "What do you say?"

The boy was not quiet for long.

"Grandmother acted like a Pharisee when she bribed Tigranes to give up Acco and Damascus. There's no honour in paying a tyrant to go away."

"And then she gave Damascus back to the Nabataeans," Aristobulus said.

"When she could have made money from it," Alexander replied. "Or kept it."

"And why would she want to do that?"

"Why not?"

"You have to do better than that, son. You are twelve now. Think like a man or I'll demote you and appoint Antigonus in your place." Aristobulus looked at his second son. The younger boy paid close attention. He would rival his brother one day, for there was no real division between the boys but a year. Aristobulus was proud of them both. "Now answer me."

"Eretz-Israel is safe when it has a buffer," Alexander said. "Like in the days of Grandfather."

"Jugurtha's Doctrine."

"We expand Israel beyond Israel's border—" Alexander started.

"—so if we fight, we fight our enemies over there, not in our own country," the younger son interrupted.

Aristobulus looked at Antigonus. "Don't interrupt," he said. "This is Alexander's time."

"It's not just about territory," Alexander continued. "It's also about revenue. Grandmother could have sold Damascus back to the Nabataeans or we could have kept it and earned taxes from it for years to come."

"Good. Why? Don't we earn enough?"

"Loyalty. Those who pay are loyal. Those who are loyal protect our borders. Protecting our borders protects the city and the Temple."

"Good. Taxes are one way to measure loyalty. The moment we stopped paying the Seleucid tribute, we were preparing for something else: our war against them. The flow of money measures the flow of intentions. Now, next question: who are Galilee and Iturea loyal to?"

"The Pharisees."

"And who actually guarantees their borders?"

"Sadducees."

"Then why are they loyal to the wrong party?"

"The Sadducees have failed—"

"Stop. Rephrase."

"The Pharisees lie," the boy said. "They claim to honour the law of Moses as he intended, but everything is different now."

"Do better."

"To apply the law of Moses in our time, you have to adapt."

"Otherwise?"

"Otherwise, the nation dies."

"Yes. If we leave the future to the stubbornness of Pharisees, there will eventually be no more Eretz-Israel. You have to adapt. If we ran this country like Pharisees, Galilee would be in chains. So what if our ways become a little Greek as a result? The whole world has become Greek to one degree or another. Now, I'll ask you again: to what are you loyal?"

"Eretz-Israel and the Temple."

"Which makes you a—"

"Sadducee."

Aristobulus stretched and contemplated the floorboards above. This was not the palace. The home was not worthy of royalty. The queen, his mother, gave him no honour. His mission to Damascus had been undermanned, a meaningless force, a ruse to keep him away from Jerusalem. He was under no illusions.

The arrangement Aristobulus made with Ptolemaeus of Chalcis, however, was a stroke of genius. His eldest daughter would one day be the queen of Chalcis—a Jew would be the queen of a gentile nation. That was a Greek move—a Sadducean plan in action. It was Jugurtha's Doctrine taken a step farther. Jugurtha proscribed war and taxes to free and then protect Eretz-Israel, but the man had not read enough of Israel's history. Every stool had at least three legs, and political marriage was the third leg.

Aristobulus looked at his boys and wondered what he should arrange for them. The Egyptians would be valuable, and the Romans were always of interest. The Parthians were impossible. He thought about the Nabataeans and considered Antipater's play: marrying the girl from Petra. It was clever. But Antipater was not a real Jew, just an Idumean. He might be the Idumean governor, but he was no threat.

Still, Cypros had been a good idea. Aristobulus would have to find women like that for his boys.

"What do people say about Galestes?" Aristobulus asked. "And Pitholaus? Nicodemus?"

"People call them traitors," Alexander said.

"Traitors?"

"They are loyal to the Sadducees. That kind of traitor. Like us."

"What else?"

"People say that a knife will find them soon enough."

Aristobulus nodded. "And yet, they are my friends," he said.

"They are all Eretz-Israel's friends," Alexander said. "Most people are just too stupid to know it."

Aristobulus smiled. He sat up and looked at Antigonus. "And you?" he said. "You're too young for this conversation, but what do you say?"

"I'm with the Sadducees too," the boy said.

"And what about the things people say about the sort of men your father calls friends?"

"Isaiah said tough things too," the boy said. "But he was right."

Aristobulus laughed. "Yes, he did and he was." He looked at Alexander. "Your brother is a smart boy."

"They killed Isaiah," Alexander said.

"Yes, that as well. You two share a dark fate with your father. We have to be Isaiah to this generation. David as well. It is up to us to save this country from itself. If the Pharisees continue to stick to old, outdated ways, the nation will fall."

"But Uncle Hyrcanus will be king after Grandmother dies," Alexander said.

"And he's a Pharisee," said Antigonus.

"Yes. Yes, he is. And he will. Unless we stop him." Aristobulus leaned in towards the boys. "We have to stop my brother from becoming the next king," he said. "Galestes will help. And Pitholaus. And Nicodemus. But I will count most on the two of you."

"You're going to take the throne from Uncle Hyrcanus?"

"Yes, we are—when the time comes. Now answer me: why are we going to do this?"

"Because we're with the Sadducees."

"No. That's never a good enough reason. Try again."

"Because we love Eretz-Israel and the Temple."

"Yes. Good. And we love Uncle Hyrcanus as well. We must make sure that he doesn't come to harm through any of this. Do you understand?"

"Yes."

"When the time comes, he can go back to a private life, like Aunt Salina. She gave up the throne for my father and lived the rest of her life in peace."

"We could give Uncle Hyrcanus this house," Alexander said. "It's a good house. He could live here."

Wrinkles appeared around Aristobulus's eyes. "You're a good boy. Yes, let's do that."

# 12

## 69 BCE

DARKNESS LAY OVER the Ashkelon palace. The stone pillars and seats down by the ocean surrounded an unlit fire platform. Dozens had celebrated here in times past, but this night there were just Cypros and Antipater. Only stars and one lantern illuminated the space.

The boys slept inside the palace under Hanne's care: Phasael, Herod, Joseph, and now Pheroras—four living children for seven years of marriage. All boys.

The small lamp that lit the space between Cypros and Antipater seemed to waver on a rhythm in time with the sound of waves in the distance. This place of pillars—the fire platform, stone seats, and stars—was their place of entertainment, celebration, and at times, private conversation. When they sat out here alone, like tonight, staff came only when signalled.

Antipater had set a small package before him when he had settled himself. He had brought the package down from the principal residence, but Cypros had not asked about it. He would tell her in time.

"Your home town is once again Nabataean," Antipater said. The lamp glowed in the middle of the otherwise unlit fire platform. They reclined across from one another, the lantern between them, the sound of the sea washing over. "The queen takes all the credit."

Cypros had eyes for the stars, ears for her husband. "Does she not deserve it?"

"The Romans were threatening Armenia. Salome's flattery and gifts were just the excuses Tigranes needed to go back and defend his homeland. The real credit for the liberation of Damascus goes to Rome."

"But Damascus thanks Salome," Cypros said.

"She takes credit. And then she gave the city back to Nabataea, for which your uncle and countrymen thank you."

Cypros wondered if the stars were cities off in the far, far distance. Or lights on distant roads. In some places, she thought she could see the pattern of paths in the light, markers to get from one place to another in those heavenly realms. Who the travellers might be in those places was a mystery to her. There was nothing in the lore of al-Qaum to satisfy that curiosity.

"Her victory with Acco and Damascus is a humiliation for Aristobulus," Cypros finally said. "Both of her sons are a disgrace: Hyrcanus and Aristobulus. Jerusalem can be grateful she only had two."

"Is it that obvious?" Antipater asked.

"That her sons are the end of the Maccabean line?"

"That Damascus is Aristobulus's humiliation."

She looked long and hard at the stars, as though winding down a conversation or train of thought that had been focused there, then looked across the platform at Antipater. "He was sent with an army to protect it from Ptolemaeus. Instead, he gave up his daughter to Ptolemaeus's son while losing Damascus to Tigranes."

"Getting things spectacularly wrong is the standard Maccabean way."

"Then Ptolemaeus decides he likes Aristobulus's daughter in a very non-father-in-law sort of way and kills his son so he can marry his now-widowed daughter-in-law," Cypros said. "That puts things going wrong at an impressive new level, even for a Maccabee."

"I see where you're going with this."

"Then his mother, who was furious at the marriage, settles not just the Acco problem, which is what she set out to do, but Acco *and* Damascus with the same bribe? One visit? No army? And she shores up Israel's relationship with my uncle while she's at it?" Cypros tucked a strand of hair away that had not escaped, that no one could see in the dim light even if it had.

"Now Aretas is happy with Jerusalem," Cypros continued, "even though she's keeping all the former Nabataean towns her husband stole from my people. She's wrapped everything up, all the borders of Eretz-Israel at peace, with no effort at all but that of thinking and talking and a few coins. She's a genius and makes her sons look incompetent. The disastrous double marriage business with Aristobulus's daughter is all he has to show for himself."

She could hear a different silence coming from her

husband. He was not listening to the waves or studying the stars. She knew this stillness and silence and stayed quiet herself as she waited for him to work through what he would say next.

A long time passed. Had there been a witness to this conversation, the thread might have appeared lost, the topic changed, or its participants fallen asleep, but that was not how things worked with Antipater. Those that understood and could be patient benefited.

"I know everything you know," he finally said. His words came out slowly. He was still thinking. "All the same information was available to me—Aristobulus's failures, his daughter's bizarre marriages, his mother's victories, the Nabataean angle—but I had not put them together before. Not until now. You are right; his humiliation is profound and complete."

"She's done everything Aristobulus couldn't. And his older brother will get the throne when Salome passes and presumably keep the high priesthood as well. But Hyrcanus is not any better than his brother."

"How so?" Antipater asked. "I understand, but I want to hear you say it. You've got me questioning my interpretation of people and events now."

"At least Aristobulus tried something."

"A complete failure."

"But he tried." Cypros made as though to sit up, then changed her mind and adjusted her cushion instead. "Hyrcanus just performs the bare minimum of the high priestly duties in the Temple but otherwise demonstrates no ambition. When he comes to visit here or in Jerusalem, he's drunk and never has an interesting idea to share. Both brothers are incompetent and useless."

"Hyrcanus takes suggestions well."

Cypros nodded at that, then realized that Antipater could not see her well enough to notice. "He helped me convince his mother regarding Damascus."

"He takes full credit for leading that conversation now," Antipater said. "I thought you should know. He simply followed your directions, but now he makes it a point of pride. As though it was all his doing to strengthen the Nabataean relationship. He might be a drunk, and he could be a useful drunk when Salome passes, but we'll have to put up with him continually taking credit for what we tell him to do." He sat up and rubbed his head. "You need to track down some of that Galilean quince wine that he likes, if there's any still left in this country."

Quiet settled then between them again. On any other night, they would have stayed quiet until the morning. Even their walk back to the palace residence would have been silent. There was a rhythm to these late-night talks near the sea, and they had used up the evening's quota of conversation. But Antipater was not yet done.

He picked up the package and held it in his lap. "You haven't asked about your gift," he said. The package was a small, wrapped box about the size of four fists.

"The weave is Nabataean," she said.

"You can tell the weave just looking at it?"

"I didn't know I could until I saw you carrying it. I remember it from my childhood."

"Well, you're right about that. It's from your uncle."

Antipater stood and walked around to her side of the

firepit. The lantern there continued to give them the little light they enjoyed.

He sat down beside her and handed her the parcel.

"It's heavy," she said.

"He's sent you a block of stone, I think."

Cypros unwrapped the package, and inside were twelve square tiles of roughly equal size but two different types of stone, four of limestone and eight of marble. Cypros said nothing, but her hands betrayed a tiny tremor. She sat up, and on the wide flat rim of the raised fire platform, she laid the first stone. The paint on the face of it was white and red. She continued laying stones like pieces of a puzzle until all eight formed a grid four wide, two high.

Antipater brought the lamp closer.

She moved a couple of the stones around until she had the image right. The picture revealed a collection of birds—some wading and a few soaring, and even some tiny songbirds. The second puzzle was a four-piece collection in red and white and blue, which revealed a palm tree, two figures below it, and a lute. Far-off in the distance were three camels.

"Does it mean something?" Antipater asked. She did not answer him at first. He moved closer to her. Tears tracked both of her cheeks as she looked at the pieces.

"What is it?" he asked.

She put the heels of her hands to the sockets of her eyes and then wiped her cheeks.

"They are from Damascus," she said. Her voice was airy and broke up as she spoke. "From our house. From the room I shared with my sisters."

Antipater wrapped up the tiles again for carrying.

Walking back to the house in the dark, Cypros spoke again. "Hanne will be the new head of staff for the women," she said.

"That's Efrat's role."

"Now it's Hanne's."

"What will we do with Efrat?"

"Dismiss her."

"At her age? She worked for my father her entire life and has done an exemplary job during the transition."

"Yes, she has. And in doing so, Hanne now knows everything she needs to know. So get rid of Efrat."

"Anything else?"

"I'd like to have her beaten, the Jewish way, with rods. I want her barely able to walk."

"No, Cypros. We can't do that. She's done nothing wrong but get crossways with you early on and stay that way ever since."

Cypros stopped and turned to face him. "You can't, or you won't?"

"I won't."

"Fine. By the time I am up in the morning, I want to hear news about Hanne's promotion circulating in the hallways. The other one can walk from here. Don't allow her any special treatment. She can leave only with what she can carry."

"She's an older woman, Cypros."

"Then she best not carry too much with her."

Antipater sighed and took her arm, and they finished their walk back to the buildings before them.

❧

Some months later, Aristobulus left Jerusalem at night with a large company. As they came to the city's moonlit gates, silent allies opened the doors. These men tasked with standing guard that night were given the spare horses, and they left the gates abandoned to join Aristobulus's throng. The men and horses entered a plain that at various times in Jerusalem's history had seen the bloody regalia of nearly all the world's armies. Perhaps only Rome had never camped outside these walls. This night, the gates were left open. No armies threatened. The plain was moonlit and silent once the men were gone.

Once on the Jericho road, Aristobulus reflected on Eretz-Israel's history of royal children vying for their parents' crown. In the days of King David, Absalom had been the first of these treacherous children. Aristobulus's namesake uncle, the first Aristobulus among the Maccabees, had been the most recent. Aristobulus wondered if Absalom would have chained and starved his father, David, had he been victorious in that first coup attempt.

*I won't chain or starve Salome.*

The decision satisfied him as he rode by moonlight towards Jericho.

*She is already ill. The old woman won't last long.*

# 13
## 68-67 BCE

THREE MONTHS PASSED. Rumours spread that Aristobulus was visiting each of the Sadducean refuge cities. When he left each city, the gates were all locked down except for the main ones.

The queen sent messengers out calling for a special meeting of not only the Sanhedrin but also the regional governors. The riders bringing word to Ashkelon had arrived late the previous day.

"The timing isn't good," Antipater said, putting a hand on Cypros's swollen belly.

She brushed his hand away. She did not like him touching her that way. She did not know why.

"The baby isn't due for another month or more," she said. "Go."

The day after Antipater left was a day of sunshine. Not being able to attend the Jerusalem council bothered her. It was not the late stage of her pregnancy that prevented her from going. It was not even her Nabataean blood. She was a woman. Salome, the queen, would be the only woman present. One woman ruled, albeit precariously now that her son seemed intent on a coup. No other women attended.

Despite these thoughts, it was still a day of sunshine. She wanted to brood on what the council members and advisors would say and do and decide, on how the queen would manage the room, but there was something in her blood that would not let her brood. She would have run along the sea with the boys had it not been for her belly. Walking was now a chore.

Still, sunshine ruled, within and without.

Two days later came birth pangs and a coldness that crept along her scalp foretelling doom.

"It's too early," she said to Hanne.

Her companion and attendant did not answer. Instead, she directed the staff to put different coverings on Cypros's bed to protect it. She sent for the doctor and informed the minder to keep the boys away until called for.

Cypros gasped near her bedroom window and squeezed her eyes closed. A contraction seized her and promised more terror to come. "Send someone for Antipater," she whispered as the attack eased.

"Already done," Hanne said. "Two fast riders."

"What is he going to do here?" Cypros asked. She glared at Hanne as though daring the woman to point out her contradiction. "He belongs at the council in Jerusalem."

Hanne smiled and said nothing. She helped Cypros back to her feet and across the room to the prepared bed.

"The doctor will be here soon," Hanne said. "This baby will come quicker."

"What do you—" Cypros stopped as another contraction gripped her. She half crouched, holding on to Hanne's arm, and let out a long, guttural moan.

Hanne stood still and supported her until Cypros could stand on her own again, panting for air.

"What do you know about how long it will take?" Cypros asked.

Hanne helped her turn around, back up, and then sit down on the edge of the bed.

"I've been here for every one of your deliveries," Hanne said.

Cypros tried to catch the woman's eye, but Hanne kept her head down, moving pillows and absorption blankets.

"These contractions are coming more quickly," Hanne continued. "It stands to reason that the baby is coming quicker as well."

Cypros wanted to argue, shout for the doctor, shout at the doctor, curse Antipater for not being here and for eventually, uselessly, arriving. Another contraction claimed her and with it her water broke, and she no longer had words or energy to fight. But it did not matter. Her body would fight her regardless. It had started. There was nothing she could do to stop it. The child would die. Cyprus's passage through this valley would come with screams and with blood, but death would be victorious in the end.

Cypros moaned after the contraction was over and noticed Hanne react. It was written clear on her face that she thought Cypros was having another contraction too quickly. Cypros shook her head to correct the misunderstanding. Before she could complain about the darkness she felt, the cause of her moan, another contraction did seize her. And so the night passed. The morning dawned. Afternoon came on. And then, early in the afternoon, the baby arrived.

Cypros woke to silence. She did not know how long she had been asleep. There was a heavy cup filled with water at her bedside. She drank and emptied the large cup, not pausing for air, then set it back on the table.

She lay back and pulled the small bundle to her. None had been able relieve her of the burden. She wiped tears from both eyes and then felt her hair and found it wet at her temples. She closed her eyes and wiped them again. Everything hurt. She lay still as the bundle was still and willed sleep to come again and erase this day and this night. It was dark in the room. All candles had gone out. She imagined that she heard vultures shuffling somewhere in the hallway. They hunted for her and her burden.

Someone came back into the room, probably Hanne, but Cypros kept her eyes closed and pretended to still be asleep. Soon she was.

"Aristobulus left his wife and children in Jerusalem," Antipater said. He paced about the room. He had arrived from Jerusalem the night before, but only come into their room this morning.

"It's a tactical blunder of staggering stupidity." Antipater shook his head. "At first, Salome had a hard time believing that her son was planning on overthrowing the throne."

Cypros slipped a finger into the palm of a tiny hand that closed its fist in response to hold her. Cypros smiled. The baby lay quietly, her sleeping breath gentle and even. "What changed her mind?" she asked.

"He's visiting each of the Sadducees' refuge cities, and when he leaves, they lock down all but the main gates."

The baby was very small—early but healthy. And small. This was her first girl. Her first girl to survive. "You're going to make it," she whispered. To Antipater she said, "Why are they convinced that he's plotting something?"

"The sudden departure from Jerusalem with an armed guard for an unexpected visit to Jericho. The abandoned gates in Jerusalem. The locked gates in the refuge cities. The sudden lack of communication between refuge cities and the palace. No word at all from Aristobulus about where he is or what his plans are."

"But the queen isn't convinced."

"Not at first. She is now. She's put Aristobulus's wife and children, including the two older boys, under arrest. Her grandchildren are her hostages now."

Cypros looked at the sleeping child. Her face did not look much different than the boys so soon after birth. She was just smaller. "Where is she keeping them? Aristobulus's family."

"In the Citadel."

"Where both of his uncles were killed."

"Including the one he's named after," Antipater said. "It's not subtle. The queen's husband walked through pools of his brothers' blood to win the throne. She will keep that throne on the lives of her daughter-in-law and grandchildren if she has to."

"Do you think it will come to war?"

"That woman has kept the peace in this country for almost ten years with words, symbols, and threats. She has not led us into a single armed conflict despite having an army half again larger than the one Jannaeus commanded."

"The Sanhedrin backs her?" Cypros looked up to see Antipater watching her and the baby. He nodded in response to her question.

"The queen may be old and ill," he said "but she knows that language is about more than words. Small deeds demonstrated early can avoid larger conflicts later. Her son should be afraid. She has his family."

"And so," Cypros said, looking back down at the baby, "we will call our daughter Salome."

Antipater opened his mouth, then closed it, and in the end said nothing.

Cypros smiled at the baby, but not about the baby. She smiled about names. She had a rule about names: she bore and birthed the children, so she named them. She did not look up to see if Antipater agreed or disagreed. She knew he would not say anything. Regardless of his opinions, the girl would be Salome, and the name applied today, not after thirty days.

"Salome," she said.

❧

Grief is a powerful emotion. Greed, betrayal, humiliation, fear, and anger are as well, but grief overrules them all. It was one thing to form a rebellion against your mother, but it was, apparently, another thing altogether to face the reality of her loss.

For Aristobulus, it seemed that grief arrived when least desired.

Eretz-Israel no longer gave birth to prophets. Its sages and poets, however, spoke eloquently about Salome's legacy. The entire nation paid their respects when she died. Seasons of good weather, years of strong crops, borders without invasions, even the invention of new dyes, weaves, and melodies were all ascribed to Jerusalem's first successful queen.

Aristobulus returned to Jerusalem for both the funeral and his brother's coronation. No one accosted him or grilled him. Cypros, in Jerusalem with Antipater for the funeral, watched the armed men trail Aristobulus in and out of public events. The city's guard ignored these men.

After the coronation, Cypros asked about Aristobulus over a family dinner. Her brother-in-law informed her that Aristobulus had already left the city.

"His wife and children are still under arrest in the Citadel," Phalion added.

"I heard he did not even ask about them while he was here," Phalion's wife commented.

"You can't know that," Phalion said.

"It was obvious at the funeral that he mourned his mother," she replied. "And from the look on his face two days ago, he mourned the coronation as well. But he didn't say anything about his wife and children. And he left without them."

"He took more than his guards with him when he left," Antipater said. "I'm hearing reports that many others from Jerusalem left with him."

"Loyalty to Salome doesn't mean loyalty to her oldest son," Phalion said.

It was an odd dinner—just the four of them together, men and women in the same room and no guests. It was more like an evening at Ashkelon than Jerusalem.

"If it comes to another civil war—" Cypros started.

"Don't say that," Antipater said. "There's no need to discuss that."

"There is. And we will. If it comes to another civil war, which brother are we backing?"

"Cypros."

"Which one?"

"Neither. They're both incompetents."

"Incompetents, leading armies, do a lot of damage. Their mother's competence is what prevented wars, civil or otherwise. We have to pick one, so which brother do we back?"

"Who do you suggest?" Phalion asked. He seemed more willing to give her topic a hearing than Antipater.

"The one we can most influence," she replied, "which would be Hyrcanus."

Antipater frowned. He made as though to take another drink, then seemed to change his mind. Cypros watched him hesitate, then look up at his brother. "What do you think?" he asked. "Do we back Hyrcanus over Aristobulus, if it comes to that?"

"Hyrcanus it is," Phalion said. "The drunk over the rebel."

A few days later, at Ashkelon, Antipater brought up the conversation again with Cypros. They were alone, walking back from the sea with the sound of waves behind them.

"I don't bring you to Jerusalem to meddle in Jerusalem affairs," he said, bringing an end to what had been a walking argument. "Leave the running of this country alone. The way you women gossip is bad enough. When you start trying to direct policy or decide our loyalties, it becomes intolerable."

# 14

## 66 BCE

"A MAN I KNOW has something for me," Gavriel said. He and Pninah were sitting in a secluded corner of a rooftop surrounded by taller parapets. They could see over the wall on an angle across the valley and on to the setting sun.

"A job?" Pninah said.

"Maybe. An opportunity. I have to go to Jericho." He gestured behind him.

"What kind of job?"

"Aristobulus is recruiting men."

"Gavriel!"

"Not as a soldier. I don't know anything about weapons. He wants runners and riders, but I might be able to get access to the stable manager. Maybe I can get in there. I'd even do cleaning to get started. The way we're living with day jobs and always looking for the next thing can't be our plan forever."

"They're not going hire you in the prince's stables at Jericho or anywhere else."

"It's a chance."

"What will I do?"

"I don't think women are going there yet. I'll send word or come get you once something is secure. Or maybe there's better work in Jericho, and we can move there and try a new start."

"Is it safe?"

"Nothing is safe with the Pharisees in charge."

"Nothing was safe for the Pharisees when the Sadducees were in charge either," Pninah said. "I know what my father did for a living."

"It will be safe for us. That's all that matters."

⚘

At Jericho, Aristobulus stood in a high area and surveyed the scene. His father, Jannaeus, had fortified the palace here with gates and high walls. An aqueduct neared completion, the work of his mother, Salome. The marble inside the palace had been faked, the work of painters.

There were two smaller palaces on the property. These were his mother's creations as well, Salome's solution for peace between her rival sons. She mirrored the separation of Pharisees secure in Jerusalem and Sadducees banished to fortresses by separating brothers at the family winter residence. The two sub-palaces were identical in size, structure, and even decoration. One for him. One for Hyrcanus. Aristobulus despised both buildings.

A path between pools, a pavilion, and a kind of miniature temple in a very dated Greek style lay about the property.

Two stiffened leather straps came together in the open field below the palace compound. The resulting crack echoed across the plain. Aristobulus watched the five runners race along the track. The one who had recently come from Jerusalem was ten strides ahead of his competition when he crossed the finish line. Over both short and long distance, the young man was fast, perhaps faster than anyone else in Eretz-Israel. They had yet to find a career runner who could beat him.

Aristobulus smiled. Sometimes all that mattered was speed. He watched the runners regather in the distance. Aristobulus's hair and beard were as wild as the wilderness that filled his mind. He thought about runners and Greek-style temples and divided brothers and the inevitable war to come.

Later, in the stables, Aristobulus walked with Galestes.

"How fares Pitholaus?" Aristobulus asked.

"He's gathering men, but few come with their own weapons. He needs more volunteers with weapons. They are arriving, but not armed."

"What of your men?"

"I've been more successful recruiting from Ragaba. The men there are better equipped. Salome retired many of her foreign men around the city. She didn't think to collect their private weapons."

"My mother thought that letting the older ones retire and stay here on Jewish soil would ensure their loyalty and deter the Nabataeans from trying to return."

Galestes nodded. "When you stop paying a mercenary, though, they stop being loyal."

"So Pitholaus needs weapons. Get him some. Artabba is a critical fortress for the west side of Jerusalem, and Kefira even more so. Controlling the fortresses isn't much help to us if the men are not adequately armed. Pitholaus needs to find a solution. How is Nicodemus faring with his locations?"

Movement at the far side of the stables caught Aristobulus's attention. He redirected their path towards it.

"Nicodemus's recruits have more weapons," Galestes said, "but not many horses or donkeys. Similar to what you've got here."

Aristobulus put his hand on Galestes's arm to alert him as they continued to walk forwards. Galestes put a hand on his sword, but Aristobulus shook his head. "You won't catch this one," he said in a whisper. The whisper gave him away, and the shape moved quickly.

"You can't outrun the horses," he said loudly.

The shape slowed, then stopped.

"Come," he said. "I want to talk with you."

The runner from Jerusalem, the new one, came into the open.

"What is your name?" Aristobulus asked.

"Gavriel," the young man said.

"What are you doing here? Spying?"

"I like horses," he said.

"You're a bit too talented to put with the horses."

"I've wanted to work in a stable all my life."

Aristobulus laughed. "How old are you?"

"Twenty."

He turned to Galestes. "His whole life, he's wanted to be a stable boy," he said. "All twenty years of his whole life." He turned back to Gavriel. "You're a runner. You would be wasted in a stable."

"I've always wanted it."

"Why?" Galestes asked.

"They are the only thing faster than me."

Aristobulus grunted a forced and unkind laugh. "I said you were *a* runner, not the fastest runner."

"There's no one faster than me. Not here. Not in Jerusalem. Not short distance, not long, especially not with obstacles. I can run across the roofs of Jerusalem if I have to. No one is faster than me."

"Why would our future king make you a stable hand when you're such a fast runner?" Galestes asked.

"When horses collapse, you still need the message to get through. Messages sometimes cross the city itself. I'm faster than any horse in the city. Try me on stone streets with crowds and corners and carts. I'll beat any horse you can provide. Twice. I can ride to the city, then run through the city. Why *wouldn't* you make me a rider?"

"Have you ever ridden?"

"No."

Aristobulus grunted. "No one is going to teach you now. Get back with the others, or I'll have you beaten as a deserter."

Two nights later, Gavriel lingered outside the stables again. Only a quarter moon and the stars lit the area. He listened to the sound of the horses, their slow movements, impatient exhalations, and the scrape of hooves on stone. He imagined that only kings rode horses. He imagined cheating on his dream by stealing one. He listened to their night noises through the stable wall and tried to come up with a plan.

⁂

Pninah stood at the edge of a field in bright sunlight and felt fear as though she were about to walk into fire. Gavriel would never let her work in a place like this. The heat was intense, and there was no shade. The plants were tall enough that if she fell, she would be lost. If a seizure lasted too long, unshaded, she could die in a place like this, and none would know until someone found her body.

"You lose a lot of water in an attack," Gavriel had explained to her.

She had frowned at him then.

"I don't mean that—you even lose water from your hands and feet. If you lie for even an hour or two in the sun with no shade, you could die. Anybody can get a seizure if they lie in the sun too long. Working in a field like that could kill you."

She stood on the field's edge like it was a cliff. There was no food in their bare room. She had not seen Gavriel for three weeks. There was no one she could ask. He was just gone. This was the work she had found.

She entered the field and bent to her task. The sun immediately reached out with long hot fingers, slid across her back, and gripped her skull in a fiery fist. The long day started with that first step.

At the end of that first day, and each of the days after, she walked, tired, after work to the Gishon Pool. Siloam, they called it now. She had yet to get used to the new name. She got into the pool with her clothes on and swam, washing as best she could. Afterwards, she climbed the southern-most steps dripping and walked home.

She bought some old bread from the merchants and ate alone in the small room she had once shared with Gavriel.

The foreman in charge of the field outside Jerusalem's walls was a lean man with incongruously wide hips. He sat in the shade of a row of olive trees, watching the field as he slowly separated dried grains of wheat from their husks, working only by feel. One at a time, he rolled a hard seed, brushed away the liberated husks and papyrus-like layers, and then chewed the hard results. He laboured not for hunger but out of boredom. He kept his eyes on the field and prided himself on performing the seed-cleaning operation without looking, each hard grain its own reward.

One of the young women in the field suddenly stood up. There was no cause for standing in this place. They did not get accustomed to this labour if they insisted on standing up straight all the time. This one was weeks in and should know better by now. She called herself Pninah. She had been no trouble so far, but now, suddenly, she stood. He watched in utter amazement as this violation of procedure was shattered by an even worse trespass: the girl began to run, not down a row but straight for the treeline, across rows. She ran like a demon pursued her.

The foreman stood to watch this offence more intently. He had a mind to shout at her, but her run was so wild that it distracted him. He looked behind her for a pursuer and ahead for a destination, but neither glance yielded an explanation. Then the picture changed again. The girl went from running to falling, and not the normal fall of someone tripping in a field. It was as though she had flung herself onto the ground. He was shocked to see her land face first in the turned earth, arms stiffly out to her sides, not trying to stop her fall. She landed hard on the ground, well before the shadowy line of olive trees, and then she began to shake.

The man dropped his remaining grains and walked to where Pninah lay. She frothed into the earth, face down, and looked like she would suffocate. He took her by one stiff and unyielding arm and rolled her over as others came to witness this spectacle. Her face was a smear of spittle, dirt, and blood from her nose and lip. Her eyes stared at some unseen place up and to the right, a reference point that stayed fixed in that same spot above her skull no matter where her head was turned. Her hands and feet dug into the loose soil, and a terrible moaning came from her throat.

"Get back to work," the man shouted at the gathering labourers. "There's nothing here but madness."

He stood and watched Pninah while the others drifted back to their place. She could be pleasant to look at, but not now.

She worked hard. He paid her less than the others, and she worked harder. But not now. This was inexcusable, and he decided then and there that he would fire her after this week.

"Not worth it," he said to the trembling body. "This is not worth it. You're not worth it."

⚬

She knew this was the end. She lay in the dirt, feeling the ache begin to spread through her body—the post-seizure muscle pain that crippled. She was very, very tired now. A few days would pass before she was at risk of this happening again, but she had heard the foreman's promise as he had talked to himself, unaware that she was not only still but could once again hear.

Pninah sat up, and the foreman watched her from a distance. He was seated again, had regathered his scattered grains, and was once again slowly hulling them by feel. "Go home," he said. His expression was not kind. "Get yourself clean."

She had worked half the day already, but he offered her nothing for the morning of labour. "You owe me at least that for the distraction," he said.

There was no one to appeal to. She stood on weak legs and walked out of the field, through the front gate, and back towards the city. She felt like an old woman. She had mud and blood dried on her face and in her hair. A woman at the valley-gate well drew water for her, and Pninah washed to make her appearance less awful. The woman asked nothing of how she got to be in this state. The woman looked at her clothes, the dirt front and back, the blood and filth, and drew her own conclusions.

The next day Pninah returned to the field and worked without incident. The foreman dropped a coin in her hand at the end of the day and dismissed her with the others.

The next day was to be her last. She felt ill towards the end of that day, but no attack came. She stood in line with the others for her day's coin.

"You wait until the end," he said when her turn came.

She stepped out of the line, uncertain.

"Back of the line," he said. His voice was harsh, his gaze on the next worker.

She did as she was told.

After everyone but Pninah had been paid, one of the older workers, a man with white hair who as a boy had once been trapped with his family between Jerusalem's closed gates and the invading Seleucid army with its gaudy soldiers and elephants, who as a middle-aged man had seen eight hundred Jews crucified outside those same walls, and who now worked for subsistence wages in this unshaded field in view of those same walls, held back. The foreman looked at him, and the old man put his head down. "There's nothing for you here," the foreman said. The old man nodded but did not move. "Nothing at all but a beating, if that's what you want." The foreman had a reputation. His wide hips made him look foolish, but he was otherwise lean and muscular and had a violent streak. Pninah had seen this man beat a fieldhand, and her fellow workers spoke of others.

The old man hesitated with this warning, and then when the foreman made a slight gesture, the old man nodded and departed.

The foreman held her coin in one hand and looked at her. "You can't come back," he said.

"I know."

"No one else will hire you."

"Someone will."

The foreman sneered. He kept the coin pinched between a finger and thumb. He reached out, and she opened her hand for it, but he held the coin there, over her open palm, and did not release it.

"I could keep your pay and send you on your way. What would you do? Who could you complain to?"

She said nothing. Her legs and back hurt from the bending, and her head ached from the day's heat.

"I saved your life the other day. You would have filled your mouth with dirt and suffocated. You owe me your life."

She said nothing.

"What will you give me for the coin and for saving your life?"

"I don't have anything to give."

"I think you do." His other hand shot out under her wrap, fixing on a fistful of hair. She jumped in surprise, and then he bent her head back. She shifted to keep from falling, neck arched, throat exposed, hips cocked to keep her balance. She tried to call out, but her voice caught against the acute angle, and barely a whisper escaped.

The foreman laughed and said something, but she could not understand what he said. She struggled to breathe and to keep her balance as he forced her head farther and farther backwards. Her back arched towards him, and then there was the sound of running footsteps and a great collision. Released, she fell backwards and landed on her elbows, jarring her back. Two bodies tangled on the ground beside her, and she had the memory then of a crunching sound like a bone breaking, and a deep bass grunt finally came from the foreman.

The two bodies rolled on the ground. The new assailant was much smaller than the foreman, a wiry shape with well-defined but small muscles like—Gavriel. She got up on her knees as the foreman finally got on top of his smaller opponent, and one fist connected with Gavriel's head before she could act. A second fist descended as she cried out and threw herself at the foreman, knocking him off Gavriel.

Gavriel was up quickly, and then it was the three of them tangled together. The foreman was roaring now. He punched Pninah once, connecting with her forehead, and when it did not knock her out or cause a seizure, she screamed back at him and threw herself forwards, locking her teeth onto his forearm.

Gavriel was doing something furious and frantic, his fists swinging, the blows roughly blocked. Pninah fell away from the foreman's arm with a piece of meat in her mouth, and the foreman's rage and noise filled the yard. They rolled and rolled again, the three of them.

The foreman finally managed to get on top of them both, with blood pouring from his arm and his nose or mouth. She did not know how badly Gavriel was hurt. He was on the ground, below her. She was on top of Gavriel, her back to his chest, the foreman with his wide hips and powerful legs straddled them both. But all was not in the foreman's favour: Gavriel, reaching around Pninah, had a fistful of the man's beard in one hand. He held one of the man's wrists while Pninah held the foreman's other bleeding forearm in both of her hands. Dominant again, the man wanted to see the source of his bleeding, and he wrenched the bitten arm free to look at it. His weight and the strength in his legs kept them pinned. She knew he would look, then he would strike, and her own body was part of the trap holding Gavriel down.

The foreman turned his gaze towards Pninah, ignoring Gavriel for the moment. She could tell that he planned to speak, to bite, to spit, or to claim some down payment on a more intimate assault to come. She feared what was about to come from that looming hate-filled face.

She saw the old white-haired man then. He had in his hand a field blade, and he came from behind the foreman. The old man had no eyes for Pninah and spared not even a glance at Gavriel. He came with the knife in both hands and seemed to be measuring his spot when he tripped over the tangle of warring feet below him and fell forwards. His knife, no longer carefully aimed, fell haphazardly into the foreman's back. Pninah's left hand acted in concert with the old man's fall. She blocked the foreman's descending face, and her hand slid across blood until her thumb found the hollow above his cheek. In the same moment that the old man's blade entered the foreman's back, her thumb drove into the eye socket and, once buried there, deliberately hooked into the softness of that place. The foreman came forwards under the old man's weight, and he screamed. It was not the foreman's familiar roar but a scream like a wounded animal. Then he jerked back and away from the two below him, and the old man fell off, and the foreman's violence met the anger of her hooked thumb. All she did was hold her hand steady, and he did the rest.

She rolled off Gavriel, or he pushed her, and then Gavriel pounced on the wounded man, who held his face in two hands, seeing nothing. Gavriel straddled the foreman, punching at the brute's hands and face, not understanding what had just occurred.

Pninah came up beside him. "Let me," she said. The bloody field knife lay beside the two men. She picked it up and, without pause, drove it into the man's temple.

They stood back then and watched, panting and blood

covered. The old white-haired man got to his feet and stood with them. Together, side by side by side, the three watched the foreman move.

"Am I like that?" she asked.

"No," Gavriel said. "It's different." They looked around, but the field was empty. All of the other workers were long gone.

Pninah's breathing gradually settled as she stood with the two men and watched the foreman die.

"It takes longer than I thought," she said.

"Living things don't like to quit," the old man said. "Cut his head right off, and his legs would kick a while yet."

When he was still, they finally looked at each other.

"Did he do this before?" Gavriel asked.

"No," Pninah and the old man both said together.

"Today was the first day," Pninah said.

"Has anyone else—"

"No. I've been okay. Where have you been?"

"You moved," he said. "I couldn't find you."

"You were gone. I had no money. You smell funny."

Gavriel laughed. He wiped his thigh and brought it up to Pninah's nose. "Like that?"

"That's gross." She pulled away from him, but not far. "Yes, like that. What is that?"

"Horse."

"Horse? Why do you smell like horse?"

"I'll tell you later." He knelt over the dead man, went through his pockets and purse, and then limped to the accounts table. There he emptied the small box. He piled up a few weeks' worth of wages for one person and then sorted the coins into two piles. He scooped one pile into his hand and walked over to the old man, who was crouching now and staring at the foreman's corpse.

"Here," Gavriel said. "Your share of what remains."

"I didn't kill him for money."

"No. But you, sure enough, helped kill him. Thank you for that. You might as well take a share."

"I don't want it," the old man said. "I'll show up to work tomorrow like normal. I don't know anything about what happened here."

The old man looked up at Pninah. "Other than I saw you leave on good terms. It was your last day. Everyone knew. He paid you fair, and you went on your way in peace. We left together. That's all I know about what happened here. I don't need any money."

With that, the old man stood and walked away. Nearly at the gate, he turned back again and looked at Pninah. "You need to wash your face before you leave here," he said, then passed through the gate, and was gone.

Pninah wiped her mouth and nose, and her hand came away covered in blood. Then she noticed Gavriel's stiff, wide posture. "What's wrong with your legs?" she asked.

"I rode a horse from Jericho," Gavriel said. "I'll never ride a horse again."

# 15
## 66 BCE

Beyond the Ashkelon palace, the night-time sea lay unusually quiet. Inside the palace, children slept. In the governor's bedroom, lamplight flickered. Neither Antipater nor Cypros could sleep. Antipater sat on the bed beside Cypros, feet on the sheets, elbows on his knees.

"Hyrcanus has the Pharisees," he said. "He leads the Sanhedrin as well. Despite a complete lack of ambition, the kingship, the Sanhedrin, and the high priesthood all rest on his shoulders. Are you listening?"

Cypros nodded and covered herself. She made a gesture for him to continue.

"My brothers and I are his strongest allies. If I were Judean, or a Hasmonean cousin, he would appoint me as king. He has that little enthusiasm for the throne. Are you paying attention?"

"I want to go back to Raqmu," she said. She closed her

eyes and breathed in deep and slow. After several months, Antipater finally wanted to talk politics again, and here she was redirecting the conversation to Nabataea. She frowned and kept her eyes closed.

"What?"

"You liked the canyon," she said. She opened her eyes and tried to even out her breathing. Her heart raced. She distrusted her tongue.

"Sure. Petra is fine. All of it. But we are talking about Jerusalem." He leaned in towards her, trying to find her eyes behind the veil of hair that covered her face. "We are the king's closest friends. Our boys will be next to the throne. It's what you've always wanted."

She swept her hair from between them and returned his gaze. "My uncle is a king, and our people are richer than these provincial Jews could ever dream of being. I don't want my boys next to a throne. I want them *on* it."

*And free to eat dabb,* she added only in her mind.

She wanted dabb, the red delicacy of the desert, but Jews were forbidden to eat lizards. She realized then that her boys would not only never eat dabb but they would also never want to. They were Jews. They knew nothing of Nabataea. Heat churned in her stomach and pressure built in her chest. Tears formed and began to roll down her cheeks.

Antipater came in close to her. He wiped her face with two hands and said words she could not hear. Just once, she wanted Nabataean to come from him, but he had not learned a word of it. His hands were on her shoulders, and he was still speaking. One hand moved to a breast, his way of jollying her out of these moments. She slapped his hand away and then got out of the bed. She pulled her wrap tighter around herself.

She looked at the doorway but did not move towards it. They used the next room only as a passageway and for clothing. Then came the actual passageway. The rest of the palace. Servants. The children. Servants' quarters. The kitchens, the butchery, the dining rooms, the burning pit, the stables, the barracks.

There was nowhere to go.

A vision of the desert came to her. It was a memory of those days of flight when she had lain beneath uncountable constellations in the dark, the sand below her, limbs pulsing, a half-limp water skin against her hip. She had been bride only to al-Qaum. Utterly alone. She had lain there, for the first time motherless, fatherless, and without siblings. Her body had not been lost, just her life.

Now her life was found, reconstituted as an Idumean Jew, and her body was lost. Parts lay buried and unnamed about Ashkelon. Other parts wandered the grounds in the form of living children. Parts of her were surrendered to this man who did not understand her. Another child would eventually come, and that child too would cause her pain and then leave, whether to live or to die, she had only to wait to discover.

Antipater wanted to talk about power now, but only his. She had none. Would only ever have none because she was a Nabataean in Eretz-Israel. A woman in any country. There were occasionally queens, but they were a rarity and usually short-lived. Salome had been the first on Jerusalem's throne not murdered.

Cypros wanted the desert again and her younger self,

alone there, her body her own, no parts taken, none owned by another. She wanted to be free. She wanted to rule.

In the desert, the environment had been her tool. Everything had been hers in the desert. No one had corrected her, penned her in, or chained her down. Raqmu's refreshments had likewise provided joy and strength. By contrast, Ashkelon and Jerusalem were shackles.

She walked over to the window and looked out at the night-time courtyard. It was the same courtyard where Jerusalem's troops had once camped the night before they had assaulted the Ashkelon temple. She wondered if the witches of Ashkelon enjoyed a better fate than she did now. Those witches no longer struggled in a world that would not have them.

Antipater's feet scuffed the floor as he moved across it. She waited to resist his touch. He rarely came to her now for a second time on the same night. Then she registered that the scuff was fading, not advancing. Shortly afterwards, she heard his voice elsewhere in the palace. Later yet, he left through the courtyard with two of his aides while she looked on. He was going somewhere in the night, doing something unknown to her.

She looked back at the crumpled bed. This was her mission now: to live for others without choices. What came of her service would be decided after. Little, if any, recognition would be given for her part in all of it.

She went again to the bed and sat down on it and wound her hair. One of the servants would fix her hair in the morning. She bundled the strands together, inserted the knife—the same one she had carried in the desert—and then tied it all beneath her scarf. The nurses frowned on her attachment to the blade. Of those at Ashkelon, only Antipater knew the story behind it.

As she sat there, feeling her tears dry, an image came to her—it was that of a peasant girl, a girl with a man who was little more than a boy himself, the two of them a pair. The girl was smiling, an awful grimace, her mouth and teeth caked with blood. Cypros did not know what the image meant, whether the pair were Jewish or Nabataean or something else, but they made her want to know with urgency where Antipater had gone.

She went to the window again, but there was nothing to see. The trio had left without even the lingering sound of horse hooves on stone.

The next day, the relentless tyranny of the Great Sea crashing alongside Ashkelon drowned out the voices of the children playing. They loved the pattern in the rock that ran into and below the surf. Phasael was the oldest of the children, nearly nine now, Salome the youngest at two. Joseph was the loudest of the lot, and Pheroras the most reckless. Herod, at five, was the moodiest. He wanted to know why the land shifted from sand to rock alongside the same sea. She had no answers for him as she stared out across the water. She looked down finally and saw him turn away with a frown. He played the rest of the afternoon with less enthusiasm.

Cypros had loved the sea when they had first moved to Ashkelon. Now its endless and purposeless noise upset her. Jerusalem was the centre of this country, and it lay far from the sea.

In Jerusalem, there was a certain quiet aura around the

Hyrcanus palace that reminded her of the desert. She who had walked the desert alone, had killed nine, had carried and delivered eight, of which the Jews counted only five. She felt the previous night's anger stir up again. She despised herself as unfit and hated her role as governess in Ashkelon. She wanted more.

A week before, she had convinced Antipater to walk with her through the Ashtaroth grove. They had passed the trees the priestesses had been nailed to while the couple had still been at their wedding in Raqmu. The scars on the trunks had largely healed now.

"Eleven years has nearly erased all signs of the women who hung here and screamed," she had said, looking at her husband, who had erased a flinch and replaced it with a scowl.

"Why do you say that kind of thing?" he had asked.

She had rested a hand on one swollen bark scar and looked up the tree, imagining the one priestess who might have hung here—one among eighty—through torturously long days and nights.

The raiders had intended their own kind of crucifixion in the desert. They had intended to torment her as a mere girl for days. She had escaped most of what they had intended, but not all. The desert followed her. Even along Ashkelon's noisy and salt-sprayed shoreline, that trial in the desert followed her. It would not leave her alone.

She wanted a replica of the dabb's tail, something on a larger scale and with a handle that she could swing at all who made her existence unbearable. It would puncture skin and crush bone like a great ancient mace. She could not fix on who she would swing it at. Perhaps the Jews' God. Perhaps that.

Her private ceremonies in honour of al-Qaum did not move her as they had before. She wanted the essence now and to drop the fiction of ritual. She wanted to become one with something that had power. Something that could protect her and hers. Jerusalem did not listen to Ashkelon. The only power in Ashkelon was the unceasing grind of the ocean's waves.

"We are talking about Jerusalem," Antipater had said last night. It was the last thing he had said before he had tried to draw her from her sour mood. She could not remember everything she had said after that, but she remembered slapping his hand away and him leaving afterwards. His words lingered in her memory. *We are talking about Jerusalem.*

"Yes we are," she said out loud.

Hanne turned and looked at her. The maid was too far away to have caught the specific words over the sound of the waves.

Cypros shook her head and then nodded towards the children, redirecting Hanne's attention.

She thought again about the crucified witches. That had been the work of Pharisees. A few years prior, it had been Sadducees crucifying Pharisees. Both parties were dangerous and fixated on slow forms of killing. Nabataea had never crucified anyone in all its ancient existence. There were no trees or iron nails in the desert. Slow murder meant nothing to a Nabataean.

Cypros doubted that the Pharisees would pull out their nails and hammers again any time soon. Hyrcanus was not that kind of king. It was not a matter of nobility or restraint. He was too lazy to bother. Hyrcanus did not inspire bold moves.

*Which is where I come in.*

She looked out at the sea towards Egypt or Rome—she was unsure which. Whatever the direction, the view was of empty sea. Empty, like the desert lay empty.

*But it's not empty.*

She thought about the dead raiders in the desert, the churning in her stomach, the burning in her eyes, the shaking in her legs as she navigated rises and falls of sand and stone in that place. The vultures had circled overhead, ever watchful.

*They circled for me. Not to consume me but to support me. They watched over me. They ate my enemies.*

Cypros looked towards the Ashkelon palace. The complex was like a miniature Jerusalem with its stone walls in stark contrast to the desert-like emptiness of the shoreline. A new thought came to her, something only partially formed.

*I need new vultures.*

She stared at the palace.

The voices of the children and the churning of the waves and the calling of Hanne all faded.

She heard something like the desert's silence.

*I did not kill nine men with a blade. I killed only one. The rest I killed with the desert.*

Ashkelon's walls wavered in the heat. She looked over at the children again but did not really see them. Her mind stayed on this new thought, sliding over its still-uncertain shape.

*I knew who to kill then. And why. It was simple.*

Then she understood her problem. A thousand blades

would not slay her enemy in Ashkelon or Jerusalem or anywhere else. Her enemy lived in the hearts and minds of every human in this country. Her children would grow up and raise new versions of that enemy within. She was a Nabataean woman in Eretz-Israel—that was her enemy. There was nothing she could do to conquer that.

Just like there was no way for a girl, alone, to kill nine men in the desert.

Looking towards the children and the sea but not seeing them, Cypros smiled for the first time in days.

# 16

## 66 BCE

DESPITE THE FUTILITY of their survey, great black birds rode the air high above Jerusalem. The scent of blood that came from the Temple Mount floated in the sky and drew them in. The bodies that still occasionally appeared in the city's alleys and ravines also beckoned the birds.

The Tyropoeon Valley ran through the middle of the city. It was a place of jagged edges and steep falls, populated by only a few small old homes, shacks, and rough passageways. The Temple Mount towered over its eastern bank. The Upper City, with its palace and administrative buildings and expensive markets, dominated the high land to the west. Between the palace and the Temple, the valley was a dim tree-studded chasm.

Scents within the Tyropoeon Valley rose in drafts of heated air. Death was not as regularly disposed of in some of the valley's darker cracks and hollows. The heart of the city and the shadow of the Temple failed to provide a civilizing effect. Its residents, though fewer, were aggressive. The birds would not land in the deep dark lands, whatever the wind offered.

❧

The route from the western royal heights across the Tyropoeon Valley to the Temple complex travelled across a bridge of stone arches. The finest people of Jerusalem did not traverse its bottom lands but kept to the bridge above the depths. The bridge shone in sunlight and looked miraculous to Pninah as she gazed up from the valley floor. She could not imagine how its construction had been achieved.

Pninah and Gavriel climbed the western slope until they had a good view of the Zion Bridge and the Temple complex with the Citadel on its northern edge, which most now called Baris.

"This is it?" Pninah asked. "You're paid a day and a half's wages to sit here all day and just watch?"

"That's it," Gavriel said. "I guaranteed them I wouldn't leave while there was daylight. Said you'd fetch us food and water if I needed it."

"And if you see it, report it?"

"That too," he said.

"If you see trouble, you have to run back to Jericho?"

"No. Just to the house near one of the north gates. They have riders there waiting—about six. If I report something, two take the message to Aristobulus in Jericho. Two go in case something happens to one of them."

"And what about the other four that stay behind?"

"They wait for updates," Gavriel said. "Others are watching other places. You'll stay here when I go with the message. If something else happens while I'm gone, you can tell me when I get back."

"What counts as something happening?"

Gavriel shrugged. "An army gathering. A speech. Something important. Something that could interfere with Aristobulus's plans."

Pninah squinted and studied the valley, the bridge, the straight-walled buildings across the valley. "Where does Aristobulus get the money to pay you? And the others?"

Gavriel shrugged again. "I don't know. He's a prince. And a lot of people want the Pharisees and Hyrcanus gone."

"People who support the Sadducees, you mean."

Gavriel nodded. "They give Aristobulus money so he can put things right again."

"My parents would have given him money." Pninah frowned at a densely packed group on the bridge—a large collection of travellers were making their way across the bridge to the Temple. Some of them were dressed in the Roman style, with flowing togas and one arm awkwardly bare while the other lay buried in fabric. Outside of the regular festival celebrations, Jerusalem attracted Jews from all over the world. Even from Rome. This wasn't new. Still, they looked strange on the Zion Bridge. "Do you think Hyrcanus is doing something like this too? Maybe he has spies posted at Sadducean fortresses, finding out things."

"I don't think so," Gavriel replied. "Hyrcanus doesn't think about these kinds of new ideas."

"He's like one of those farmers who doesn't turn their field over after harvest. He wants to harvest in the fall and plant again in the spring and not do too much about the bits in the middle."

Gavriel laughed. His voice carried out over the valley. "Not even the planting part for this king. He only wants to do the harvest. He's harvesting what the queen laid down in her lifetime. Aristobulus, though, is a different kind of man. He has energy and ideas and makes people follow him. He'll restore the old ways and bring about the new at the same time. He's better than his grandfather. Or great-grand-father even."

"He didn't let you become a horseman."

Gavriel's lips tightened, and then he relaxed. "He was right about that. One long day riding behind an actual horseman was enough for me. I hated it almost right away." Gavriel turned to Pninah. "See, that's what is so great about Aristobulus—he knows things, he understands where things and people fit, and he can make things happen. Other than Hyrcania, Alexandrium, and Machaerus, every other important fortress has gone over to Aristobulus. That's twenty-two fortresses and all the men in them against three fortresses, plus Jerusalem and Idumea. Aristobulus has already won a war that hasn't even started. Hyrcanus just doesn't know it yet."

"I didn't realize," Pninah said.

"And Ptolemaeus of course."

"Why 'Ptolemaeus of course?'"

"Aristobulus's daughter married Ptolemaeus. That makes her his queen, which makes the whole country up there another ally for Aristobulus."

"Oh, right. That's weird, though. The king kills his son to steal his son's wife. That's weird."

Gavriel's gaze continued to survey the bridge and Temple beyond. "Yeah, but it's an ally all the same. If it comes to a straight war, Aristobulus will win. Add in all the planning ahead and the allies and the people like us keeping an eye on the Temple and the palace and every movement everywhere, and Hyrcanus has no chance. There's more than lookouts and treaties going on in Aristobulus's favour. He's doing something else, right here in Jerusalem."

"What?"

Gavriel smiled. "Can't say. Sworn to secrecy."

Pninah frowned again. "I'm the one who has to climb back down to get our dinner and climb back up."

"He's paying us to watch, run messages, and keep quiet about it all."

"Fine. What is it we're supposed to be looking for then? Is this like that old game of trying to guess the next Jerusalem assassin?"

"Yeah, but different. Think bigger. Not one person but a movement, an army, some kind of major move that Aristobulus would want to know about ahead of time. If we are the first to report something significant, there's a bonus payment."

They could see a new group of people crossing the bridge. The Roman Jews were now circulating on the far side of the Temple complex. Other groups were crossing the second smaller bridge between the Temple Mount and the Baris Citadel. "Why don't I go get a job in the Citadel as a cleaner or kitchen hand?" Pninah asked. "I could keep my ears open and hear things and report them to you. Actual things. Not just what we think is happening from a distance but what is actually happing while they're still discussing it."

Gavriel laughed. "You'll just walk up and ask for a job there, will you? Even if you somehow got one, you'd have one seizure in the Citadel, and they'd throw you over the wall for having a demon. They're Pharisees, Pninah. Think about it. They would hate you in a minute. Go get us something to eat later. I'll look after the running and reporting."

They were on the lookout for two weeks before something worth reporting occurred. There was a rustling in the brush behind them, and a young man, only a few years older than Gavriel, appeared.

"Found you," the newcomer said.

"Right where I said we would be and have been every day," Gavriel replied.

"We believed you, but that's not the same thing as finding you. Listen. About a thousand have shown up from the south. They'll probably come through the gate and go on to the Citadel. I'll stay here and try to count them." The stranger looked at Pninah. "With her. You get down to the bridge before they arrive and confirm who they are."

"How do I do that?"

"You go fast and don't fall off any ledges. Then get back here just as fast."

"How do I tell who they are?"

"That's for you to figure out. Now go."

Gavriel and Pninah exchanged glances. Pninah nodded, and then Gavriel left.

The stranger settled himself beside Pninah. Between them lay a bag she had brought up earlier in the day. The stranger opened it. Without asking, he helped himself to a corner of oiled and salted bread and all the dates along with a long drink of water from his water skin.

"No wine?" the stranger asked.

Pninah shook her head.

"You're the roof runner," the stranger said. "With him."

"Not really anymore. That was when we were children."

"You got any?"

She did not answer at first.

"Children?" he clarified.

She shook her head. She could feel the man's eyes on her while she tried to focus on the way Gavriel had gone and the bridge that was his destination.

"Soon enough," he said. "I'm sure children won't be a problem. Not for someone like you."

A rider crossed the bridge coming from the eastern side, the Citadel side, moving faster than the regular foot travellers. Pninah focused on the passage of the horseman, and the stranger grew quiet then. After a while, the rider passed from sight.

The stranger started talking again. "What did you do before this?"

She made an expression of not understanding without saying anything directly to him.

"You're working for half wages, sharing with him. It's not a lot, so whatever you did before this cannot have paid very well. I imagine a woman like you would have various ways of making some money down there."

When she looked at him, the man wore a half-smile and gestured at the Tyropoeon floor below them. "And a few other places in the city as well."

Pninah reached for her bag as though to take something from it to eat, and then she suddenly stood, bag in hand, and took several steps away from the stranger. The man stood with her and started to advance. "Listen—" he said, then stopped, seeing the knife in her hand.

"The last man to cause me trouble was twice your size," Pninah said. "I put the point of this blade through the side of his head." She touched the blade's tip to her temple, then slowly brought it back down to waist height, pointed at the man. "Right behind the eyes, where the skin is soft."

She waited until his eyes came up from the blade and met hers. "A man doesn't die right away when that happens," she said. "It takes a long time to die. A demon comes first and carries that man all over the ground, into fire, off a ravine's edge. It doesn't matter. It takes longer than you would think, but there's nothing any doctor can do about it once it starts. Once it's done, it's done. Even if it takes a long time, the end comes eventually."

She had never spoken anything so cold in her life, and she could see the dying supervisor as she said it. She felt herself shake, but it was not the shake of a seizure—it was the shake of fear and anger and memory together. Knowing it was not a seizure gave her a strange confidence. The stranger backed up several steps and sat down.

"I didn't mean anything." He said it to the valley as though soliciting confirmation from a witness. "I was making conversation. Gavriel talks about you as though you're something miraculous, and I thought I saw what he sees was all."

The stranger looked at her with a new expression. "Zeus confounded," he said, then looked away again. "I thought he was saying you were a flower. I didn't see all of what he was saying. Well, he can have it." The man was talking to himself now, staring at the bridge again.

They stayed that way for the rest of the afternoon as they waited for Gavriel. The man brooded and stared either at the valley or the bridge. Pninah stood apart, the bag still over her shoulder, one hand inside the bag.

Gavriel returned late in the afternoon, sweat-covered and dirty. He dropped down on the rock between them. "Idumeans," he said, still out of breath. "A contingent from Ashkelon, with Antipater the governor with them. They won't be crossing the bridge, so you can't count them. They're camping outside the city, about five thousand."

"Five thousand?"

"That's what eight different people reported. A couple guessed higher, but the reliable ones had talked to some of the southerners. Five thousand. Governor at the head. They're expecting to ride out again in a day or so."

"Where to?"

"Jericho."

The stranger stood, said nothing else, and was soon gone through the brush towards the high road.

Gavriel gazed into the ravine in a manner identical to the stranger's pose. He reached for the bag without words, and Pninah set it down.

"Where are the dates?" he asked.

"Your friend ate them all."

# 17

## 66 BCE

IT WAS ALREADY noon on the Jericho Plain. A horse to Aristobulus's left had a long, wet line trailing from its lower lip. From his own horse, Aristobulus studied the animal, wondering if it was diseased or like a dog drooling from the heat. He looked at the captain riding the horse, but the man only had eyes for the army assembling against them on the far side of the plain. The man looked worried.

Aristobulus smiled and looked skywards. Four vultures circled high above. They were so high they were barely identifiable. But they clearly circled. They knew this formation of men.

Aristobulus avoided looking back at those assembled behind. He knew their count.

Across the plain, his pathetic brother was still organizing his units. The Jerusalem guard had been expected, as were those from Alexandrium and Machaerus. Idumea had been the unknown factor. That contingent turned out to be far larger than anticipated. The Idumeans outnumbered Jerusalem's guard by almost double.

Antipater.

Aristobulus might have said the name out loud. He looked at his nearest captain again, but the man gave no notice of having heard him. He was studying his drooling horse now.

The army gathered on Jerusalem's side of the plain outnumbered Aristobulus's rebel forces three to one. He wanted to look behind him to see the fear that must reside on the faces there. The spearmen would be stiff faced. The slingers and archers would stand and shoot and then run. There was no shame in a slinger or archer running when overwhelmed. They were not armed for close quarters. There was a restlessness in the front line of cavalry on either side of Aristobulus, but his men held their positions. They were outnumbered, but they stood steadfast.

Aristobulus squinted, studying what he judged to be the Machaerus contingent. They had more cavalry than he had expected. Far more. Easily double his own. Alexandrium was as predicted. It was close to Jericho and easier to survey.

One fortress was missing: Hyrcania. Named after Aristobulus and Hyrcanus's grandfather, it was one of the holdings their mother had retained for Hyrcanus. Hyrcania should have been on the field with its king. It was not.

Aristobulus smiled.

"Spread the word," he said to the distracted captain. "Let them know that Hyrcania stayed home and the plan is now in motion. Tell them all to remain calm and wait."

The captain moved off, and Aristobulus turned then to the signalman on his right. He was a slightly built man who had no business on a horse except for the horn he held in his hand. Aristobulus nodded at him.

The man straightened up, inhaled deeply, and then let loose a long blast from his trumpet followed by two short staccato conclusions.

Aristobulus waited. His whole army waited. None moved. Aristobulus squinted and studied the field. He tried to imagine what his brother was thinking: an army had signalled battle and then not moved.

*He thinks we've quit. My men refuse to advance.*

He turned and nodded at his signalman a second time and the man repeated the long blast followed by two short ones. Again, the announcing army did not move. Aristobulus leaned forwards as though he could see better this way. Squinting, he watched as Machaerus and Alexandrium lowered their Jerusalem flags.

"Okay, once more," he said. He did not watch the trumpeter this time. This time he tried to watch both edges of his brother's army at the same time. When the trumpet sounded, Machaerus on the left flinched first. The entire company surged forwards, cavalry at the fore and men on foot behind. They set out at a quick pace across the plain, and as they did so, they unfurled a yellow banner.

Alexandrium on the right moved next. As they separated from the Jerusalem and Idumean forces in the middle, they unfurled a white and green banner.

The two companies advanced across the field but did not aim themselves at Aristobulus's centre as though intending to break it. Instead, they spread apart from each other, making for Aristobulus's flanks.

Aristobulus leaned back and directed his gaze skywards.

The vultures turned and turned. He smiled up at the birds. He wanted to say something to them, as though the birds were confederates in this affair. As though they would hear and understand him. He kept looking upwards long after it became uncomfortable. He waited until he could hear the horses, then he looked back down.

The cavalry was three-quarters of the way across the field. Then, as Aristobulus watched, they swung wider, moving out of the way, revealing the foot soldiers that followed. The men on foot moved at a fast pace, charging out ahead of the halted cavalry. Their swords remained sheathed, bows and shields slung over their backs. Men marched this way. They did not run this way. They did not approach combat this way.

There was a bristling of shields and spears among Aristobulus's men.

"Stand down," Aristobulus growled. "Wait." The captain spread the word to his peers. "Wait and trust."

Aristobulus realized that his own hand was on the hilt of his sword. He closed his eyes and let go of the weapon.

He wanted to give a speech, but only those around him would hear. A speech could create confusion if it was misheard or misunderstood. He stayed quiet and let the trumpet do his talking.

Once the new spearmen, archers, and slingers were settled alongside Aristobulus's men, tension turned to calm and then a new excitement. The Machaerus and Alexandrium cavalry still milled about. They had a quarter of the field yet to cross. They waited. Both armies waited with a stranded cavalry between them.

Aristobulus turned and nodded to his signalman once

more. Two quick blasts echoed back from the far mountains, and the Machaerus and Alexandrium cavalries rallied. They came together and then galloped the final distance in a rush of energy and power, charging towards Aristobulus's centre. Towards the trumpeter. Towards Aristobulus himself. Fear and exhilaration swelled in Aristobulus's breast despite his secret knowledge, and just before the new cavalry clashed with his, they broke off. Alexandrium made for the right flank, lining up in front of its own spearmen, archers, and slingers. Machaerus did the same on the left.

There was a cheer from somewhere behind Aristobulus, something spontaneous involving perhaps only a few hundred men. He smiled. He took a moment to stretch his back, working out a stiff bit near his left hip.

"Okay," he said, and signalled with his hand for the trumpeter to lower his instrument. "We don't want any miscues. Put that away for now. We'll wait and see if my brother has the sense to run."

❧

"It was over before we started," Antipater told Cypros later in Ashkelon.

There was a pool along the shoreline, fed by the tide, heated by the sun. The two of them sunk into its saltwater comfort. Overhanging palms on the eastern side provided shade when needed. Attendants remained at a distance. The guards waited some distance beyond the attendants.

Cypros waited Antipater out. When it came to important topics, she was always waiting him out. He was not stupid, but he spoke slowly. She waved her hands about underwater to hurry him up, but he could not see the gesture. Above the water, she smiled and then adjusted her expression and tried to look concerned.

"The men from Hyrcania did not show up at all. There were no messengers, no explanation of any kind. That they all were able to keep such a large betrayal secret staggers the imagination."

"Galilee didn't come either?" she asked.

"No, there was no time to test their loyalty. We didn't send anyone to call them. We didn't think we would need them."

"What fortresses are there to call on in the north?"

"There aren't any."

Cypros caused a slight wave in the pool as she moved in response, but Antipater waved her quiet. "It's an old story," he said. "Jerusalem has never built a proper Galilean fortress. It's a policy from Jannaeus's time. Earlier, I think."

"Someone has to have paid them," Cypros said. "Machaerus, Alexandrium, and Hyrcania. And you just watched while they switched sides?"

"We were stunned. I've never seen anything like it. I've never even heard of anything like it. How would you even organize such a thing?"

Cypros laughed and then let herself sink under the water. She rubbed her face underwater and then slowly resurfaced again. She wiped the salt water away from her eyes.

"Go on," she said. "You just watched them."

"We didn't know what to do. We didn't know why they'd left, why they surrendered. Then they changed sides and both groups raised new flags. They were Aristobulus's men the whole time. Not ours. They already had their own flags." He stopped talking.

Cypros laughed again and pulled her hair back, pressing water from it pointlessly. Hanne would need to wash the salt from it later. "That's what happens when a country relies on gentile mercenaries that it not-so-secretly despises. Better money and no fighting—why wouldn't they defect to Aristobulus? So half of Hyrcanus's mercenaries didn't show up, and the other half defected, and the rest of you ran home."

"Cypros."

"Those with horses rode home. The rest ran home."

Antipater slammed his hand down on the water and created a great splash, which made her laugh again. None of the distant attendants took notice.

"Where is the king now?" she asked.

"The Citadel with his guard, as far as I know. Aristobulus's wife and children are still locked up there. Hyrcanus can use them to negotiate a deal."

"A deal." Cypros's upper lip curled. She knew it was an expression he hated.

Antipater looked away towards the sea. She could tell that he was working hard to control himself, but she did not fear him and did not hesitate to goad him further. "So you backed the wrong brother."

He said nothing in reply.

"Aristobulus is not going to ask for a few more cities. He's going to demand the throne. And Hyrcanus will give it to him."

Antipater nodded. "Our job will be to hope for peace with Aristobulus and keep our position here."

"We hope for nothing," Cypros shouted. She stood in the water, her hands in fists, and then sank back under the surface again. When she rose again, she wiped the water from her eyes once more and again squeezed the excess from her hair. Then she sunk back down, letting her hair float once more. "The Idumeans have little love for Jerusalem. Your father was away when Jerusalem came through here and destroyed the Ashtaroth Temple. The feeling in this country is that if he had not been at our wedding, he would have stopped that slaughter. Idumea is with you, as are the Gazites. And through me and the trade agreement that now connects Nabataean routes to Gaza's ports, you have the Nabataeans. If Aristobulus wants an Arabian war, let him make trouble with us. My uncle does not rely on mercenaries. A camel can outrun and outlast a horse in desert battle."

She swam over to Antipater and pressed herself against him, her face nearly touching his. "I was a thirteen-year-old girl on foot when I killed nine Moabite men in the desert with a child's knife. Imagine what a Nabataean soldier on a camel can do with a long blade, a spear, and a bow. If I can kill nine, such a man will kill ninety."

She kissed him then, hard and not pleasantly, before pulling back so she could see his eyes. "You don't hope for peace with that Jew. You command it."

She pushed off to the edge and then climbed out of the pool. As she did so, one of the attendants came running.

Jerusalem's nights no longer concealed the living nightmares that had lingered when Salome had been queen, when the Sadducees had walked the darkened streets in fear, when morning had found the bodies of those slain by their fellow countrymen. This night was not like those dark days of Pharisaic retribution. This night was full of joy and celebration.

Pninah walked through the night with Gavriel, and her eyes shone as the city glowed. There were so many torches and lamps burning that the entire city seemed to be on fire. Hyrcanus and the Pharisees had been bloodlessly deposed.

"That's Aristobulus for you" had been Gavriel's pronouncement.

The city had crowned their hero earlier in the day, and the new king claimed the high priesthood as well. As a result, the city this night was alive. It was as though the coronation oils infused with myrrh, aloe, and cassia had expanded with nightfall, their fragrance now crowning the entirety of Jerusalem.

"Over there," Gavriel said. At first, it seemed that he was pointing towards a group of dancers, a wild collection of girls and women, not just poor women from the valley but merchants' wives and some who appeared to be Sadducean. They were all dancing together in their poor clothing, their merchants' clothing, and their fine white, scarlet, and blue linens. Their skirts swirled and heads swung with such abandon that they risked exposing their hair.

It took Pninah a moment to see past the women and locate Gavriel's group. They were mostly men, though a few had wives with them. They had assembled around a makeshift fire built right in the street, up against a stone wall.

Pninah recognized the man who had insulted her and her valley some weeks before. "You found us!" he exclaimed and handed Gavriel a wooden skewer of roasted lamb.

It was well past dark, but music flooded the street, musicians at one end competing with another group blocks away. The mixed group of women-dancers had chosen this cross-current of sound for their stage. They were as jubilant as wedding guests. Pninah wondered if their men were at richer banquets or just not social. A lack of invitation or escort would not stop these women from rejoicing at Aristobulus's bloodless coup.

One of the women among Gavriel's friends came alongside Pninah. She wore a bright smile and wrapped herself around one of Pninah's arms. "I'm so glad you've come to be with us," she said. Her eyes shone and her touch was soft. Pninah felt herself relax.

"So you're the delicate pearl," the woman said. "Gavriel has told me all about you. My name is Rachel."

The following day, Pninah rose late. Gavriel was already up and gone. They had agreed that she would meet him at the baker's this morning, where they would extend the previous day's celebration with sweet bread and salted jam.

She put herself together slowly and then climbed up to the Upper City and walked along the street. Her eyes were heavy, and her head hurt, but there was still an afterglow from the night before. Her body ached, but in a good way. Her mind felt free. The Sadducees had finally restored order to her city. She thought of her parents then, and a fleeting sad ache pressed in her chest before she let the memories go.

She took in the warming air and noticed litter spread up and down the thoroughfare. There were discarded fruit pits and bones, shards of broken pottery, almond husks, and the remnants of burned-out torches. There was even a shawl that in another time she would have claimed for her own to clean and wear or resell. She was too tired now and their prospects too fine with Aristobulus's ascent. She did not need to worry about collecting discarded clothing. She could buy her own new shawl in the days to come if she needed one.

❧

Two nights later, Cypros and Antipater were in the place of stone chairs and the raised fire platform outside the Ashkelon palace. Only one lantern lit the space between them. They were otherwise alone in the dark.

"It's probably all Hyrcanus wanted to begin with," Antipater said. "An income, a home, and no responsibility. He should have been the second brother."

The deal was everything Cypros had expected. Hyrcanus gave up the Citadel and his hostages, the palace, the kingship, the leadership of the Sanhedrin—even the high priesthood. Hyrcanus had turned everything over to Aristobulus in exchange for his life, the high priest's income, and Aristobulus's old house.

"We backed the wrong brother," Antipater said.

"No, we didn't." Her voice was low and firm and carried itself across the space between them with force. Antipater looked up at her. She could barely see his face in the dark, but his eyes held hers.

"You're always full of ideas and confidence," he said. "But when the time comes, you don't hold a sword. Don't tell me what's right. Mind your place."

Cypros thought of the knife in her hair. She felt acid in her throat but calmed her instinct to respond. Tonight, her husband's failure was official. Tonight, he could have his darkness. Tomorrow, she would explain the sunrise to him.

# 18

## 66 BCE

IN LATE FALL, after the Sukkot Festival, the residents of Jerusalem reclaimed the city's streets. The relative quiet after the crowds paralleled the changing of the season. Blood cooled. Voices became quieter. As the branches and leaves of the cut-bough festival were cleared away, newness descended. It was like spring but colder and more barren. The city became livable again.

"It's nice to have a day off," Pninah said.

She and Gavriel walked the Tyropoeon Valley floor together. She considered holding his hand like she had when they were little, but they were not children anymore.

Their home was behind them, up a few steps higher than the valley's bottom gully, as were all but the poorest homes here. The gully lay dry on most days, but the valley flooded during the rainy season, water rising high for an hour or two before draining away. Occasionally, during bad spells, the water would remain for days or weeks at a time.

Gavriel and Pninah walked below the houses in the smoothed natural path of the dry ravine, the most direct and best maintained road in all the valley. They soon approached a small footbridge that stood crossways in their path, serving a purpose only in the rainy season and creating a roadblock in every other. They would have to go around.

Gavriel took Pninah's hand as he tested the slope with one foot and then began climbing up. He helped Pninah steady herself on the rock as they climbed together until they were both up the bank. The hard slope rose steeply beyond, but they did not need to climb any farther. She followed his lead past the footbridge, trailing behind him, and then they went back down into the dry channel. He did not take her hand going down. She held on to his shoulder until the ground was flat again, and then she let go.

A few minutes past the footbridge, a dirty patch of clothing and a tangle of branches appeared—debris from a previous flood swept to this place and no farther. They were heading towards the north market but stayed in the valley longer than the route required.

"I like the stillness down here," Gavriel said.

Pninah looked up. Though the Temple Mount and the Citadel loomed over the right bank, she could not see any sign of the city on the left. She imagined that they were not in Jerusalem at all.

Ahead loomed the tree that she loved. She did not know the name of the tree. It reminded her of oak, but the small pale nut that it produced—in the rare year that it produced anything at all—was edible. The tree's bark was thick and grey with hints of brown in the deepest cracks. It was deeply grooved, even up into the branches, as though it wore the skin of some fantastically ancient lizard famed for an impenetrable but deeply cracked hide. The tree grew out of a soft place at the base of a boulder. It leaned out towards the middle of the valley before curving up towards the light. Gnarled roots snaked along the slope and disappeared into what seemed to be solid rock.

An old woman often sat in its shade and ate from supplies she kept wrapped up in an old rag. Afterwards, she would climb to the Upper City where she begged for a living. The woman was not at the tree this morning.

"The tree looks like something from the days of Elijah," Pninah said. "It looks so old."

"We've been watching Hyrcanus's house for a while now," Gavriel said. He was never interested in the tree.

"Half a year," Pninah said.

"People come and go, but nothing interesting happens."

"He's lucky to be alive."

"The one odd thing is that Antipater's brothers keep visiting. Antipater only twice. But lots of other Idumeans."

"Antipater is still Idumea's governor?"

Gavriel did not answer right away. Instead, he climbed up a line of rubble that crossed their path and then reached a hand down to help her again. There was no room on the top rock for both of them to stand, so they executed the manoeuvre as they had on other days before: she came up trusting his handhold as he tilted back in the opposite direction, pulling her up, and at the last moment, once her momentum was sure to carry her safely the rest of the way, he let go and jumped down to the other side.

The valley was shallower here, and soon they would have to either cut up the bank to their left to get to the market or eventually pass through one of the northern gates and be outside the city.

"I'm surprised that Antipater is still governor of Idumea," Gavriel said. "He's Hyrcanus's friend. If Hyrcanus tried to reclaim the throne, Antipater would help him."

"Do you think that's likely?"

Gavriel laughed. "No. Hyrcanus wants to drink and listen to musicians. I don't think he's even interested in women. Just food, drink, and music. He's the laziest Hasmonean ever."

"Do you think all the Pharisees are like him?"

Gavriel looked at her and then at the road ahead. "Could be. Salome didn't conquer anything when she was queen," he said. "Even Hyrcanus's grandfather, John Hyrcanus, didn't do much in his early days when he was a Pharisee. It was not until he switched to the Sadducees that he got serious about expanding Eretz-Israel. Maybe you're right: the Pharisees are lazy."

They stopped well past Pninah's tree for a rest and a drink, though they had not walked long enough to need a rest. Pninah looked up the left bank. She could see the sides of buildings now through the trees. The streets there were busy. The old tree was the last nice place for contemplation and conversation on this path, but Gavriel always stopped well past it before moving up into the city. He knew she liked the tree, but he never let her linger near it.

The leftward hill of Jerusalem was the Upper City, though both the western Upper City and the eastern Lower City were "upper" when viewed from the Tyropoeon Valley floor. Both eastern and western sides of Jerusalem looked down on the valley's disorder, floodwater debris, and poor houses. Rumours of violence in the darker recesses of the valley kept the curious away. Those that lived there walked there, and no others. Though misinformation about the place impeded its prosperity, it also served to insulate the valley from many of the city's excesses. In Gavriel and Pninah's pickpocketing years, they had worked in the city above, not down in the valley. In the streets above, they could work unmolested, usually undetected. But the valley's inhabitants had different skills. Tyropoeons observed more alertly. To steal from a Tyropoeon would get you a blade in your side before you earned enough for a meal. More than once, Pninah and Gavriel had discussed whether the valley or the upper parts of the city were safer, and it always came down to one's point of view. You could steal more safely above, which made the upper streets better for thieves. You could hide more reliably in the valley, which made the valley better for fugitives. She and Gavriel had moved to the valley after the murder of the supervisor.

"Ready?" Gavriel asked.

Pninah nodded and handed the water skin back to him. He took her hand and helped her with the first big step up. So they climbed together to sunlit streets where they let go of one another in accordance with the custom of that place.

The next day, Pninah and Gavriel were back on duty outside the home of Hyrcanus, the relatively humble building that had once been the abode of Aristobulus.

"It's bigger than our place," Pninah said.

Gavriel laughed. "It's bigger than ten of our places."

He took another bite of the flatbread, then wiped his mouth. He passed a small bag back to her.

"That's Malichos," Gavriel said, speaking through a mouthful and pointing. "Another Idumean, but a Nabataean as well." The figure he pointed at was on foot, attended by two men, heading towards Hyrcanus's home.

"Nobody makes easier money than you," Pninah said. "You just sit here and watch."

"A labourer is paid for their back and muscles," Gavriel said. "I have to watch, recognize faces, remember names, report on what matters. Seeing and thinking work pays more than running or labouring."

"Is he important?"

Gavriel's eyes followed Malichos's group. "No. Just a Nabataean living in Idumea."

"Antipater's wife is a Nabataean. Maybe there's a connection there."

"No relation to her."

"I mean, being Nabataean connects him to Cypros and through her, to the governor."

"Like some kind of conspiracy?" He laughed.

She tried to speak, but he continued. "You think that Hyrcanus the Lazy and Malichos the Nobody are plotting something? Through Malichos, you get to Cypros, and so Antipater is now in on the plot?"

"It could be."

Gavriel laughed again. "Malichos has something to do with the ports and Nabataean trade. He ships wine. And he visits Hyrcanus a lot—probably to sell wine. That's all."

The regular traffic of Jerusalem's Upper City continued to flow past them. Few of those passing turned in the direction of Gavriel and Pninah. The pair were regulars, no longer seen by locals as they perched throughout every long day, dozing, eating, and conversing.

"What will you do after this?" Pninah asked.

"After what?"

"After Aristobulus decides he doesn't need to spend money spying on his brother anymore?"

"You worry too much," Gavriel said. "I know what I'm doing."

While Gavriel and Pninah staked out Hyrcanus's house, a caravan formed outside the Ashkelon palace. Early the next morning, it left Ashkelon altogether.

Five hundred of the Idumean guard accompanied this caravan. Cypros preferred the swaying gait of camels, but the Idumean palace kept no camels. The children were better corralled in the shaded horse-drawn wagons anyway. Phasael, the firstborn, was almost ten years old now. Salome, the youngest, was nearly three. All five of the children began the journey enthusiastic about a new adventure.

Two days in, the children became disgruntled and wanted to be free of the confines of their relentless transport. Raqmu was still a week away.

Eight days into the journey, a small dust cloud appeared on the horizon ahead, and their caravan of wagons and horses slowed but did not halt. A reshuffling of wagons positioned Cypros and the children farther back in the crowd of men, horses, and equipment.

"What's happening?" Phasael asked.

"Shush," Cypros said. She wanted to stand up in the wagon to see better, but there was no reason to. With the slope of the lands, she could see the road ahead clearly enough. She felt that her eyes simply worked better standing. Out of respect for her husband, who rode with his men, she stayed seated.

"Those are camels," she said in a voice not for her children or the staff but Antipater. He was not near enough to hear her.

She squinted in the bright sun, studying the riders, satisfying herself with their posture and the colour of their saddle blankets. Outside of bowshot range, two of the riders brought their camels to a halt and waited. The remaining two continued towards the Idumean caravan.

"Five hundred is too much," she had complained to Antipater before they had set out from Ashkelon. "My people will think it's an invasion."

"If we encounter raiders on the way," Antipater had replied, "five hundred will be a good number."

The two riders approached quickly, only slowing as they came within shouting distance. Their weapons remained sheathed. She knew that if the caravan attacked the advance riders, the distant pair would pass the message back through the Nabataean lands to Raqmu. No horse could catch a Nabataean camel on this terrain.

Cypros's youngest brother had wanted to be one of these advance messengers. Thinking of him made her remember her last moments with her family in the open desert. Her brother had jumped down and run when she had, he in one direction, she in another. She remembered that day and her sisters and parents. She swallowed and felt a burning in her chest.

The riders came closer. With watery eyes, Cypros saw their distinctive yellow and grey saddle blankets and the small tassels on the camels' reins. She took in the sharpness of the men's cheeks and the deep set of their lined desert eyes. She felt her throat tighten. These were her people. Contradictory tears threatened, a commingling of tears for both grief and joy. Her chest grew tight and hard.

The caravan came to a stop, and the two advance riders conferred with Antipater's front row of men. The Idumean horses, unused to the smell of camels, stamped and snorted as though to clear something from their nostrils. The two advance riders looked up, scanning the crowd before them until they found Cypros in her wagon. They gave no expression that an Idumean would notice, but Cypros saw them smile. It was a change of the light in their eyes, nothing more. A daughter of their people had come home.

One camel rider then turned and trotted away, returning to the pair waiting up the road. The other joined Antipater's caravan and began to lead them on to the stone city of Raqmu.

"Are we almost to Petra?" Phasael asked.

"Raqmu," Cypros said. "It's called Raqmu."

# 19

## 66 BCE

THE *SHARQI* WINDS blew dry and dusty two days after the Jewish caravan arrived at Raqmu. This year, the southeasterly force came more from the south than the east. It came sliding over the mountains, lifting vast clouds of fine-grained sand, and then twisted and fell straight down in a relentless onslaught of sand and dust. It pounded the stout roofs of Raqmu's tent city and created billowy clouds in the valleys between tents.

The constant noise and motion of the tent walls and roof delighted the children.

"It's like a snake," Phasael said. He turned to his little sister. "Hissing. Can you hear it hissing?" He raised his hands in mock, incongruous claws, and Salome screamed and ran across the floor of the vast tent, and Phasael pretended to follow her, then seated himself beside Cypros.

"How long will this last?" he asked.

"A day," Cypros said. "No more. Then you can learn to ride the camels."

Phasael shrugged as though such a thing was below him.

The children had played with the Nabataean children at Raqmu from the day of their arrival until the dust storm had cut off each tent from the other. When able to be together, all the children used the common language between them, a running confusion of Idumean- and Nabataean-accented Aramaic.

"They just need to burn off energy after eight days in a wagon," Antipater had explained, though Cypros had not asked for an explanation.

This running was not a result of time spent in the wagon. They had travelled nine days, but not nine days straight. On the sixth day after their departure, they had rested. It had been the Sabbath, from one evening until starlight shone the following evening. The children had not run wild on the Sabbath after six days in the wagon. They had only begun to race like this here, at Raqmu. Nabataea spoke to their blood, and what it said made them run. There was nothing they could do but run. She had smiled when Antipater had spoken of what he did not understand. She had said nothing about what she knew.

Before dawn on the morning after their arrival, Cypros had gone for a walk, alone, away from Raqmu's tents. Or rather, she had walked as alone as her position allowed her. As both the governor's wife and Aretas's niece, she was never truly alone, not as she had been as a girl alone in this desert.

Women from Nabataea followed at a distance. They respected her need to worship in isolation but would not entirely permit it. A group of Nabataean guards followed as well, behind the women. Though no raider would dare approach Raqmu, there were leopards in this dry desert and hyenas and other dangerous creatures. Distant but alert, the men rode camels and carried weapons.

The mad frenzy of her children with their Nabataean cousins made Cypros feel warm inside. She walked north from the tent city, looking for an unobstructed view of the mountains as dawn appeared. She had no rooftop or other high place, but she made do.

Cypros bowed herself down to the ground in prayer to al-Qaum. There were no Jews to observe her here. Only Nabataeans watched her this early morning.

Cypros spoke to the ground with tears in her eyes. Then she chanted to the rising sun, and then again she bent into the sand below her. Her palms held the cupped sand the way Antipater sometimes held her, both hands wide open and fingers as splayed as though to hold everything in two palms. In this way, she held the desert—innocently, intimately, passionately—and she spoke to the desert, spoke to the sun, spoke again to the desert, and so prayed to al-Qaum.

Her children might never desire dabb or worship al-Qaum. Her children might develop emotional memories better attuned to Sukkot, Passover, and the other Jewish festivals, but they were still Nabataean—even if Antipater could not see it. Their blood awoke in this land of sun-whitened sand, red cliffs, and relentless heat. Their minds did not find Nabataean accents strange. The sound of the Nabataeans was the sound of their mother, the sound of their strongest history. It spoke with a rhythm that echoed in their blood. They might not worship al-Qaum, but he lived inside them, through her.

In the great tent, below the snake hiss of sand all around them, Cypros looked at her children. Phasael sat beside her. He was clearly interested in discussing camels further but would not initiate the conversation. He waited for her to say more. Herod worked on a collection of rough rose-coloured stones he had gathered the day before. He tested various dry-fit combinations as he sought to assemble the highest and most stable tower possible with his limited collection. Joseph played with a cousin who had braved the sand, bringing a game of bones and stones that he was now teaching. Salome sat slumped against the far side of the tent wearing an exaggerated frown.

As Cypros watched, Salome wiped her hands across her eyes and then stood up and began a slow circuit through the tent. When she got to Herod, she stopped. Her brother stayed focused on his project. When she sat down beside him, he moved a few of the stones away from her. He placed a new block in place. Then he looked at her and said something to her that Cypros could not hear. Salome responded with a smile on her face. Herod was at his best with Salome. Though the little girl took no interest in his building fixations, she was a sponge for his attention.

Antipater was not here. He had gone to her Uncle Aretas's tent earlier in the day. There, the Jewish governor and Raqmu's king discussed matters that Cypros had already laid the groundwork for with both men. It was good for Antipater to feel that he had influence in this place.

෨

After dark, windblown sand continued to hiss against the rippling walls and long roof. Hanne had extinguished the lamps. The children were asleep. Antipater sat at the end of their bed, not crouching like the desert dwellers but seated like a Jew, his knees halfway to his chest.

Cypros came to him at the end of the bed, wrapped in a linen sheet. He had come from the meeting with Aretas tense and uncommunicative. The children had steered away from him and quieted their conversation and play.

She and Antipater had tried to make love. Almost immediately, he had pulled away and re-dressed as though to leave. In the dark, he stopped, appeared to listen to the sand, and then sank to the floor.

Cypros put a hand on his shoulder and settled herself beside him.

"Tell me," she said.

There was one small lamp still burning near the tent's central pillar. It leaked weak light that faded to almost nothing by the time it reached the walls of the tent. Cypros could barely make out the silhouette of Antipater's head and neck.

"Tell me," she said again, her lips close to one ear, her voice a whisper. Her emphasis was on the first word. *Tell* me.

He put a hand on the inside of her leg, a careless gesture, and then he took it back to himself.

She whispered again to him, reversing her emphasis: "Tell *me*."

"Your uncle," he said.

He said nothing more. He had said enough. Now he needed time.

She relaxed into him, both hands holding his closest

arm, her head against his shoulder. His hand returned to her leg.

*What is it?* She wanted to ask. She stayed silent and waited.

"At the wedding," he finally said and then said nothing more for a while.

Cypros did not move. Her ears read the rhythm of his breathing; her skin read the stillness of his one hand on her thigh. Her fingers wanted to seek out the pulse on the inside of his arm, but she restrained herself. She wanted to see him but did not move her temple from his shoulder.

"At the wedding," he finally continued, "Aretas was as you would expect. Like my father."

He sighed and shifted, but not enough to signal that she should move away from him.

"Afterwards," Antipater continued, "on his visits to Ashkelon, he was my guest."

"This is your first time in Nabataea, not at our wedding."

"And I am not a young man with prospects anymore. I am the governor of Idumea." Antipater's quiet pitch became lower, the pace slower. Not quite a growl.

"Yet you are in Nabataea now."

"In Nabataea."

"Seeking help."

Cypros felt him shift in the dark. "Help. But not humiliation."

"Tell me," she said. Her voice remained quiet, but the heat of her previous whispering was gone.

"He asked a lot of questions about Jericho," Antipater said. "The preparations. How many spies we employed."

"None."

"None. How many they employed."

"You don't know."

"I don't know. And I don't know how they organized the betrayal. How entire fortresses were brought into a plot to betray Hyrcanus without us catching any hint of it. Who supplied the flags. Who organized the scheme by which Hyrcanus's troops changed sides."

"None of which you know."

"None of which I know. And then he wanted to know how long it took us to get from Jericho to Ashkelon."

Cypros held her breath at that and did not move. She waited for him to take his hand from her leg. Perhaps now he would stand and go face the windblown sand. He did not move. He did not stand.

"They were just questions," Antipater continued. "He did not sneer. It was only the two of us. There were no other Nabataeans to overhear or for him to laugh with. He only asked questions. But such questions."

# 20

## 66 BCE

THE WIND LASTED longer than Cypros had forecasted. But after a few days, it did finally die. The last of the sand fell from the sky like rain. Following the fall of sand, a fog of dust remained, leaving a haze up high to dim the sun's rays.

Released from domestic captivity, the children scattered.

Antipater stood outside their tent, studying the red walls of Petra's mountains. Cypros stood half a step behind him.

"I'd rather go with you and the children," Antipater said. He was looking towards the canyon that led into Raqmu's interior.

"Instead, you've got eight days of riding ahead," Cypros said.

"Seven. We won't have wagons. Here to Jerusalem is only half the journey. Coming back, we'll have wagons."

"Hyrcanus is going to flee Jerusalem at night, like a fugitive." She let the rest of her thought go unfinished.

"We've convinced him that Aristobulus means to kill him. He'll be the first Jewish king—former Jewish king—to visit Petra."

"Raqmu."

Antipater half turned towards her, then looked back at the Siq. "Raqmu. He knows it as Petra." He laughed then.

"What is it?" she asked.

"History," Antipater said. He shook his head. "The first Aristobulus to sit on the throne killed his mother to get that throne, then his brother to keep it. Now we're spreading rumours that the second Aristobulus is planning to do the same thing. Hyrcanus is certain that the family history will repeat. The message I got indicates that he expects my escort to be in Jerusalem by tomorrow. He doesn't understand the distance involved."

"After he's been here a while, he'll want to go home again," Cypros said. "The lack of wine in Nabataea should make him angry enough to start a war."

Antipater laughed again but lightly this time. "Give him a few months sober, and he'll be ready to carry a sword himself. He might be the first Maccabee in a hundred years to do so."

"When he comes, make sure he comes to negotiate what we've already worked out with Aretas."

"Your uncle won't change the bargain?"

"He won't give the game away. And he won't change the bargain. He won't try to get more out of Hyrcanus than we've arranged. But he won't accept anything less either."

"We'll have days of travelling together. He'll have no choice but to listen to me."

"Remind him that he will be negotiating with an actual king. With an actual kingdom."

"Aretas would rather have our sons on Jerusalem's throne. If he is going to fight for Eretz-Israel, winning the whole prize would suit him better."

Cypros laughed this time, a low sound, and then she was quiet. But only for a moment. "They're too young," she said. "Not yet."

Antipater turned around to look directly at her. He arched one eyebrow. "I was joking," he said. "An Idumean-Nabataean on Jerusalem's throne?"

Cypros met his eye without deference. "You do your part. I expect more than Idumea for our efforts here. And your sons will inherit what we earn."

⸛

After the lashing of desert winds and sand, the wilderness revealed creatures beaten by the elements and laid out like feasts for those who could see and scent. The desert's great black birds rose together and searched for such carcasses to scavenge.

Passing over the arid valley, they spotted a small company of men riding towards the inland sea. The men did not ride laden camels like traders. They rode horses. There were no wagons. This company of men looked like raiders, and raiders often left bodies. The birds flew past, scouting the route ahead. Finding the road empty for some hours to come, they veered from the path of men to explore other wastes.

Later in the day, the birds returned and again followed the path of the travelling horsemen. When the small company passed two smaller groups without incident, the birds reconsidered the potential of this grim band. They were horsemen, but not raiders. There would be no feasting on the spoils of small war here.

The birds returned to tracking pathless places, looking for other sand-scoured offerings. There was always something for them in the desert.

Cypros stayed out of the bright sunlight, below the overhang of a tall extended tent roof. She stood unnoticed behind a small crowd of boys. Their angular poses leaned this way and that, eyes and voices all directed at her eldest son, Phasael. She sensed the excitement of the boys around her, and it made her stomach churn.

A camel rested on the ground with its legs folded under it. Phasael sat on its back with a yellow and grey blanket between him and the beast. He gripped camel hair with one hand and the blanket with the other. Cypros shook her head but said nothing. She eased farther back into the tent's shadow until tight fabric touched her back.

Herod was bouncing on the balls of his feet in front of the crowd, but he was the younger of the two. Phasael went first.

Phasael had never been a great listener, and his ears were closed in this moment of excitement. The boys all yelled different instructions at him. She knew from his expression that he did not hear any of it.

*You're not going to lean back, are you?* She unclasped

her hands at her stomach and tried to find somewhere to put them that did not make her look worried. No one was watching her anyway. She stared at her oldest son and restrained herself from speaking or acting. There were no men present.

One of the Nabataean boys smacked the camel on its hindquarters. Another pushed against its jaw, signalling the beast to stand. It moaned loudly at the two boys and then sullenly responded, hind legs rising first. The motion was abrupt and unbalanced.

*You weren't listening.* She put her hands back on her stomach.

Everything happened quickly, but she saw it all clearly as though by way of a very slow demonstration. The camel raised up its rear end, front knees still on the ground, and Phasael lost his grip. He fell over the camel's one hump and into its neck. He still held the blanket but quickly dropped it as he scrambled for a fresh handhold. He clutched here and there as the beast's front legs finally engaged, and then it stood, and in a moment, Phasael was hanging by the animal's thick neck. Then he lost that grip as well and swung to the ground, landing on his side in a cloud of dust.

The boys burst out laughing. Two of the younger ones theatrically threw themselves onto the ground, trying to create the same or bigger dust clouds with their antics. The camel did nothing but stand in place, relieved of its load and disinterested in further action except to release a large stream of drool.

Cypros watched, mortified, as her oldest son gathered himself in humiliation. He started to sit up, and then a long rope of saliva slapped across his face and chest. The boy reacted slowly, but once he realized where the wet had come from, he jerked away from the camel, rolled several lengths away, and then stood.

The laughter of the children increased, and Herod laughed the loudest.

They had been told to wait for the camel trainers. But the boys would not wait.

Phasael looked around, clearly shaken by his sudden impact with the ground and the resulting scene. He wiped his cheek with one arm, looking wounded, looking like he might cry, and then he pounced on Herod. He slapped his brother twice before Herod reacted. Then both boys were fighting, rolling in the dust, punching and pulling at one another with more energy than skill.

The laughter of the other boys changed and then stopped as they circled the pair. The short crowd watched as the two brothers mauled one another. Then the camel trainers finally arrived, parted the crowd, and separated the brothers.

Cypros moved along one wall and then disappeared into an alley between the tents.

Later in the day, she got reports on the progress of her boys. They had both learned to get on and ride the camels. The animals would not listen to the half-Nabataean, half-Jewish boys—often, they would not listen to anyone but their trainers, so this did not bother her.

Other reports came as well. The boys had continued to trade insults in front of the other children. Partway through the day, Herod had pointed out the camel drool and dust stain across Phasael's chest again. The youngest boys had enjoyed this opportunity to goad one older than themselves.

When the brothers had started to fight again, the camel trainers had separated them.

She heard them coming back to the family tent as shadows lengthened across the land. Phasael was speaking, something in harsh tones, and Herod's response was pure contempt. Cypros did not catch the words, but she knew their voices.

They came into the tent while her back was to them and she was fussing with a small lamp that Hanne had already filled. They went quiet upon seeing her and shuffled towards their end of the dwelling.

Cypros turned slowly. Joseph, Pheroras, and Salome were already in the tent. They stayed quiet as Cypros faced her two oldest boys.

"Come here," she said.

Herod watched her with alert eyes while Phasael hardly seemed to notice her as he launched into explaining how they had both learned to ride that day.

"Come here," she said again and pointed at the ground in front of her. The boys approached her.

When they stood before her, Cypros could see that they were still shorter than her, but not by much. Cypros put her hands on their shoulders. She looked at them each in turn and lightly ran her hands along the tops of their shoulders and then up their necks. When she got to their hairlines, her hands remained gentle, fingers sliding along their scalps, gathering great fistfuls of hair. When she had what she wanted, she closed her fists slowly, squeezing them tight, watching the boys gasp and buckle in front of her. She imagined the roots starting to tear from their heads.

They said nothing. She held them that way, fixing them

one at a time with a fierce expression. Then she spoke. "The blood of Antipater runs in your veins," she said.

She turned her attention on Phasael and his pain-distorted expression. "Your deaf ears pitched you into the ground today. You heard laughter, but not the instructions that would have saved you the fall."

She turned then to Herod. "And you betrayed your brother to entertain a crowd you only met last week. He protected you along the sea when you were a baby, and when he was hurt on the ground today, you mocked him. In front of others."

She held them at an odd angle, tilted in towards one another, and when she released them, they stumbled into each other. They were unprepared when Cypros swung with one fist, striking Phasael in the face and sending him sprawling to the ground.

While Phasael was still falling, she grabbed Herod by his throat and threw him at his brother, hooking one foot so that he fell. Both boys gasped when Herod landed on Phasael. Before they could recover, she fell on them herself, straddling them in a way that was as rough as it was indecent, hands back in their hair. She pressed the sides of their faces into the ground.

"You're going to do something tonight, both of you, together," she said. "You're going to erase this day. When your father returns, he will be able to focus on the business that he is about. You will not be his concern."

Both boys made nodding motions to the degree that they could.

Cypros stood, and the boys stood with her. Phasael looked like he wanted to cry, and Herod was pale and shaking. Cypros reached out again, and the boys flinched as she once again took handfuls of their hair. She held them firmly but did not pull this time. She turned them towards each other.

"Kiss," she said.

The boys looked at her in surprise, but her face remained emotionless. They pecked at one another, and then Cypros turned and walked them out of the tent, hands still in their hair. They walked through various alleyways among the tents until she came to the periphery of the tent city. The guards that followed remained silent.

The sun hung low in the sky. There was less than an hour left in the day. Cypros pointed the boys' faces across the flat wilderness to where a spire of rock arose, perhaps an hour's hike away.

"You're going to go to that rock," she said. "I left something there for you in a jar. You will not return to us until you have found the jar and done with the gift what the gift is for."

"It's going to be dark soon," Phasael said.

"That it is," Cypros said. "Don't get lost in the sand."

She let go of the boys' hair, and they turned to face her. They did not look like the eight- and the ten-year-old that they were. They looked like much younger children. She put her hand lightly, kindly, on Herod's cheek as she held his eyes. "Since you forgot who your blood was today and who protected you when you were young, when the sea tried to steal you from us, your brother will be all you have when you go into the desert tonight."

From inside her tunic, she removed a short length of rope and signalled Herod to turn around. He did so, and she bound his wrists, wrapping, overlapping, and knotting the cords up his forearms so that not only were his arms bound, but his shoulders were uncomfortably pulled back.

"There are wild animals in the desert that would fall upon two boys like you as though you were gifts from heaven. Your brother is all you have tonight. You cannot even run fast like this."

She turned then to Phasael. She held his gaze longer, and he looked terrified before her. "Since you refused to listen to your teachers today," she said, "your brother will be your ears tonight. You will not know what is coming. You will only be able to see, dimly, in the dark."

She reached inside her tunic, removed a linen strip, unwrapped it, and removed two wax plugs. She adjusted the shape and pressed one of them into one of Phasael's ears. Before she plugged the second ear, she looked closely at him again. "Find the jar, use what's in it, and come home. Don't ever let today happen again." She looked from one boy to the other. "Do you understand?"

Both boys nodded. "Good. Go. Come back to me. Don't ever again act like the animals I saw today."

With that, she plugged Phasael's other ear and then wrapped his head with the linen, covering his ears with extra layers.

She pointed. The boys began to walk. Their posture was stooped, their gait unsteady. They walked very closely together. Phasael had a hand on Herod's nearest shoulder as though to help him if he lost balance on the uneven ground. They walked forwards and did not look back, the armless boy and the deaf one, each dependent on the other.

When Cypros turned around, the guards were well back,

eyes downcast. As she approached them, one looked up and gestured towards the boys as though he would follow them.

"Leave them," she said. "They'll return on their own."

She said nothing else to the guards as she returned to her other children.

*They are al-Qaum's tonight.*

# 21

## 66 BCE

IN THE MORNING, Cypros sat with the children while they ate their morning meal. The scent of flatbread and za'atar spice and salt filled the air. The disks were both spice encrusted and honey coated. Herod insisted on dipping his in his bowl of cream. The others drank their cream properly. The sweet spice loaf was a treat, as were the ripe pomegranates. Rich juice smeared their faces, Salome's above all, her hands a mess of sticky red syrup, crumbs, and flakes of dried green spices. A slick of white clung to her lips when she smiled.

Cypros watched her two oldest sons. They had come back late in the night. She had heard them coming, sensed them outside the tent, putting out the torch they had found in the jar along with the flint, kindling, and knife. Phasael's wax earplugs and headband had contributed to the torch's longevity on their night journey home. She had said nothing to them—pretended to be asleep.

In the morning light, she studied their faces and saw calm there and new confidence. They had missed the evening meal last night. There had been no food in the jar, and nothing had been left out for them. This morning they looked hungry and happy.

They talked with their sister and brothers, interacted with Cypros and Hanne, but largely they focused on the food. They looked at one another when they thought Cypros was not looking, and there was a light in their eyes. As they talked, she heard a different layer of humour pass between them.

The side of Phasael's face was swollen. Cypros surmised that the redness there would turn into a bruise. His eye might blacken. She told herself that it was from his fight with Herod the day before, perhaps also from his fall from the camel. But she had struck him there as well. She tried to remember if it was his jaw or his cheek she had hit, but she could not remember.

Herod was worse for wear. More than just the fights marked him. Besides normal bruising, he had several scrapes along his face. When he had changed his shirt in the early morning light, she had seen that one shoulder was raw as though he had fallen on it more than once in the night. If he had cried in the desert, there was no sign of it now, and there had been no sound to indicate it last night. The boys had crept into the sleeping tent and settled themselves silently. Phasael had seen Herod through to the rock and the jar. He had cut his brother's bonds, and they had left the cut ties, knife, and flint near the tent's central pillar.

Servants, Hanne among them, cleared away the breakfast.

Later, a man she associated with Obodas, Aretas's oldest son, came to their door. Joseph left, taking the man's hand and going out to learn to use a smaller version of the Nabataean rider's bow. Salome left a short while later with a group of young girls, a few of them cousins. There was an oasis farther up into the mountains from which water was piped down to Raqmu. A group of women and girls—with escorts in attendance—would take camels there, and one of the women had offered to show Salome this miraculous place of water in the desert. Pheroras, nearly four years old, wanted to stay with his mother and his oldest brothers.

"Not where we're going," she said. "Not today."

The boy left pouting, but before he was out of earshot, she heard him talking with the other Nabataean boys. He too would go a long way on a camel today, on the lap of a caretaker like his younger sister. They were both too young to ride alone, but it was important to Cypros that they learned the camel's strange sway at this early age. Starting this young, they would be naturals at it later, better even than Phasael or Herod. Brother and sister left on separate adventures, to learn the same swaying lesson.

"Let's go," she said to her eldest sons. "I have something to show you that is unlike anything you've seen yet."

"The Siq?" Phasael asked.

"The Siq and beyond. Don't keep your uncle waiting."

Obodas, Cypros's cousin, accompanied Aretas, Cypros, and the boys on this walk. A group of guards trailed, though there was no practical danger in the city. A few advisors followed alongside the guards in case Aretas needed them.

They passed beneath the vast archway at the entrance of the Siq. Great stones bigger than ten men supported the curving structure. Intricate lattice patterns inset with baetyl stones ran down the carved arch and into the sides of the cliffs. The Jews called those sacred stones idols. Cypros resisted shaking her head. Her boys were the closest things to Jews in this canyon today.

They passed beyond the archway, but the guard lingered behind. One of the advisors finally called out, and the group realized that Herod had stayed behind. He stood beneath the archway, looking up at the structure above him. He squinted and studied the stones.

It was unnatural for the Nabataeans to let a child lead, but Aretas was of a generous mood. He returned to his grandnephew and crouched and looked up at the arch with the boy. If he noticed the boys' new injuries, he said nothing about them.

"What do you see?" Aretas asked.

"How did you get them up there?" Herod asked.

The stones were massive. It seemed that a hundred men would not be able to lift one, and dozens of them formed the archway, spanning the distance, held in place by the angle of their position, wedged one into another.

"Angels of Dushara did it," Aretas said. "Dushara is the Lord of the Mountain."

Herod ignored this answer. "When you put one up, it would just fall. You need them all up at the same time before they will stay there."

"Maybe it wasn't his angels after all," Aretas said. "Dushara must have set them all there himself, at once." He looked up at the stone arch above.

"No," Herod said. "How did you do it?"

Aretas smiled and looked up at Cypros, then back to Herod. "Come," he said. "I'll show you. The answer is inside."

He stood and returned to the others. Herod followed him. The guards and advisors trailed behind.

Cypros had kept an eye on Phasael during this exchange. He shifted on his feet and looked several times up the Siq in the direction they were going, but he said nothing. Grand-uncle and grandnephew had discussed the arch, and now the group started walking again. Phasael was not great at listening, nor was he good with patience either.

They were not far into the Siq when they encountered the bow of rock many times higher than a man and ribbed with vertical ridges. "Your father described this once as looking like a beast trapped in the rock," she said. "It looks like one, don't you think?"

They all walked up to the formation and stopped.

"The front legs could be over there," Phasael said. "Eroded."

"Perhaps a beast like this made the archway," Aretas said with a smile at Herod.

"You said the answer was inside," Herod said. "This just looks like a beast. It's not actually one."

The farther they walked into the Siq, the more tension welled in Cypros's throat. She felt her eyes water and willed the water away. This was another part of home for her. The tent city before the cliffs had been her first welcome. This was her second. If she ever got back to Damascus again, that would be her third.

As they passed out of the Siq sometime later, the narrow

channel through the mountain opened into a wide square. In front of them lay a pile of rubble somewhat taller than a man. Cypros turned and looked back. She had forgotten to look up and see the beauty that Antipater had once described as a river in the sky. Her man was not a poet, but he had his moments.

Herod and Aretas were discussing the massive carving in front of them. Above a rubble pile, the peak of a building was revealed, emerging from the cliff face.

"You lower carvers from the cliff above." Herod pointed at the pile of debris at the building's base. "This is what they cut away."

"Your boy has an eye for architecture."

Cypros smiled at her uncle and son, then made as though to give Phasael her attention. Her mind was elsewhere. She worried about Antipater. The ride was long. Their band was small. They were going to secretly escort a former king out of Jerusalem and set in motion a chain of events to topple a throne. *To reclaim a throne.*

"You'll carve it right down to the ground?" Herod asked.

"That's right," Aretas said.

"When will you finish?" Herod asked.

Aretas laughed. "I won't ever finish. I started, but now I've stopped. My son will continue this work." He gestured at Obodas. "Or his son after him. Instead of finishing this in a hurry, my attention is on other buildings and dams and waterways. And some business in Jerusalem with your father."

"I didn't know Nabataeans were builders and carvers," Herod said to his mother.

"We're not," she said. She thought about Damascus.

The Nabataeans had taken the city from the Seleucids decades ago. For the first time in her life, she wondered who had lived in her room in that city before her. Generations had called Damascus home before Nabataea had claimed it.

"Some of us are builders," Aretas said. "A few and perhaps more in the future."

Cypros looked at her uncle and saw that he was talking not only to Herod but about him.

"We hire the best from other places," Aretas continued. "We are better at camels, the desert, and the spice routes. That keeps us free and keeps us strong and keeps us rich." He burst out laughing and ruffled Phasael's hair. The boy seemed bored with this dialogue.

"Then who are the main builders and carvers?" Herod asked.

"Greeks," Aretas said. "And Egyptians. We have a man in Rome recruiting craftsmen from there to come as well. Raqmu will one day be the centre of the world. Greece, Rome, and Egypt will intermingle. Dushara will dance with Isis and Diana. At the end of a long dry journey, the dignitaries of the world will come to Raqmu and find it overflowing with water. It will be crowned by the finest buildings in the world—buildings carved from the mountain itself."

"Water?" Herod asked. He looked around with a frown.

"I'll show you," Aretas said. "You heard the water in the pipes in the Siq."

"That's not 'overflowing with water,'" Herod said.

Aretas laughed again. His mood was good, and he did not abandon the dialogue.

"It's a start. I'll show you the future. That is what I will build. My son will build the rest of this building and others like it one day. After we finish with this Jerusalem business."

Cypros felt herself getting frustrated. She had intended to introduce the boys to Nabataean wonders, to lift their minds above petty sibling struggles and the challenges of camel riding. Instead, Phasael looked bored, and Herod's endless questions were steering credit to Romans and Greeks and Egyptians rather than Nabataeans. She turned to go on, to lead the group onwards, but Herod stood still within the Siq's shadow. "What about the archway?" Herod asked.

"Ah, yes." Aretas pointed at the pile of rubble at the base of the carving before them. "An amazing amount of rock comes off the mountain when we carve a building into it like this. We started from the top like you said, hanging men from ropes, and they carved their way down until halfway down they were standing on their own rubble. Then we took rubble from other works and piled it up until the Siq was completely blocked."

"Then you dragged the archway blocks up your rubble pile," Herod said. "They didn't hang in the air; the rubble supported them."

"Your son understands how to build," Aretas said to Cypros.

She liked the Angels of Dushara explanation better. Or the Siq's beast come to life. This talk of men at labour stole the magic from the place. She thought again about Antipater's river in the sky. Her sons were not like her or Antipater. Herod at least was different.

"Then you took all the rubble away later," Herod said. He was speaking to himself now, though the others could hear. He seemed deep in thought.

They started on their way again with Aretas leading. Cypros watched Herod as they continued through the interior of Raqmu. There were many construction projects under way, some grand, some merely a maze of underground piping and foundation work soon to be covered with street-level paving.

Herod only seemed to rouse himself from his thoughts when a new sight prompted a new question. Each query made Cypros's mood grow a little more sour.

"I can put you with the workers for a day or a week if you like," Aretas said. "And you can spend time with the architects. It will be a long time before your father returns with our special visitor. You can learn everything you have the energy to absorb."

Cypros was unsure if Aretas was serious or not, but Herod nodded and thanked the man as though what he offered was only a small trinket. "That would be good," Herod said. "I can start tomorrow. Who should I meet?"

Obodas laughed. "I'll bring you," he said. "I'll meet you at your tent as the sun rises. Have an early breakfast and bring a lunch and plenty of water."

Later that evening, they gathered in Aretas's grand tent and feasted by lamplight. The children were with them this night and they shared food and stories. As the meal wound down, Aretas leaned towards Cypros and got her attention.

"Don't let that one," he said, pointing towards Herod, "become a Jew. He's a Nabataean. Make sure he stays that way."

"He's growing up a Jew," Cypros said.

"I know. And his father will teach him Jewish things. But he's a Nabataean. Make sure that whatever he does in Eretz-Israel, they are Nabataean things."

Aretas leaned back and took a mouthful, chewing as he surveyed the room. Cypros tried pretending to focus elsewhere, but he caught her eye again.

"Don't forget," he said in a voice that others heard, though they did not know what he was referring to. It almost seemed like he was angry with her for a moment.

"I've never forgotten," Cypros said. "Not even for a moment."

# 22

## 66 BCE

IN THE GLOOM of the Tyropoeon Valley, shadows fell early. Trash from both the Upper and Lower City found its way down here along with a fine layer of soot from the Temple's ever-present fires. Pninah sat in their small house near the valley floor with Gavriel, contemplating his question.

A single lamp lit the room. The lamp guttered before some phantom breeze. She watched the flame sway, then straighten, then stand a half size taller and hold itself there for the space of several breaths. Then it guttered again, shrinking back and splaying across the lamp's surface before recovering itself and standing tall once more.

"No," she said. "I don't remember a wagon full of baskets." She wanted to remember such a wagon. Or the one full of wine amphoras that he had asked about. Or the one taking away rubbish: old rags and tangled cuttings from

Hyrcanus's garden. These sightings mattered to him. *I don't see these kinds of things—they are not the sort of things I notice.*

Gavriel snorted.

"We can't guard Hyrcanus's house anymore now that he's gone. If they don't have any other work for you tomorrow," she said and then did not finish the thought. She looked at the door, thick and barred on the inside with a branch Gavriel had found outside Jerusalem and carted home. He had notched it so that it fit inside the brackets anchored into the door's thick jams. She looked at the sturdy stone walls and then up at the low roof that kept them safe.

"What if they don't have any work for you at all anymore?" she said.

Gavriel shook his head. "Don't be stupid. Kings always have work for people. The Citadel is overrun with Aristobulus's people. They're trying to figure things out. Where did Hyrcanus go? Who did he leave with? How come the two people put in charge of watching the house didn't see him leave?"

Pninah avoided looking at Gavriel. She looked around their small room instead. There were no windows. There was the one door and the two drafty cracks down low and up high where the stonework needed repair.

"There's no work for me tomorrow," Gavriel said. "We'll make it a proper day off. We'll go around the city like before."

Pninah felt the mood in the room lighten at that. It was as though there were now two lamps in the room and not just the one. But the change was only that. The air was still heavy between them. The scent of the valley lay unchangingly stale. The stone walls of the house could not block its scent.

⌘

The next morning, sunlight filtered down into the valley.

"Which way do you want to go?" Gavriel asked.

Pninah walked through a shaft of light and opened her mouth to answer, then saw Gavriel had already turned to the right. He was leading them to the Upper City.

She thought about the shaft of light for several minutes as they walked. She wondered why her mind could not be more like the air in that bright beam: clear and clean and confident. Instead, she felt like her head swirled with muddy water. She thought foolish things.

In the Upper City, they began to follow strangers as though they were still in the business of pickpocketing. A man dressed in the severe whites and blacks of a Pharisee entered the street ahead of them, and Gavriel nudged her.

"Nobody told him that Pharisees are not welcome anymore," Gavriel said.

He kept his voice low, but Pninah still looked around to see if anyone had overheard. She smiled and then remembered to make a small laugh.

"What do you think?" Gavriel asked. His tone was like that of his younger self when this had been a way to make a living.

"They never have much money," Pninah said.

"How about her then?" Gavriel said. The woman was pregnant, well dressed, clothed in a style that Pninah associated with wealthy Egyptians. It wasn't the usual *kalasiris* sheath dress—she was too pregnant for that. But the dress was based on that design and even had the breast caps that would have been offensive in Jerusalem except she mostly covered it all with a very light pleated linen shawl. She was flanked by Jewish bodyguards, but everything else about her suggested an Egyptian nationality.

"Is she from here, or there?" Pninah asked. The woman was a puzzle.

"There's a nurse with her," Gavriel said, nodding towards a clearly Jewish woman nearby.

"And extra guards," Pninah said. Two additional men trailed the nurse and the woman.

The pregnant woman said something to the nurse.

"How about we do the Stumble?" Gavriel said.

"With two layers of guards?"

"I can outrun them. If anyone even notices."

"Have you figured out where she keeps her purse?"

"I'm working on it."

"You're picking the ploy before you know where the take is?" Pninah asked. "What happens when people realize I'm the distraction, not the main event?"

"Have you lost your taste for a hustle?"

"No," Pninah said and shrugged. "It's just a question. Besides, we don't do this anymore. You have a proper job now."

"Let's do it by feel," Gavriel said. "Let's go for the nurse instead. Whatever she's got. She's closer to the edge."

Pninah considered this. She tried to consider it—tried to understand how this approach was to their advantage and why this old game was back on the menu. Gavriel continued talking, leaning into her as they walked. Pninah's vision narrowed. She tried to focus on the pregnant Egyptian woman. She tried to take in the nurse as well, but she found it hard to fit them both in one frame of vision. Her limbs felt loose. An exhilarating feeling rose within her. Then a floating feeling. Then no feeling.

❧

"She with you?"

"She's my wife."

Pninah opened her eyes at the sound of Gavriel's voice. She could not remember anything. Then she felt the strangeness of memory coming back.

The sky shone blue. It was always blue. Looking straight ahead meant she was looking straight up, and the sky was very blue. There was not a wisp of cloud. *Is it late in the day?* The blue was dark and not the faded blue of midday.

She looked around. Gavriel was talking with a large man while two others held him, one on each arm. Two other guards stood nearby, watching over her. He had given her up. Just like that. *She's my wife.*

She wondered how far into their ruse they had gotten before her seizure. It had always been a risk. They had discussed in their younger years how to use it if it happened. The Stumble was perfect. There was no acting in a seizure. Well handled, the plan had been for Gavriel not to run away. Demon attacks were riveting and crowd drawing.

"I could pick two or three extra pockets in the confusion," Gavriel had once said. "I wouldn't. I'd make sure you were safe. Stop you from banging your head on the street. But I could."

Now it had occurred. And he got caught. And gave her

up. That was not in any of their plans. *I don't understand why we went through with it. We don't need the money. Not today.*

She looked around for the pregnant woman and her nurse, but they were nowhere around. Others were watching, but they focused on her, not on Gavriel or the guards.

The guards looked different from those she was familiar with. They weren't the Egyptian woman's guards. They wore clothing that suggested Sadducees. Not actual Sadducees, who were all priests, but something like Sadducees. They wore the same blues and bright whites as the Sadducees, but with none of the purple or scarlet details.

She scowled and tried to remember what had happened. Where had these men come from? She did not know if they had even gone ahead with the Stumble. *Did we change ploys?* She could not remember any of it. *How am I supposed to play my part in the aftermath if I don't even know what it is the aftermath to?*

"What do you want us to do with her?" one of the guards asked, talking to the interrogator.

"Will she recover?" the interrogator asked Gavriel.

"She's okay now. Pninah, you're okay, right?"

*He's giving them my real name?*

"I'm okay," she said. Her voice was quiet even in her own head.

"Take her home then. Is she okay home alone?"

"She's okay now. She'll be okay," Gavriel said. "You can walk on your own, right?"

"I'm okay."

"Take her home," the interrogator said. He was one of the Sadducean royal guard. Obviously. She felt very slow as she tried to piece things together.

"She'll be okay now," Gavriel said. "She can walk on her own."

"No." The interrogator gestured to two of the guards. "You two, take her home."

Pninah sat up, trying to do her part. Her head swam, and her limbs were weak. Her stomach and major muscles hurt. She was wet and did not want to stand.

"It's okay, Pninah," Gavriel said. He used her name again. "She needs a blanket to wrap around her," he said to the interrogator.

Pninah waved them away. She always kept a cloth with her just in case. She unwrapped it and wound it about her waist, covering her shame as she stood. She looked briefly at Gavriel and then caught the expression on the interrogator's face. He looked like he had seen something foul. He had seen nothing. She had covered herself properly when she had stood, but it did not change what he imagined.

"Okay," the interrogator said. "Take her home."

The guards escorted her to the top of the trail leading down into the Tyropoeon Valley. There, they conferred with one another when she began to descend.

"I'll be okay from here," she assured them.

They made no response. They did not agree to this procedure, but they did not stop her from descending on her own. They did not follow. After a short while, she was free of Gavriel's captors and alone again on the valley floor.

In the house, she cleaned herself and then made the evening meal for two. She ate her share, then put the rest away. Then she waited.

"Come home, Gavriel," she said to the quiet room. "Come home."

She got up slowly from the table. Her legs were stiff and weak. She walked woodenly over to the bed, knelt to pull the covers aside, crept onto the mattress, and lay down. Pulling the covers over herself, she moved slower than she ever had before. She wondered if this was some new kind of seizure. Then she felt her eyes close and understood: this was sleep and nothing more.

"Come home, Gavriel," she murmured to the dark room.

Gavriel did not come home.

# 23

## 66 BCE

From dawn's first light, Pninah walked for hours, criss-crossing the Upper City. She sat by a well at mid-morning and quenched her thirst. Afterwards, she went to the bakers to quiet her hunger, then went back down into the valley. The house remained still and empty.

*I don't even know who to ask.* She looked in the direction of the palace, but she could not see it from the valley floor. *They would not have taken Gavriel there.*

She could see a section of the Zion Bridge, but she could not make out faces from this distance. *Perhaps the dungeons or the Citadel.*

Neither were places that she could simply approach to ask questions. There was no procedure at all for finding someone taken to those places.

Instead of seeking where he was, she turned her attention to who she could ask and then realized that she did not really know any of Gavriel's associates. She had met the offensive man twice, the second time while celebrating Aristobulus's coronation. He had had his wife with him that celebratory night, but Pninah could not remember her name nor his either. She did not know where to look for him. Then she remembered Rachel, the kindly woman who had held on to her arm most of the night as though they were sisters.

Pninah wiped her face, smoothed her hair, and then went looking. The woman lived in the Lower City. She did not know exactly where, but it was somewhere in David's old city.

She walked the streets of the Lower City until her feet ached, and still she walked. Finally, late in the afternoon, Rachel came out of a low building and passed Pninah with her eyes down.

"Rachel," Pninah said.

The woman stopped. There was the barest of pauses, and then their eyes connected, and a bright smile flashed across Rachel's face. "Oh. You're Gavriel's. . ." She did not finish the sentence but kept smiling at Pninah.

"I've been looking for you," Pninah said.

"What for?"

"Gavriel is gone."

The woman flinched and took a step back. One hand came up between them, palm out. "I don't know where he is."

"Do you know any of his friends? People he works with?"

"Don't you?"

"No."

"No, of course not. You wouldn't. I'm sorry." The

woman lowered her hand, shook her head, closed her eyes, pinched the bridge of her nose, and then opened her eyes again to look at Pninah. "Where did he go?"

"I don't know. He was arrested yesterday."

"Arrested?" The woman's smile vanished. Her eyes narrowed and held Pninah's gaze. "By who? For what reason?"

"I don't know. I need to talk with people he works with. They would know something."

"Why would they know?"

Pninah looked at the wide serious eyes staring at her and then it came to her. "I think it has something to do with Hyrcanus. We were watching his house, but somehow Hyrcanus escaped. Maybe they think it was Gavriel's fault."

"Then they would have taken him to the Citadel," the woman said. "Looking for him won't help you." The woman turned away and gestured for Pninah to follow.

She led Pninah up a series of stone stairs and into a small room. It was not much bigger than Pninah's tiny house in the valley. The walls of this house adjoined the walls of other houses, as was the style here. It was like the home Pninah had grown up in, but smaller.

A water-pot sat on a low fire, nearly at a boil. From her bag, Rachel removed a small packet, presumably the purpose of her quick trip. She made a tea from the water with the contents of the packet, and together they sat near the open doorway, letting the light fall equally across them.

"He'll be okay," Rachel said. She said it contemplatively, as though talking to herself. Then she looked at Pninah. "We're all impressed with how he looks after you," she said.

Pninah nearly spilled the tea. "Who is 'we'?"

Rachel smiled. But not with her eyes. "The people he

works with. He talks about you a great deal. His love for you is stronger than most. You're lucky to have him."

"You work with him? I'm with him most of the day, and he works alone. With me."

Rachel looked away. Her brow wrinkled. She looked like she was going to put her tea down. She smoothed her appearance and returned the smile to its place. "Yes, I know. You provide wonderful company. Still, Hyrcanus got away."

"He got away at night."

Rachel frowned again and this time did not erase it. "Then why was Gavriel arrested?"

"I thought you could help," Pninah said.

"He's the one who helps you," Rachel said. She leaned over, rocking on one hip, and then stood. Pninah stood as well. She still held the small cup. Her legs were stiff from yesterday's attack and then this day of endless walking. Rachel reached out her hand for Pninah's tea and then set the cup on a stone by the fire.

"Go home," Rachel said. "Wait for him there. He'll be home again to look after you soon enough."

The woman did not step towards Pninah, but Pninah felt her presence as though she had. Pninah took a step back, and then another, and found herself in the doorway.

Pninah expected the woman to say something else, but she said nothing. The woman's expression was placid other than a quiver at her throat. It betrayed some emotion unstated. She revealed nothing else. When Rachel reached out, it was not to touch or embrace but to rest a hand on the open door. Pninah tested her intention by taking a farther step back, and the woman moved the door the same distance towards her.

Confused, Pninah turned and stepped completely from the house, and the door continued to close. She had not gone two steps down from the doorway when she heard it completely close behind her.

Back on the street, an older Jewish woman crossed Pninah's path. She glanced at Pninah, then up the stairs to Rachel's place. She curled her lip in a sneer and muttered something under her breath. Then she turned away with a sour expression.

Pninah stood still on the street, watching the old woman walk away. She felt her hands tremble, not with a seizure. With something else.

She began walking again. A slow pace. It had been a long day. She shuffled along. She tried to focus her mind on Gavriel, but she now found that her image of him kept sliding out of focus. *I'm just tired.*

Another woman crossed Pninah's path. The woman wore an ankle-length chiton. The cut, the high gather at the waist, the exposed skin at the woman's throat all clearly said that she was a gentile. Probably a Greek. Perhaps even a Seleucid remnant left in the city from years gone by. Pninah felt her lip curl like the old Jewish woman's expression. The city's ills were always traceable back to gentile trespassers with their uncleanness, foreign gods, and filthy habits and children. She wanted to lash out at the stranger, but the woman looked wealthy. Pninah needed help finding Gavriel, not new enemies.

She kept walking and passed the Greek woman. She said nothing, but the woman continued to occupy her mind. *Think of something else.* Turning her mind from the Greek woman brought her to Idumeans—they were foreign as well. *They call themselves Idumeans now, but they're just filthy Edomites with fresh names. Gentiles. Fake Jews.*

She thought about how the Idumeans—it had to be the Idumeans, Antipater and his brothers—who had spirited Hyrcanus away. *For what purpose?* The gentiles were always about something evil—even their good deeds were evil. *They cost me Gavriel.*

Walking towards the valley, she wanted to scream then and turn and run back and attack the Greek woman. She wanted to assault the old Jewish woman and Rachel as well. She wanted to march on the Citadel and reclaim the man she claimed as her husband—even if there had been no real wedding between them. She wanted to stand in the city gates, any of the gates, all the gates, and proclaim the wisdom and right and might of Aristobulus, leader of the Sadducees, king of Jerusalem, the man her father would have followed if he had still been alive.

She felt tears come, thinking of how her father would have thrived under this new king.

She chose the first route down into the valley, though this way was longer. She wiped her eyes, though no tears had fallen. She wanted to be away from the upper lands. She needed the quiet found below.

As the noise from the city receded, a new spirit came upon her. In the quietness of the valley, it occurred to her that the Pharisees would be more apt to clear Jerusalem of its gentiles. The Sadducees were not concerned about gentiles—integration with foreigners was their strength. Aristobulus had even married off his daughter to a gentile.

*And Aristobulus took Gavriel from me. Why do I believe in him?*

She frowned in the valley, sensing an argument contrary to the blood that surged within her, then she let it go. Rachel, the Jewish woman, the Greek woman, even Jerusalem's politics—these were all distractions. Kings were not her concern.

*Just get Gavriel back. Gavriel is all that matters.*

# 24

## 66 BCE

As evening slipped towards night, the atmosphere past the Siq and up the canyon was like that around the stone tables and fire pits outside the Ashkelon palace. Unlike the quiet nights of Cypros and Antipater hosting Hyrcanus and her uncle, on this night the canyon was crowded.

Cypros noted the stone pillars and skeletal roof marking the boundaries of this space, just like at Ashkelon. Both locations followed an even older civilization's pattern. The usually suspended sunshades overhead had been removed, and looking up, Cypros could see stars, clear and bright in the late autumn air. She reclined some distance from Antipater, surrounded by cousins and other Nabataean women.

"Is she like this often?" a cousin asked. The question was about Hyrcanus's wife, the only Jewish woman invited to this feast. She had remained behind, with her children, in the tent city on the plain before Raqmu's cliffs.

"I don't know her well," Cypros said. "I hear that she has a weak stomach."

Another course arrived, and the servers started with the men.

Several women around Cypros stirred, shifting as though to get up, then just moving to adjust their weight on one hip more comfortably. *They're not used to being served.* Cypros smiled and waited and said nothing out loud.

Hyrcanus's wife never came with him to Ashkelon. *It is a poor Pharisee that would accept the hospitality of a Nabataean and her Idumean husband.* The thought came to her fully formed, as though handed to her from someone else's store of knowledge. She frowned and looked across to where Hyrcanus sat beside Aretas. The deposed Jew was just drunk enough to be comfortable, as on so many nights at Ashkelon. He was the only one drinking. The meagre supply of wine he had brought with him from Jerusalem would only last tonight. It would be his last drink for a long time to come. Cypros ignored her husband and looked around at the other men, trying to read what they thought of Israel's past and future king.

Obodas, Aretas's eldest son, was engaged in conversation with Antipater. Her cousin was trying to sketch something using his finger on stone as though he could leave a mark there. He nodded and talked and her husband replied with nods and hand gestures.

". . . fifty at least," one cousin said near her. "From a stronghold deep in the desert."

"Half of Damascus will be emptied," another woman said.

"Trade is going to suffer with all these men gathered in one place," a third contributed. "I hope this Jerusalem campaign is worth it."

"Twelve cities," Cypros said. She took a drink and waited until she had the attention of the other women. "That is the deal between Aretas and Hyrcanus. We contribute fifty thousand Nabataean soldiers for a short siege. Once Hyrcanus is back on the throne, he will return twelve cities to us. To Nabataea. Taxes from those cities will go a long way towards compensating for gaps in trade."

"Fifty thousand," the first cousin said, eyebrows raised as she looked at the friends around her. "That's a lot of men with no women to comfort them."

There was a brief, aborted squeal from the youngest of the cousins, who slapped a hand over her mouth.

"They're not coming until later in the season," Cypros said with a smile. "The ones you see now are here to set up sanitation, food stores, logistics for when they march. Damascus, Gaza, and those from the desert will come closer to the day."

"After—" one of the cousins started, then stopped. "What do the Jews call it? Their festival?"

"Passover?" Cypros asked.

"Yes, after Passover?"

"No. Before it," Cypros responded. "Aristobulus will lose in the field and get bottled up in Jerusalem. Then he'll work out a deal and surrender. The rest of the Jews will come for Passover. Hyrcanus will be seen on the throne again.

Hyrcanus will lead the Passover as high priest as well and everything will be back to normal for the Jews."

"They're going to start during the rainy season?"

"Yes," Cypros said. "Al-Qaum willing, the rains will end early."

"'Al-Qaum willing'?" her cousin to her left asked. "Not, what do the Jews say, Adonai? Hashem?"

Another cousin chimed in. "It's always al-Qaum with her. She's old-fashioned. Not even Dushara will do. It's always al-Qaum."

"Don't tell her husband," another said, laughing, then put her hand on one cheek and glanced across the room at the men who paid no attention to the women's Nabataean chatter.

"My husband has no concern for my private practices," Cypros said, "as long as they remain private."

"What do you teach your boys?" her leftward cousin asked.

"I teach them what any mother teaches her boys. I teach them to be men."

Sparks from one of the nearby fires leaped into the air as though someone had dropped a log on the flames. There seemed to be no cause for this display of hundreds of tiny points of light suddenly rising in the air, zigzagging as they reached the apex of their flight, then falling and winking out in quick succession.

Talk among her cousins and other Nabataean women continued around her while Cypros grew silent. She thought about the thousands of hard sun-darkened Nabataean men that would soon gather at Raqmu to serve in a Jewish civil war. To pay for it, Hyrcanus was giving up his father's legacy east of the Jordan. All this to reclaim his mother's Jerusalem throne.

*We're going to do more than free Nabataean cities from the Jews.* She was glad that the conversation had moved on. Had any of the women around her asked, she would have had a hard time staying silent. *We're going to change Idumea's relationship with Jerusalem as well. Idumea does not need to become free. Idumea needs to take over.*

"That's foolish thinking," Antipater had warned her when she had shared her intentions.

She had discussed the same ideas with her uncle, and he saw things her way.

"Nabataean blood controlling Temple and throne," Aretas had said. He had nodded gravely, taking her seriously. "No nation has done this. Only Jews have sat on the throne and controlled the Temple."

"The Seleucids controlled both," Cypros had said.

"Controlled," her uncle had replied. "But they didn't occupy the positions."

"Occupation is relative. Hyrcanus is weak. Let him hold the titles. Antipater and my sons after him can do the actual work, provide the practical direction. Power is more than appearance."

Remembering those discussions with her uncle made Cypros feel warm and contented. She reclined among her cousins and the other women, but her thoughts kept drifting elsewhere.

Sweets and teas were offered. Cypros selected a few honeyed pastries with her tea. She tried to focus on the women's discussions. They had moved on to the topic of how marriages worked for men in the strongholds and men who crossed the desert in the trading caravans, their wives and families fulfilling the role of human oases in otherwise nearly barren lives. The men entered the communities of their own families like rare interlopers, disrupting the regular patterns of life with their oversized presence. Then they returned to their lonely existence between the sun and the desert sand.

By these sacrifices, the Nabataeans were among the richest of any nation. Their wealth was revealed only in their diet and the awe-inspiring waterworks and spectacles of architecture carved into the mountains at Raqmu. They had other places like this planned.

There had never been a people like the Nabataeans. When the camels and foot troops of Nabataea descended upon Judea, Cypros wanted to be there to see what fear they inspired.

The conversation around her returned to the topic of war. "What if Aretas loses the initial battle with the Jews?" one of her cousins asked.

Cypros cut this conversation short. "Aretas won't be fighting Jews," she said. "He'll be up against mercenaries. These mercenaries accepted money to betray their master once. They'll do it again. It pays to be rich. Nabataea can buy Aristobulus's defeat."

"And the siege?"

"The siege won't last long. Jerusalem is useless in a siege. Always has been. There is no room to store up the volume of food that they need to support a long siege. If they try to operate the Temple during the siege, they burn up their already limited food supply. The flocks and herds for the sacrifices are outside the city. It's a hopeless place to defend in a siege."

"If the vulnerability is that obvious," another cousin said, "why don't they do something about it?"

Cypros smiled. "That kind of practicality is Nabataean, not Jewish. The Jugurtha Doctrine taught them how to make war and take territory. But even Jugurtha didn't teach them how to fix the vulnerability of Jerusalem. He was a Seleucid advising Jews. Solving the Jerusalem problem will take Nabataean minds. Later." She had almost said too much. "As allies and advisors. After Hyrcanus is back on the throne."

Then she closed her mouth and waited. Feasts could be dangerous places, even without wine.

# 25

## 66 BCE

For days, the sagging house in the Tyropoeon Valley bore witness to the comings and goings of a young woman. She lived there, alone now. She left early each morning looking tired. She returned home late, carrying a few things. Her movements were slow and stiff. She ate alone now and slept alone.

One morning there came a seizure, but unlike times gone by, no one held her. No one protected her or murmured to her as her body sought to escape her mind. Afterwards, she lay for hours in recovery with no one to organize her limbs or help clean her.

Later that morning, Pninah roused but felt like she could not move. Her head hurt. Her body hurt. This one had been worse than normal. She looked at the bucket of water she had drawn earlier in the day. Or the day before. She could not remember. She watched it wait for her, and then eventually she fell back to sleep.

She awoke again some time later to the sound of footsteps. Judging by the light, it was early evening. She started to sit up, but her stomach clenched. Without a chance to stop herself, she vomited across her front, and then the door opened.

Two men stood in the doorway, and they stayed there, blocking the light. They squinted, working it seemed to grow accustomed to the gloom inside.

"It stinks in here," one man said. He stepped into the room. He was a small man and very thin. He had light hair that drifted away from his skull as though seeking somewhere else to be. He looked like a bird too young for mature feathers. If he was a bird, he was half-plucked. He looked vulnerable and grotesque.

His companion entered the room behind him. The second man was also small, shorter than the first and thin as well. He had wrapped his head in a style popular with wealthier classes, but the fabric was threadbare and stained, like a mockery of Upper City finery.

Pninah sat the rest of the way up and moved her back against the wall.

"There she is," the bird-man said, pointing. "The stink comes from her."

"You were right," the shorter man said. "She stayed in all day." He stooped and poked his nose in her direction, eyes narrowing to see her better. "You picked a bad day to stay home," he said. "The day we're coming in, you stay home." He shook his head and stood up straight again.

"Where is it?" the bird-man asked Pninah.

"Where is what?" she asked. Speaking, she became aware that she still had vomit on her lips. She went to wipe her mouth and saw what was on her arm and stopped.

"Disgusting," the bird-man said. "What's wrong with you?"

"I'm sick," she said.

"She has a demon," the shorter man said. "I'll bet she's had one of those attacks."

"Is that it?" the bird-man asked. "Or is the demon still here?"

"I don't know," she said.

The bird-man laughed. "That's right." He turned to his companion and pointed at Pninah. "They don't even know when they have it. That's part of it."

"It's too bad," the shorter man said. "I've seen her in sunlight when her man used to be around. I could go for a while with her. Quite a while." He stooped again to get another good look at her.

"With that mess on her?" the bird-man asked.

"When she's cleaned up, I mean. When I seen her with her man. Before."

"Where's your man?" the bird-man said to Pninah.

"I don't know."

"She doesn't know." The bird-man laughed again. "No guile at all. I see what you mean. She's got some qualities. Cleaned up, she'd be pretty good. But not with that demon."

The shorter man took a step towards Pninah, and the bird-man put a hand on his shoulder and backed him up again. "Not with that demon," he said. "I've seen them go wild and kill a man who tried to hurt their host. And I've seen them change hosts. You get a demon like that inside you, from her, and I'd put a blade in you to get it over with quickly. So don't be touching her. Kill her if you want to but keep your distance doing it."

The small man relaxed and frowned, and then contrary expressions passed across his face that seemed to convey both pain and relief. A moan escaped him. "Now what, then?" he asked, looking up at the bird-man.

"The money," the bird-man said to Pninah. "Your man saved up some good money in here. You're not selling yourself that we can tell. You're not working anywhere up above. So you've got it stashed here somewhere."

"I don't have any money," Pninah whispered.

"Were you planning on eating tomorrow?" the bird-man asked.

Pninah nodded.

"You got people up above who give you food for free?" he asked.

She shook her head.

"Then you've got money. So where is it?"

She pointed to the wall and the loose stone there. It took the bird-man a few guesses before he figured out which stone was loose, removed it, and retrieved the small pouch.

"Not much," he said, looking inside. "But more than you'd guess from the looks of you."

Steps then came up from outside the house, approaching from the north end of the valley. The thieves were busy sorting the various coins they had collected when the new footsteps approached the house. Pninah squeezed her eyes closed, straining to recognize the weight and rhythm of those steps. She willed Gavriel to appear as he had once before.

The steps kept coming, the weight suggesting a man larger than the intruders. The footwear sounded sturdy. A large shape then filled the doorway. Though the sounds and the shape bore no resemblance to Gavriel, Pninah felt a surge of excitement within her. She gasped, eyes wide to take in her deliverance.

"You're late," the bird-man said without looking.

Late-day light left the shape in shadow, its arms out-spread, hands resting on the door frame.

"Well?" the big man asked.

"A week's wages," the bird-man said.

"A bit more," the shorter man said.

The large shadow grunted and nodded in Pninah's direction. "What about her?"

"Can't you smell her?" the bird-man asked. "She's pissed and vomited on herself, and she doesn't even know if the demon is gone or still lurking."

The big man grunted and then held out a hand. The bird-man swept the coins he had been counting back into the pouch and handed it to the big man.

The bird-man and shorter man made as though to leave, but the big man blocked the doorway. He seemed poised to enter farther. "You're sure about her?"

"Something wrong with your nose?" the bird-man asked.

The big man removed a hand from the doorway, and the bird-man flinched, backing up a quick step.

"Everybody knows about her," the bird-man said.

The big man grunted again, put his hand back on the door frame, paused, and then pushed off with both hands, propelling his bulk away from the house.

With the doorway clear, the two thinner thieves left the

room, left the door open, and left the small stone house to its usual silence.

Time passed, and Pninah did not move from her place. She continued to listen. Her eyes watched the doorway, but after the footsteps had retreated, there were no other sounds outside but the usual rustling of birds as they navigated the shady areas at the end of the day.

After a long wait, Pninah finally moved away from the wall. She left the house, taking the small bucket of water with her. Beyond the house she rinsed off her face and arms with the water in the bucket. Then she went down to the creek bed on the valley floor. Recent rains had left pools of standing water there. Later in the year, the creek would run free and flood. In summer, it would be dry. For now, it held water in temporary stone pools. She refilled the bucket, drank from it, and then returned to the house. She got the fire restarted and poured the bucket of water into a large pot to boil. She returned to the nearest small pool repeatedly, washing and then rinsing her bedding and clothes outside as the day darkened. When she finished, she washed the stone floor, the lower part of one wall, and then herself again.

The water never boiled. She needed to get more fuel. The water was at least warm enough for a weak tea. She drank the tea slowly. The house hung festooned with drying bedding and clothing. She wore her only other shift with a shawl thrown over for warmth though the air was not very cool. Despite the effort of hauling water and cleaning, she felt cold. And she felt hungry.

The following day, Pninah could not decide what to do. She considered going back to Rachel, but Rachel clearly did not want to help her. She thought about the old man outside of Jerusalem's walls who had helped protect her from the supervisor. It was a long way to go to that field. She had no idea if the field was still worked, who worked it, or if the old man would be among them. And he had no reason to help her. Then she thought of Anna. She had not seen the woman in a long time. She resisted going to her now for reasons she could not explain, but as her hunger grew greater, she stood and left the house.

The path up to the Zion Bridge was only a short distance from her house. The Temple lay to the east, but that bank was not climbable. To get to the Temple, she had to climb the steep path on the west side. She pointed herself up the slope and began to climb. She had to stop far more often than usual, but soon she was back on Upper City streets.

She stood there for a while on trembling legs. She looked across the valley at the Temple. Her legs shook, and her stomach protested its emptiness. She caught her breath, let the trembling ease, and then walked to the Zion Bridge and across it. She bypassed the usual routes through the Temple, making her way instead to Anna's quarters.

Anna looked up when Pninah came to her door. The woman squinted at Pninah, then smiled.

"My child," she said and gathered Pninah in her arms. "I haven't seen you in years. I thought you were lost. Where have you been? How are you? Where is Gavriel?"

Pninah told her everything. Of her and Gavriel, she maintained the lie about a marriage in a small village outside of Jerusalem. Otherwise, she told Anna everything.

When describing the marriage, Pninah saw Anna's eyes narrow and her lips flatten, but she did not interrupt. Some said that Anna was a prophetess, but Pninah had only ever known her as Anna. She was the woman who lived at the Temple. She was the one who had assured Gavriel that Pninah only suffered from a muscle sickness and not a demon.

When Pninah described Gavriel's arrest and disappearance, leaving off what they had been about when the arrest occurred, Anna's eyes stayed narrow and focused, but her mouth softened.

When Pninah described her searching, her vague rejection by Rachel, and then the robbery, Anna's full expression grew warm again. After her report, Anna reached out her arms and pulled Pninah close. She held Pninah the way she had not been held since her mother had been killed, and not often even with her mother. Anna, the childless widow, projected a warmth that was complete. With her face against Anna's shoulder and neck, Pninah cried. She wept into Anna's shoulder as though she were still little, a girl young and foolish but just old enough to discover that she was of no account in the world.

"Don't think that," Anna said, pulling back from Pninah, one hand on Pninah's shoulder, one hand on her neck. She studied Pninah's eyes, her gaze shifting from one to the other as tears spilled down Pninah's cheeks.

"You need food," Anna said.

She let go of Pninah and left her alone in the one room among the warren of the Temple Mount residences. She returned a few minutes later with a small stone bowl overflowing with a bit of lamb and roasted vegetables, both still hot as though they had just come from the fire.

"Where did you get this?" Pninah asked in awe.

"Never mind that child. Eat." She poured a cup of wine

from a small flagon, then mixed in an equal portion of water, and set it beside Pninah. "Eat and drink. It won't bring Gavriel back quicker or make the hurt go away, but it will help."

When she had finished eating, Pninah sipped at the wine while Anna busied herself about the small room. Afterwards, Anna came and sat with Pninah again.

"I've eaten your dinner," Pninah said. "Your allotment."

Anna smiled. "I had a morning meal," she said simply. "And I'll have another one tomorrow."

"Can you help me?" Pninah said.

"How would you like me to help you?" Anna asked.

"Can you tell me what to do? Where Gavriel is? How to live?"

"You know how to live," Anna said. "Your parents had many years to teach you, and you've been to the Temple and heard the priests many times. You know what to do."

"I don't," Pninah said. "I don't understand things."

Anna smiled. "You're naïve and rebellious both. But mostly scared."

"Explain it to me," Pninah said.

"Explain what?"

"Anything," Pninah said and burst into tears again. "Everything. Make me understand."

Anna sighed and relaxed.

"Prophets come to those who are hungry and ready," Anna said. "Or to those who are too far gone to hear, to make an example of them. I would not make an example of you, dear girl. And you're not hungry enough yet to hear."

"I am," Pninah said. "I'll listen to you."

Anna sat back against the stonework surrounding her

unlit fire. She crossed her arms over her chest. "The Greek woman," she said. "What is a Greek woman, dressed as she was dressed, doing in the Lower City?"

Pninah shook her head. "I don't know."

"Alone."

"I don't know."

"Did she have a basket for the market or a water jar for the well?"

"No."

"Then what?"

"I don't know."

"In the Lower City. Dressed as she was. Exposed as you described her. Think, Pninah. This is Jerusalem, not Antioch."

"I don't know," Pninah protested.

Anna sighed again, and it looked like she would stop her instruction.

"Just tell me," Pninah said. "I'm no good at understanding the teachers' roundabout ways of saying things."

"The old Jewish woman who was disgusted with you leaving Rachel's home," Anna said. "Does that not mean anything to you?"

Pninah shook her head.

"Was she disgusted with you or with Rachel? Or with Rachel's house?"

"I don't know. She couldn't have been disgusted with me. She'd never met me before."

"Your marriage, this mysterious unnamed village, is a lie," Anna said.

Pninah's eyes widened, and she felt her face flush. Her

lips stayed pressed together. She nodded her head despite herself.

"Some men like women from Ethiopia and places even farther," Anna said. "Some men buy slaves not for what they can carry but for how they lie down."

Pninah started at this and stared at Anna. Blood left her face at this turn in the conversation. Such language was unheard of, and coming from this woman, in this place, was even more shocking.

"Some men like Greek women. They like conquering in bed the people who used to conquer us in life. The Greeks are gone now, but their women still find a living here. And then there are women like Rachel and yourself."

Pninah stared back at Anna, not moving. Even the muscles in her throat were rigid.

"A young woman who sells herself one interaction at a time, and a woman who sells herself on a salary to the same man, are similar. They both lie down for their security."

"You can't say that about Gavriel," Pninah protested. She felt fire come to her chest and suffuse her face.

"How does Gavriel know Rachel? What was the occasion of their meeting?"

"I don't know."

"You've known Gavriel since you were both children. How can you not know?"

Pninah stood then. "I need to go," she said. Anna stayed seated and said nothing. Her gentle eyes watched Pninah's face.

"You're wrong about Gavriel," Pninah said.

Anna gave no reaction but continued to regard Pninah with a gentle, unfamiliar expression. Pninah took a step towards the door, and Anna held out a small packet. Pninah opened it and saw inside a small loaf. She smelled sweetness there. It was a spiced, sweetened loaf of the type she and Gavriel would share on special days. Tears came to Pninah's eyes again. She tucked the packet into her tunic and then fled Anna's home, the Temple courtyards, the crowds outside, and soon even the Zion Bridge, descending into the gathering darkness that was the Tyropoeon Valley.

# 26

## 66 BCE

PNINAH STAGGERED UNDER the weight of a clay jar brimming with water. She could lift it, but she had carried so many things this day that her arms shook. A small pain radiated out from behind her left shoulder blade as though a muscle had been torn. She settled the jar on her shoulder and stood up. The one sharp pain in her back was a counterbalance to the trembling weakness in her arms. Sweat soaked her arms and back. This was the day's last jar. For several days, she had worked small jobs here and there throughout the Lower City. At the end of each day, she turned her meagre earnings over to the bakers and market-stall owners. She selected older or damaged items that came discounted to fit the little she had been able to make. She tried to save a little each day, but it was nearly impossible. She worked to eat and did not know how she would pay her rent when it next came due.

She carried the jar through Jerusalem's crowded streets. Earlier in the day, she had seen Rachel. She knew that Rachel had seen her as well, but the woman had said nothing and gone on her way.

At a small shop, Pninah ducked her head and entered the room. She made her way to the back of the shop and poured the jar out into the nearly full tank.

"Your family were Pharisees," the shop owner said. He was a squarely built man, his forehead dented into a permanent frown.

"No," Pninah said. She did not understand the reason for this accusation in a newly Sadducean city. There was nothing about her dress that suggested anything Pharisaic.

The man sorted a few bronze coins and then set one on the stone slab beside her.

Pninah picked up the tiny coin and looked at it. "This is half of what you promised," she said, not looking directly at the man. It was not even enough to buy a day's worth of bread.

"You're the one who gets seizures," the man said.

Pninah started to look up at him, then stopped herself.

"You didn't warn me," the man continued.

"I didn't break anything," Pninah said. She closed the coin up in her fist and felt a numb weakness even in her wrists. She was afraid she would drop the coin. "I was careful. I did everything you said."

"You could have broken one of my jars. Then what? How would I hire someone tomorrow to carry water for me? With no jar?"

Pninah looked around the room. There were many jars

in the room, and she knew the price of them from her mother's shop. They were not inexpensive, but there were extras.

"I didn't break anything," she said. "I carried all that you asked." She slid her thumb inside her fist to make sure the coin was still there.

The man snorted and set the other coin he owed her on the stone slab. "Go," he said. "Don't come back. I can hire other people who don't hide their demons from me. Don't come back."

Pninah picked up the second coin, then retreated to the street. She put the coins together in one hand and then went to the baker.

The baker studied her offering and frowned. He selected a half-sized loaf that had collapsed in the oven and partially burned on one side. She went then to the stall a few steps farther down and bought the discards of leeks, onions, and herbs. The vendor was kindly and let her search the bottoms of baskets for stray bits discarded by others.

She wound her way north then, down into the valley, and along its dimming bottom until she came within sight of the little stone house. Smoke came from the small chimney, and she gasped, and her face lit up. She started to run, then stopped herself, slowed her pace, and stood for a moment, not moving.

*Please, do not take my house,* she said to herself. *Not yet. I'll find a way to pay.*

She clutched her small dinner and crept up to the house. She set the bread, leeks, onions, and herbs down and then very slowly opened the door.

Inside, the house was empty. She pushed the door open farther and still saw no one. She stepped into the room and looked around, but there was no one inside. The fire consumed the last of her wood. She needed fire for her tea and to make a soup of the leeks, onions, and herbs.

There were steps behind her then, and she whirled around. Gavriel stood there. He dropped his armful of wood, and Pninah screamed and leaped from the doorway and ran into Gavriel's arms. He caught her wearing an enormous grin and then steered her back towards the doorway. They staggered into the house, Gavriel half carrying her, her arms and legs wrapped around him in a brazen display that would have shocked even the prostitutes of this or any other Jewish city. Their reunion was physical, clothes shed in aggressive haste, the door left half-open, the sounds from their mouths in some language known only to lovers.

Afterwards, they lay together, sweat slicked and quiet, then Pninah stood up and stripped the blanket from the bed. She wrapped it around herself, exited the house, and gathered up the dropped firewood, bread, leeks, onions, and herbs.

Gavriel watched her with a bemused expression on his face.

Pninah set old water in a pot and stoked the fire with some of Gavriel's new wood. She dropped the leeks and herbs into the pot and then tore the bread and gave half to Gavriel.

"That's it?" Gavriel asked, looking at his piece of bread and the pot with its thin ingredients.

"I only got for me," she said.

"The money is gone," Gavriel said. "I was going to go get things, but it's all gone."

"We were robbed."

Gavriel looked at her.

"When I was out," she said. "Someone came and found the money. It's gone. I've been working in the Lower City."

"The Lower City?" he said. "Why go there? You usually work in the Upper City. When you used to work."

Pninah shrugged. "Did you hear the part about being robbed?"

Gavriel nodded and frowned. "Do you know who it was?"

"I said I was away when it happened."

Gavriel nodded again.

"Where were you?" she asked. "Where did they take you?"

"The Citadel. The night shift blamed me for letting Hyrcanus go. They put a lot of effort into finding the traitor among us, but we just got outsmarted. Now they think Hyrcanus's family went out one at a time, over several days. Do you remember the wine delivery?"

Pninah nodded.

"That wagon leaving, with the empty jars, would have been an easy place to hide one of the children. Among the jars. That kind of thing. A little bit at a time."

"Where did they go?" She sat down on the bed, and he rested his head against her hip.

"Aristobulus isn't sure. Probably Petra. Antipater is gone from Ashkelon, so there's a connection there. His brothers are gone too, even the one who lives in Jerusalem."

"So I was right!"

Gavriel snorted and said nothing in reply. "This is all we have to eat tonight?" he asked. "Bread and boiled leeks? You couldn't do any better than that?"

❧

The following day, Gavriel was slow to awake. Pninah got up and restarted the fire and put water on to boil. There was a little they could make tea with, but nothing remained from their small dinner.

Gavriel stirred and sat up in bed. "At least at the Citadel there was a morning meal," he said.

Pninah looked for the humour in his eyes. No humour lurked there. He sat up and frowned at the floor, then stood and took the tea she offered him. Without another word, he went outside and drank it, frowning at the valley.

Pninah went out and stood beside him, cupping her tea in two hands. "Don't you have to report somewhere?" she asked. "To work?"

"Where?" Gavriel said. "My job was to watch Hyrcanus. He's gone."

"Isn't there something else for you to do? Some other kind of work like you were doing before? Thinking work, like you said. Hyrcanus was not your fault."

Gavriel looked like he was going to speak, then he took another sip of tea instead.

"Don't you work for the palace anymore?" she asked.

Gavriel laughed, a bark as much as a laugh, but it quickly terminated, ugly in its tone as his eyes continued to stare at the valley bottom. "Hyrcanus and the Idumeans have put an end to that dream," he said.

"There must be other work you could do."

"There's plenty, Pninah," he said, throwing the rest of his tea to one side. "But not for a person like me. Not for someone who can't fulfill an easy assignment. I spent too much time talking to you and not enough time on the street making sure that carts leaving the house did not have people in them. I could have been a personal messenger for the king. For the palace, at least. For the army even. I cannot even get a job in the stables now. They don't pay thinking wages to people like me who can't think."

"What about—" Pninah began.

"What about what?" Gavriel growled, turning to face her. "Everything is gone."

"What about Rachel?" Pninah asked. She had had no intention of asking the question. She was shocked to hear herself say the words.

Gavriel's mouth opened, then he stopped and looked at her. "What about Rachel?" he asked. His voice was low, and his hands came up as though to grab her or resist her. She could not tell which. He did not retreat or advance but kept his hands poised for some unclear action.

"Or one of your other friends," Pninah said.

"What about Rachel?" Gavriel asked again. He stared and did not blink. "What do you know about her?"

"I just thought," she whispered. "I thought she might know someone."

"A prostitute is going to find me a job?" he laughed. "That's what you think? I'll go to her and get some work?"

He seemed to catch the expression on Pninah's face and laughed again. A forced laugh. His eyes did not leave hers.

"What kind of work is she going to find for a man?" he asked.

His eyes shifted away from her, then back. "Maybe for you, but me?"

His eyes were alive. A fire danced in them as he watched her.

Pninah felt the blood drain from her face. Weakness slid down to her knees. This was not the foreshadowing of a seizure or a signal of hunger but something worse. Her arms hung slack at her sides, and though she wanted to raise her hands to his, she stood limp. She could feel the pulse in her legs.

"You sometimes go away," she said, "to meet people."

"People," Gavriel said. He formed the word slowly like it was a word to savour. "People. Sure."

"You were going to see her."

A smirk crossed Gavriel's face. "You came to me," he said. "In an alley, late at night. No one else dared to take you in, not in those days with the Pharisees searching the city for Sadducee supporters like your parents. I took you in. Me."

"You looked after me."

"Yes, I did. And who looked after me?"

"I—" she started, then stopped.

"I worked, and you took," he said.

"I helped," she said.

"A lot of help you were," Gavriel snorted. "Everywhere I went, I had to worry about when you were going to have an attack. Everywhere I went, you were my problem. I did not ask for you. You just came. And took."

"You went to her," Pninah said, "to feel better."

"I paid her," Gavriel said.

Pninah struggled to interpret the strange answer.

"I did not take," he insisted. "It was a fair exchange between her and me."

He looked up the valley, then down, then back at

Pninah. "Oh, get that look off your face," he said. "Do you have any idea how good the Citadel was this past week? I did not have to think about your attacks, plan for them, respond to them, explain them to people—I was free. I did not have to worry at all. I'm done with being responsible for you."

Pninah looked at the ground, the shape of loose stones there. Some of these stones had slid, perhaps, from the Temple base, tumbling over centuries to here. *I thought you loved me,* she wanted to say. She imagined him laughing at her again, that cruel laugh.

"Will you go to her now?" Pninah asked.

Gavriel laughed again, the very laugh she had sought to avoid. "How?" he asked. "You lost all my money. In less than a week."

He waved his hand first at her and then in the direction of the Upper City. "Go," he said. "It's getting late, and you won't find work if you don't get yourself up there in a hurry. Get some work, get paid proper wages, get some decent supplies, and don't come back down here until you've got enough for a better meal, not like last night. I'm tired. Go."

He turned away from her then, went into the house, and closed the door.

# 27

## 66 BCE

PNINAH STOOD IN the valley beneath the shadow of overhanging trees and much more.

She did not look at the door when Gavriel closed it. She heard it. Hearing it was enough.

She took in the valley, the smell of the creek bed and the trees, and the distant partial view of Zion Bridge. Then she took a deep breath, exhaled, trembled, and closed her eyes. She wiped her face. She knelt on the valley floor and set her cup down and then stood again. One tentative step forward was all it took. A quiver fluttered at her throat. Her nostrils flared. She made no sound except for one more step on dry ground. And then another.

The shade of something dark blossomed within as she walked. With each step away from the house, this night flower grew. It rose from some deep and secret place. It spread itself and enveloped her. The weight of this shade muffled her shock. Her return to the house was impossible. She had not known that she had this bloom within her until now.

The petals of this flower were the shadow of her father. He had helped crucify eight hundred Pharisees on the roads outside Jerusalem. He had hung the priestesses of Ashkelon on eighty crosses. Her father had not been a man whose daughter should crawl.

This flower's vine was the deformed intensity of her mother, the ungainly potter, the slow killer's wife. Not a nice woman. Also not a woman who would beg.

Pninah walked the valley floor with this new growth within her. She would not return even to claim her few things. He would never know what became of her.

She thought of Anna as she passed below the Temple and then put the woman out of her mind.

Another two steps on, an image of her mother came to her again, fresh and alive and intense. Her mother's ungainliness had been partially a function of her profession. The one-sided leaning on the large stone wheel had made one half of her muscled, the other half weak. Wine had contributed to her misshapen appearance. She had walked into things when drunk, had fallen over objects. Beyond the injuries, drinking had laid a thickness upon her cheeks and settled a flatness in her eyes. Her mother had been no beauty at the end. As Pninah walked, however, she remembered the last conversation between her parents. They had made a plan to move to the sea and start over there. Even in her world-worn state, her mother had tried for something better.

Something not beholden to the Sadducees.

That last thought struck Pninah hard, and she nearly stopped walking.

She looked up at the morning sky and wondered why she was here. Not here in the valley—here in Jerusalem. *Why did I stay?*

She resumed walking north, away from the Lower City, on towards her favourite tree. The Temple stood high above her to the right, the Upper City to her left. The tree would come soon enough.

*Why do I stand with them?*

*Them* could only be the Sadducees. A Pharisee, or at least a sympathizer of the Pharisees, had killed her parents. That was reason enough for her to align with the Sadducees.

*I know the killer was a Pharisee based on what?*

The only words Pninah remembered from the man were the words he had spoken to her mother about her father's crimes, crimes her mother had been complicit in—the work of killing Pharisees. Crucifying them. Putting a blade to the women and children while tortured husbands and fathers hung and watched.

Pninah put a hand to her mouth and stifled emotion. She was not mourning the agonies of a previous generation. She knew it was her encounter with Gavriel that sought to ride history like a stowaway, carrying pain and searching to express the corners of her heart by crying over an imagined memory of crucifixions. She swallowed and stiffened her face and curled her hands into fists. She would not cry for Gavriel.

"My father was a killer," she whispered. She spoke it as an affirmation, not a revelation. Over the crunch of leaves and dry twigs below her feet, she turned the sound of her voice over again in her mind, looking for a way to fit her father's darkness and her mother's toughness into a reawakened frame.

She walked to the north end of the valley, and only as she was passing through the gates did she realize that she had walked the entire distance, right past her favourite tree, and had not said goodbye.

❧

Late in the day, Pninah was dry mouthed and hungry. She had eaten nothing. She had taken water from a stream beyond the city walls, but she had no vessel to fill and so no way to bring any with her. The late-fall air was cool, which spared her. But she remained hungry. And thirsty.

She had found the canyon road to Jericho. Taking the road had not been a deliberate choice. She had simply found herself there. She had walked as though in a dream, turning over the events of the past days and weeks. Then she was in the canyon.

After a while, she grew tired of reviewing her personal story. She thought instead about the royal events that had led from Salome to Hyrcanus to Aristobulus.

As she contemplated these things, the strangeness of these past seasons finally became clear to her. A brother defying the will of his deceased mother and overthrowing his brother. Another Jerusalem betrayal. After some hours in the canyon, her mind drifted back to personal pain. She did not think directly of Gavriel, but when she obliquely encountered the shape of him, hurt was joined by hate.

She redirected her attention to the canyon road ahead. Tears blurred her eyes as she walked. Her mind churned.

She had walked this road once before. It had been years earlier, with Gavriel, when her parents had still been alive. They had made it to the outskirts of Jericho in one long day. Her pace this time was slow. She slept that first night far short of her goal, curled up with no pad or blanket. She lay behind a bush whose name she did not know. When she awoke the following day, shivering with cold and hunger, it took her a moment to reorient herself. She stood up on tired legs, found the downward slope, and then continued with leaden feet.

Later in the day, when the way began to open much wider, she could see Jericho in the far distance. Other travellers were approaching from the opposite direction. She had slept on the ground in her one tunic with nothing to wrap around her. She was cold and dirty. She needed to bathe and did not want to meet others in this manner.

A goat path appeared to her right. It was a narrow path that led across foothills that stretched out towards the Jericho Plain. She was cold and thirsty and hungry. She took the track and walked for some time with her eyes down, tired and shivering and silent.

An old woman approached Pninah then from another intersecting goat path. The woman talked to herself and fanned her throat with a piece of bark as though the day were hot. She walked with a gait that suggested that she was about to trip. Each step was a hazard. Her strange stride had nothing to do with her shoes or her footing but appeared to be caused by something in her hips, a flaw that the woman had grown accustomed to. Watching her made Pninah tense.

The old woman came alongside Pninah. The energy of her gait made it seem that she would pass by, but the woman's effective pace only just matched Pninah's stride. The woman kept talking, a repetitive conversation that was barely more than a murmur. It called for no response.

"I need something to eat and drink," Pninah finally said.

The old woman stopped so suddenly Pninah almost stumbled as she halted her progress. Their trail followed the curve of the hill—a hill surrounded by other hills. She looked at the old woman who studied Pninah.

"You carry no things," the woman said. Her face was deeply grooved, a map of her life etched in living flesh worn loose. Her eyes were clear and focused. "And you need to wash."

"I have nothing," Pninah said.

The woman leaned this way and that, looking to either side of Pninah as though she might be hiding some bag or other goods.

"Nothing in your hands," the woman said, though whether this was a statement or a question was unclear.

Pninah opened her hands to show the woman.

"You won't last long on the road like this," the woman said. "You're not from around here."

"I'm from Jerusalem," Pninah said and looked in that direction as though she could see the city over the mountains she had just passed through.

"All that way, just today," the woman said.

"Two days," Pninah said.

"With nothing."

"Nothing."

"I don't need to know the reason," the woman said. She unslung a bag from her back and pulled out a water skin. She held it up as though to pour some into Pninah's mouth, but the old woman was too short. She gestured for Pninah to kneel on the path. Pninah did so, and the old woman gave her water the way she might have given it to a sheep or a goat.

Pninah stood again, wiping her mouth and brushing off her knees. She kept her head and eyes down. "Thank you," she whispered.

"I'm not deaf," the old woman said. "But you won't get far talking to old people that quiet."

"Thank you," Pninah said more clearly.

"I said I'm not deaf."

The old woman took a drink from the water skin, then put it back in her bag and shouldered the pack.

"You've got a plan?" the old woman asked, forming her first clear question.

Pninah shook her head. "No. I just can't go back to Jerusalem."

"That's a plan," the woman said. "It may seem like only the start of a plan, but all plans are just starts. Things happen. Plans change. Every plan is just a start. Your start is you can't go back."

"That's my plan."

"It's a poor plan," the woman muttered quietly. She had looked away as she said it as though that would ensure that Pninah could not hear. She sucked at her few teeth. Her deeply ridged lips pursed and moved in something like a mockery of a kiss. She cast a sideways glance at Pninah.

"You go on much farther in the direction you're headed," the old woman finally said, "and you'll find yourself caught up by Nabataean bandits." The woman paused and studied Pninah with squinting eyes. "Or Moabites. They'll take the flesh off your bones, but only after they're done with the rest of you."

Pninah felt her hunger and a return of the fear she had felt during the robbery just days before.

"You're weak, and it's not just hunger," the old woman said.

Pninah tried to speak, but nothing would come out.

The woman kept watching, and then after a while, she nodded. "I don't need to know about it," she said. "I can see it. Jerusalem is the Sadducees' city now. I can't imagine what horrors stalk its streets as part of its regular business. Might as well cast yourself to the Nabataeans as deal with the Sadducees."

The woman looked behind her as though considering her pack. Then she looked ahead. Then over the hill to their right.

"Your plan," the old woman said, "needs a second part. But the first part, the starting part, the leaving Jerusalem part, that's a good first part. The Sadducees stole the throne and the Temple, and Adonai will deal with them. In the meantime, there's no place in a city like that for a girl like you."

"—second part," Pninah said. There had been a beginning to that sentence, but it came out as air, and only the last two words were clear.

The old woman nodded at her. She did not smile, but she seemed to approve. She turned and pointed over the hill to her right, and when she next spoke, she had her back to Pninah, looking in the direction she was pointing.

"You go over there," the old woman said to the hill. "Just cut across the rocky ground there. You see it?"

Pninah came up beside her and nodded. "Over the hill, there," Pninah repeated.

"When you get to the top of the hill, you'll go twice that distance yet," the woman said, "then you'll come to a house. A rundown old place but solid. A good man's place. His name is Onias. He and his little girl live in the house."

The old woman turned to Pninah and put a hand on her forearm. The old woman's grip was dry and firm.

"You'll have no business in the house. The man and the girl live there. But there's no reason you can't sleep in the sheep shed. They probably let the sheep in the shed nowadays, but there's no reason you can't close the gate and keep the sheep in the pen. You'll have to clean it up some. They'll feed you if you can work."

The old woman pulled on Pninah's arm, forcing young eyes down to engage hers.

"You might go in the house to clean when Onias is away. You don't ever go in there when they are home. You're no wife to him. You're no sister to the girl. Do you understand?"

"Of course," Pninah said. "Where is the girl's mother?"

"She's buried with her two littlest ones," the old woman said with a nod. She let go of Pninah's arm and put two fingers to her lips as though to kiss them, then let the hand fall by her side. "You tell him Bilhah sent you. You tell him you've fled the city of the Sadducees, and he'll take you in as his own daughter. But you'll sleep in the shed."

The woman began to walk again, that tripping gait overlaid with the woman's odd murmur. She directed nothing further in Pninah's direction. She just walked away, solemnly conversing with herself in a determined tone.

# 28
## 66-65 BCE

AT THE FARM overlooking the Jericho Plain, Onias looked at Pninah with a frown.

The old man called the little girl at his side Salema. The girl clung to her father and looked as dirty as Pninah felt. She stared at Pninah with dark unblinking eyes.

The old man was missing more teeth than he retained, and he had the old woman's slack and wrinkled complexion. Pninah wondered if it had something to do with living this way on the land with a view of Jericho, the plain, and the Dead Sea to the south.

"The sheep shed," he said doubtfully—his manner of speaking made little distinction between statements and questions.

"His leg is bad," the girl said. "You could help me with the sheep. They know my whistle, but I still shouldn't go alone."

"Shush," the old man said. He laid a gnarled hand on her uncovered head. "It will get better soon enough."

"He fell," she insisted.

"Shush."

Pninah felt dizzy and hungry, and for a moment, she swayed on the rough ground in front of the father and daughter.

"Is there something else I should know?" the old man asked.

"I'm just hungry," she said. "And thirsty."

The old man studied her with an intense gaze. "There's something else."

Pninah did not meet his eyes. She looked at the ground, the stony hardness of it. The loose rock and base rock. The little greenery still forcing its way into sunlight even this late into the year.

The old man stayed silent, and the girl offered no further interruptions. Pninah looked and saw that the man had rested two fingers on the girl's lips. He would have his answer before his family broke the silence.

"I get seizures," Pninah said. She felt tears threaten, and she stiffened herself to keep them back.

"The demon kind or the muscle-sickness kind?" the old man asked.

"I don't know. Anna says it's the muscle kind."

"Who is Anna?"

"She lives at the Temple."

"Anna bat Phanuel," the old man said. "The Galilean. From the Asher tribe."

Pninah looked up and met the old man's eyes. "I don't

know those things," she said. "Some say she's a prophetess. She knew about my life, even the things I didn't tell her."

The old man nodded and frowned. He worked on his teeth with his tongue in a manner like the old woman's habit, lips working to match the frown. "If Anna says it's the muscle kind, then it is. You'll need to pay attention," he said to his daughter. He looked down at her, and the girl's dirty but bright face tilted up towards his. "If something happens to her, you need to look after her like you would one of the sheep."

The girl nodded. "I can do it," she said.

The girl stepped forwards and took Pninah's hand. "Come," she said. "I'll show you the shed. I can help you get it cleaned up, and we have extra blankets."

"Salema," Onias said.

"She can have some of mine," the girl said.

"Salema, she's hungry. Get her some milk from the goat and some bread." The old man looked at Pninah. His eyebrows seemed to swell as he stared into her eyes. "For the muscle kind, you need more than milk and bread. It's not the right season for the proper greens. There will be more in the spring. Maybe they will help."

Winter passed. Raqmu continued to play host to the governor and governess of Idumea as well as Jerusalem's former king and high priest. Nearly seven hundred other Jews had accompanied them: soldiers, servants, associates, and royal family members.

With spring came the Feast of Unleavened Bread. Passover. The Nabataeans escorted the tutor that Hyrcanus had brought for the children back to Eretz-Israel. Others would take the scholar on from there to Jerusalem. He was to attend the festival in secret, then stay another two months to attend the Festival of Weeks.

Cypros did not care about Passover news. She cared only that the Passover had nearly arrived, and Jerusalem had not yet fallen. The Nabataeans had not even gathered in large numbers to start their march. It was all taking too long.

Antipater smiled at her in amusement. "They are your people," he said.

"They can't travel with the caravans in the rainy season," she said. "They'll be on their way now, but it's a big desert. We have to wait for them to assemble."

She did not look at her husband as she said this. His amused expressions irritated her. She had gone from berating the Nabataeans for their delays to defending them in one breath.

When the tutor finally returned from Jerusalem, he gave his report first to Hyrcanus and Antipater. Later, the three presented and interpreted it for Aretas. Cypros heard it second-hand from her husband.

"Everything is as before," he said. "Only minor differences."

"Such as?" Cypros asked.

"They've added a kithara to the Temple musicians," Antipater said. "Hyrcanus is upset about a Seleucid instrument in the Temple."

Cypros did not care about Jewish Temple traditions.

Antipater seemed happy to be idle at Raqmu. He let their second oldest, Herod, pour out the things he was learning at the end of each event-filled day. The boy served as an eight-year-old guide. He took his father's hand to show him the forethought put into Raqmu's construction. Sometimes he drew pictures. Other times he took Antipater to view the actual projects. The work of Aretas's lifetime would be dams and plumbing. The work of Obodas, or his sons after him, would be the rest of the grand sculpting plans beyond the Siq. An entire city was to be carved into the mountains. Herod loved it all.

"But it's taking too long," the boy had complained. "They should just put more people to work on the digging and hauling. Get it done faster. They need at least three times as many people. Otherwise we'll all be dead before it's even half-finished."

Antipater had laughed a genuine delighted laugh. "And who would pay for these extra people?"

"Uncle Aretas is rich," Herod had said. "Richer than all of Jerusalem."

In the tent, Cypros looked at her husband. He caught her eye and smiled at her.

"Do you think there will be anything left for us in Ashkelon?" she asked. *Take something seriously,* she thought. *You're too at ease here.*

"Ashkelon conducts its business the same as if we were present. Our people know what to do." He was studying a drawing that Herod was sketching in a tray of sand to illustrate this day's discoveries. It had something to do with the mathematics of arches. Cypros could not see from across the tent and did not care to investigate. This was Antipater's place with his son.

"Aristobulus is not going make trouble with Idumea," Antipater said to her, "even with us absent. Trade is good.

Taxes flow to the treasury. He has other matters to attend to. Like where his brother disappeared to."

"You think he doesn't know?"

Herod tugged at his father's sleeve to draw his attention to a detail.

"I see it," he said to the boy. "It's a good design. Will you remember what you've learned?"

"I will," Herod said and wiped the sand image away. "I'll build it myself one day. Bigger."

Antipater got up from his knees and stretched. "Aristobulus may have an idea. But he hasn't sent messengers here to confirm. No official demands have been sent to Ashkelon either. He has other business to attend to. He's never been a king or high priest before."

"You think he's stopped being ambitious now that he's achieved his goals?"

Antipater walked across the great tent to their bed. The other boys were gone. Herod left the sand tray where it lay and went to join his siblings outside.

Antipater lay down on the bed and crossed his ankles, one arm across his eyes. It was not an invitation. "When you are the man in charge, people bring you a lot of things to think about," he said. "One day becomes a month, becomes a year, and you don't know where the time went. It takes years to learn to manage time."

He switched which ankle crossed the other.

"He'll need a year to find his footing," Antipater continued. "And that only if he's a genius. Taking on both the Temple and the throne means double the questions, double the decisions, double the controversy. It's a tiring business being on top. Answering questions all day makes it hard to organize your next conspiracy."

"So, in the meantime, you're just going to sleep at Raqmu?"

"While I wait for your uncle to assemble his army," he said into his arm, "yes, I suppose that's a good idea. Sleep and take an occasional architecture lesson from my son."

❧

Pninah sat among the sheep on the hillside. The late-day sun sent her shadow sliding down the slope. Salema was with her father, learning to sharpen blades for tomorrow's shearing.

*I can't shear sheep.*

But she would. Tomorrow she would.

These were Onias's sheep, and Onias had a name for every one of them. They listened to Onias. They followed Onias. When he called one of them by name, that one sheep would separate from the flock and come to the nearly toothless old man.

Salema knew most of the names. The sheep listened to her voice as they did her father's.

The sheep had heard Pninah now for six months. Only in the last few weeks were they starting to show signs of accepting her call. She could not draw one individual out by name yet. When she took them to the stream, or back home at the end of the day, they followed her as a group well enough. That was an improvement. She wondered if she might be a shepherdess forever. If she might get her own sheep one day or always hire herself out to tend those of others. She liked it better than anything she had ever done in the city.

Watching her shadow grow, she tried to estimate the time until she could take the animals back to their pens. First, they would go to the stream for a last drink before nightfall. She had learned to avoid the sections of the stream with rippling water. Water that gurgled or splashed spooked the sheep. Salema had taught her to take them to the pool above or the smaller one below. There they would drink freely. Hours remained until it was time for the day's last trip to the stream.

Pninah looked around at her charges, and then a smile crept across her face. She put a hand on the ground to steady herself and stood. She looked about for a clear path. Her smile expanded, and then without warning, she took off running across the hillside. She ran like her life depended on it. She sensed alarm in the sheep and ran faster. She almost burst out laughing. She did not call out for the sheep to follow her—she just ran. She could hear them coming but did not look back, kept running, intending to run until she was out of breath. But the sheep caught up to her and blocked her way. She burst out laughing as they crowded around her, jumping and pushing and pressing against her. A way opened, and she ran left a few steps, then dodged again to the right, and the sheep followed. They encircled her again. She danced with the flock, and they danced back with her. They would not let her escape but insisted on keeping her near. The sheep shepherded the shepherdess.

"If I had a lover, you'd give me no privacy," she said to the energized flock. She collapsed on the ground, out of breath, still laughing. Big woolly bodies pressed around and over her, and noses poked against her neck and chest.

"You're going to be all naked tomorrow," she laughed.

She grabbed fistfuls of wool, pulled herself up onto her knees, then let them go. The sheep lingered, drifting away only a few steps. On her knees, she was no taller than the sheep. Their shadows, hers and theirs, were one solid mass stretching down the hillside below them.

"Go eat," she said finally, and the sheep began to separate, discovering the fresh grass that she had led them to. "Tomorrow, I'll try my best not to cut you." She shivered and made a dismissive hand gesture. The nearest sheep stared at her and bleated before returning its attention to the grass. A smile returned and lingered in Pninah's eyes.

The next day, the shearing was everything she feared it would be. The sharp shears were too big for her hands. Though Salema was smaller, she seemed to manage them without trouble. Getting a chosen sheep off its feet to start the shearing was an exercise that involved pulling hands and tripping feet, trying to upend the creature. Once the sheep was on its side—or back, or at least forced onto its rump—it stopped struggling. Getting the animal upended to begin with was the thing she could not seem to accomplish.

"You're either going to break one of their legs," Onias complained, "or wrestle it all day and do nothing. Do like this," he said, showing her again, but she could not follow the move. In the end, he or Salema would upend her next sheep, and then she alone would shear it.

She had not started straight into shearing on her own. For the whole morning, she had watched, and then in the afternoon, she had begun to work on her own.

"Put your left hand over her teats," Onias had warned. "Don't cut them off."

"Slide your hand along," Salema had said as she worked

on another animal. "Watch the tendons there. Don't cut the skin at all."

The ways to cut, maim, or even lame an animal seemed endless. The process of shearing, despite its bloodless result, felt like an act of gross mutilation. With the sheep on its back, legs already sheared and bound together, Pninah's left hand pulled a fistful of wool taut while the shears in her right hand slid under the wool, cutting away, slicing a path along the animal's chest and up to its throat where her shears appeared from beneath the thick wool as though rising from the animal's body or from underneath a woollen cloak that the sheep had been wearing rather than growing. With a roughly straight line achieved, she then began working sideways, around the animal, cutting and pulling so that the wool came away like a great thick rug as she worked her way around to the animal's spine. Once there, she rolled the sheep over and continued cutting in the other direction. She had to adjust her position, one knee braced on the sheep's ribs, and the wool flopped over. It looked like the sheep was unshorn again. She flipped the wool back, and the effect was startling.

*You're almost naked now,* she thought and nearly burst out laughing but kept quiet. She was shearing one sheep to Salema's three and Onias's five.

Finally finished, she unbound the sheep's legs and stepped off the animal, letting it struggle to its feet. It bounded once in a circle around Pninah and then a second time into the air. As it did so, Pninah's eyes flew open, and Salema squealed with laughter. Onias looked up, and for the first time in all the time she had known him, Pninah heard him laugh. Pninah chased after her sheep as it ran away. The animal was delighted in being mostly relieved of its burden. Pninah had sheared it according to the pattern, the wool coming off in one solid sheet, except for one error. A small section was still attached to the sheep's rump, and as it ran, the wool followed. The following wool alarmed the animal and made it jump and turn in fright. Salema continued to squeal and laugh as the sheep dodged right. Pninah tried to follow it, but then the sheep dodged left, right into Pninah, and the two of them fell to the ground with Pninah's arms around the animal's neck.

Lying there, the sheep grew quiet, its face against hers. Pninah looked over at Onias and Salema. As far as she could tell, the little girl was going to give herself a laughter stomach ache. Onias was still laughing as well.

*Made you laugh.*

A new smile lit up her features. She had been trying for many months to make the old man laugh, though this attempt had not been intentional. This had been a mortifying mistake.

"You got the sheep down on your own," Onias shouted over to her, and then he doubled over, laughing even harder, and it looked like he too would give himself cramps.

"Bring me my shears," Pninah called.

The old man's grin was ear-to-ear. "No, you bring that sheep here and finish the job," he called to her. "I've got my own sheep to look after."

Pninah wiggled out from under the sheep and got it onto its feet, one ear held in her fist. She walked the sheep across the lot with the wool dragging. She picked up her shears and snipped off the last bit. Released, the sheep bounded away a second time. Pninah shook out and then rolled up the fleece in a bundle and placed it with the others. It was as big as her torso, a huge amount of wool.

She saw that Onias was staring at her with his almost toothless grin. "You did good," he said. He gestured at Salema. "Her mom, she never would have sheared a sheep if she ever saw one. She wouldn't have had anything to do with it. But she never saw this farm or these sheep." He looked back at Pninah, his expression a little quieter but still a light in his eyes. "You did good." Then he broke out into a full smile again and started back to work on his animal.

Pninah dusted herself off and went out among the flock. She chose a smaller one this time. With its thicker-than-normal growth, it was shaped like a ball with stumpy legs, its eyes peering out at the world from below an overhang of wool. Pninah liked the shearing. There was something about finding a completely different animal under all that wool and seeing the freed, newly defined creatures bounding white and happy across the yard. It eased old pains. It made her feel like she mattered.

The plain before Raqmu's red cliffs, beyond the tent city, teamed with camels, rough tents, men, and weapons. The endless noise of men calling and camels bawling and crates creaking filled the staging ground. Heat lay over everything like a blanket. Av, that furnace month of merciless burning, lay around the corner.

"Phasael let slip that you plan to follow the army across the desert with the children," Antipater said.

Cypros glanced at her husband, then away again. She focused on the churn of activity before her.

"Stay well back," Antipater said. "I won't bother trying to dissuade you. Make sure you don't give the scouts a cloud of dust to our rear to distract them. War is not Greek theatre."

"Do you expect to fight Aristobulus?"

"No. The disloyalty of mercenaries works both ways. They'll will switch sides before the battle begins."

"They get paid twice and work less," Cypros said.

"Aristobulus will flee back to the city."

They were quiet then for a while. It seemed the conversation was over. Then Antipater said one last thing. "When Aristobulus goes back up the canyon to Jerusalem and we follow, stay in the foothills near Jericho. Go no farther. Or come back here if you like."

"Why? You may need my help at the siege."

"I won't need you at the siege," Antipater said. "If any of Aristobulus's people find you, you would be an ideal hostage. Stay on the Jericho side of the mountains."

In the foothills overlooking Jericho and the plain, the small house with its attached shed and pen were quiet. The sheep in the pen milled about or stood waiting for the night to fully descend. Smoke came from a fire in the yard. It was a small fire for heating tea, and around it sat an old man with a young woman and a much younger girl.

"You both recite something," Pninah said, breaking the silence, "every night around this time. Then you recite it again in the morning. You say it in a language I don't understand."

"The Shema," the old man said quietly, gazing into the fire. "In the old Hebrew."

"What is that?" Pninah asked.

"The old Hebrew? It's what our people used to speak, years ago. The language of Isaiah and David and Moses."

"No," Pninah said. "The Shema. What is that?"

"The Shema?" He looked up at her and his thick brows furrowed. "You don't even know what the Shema is?"

Pninah shook her head. The evening air was quiet. Though it was not quite dark yet, the city of Jericho already glowed in the distance. A faint breeze wafted over the farm. It carried the sweet scent of the fading lilies from a hollow not far away.

"Who were your parents, child?" the old man asked.

Pninah lowered her head.

"It does not matter," Onias said. "But they didn't teach you the Shema?"

Pninah shook her head.

"It's a prayer," Onias said. "A prayer that every faithful Jew must pray, morning and night, and on other holy occasions. Anna never taught you?"

"I didn't see her early or late. Only during the day. I understand what they do at the Temple."

"Then you've heard the Shema but did not recognize it. The way we pronounce it. We do our best."

"Will you teach me?" Pninah asked.

"Of course we will. And what it means."

∾

Three nights later, near dark, Pninah was alone. She said her prayer alone, outside her small shed home. She spoke slowly, as Onias had taught her. She said it in old Hebrew. She pronounced the phrases at least as good as Salema. Afterwards, she recited to herself the standard translation. She tried to think carefully about each idea within the prayer as Onias had said she must.

Onias had quizzed her about other matters of her family and home, always sensitive not to force revelations. He often drew from her more than she intended to reveal. She had not confessed that her family had been Sadducean allies, but she suspected that he knew.

"I'll teach you to read," he had promised. He had started her on just the letters. "Words will come later," he had said.

Later, in the fields with the sheep, Salema had added to her learning, the girl teaching her elder. The next day, Onias had been impressed by her progress.

After her prayer, Pninah got up off her knees. It was near dark. She suddenly saw two men towards the east. They were on foot, not far from her, hands on the reins of camels. They were Arabs—Nabataean men.

She stood in shock, not having heard them approach. They watched her, looked over at the candlelit house, studied the sheep in the pen, and then spoke between themselves. They made gestures that she did not understand. Then they moved off. Soon, they disappeared into the night.

When they were gone, only the lingering odour of their camels remained.

# 29
## 65 BCE

RAQMU SAND AND stone baked below the Av sun.

"I want to come," Herod said, shielding his eyes as he looked up at his mother.

Cypros smiled. She was not looking at the boy but at the Jewish guards Antipater had left with her. They were trying to sort out how to accompany their governess on this expedition without polluting themselves among the more than one hundred Nabataean messengers and warriors that composed the bulk of the expedition. A few Nabataean women were also joining Cypros. Their presence resolved some of the tension that a woman travelling alone would have created, but it also added to the guards' uniquely Jewish problem.

"What is it you want?" she asked Herod.

"To come with you."

"No. You can't."

"I want to see the battle."

Cypros renewed her smile, still watching the supervisor of the Jewish guard as he debated with his Nabataean counterpart. The remaining point of tension appeared to be whether they should bring one tent or two for the women. For the Nabataeans, one large tent was the only reasonable solution. For the Jews, letting Cypros share accommodations with gentile women was unthinkable, even if they were her relatives.

"Hmm?" She turned finally and looked at Herod, then remembered. "No. The tutor is staying here. You'll continue your studies along with Hyrcanus's children."

"It's too hot here," Herod complained. "At home, there was the sea and the breezes. It's not as bad as here."

"You'll continue your ventures with the architect if you maintain your studies," she continued. "If you fall behind in your studies, then Hanne will tell the guards to cut off your access to the building sites."

Herod scowled and slouched.

Cypros could not overhear the resolution to the one-or-two-tents conflict. Judging by the expression on the Jewish captain's face, he had accepted a compromise that did not suit him. She deduced that she would share a tent with her relatives. It would be large enough to satisfy the captain's insistence that Cypros maintain a proper distance within its walls. Even if he could not see inside at night to verify that Cypros followed the custom herself.

Cypros shook her head. Jews and Nabataeans had nearly touched at Aretas's feasts, sharing space and food. Even Hyrcanus, the former and future high priest, had participated. But not Hyrcanus's wife. She was forever ill, but only during the feasts. She would not accompany Cypros on this journey either.

Phasael joined his mother and brother outside the tent, blinking in the sudden brightness. "You're leaving tomorrow?" he asked.

"Yes," Cypros said.

"I'm the oldest," he said. "I think it would be good for me to come with you. To help you, and to see what happens in this kind of thing. So I can learn."

Cypros laughed and looked at Herod, who watched this exchange with dark eyes. The boy finally smiled and looked away.

"Your father has his persistent qualities as well," Cypros said to Phasael. She turned her attention back to the camels and baggage and general preparations.

Early the next morning, darkness shifted to grey. The change was not evident inside. Cypros could tell by the murmurs of men and animals assembling, by the clatter of baggage being loaded, and by the scratching of ropes being stretched, tightened, and tied that morning was coming. She rose from her bed, crossed the dark tent, pulled back the curtain, and looked in on Hanne's small chamber. There was nothing to see there but darkness.

"I'll look after them," Hanne whispered.

Cypros nodded, though she knew the woman would not be able to see her. The children stayed sleeping as she dressed. She tucked a few final things into a small bag and then slipped out into dim morning air. It was not so much already warming as never having cooled. So it would remain until Av passed and the furnace of this land relented.

When she left the tent, she did not go straight to the

camels. They were not ready for her yet. She went to an open place beyond the camp where she could be alone. A lone guard trailed her, one of the select few who always remained at her tent door when she slept. He was Nabataean, which simplified things. At a distance, her worship of al-Qaum in the semi-darkness was indistinguishable from the prostrations a Jew might make before their revered God. Still, having a Nabataean watch her reduced the complications.

Once finished with her prayers, Cypros searched out her relatives' tent, where she shared tea and a quick meal with them. Afterwards, the women drifted out to the waiting caravan. Her relatives knew how to take their places, how to balance as the ungainly beasts lurched awkwardly to their feet. They were not Jewish women. They were Nabataeans.

The caravan set out westwards. They threaded through gaps between rock pillars and other obstacles in the landscape. Once in the Arabah Valley, they turned north, towards the Dead Sea. As they did so, the sun finally peeked over the red mountains to their right. It revealed its presence with not merely light but a new wave of heat. This early warning signalled the disk's intention for the rest of the day. And the days to come.

Nearly a week later they stopped at the southern tip of the Dead Sea. When they left the next day, they entered the trail that led along the eastern shore of the sea. It was a passage between the saltwater on their left and the steep mountains of Moab on the right.

*He said not to raise a dust cloud behind the army.*

The way here was narrow and dustless, paved with bare rock and salt.

She repositioned herself on the camel and forced herself

to sit sideways so she could watch the westward sea. The water here was shallow—a combination of thick salt water, floating bitumen, and another substance that she could not identify. This combination created strange milky shapes like a skim of congealed fat floating on the water. The irregular, undulating whitish shapes were ringed by borders of brown, black, and golden hues. Black bitumen spotted the milky centres and golden rims. In some places, the black spotting was not small and the inky substance floated instead in large blocks. At any other time, the Nabataeans would have sent harvesters to gather up this floating wealth to sell to the Romans or Egyptians. This was not a season, however, for harvest or trade. The Nabataeans were going to war.

*But this is not a good time for war,* Cypros thought. Av was a merciless month to be in transit. Perhaps in this the Nabataeans held a small advantage. Not only would Nabataean camels perform better in this heat but so would Nabataean men. There were no seaside or mountaintop escapes for the traders of the world's Great Desert. The men Aretas had taken so long to draw from his vast territory were inured to this relentless exposure.

*But I am not,* Cypros admitted to herself. After more than a decade at Ashkelon, that city by the sea with its plentiful palms and a smooth palace cooled by fountains and slaves working large fans when the breeze failed—all that luxury had softened her. She was no longer the girl who had walked the desert alone, killing raiders one by one as she led them deeper and deeper into the oven that was the Arabah.

By the middle of that second day alongside the sea she felt dizzy and squeezed her eyes shut. She tried to focus. She gripped the smooth wood at the front of her saddle and adjusted her position again. Then her eyes flew open as she nearly fell, having adjusted wrongly as her mind had wandered. The heat was getting to her.

Later she reflected that she would have eventually fallen if it had not been for the dead man. One of the men near her might have caught her. That contact would have been a scandal. Or she might have struck the ground and broken a bone. The caravan would have had to halt to attend to her either way.

In the minds of the men, there was no good reason for her to go on this journey. Her relatives accompanied her as female escorts and an outlet for conversation. They at least had a purpose. Her purpose, and therefore theirs, was without justification.

She no longer cared to be cooped up at Raqmu, honoured but not in charge. She no longer wanted to be housed in a vast tent that included her children. She wanted to visit them, not live with them—to plan for them, not have them underfoot. But there were more than these domestic complaints that set her on this scorching route. She wanted to take part in what she had prepared. And whatever he said, Antipater and Hyrcanus needed her at the Jerusalem siege.

The caravan dropped groups of five men off at each overnight stop along with supplies to sustain them. These deposits of men were message posts that would dot the route from Jerusalem to Raqmu. Aretas remained at Raqmu. This line of message posts was for his benefit alone.

The rest of the caravan intended to observe the events on the Jericho Plain from a distance. That battle was already foretold; it would be a remake of the first confrontation between the brothers with royal roles reversed. Aristobulus would come from Jerusalem, be betrayed by his fortresses, and flee back to the city. A short siege would commence. Aristobulus would surrender, and Hyrcanus would be king again. Aristobulus and his sons would return to their old house if they were not imprisoned. The future was certain.

This new plan was as much hers as it was the work of her uncle and husband. Antipater had negotiated on behalf of Hyrcanus. Aretas had taken counsel from Cypros directly. Both sides of the Aretas-Hyrcanus transaction had had Cypros as their counsellor. When the time came, Jerusalem's one-time and future king had signed where directed. Afterwards, Cypros had sent him a private gift, congratulating him on the victory she had privately prearranged on his behalf. She had sent the gift, of course, through her husband. It had been a small bottle of the distilled Galilean quince. The Jew had drunk it gratefully in that dry Nabataean land.

"Consummating a deal is as important as making it," she had told Antipater. He had shrugged and taken the bottle without further comment.

Still, despite her pride regarding the events that she was on her way to witness, she would have fallen if not for the dead man.

The man was seated, leaning back against a large rock, his head wrapped in a sky-blue and white cloth. The colours repeated in the fabric of his robe. It was the same blue as that of the woven adornments on Jerusalem's priests and the tassels found on clothes of the most devout. But this was no Jew. The man was a lone Moabite, dead at the base of the mountains that bore his people's name.

*Your people killed my family.*

She did not say anything out loud as she looked down on the dead man. But watching him cooled her and woke her up.

It was unclear at first whether the man was dead. He sat with his head down and to one side as though sleeping. His camel stood nearby, a female beast, perhaps six or eight years old. There was no mark on the man. The camel still bore her load.

After words did nothing to rouse the man, two Nabataeans got down with knives drawn. They approached carefully to inspect him. One Nabataean gave the body a slight push with his foot, and the Moabite tilted and then made a double thud as his shoulders and then head connected with rock. He had not been dead for long. The Nabataean army had passed this way three days before. This man had come along after, perhaps only the evening before. There was no sign he had drunk or eaten anything—he had simply dismounted, seated himself, and died.

It was an omen, and Cypros sought to read it. Her parents from Damascus had done little to educate their children in the ways of reading signs, and though the Jews were fantastically superstitious, she had learned next to nothing of their lore either. Hanne had been no help. The girl had vast sections of the Torah memorized but could not read the simplest of occult symbols.

A Moabite raider's death, following the army's passage to Judea. *We will conquer more than we set out to achieve, and the victory will be for both Israel and Nabataea. Against all our enemies. We will beat more than Aristobulus and his renegades. Moab will sustain losses in this conflict as well.*

Cypros looked up and saw the great black birds of the

desert floating high above. They had not yet claimed this body. They had kept it preserved. For her to witness. His blue was unmarked that she might know that overcoming the killers of her family would be part of this season's victory.

She did not share her revelation with any of the Nabataean or Jewish men in their company. Later, she would not say anything about it to the women either. Instead, she let the vision filter through her tired and overheated frame like cool water, chilling her veins and clearing her head.

*I'll have my victory.*

She stared at the Moabite. A serene expression settled onto her face, widening her eyes, softening her lips, and giving her cheeks an inviting glow.

# 30

## 65 BCE

OVER THE STONE sheep-pen walls, Pninah watched the day's events unfold alongside Onias and Salema. Sheep bumped into her legs, but sheep were not the focus this day.

Two armies assembled on the plain below. The army closest to the farm assembled in colour-coded formations. A cavalry of horsemen populated the far left and right flanks. The opposing force was less colourfully uniformed. From what she could see, camel riders dominated the distant group.

"Nabataeans," Onias said. "With Jews among them."

Something in his voice drew Pninah's attention. She saw distress on his face.

Salema grew bored as the morning wore on. The armies maintained their formations but gave no indication of an imminent fight. She went to fetch water for the three of them, then made trips for the sheep, filling small stone troughs.

"Here it comes," Onias said late in the morning as the Jewish cavalry rode out. A group of foot soldiers followed, but only one group. The rest did not move. Those advancing made various motions with flags. Onias grunted as though this meant something to him. The advance did not look like a charge but was too large for a communication delegation.

"What's happening?" Pninah asked.

Onias grunted again. "Quiet," he said to Salema, who had finished with watering and was talking to the sheep. "Listen."

There was no way to hear voices from this distance. Pninah wondered if even the clash of swords would reach them. Then a lone trumpet sounded from the Nabataean side.

"There it is," Onias said.

The advancing Jewish cavalry responded to the horn by moving wide and then halting. The foot soldiers continued to advance.

"They've got their shields the wrong way," Pninah said. The foot soldiers wore their shields on their backs. The cavalry seemed to have left the foot soldiers unsupported. The rest of Aristobulus's army remained standing as before, watching this strange contest play out.

"I don't understand," she said.

"Listen for it. After the swordsmen and spearmen are absorbed."

"Absorbed?"

The word sounded like suicide, and in fact the out-numbered foot soldiers, abandoned by their cavalry and not supported at all by the remaining army behind them, were well positioned for a massacre.

"I don't think they even have their swords out," Pninah said.

Salema pushed up to the wall beside her. She stood on tiptoes and put her elbows on top of the wall and rested her chin on her wrists like an older girl. "This is like before," she said. "They're changing sides."

Sure enough, the defecting foot soldiers moved through the camel riders' front line to places in the rear. Absorbed. The trumpet sounded again, and the defecting cavalry lined up on the flanks of the Nabataean army.

Onias snorted. "The rebel king was smart enough to pay the mercenaries to steal the throne. He wasn't smart enough though to anticipate the same manoeuvre applied against him."

Pninah remembered Gavriel telling her something similar. "This is how Aristobulus got the throne," she said.

Onias nodded.

"Boring," was Salema's judgment. She stepped back from the wall and drifted back among the sheep. "Can we take them out in the fields now?" she asked.

Onias nodded again, still facing the plains below. "But stay close," he said. "And keep them off the hilltops. Stay to the backside of the hill, out of sight."

After both armies disappeared up the canyon route to Jerusalem, a new group appeared from the east. They too came as a mixed group of camels and horses, Nabataeans and Jews.

Onias shook his head as he watched the group assemble large desert-style tents on the plain below the farm.

"Why are they here?" Salema asked. "Someone should tell them that everyone went to Jerusalem."

Later that day, three camel riders did take the canyon route.

❧

Two days later, Pninah sat with Salema as the sheep grazed below them. They kept close to stream beds and hollows where green still grew in irregular patches. The two shepherdesses sat halfway up one hill, above the flock, watching over them rather than sitting among them.

"I could keep being a shepherdess," Salema said.

"Not for your whole life," Pninah objected.

"Some girls do."

"Not their whole lives. They have families and other things to attend to."

"Not all of them."

Pninah tried to imagine a middle-aged shepherdess.

"What about you?" Salema asked.

"Me as a shepherdess?"

"No, the families part."

"I can't have children," Pninah said.

"How do you know?" Salema asked.

Pninah thought about Gavriel and the age and innocence of Onias's girl. "I just know," she said.

"Oh. The seizures."

A face then appeared cresting the hilltop opposite them. A woman emerged and crossed the top of the hill, followed by several Nabataean men who trailed some distance behind. The men appeared to be chaperones or guards. The woman wore Nabataean clothing. Her robe was long. Her head covering was tied up with elaborate strings of beading that trailed across her shoulders. She made her way down the hill towards them with careful steps as though she was unused to sloping ground.

Sheep dotted the ground between them, concentrated in the dip between hills where the thickest grass patches could be found. The woman stopped before the collection of sheep and looked across the divide towards Pninah and Salema.

"I thought I might find you here," the woman said.

Pninah opened her mouth to answer but then did not know what to say. The woman spoke Aramaic clearly enough, but it bore a Nabataean accent.

"It gets wet down there in the rainy season," Salema told the woman, pointing in the direction of the tents.

The woman smiled the sort of smile adults reserve for children too young for sensible ideas. "We won't be here in the rainy season," she said. "When my husband finishes with Jerusalem, we'll join him there."

The woman seemed to want to pass through the flock of sheep. She looked up and down the small valley. She put a hand out as though marking a potential path between the animals or directing them to part before her. Whatever the intention, it resulted in no movement from her or the sheep.

Salema watched the woman with one eyebrow cocked, as though the sight before her was the most ridiculous thing she had ever seen.

"They won't hurt you," Pninah said. "I wasn't used to

them a year ago either, but now I'm used to them. Just walk where you want."

The woman did not outwardly acknowledge the direction, but after a brief pause, she did begin to thread a path. It was as though she was expecting the animals to kick or bite.

Once on their side of the flock, the woman crouched down before Pninah and Salema.

"I am Cypros," the woman said. "Governess of Idumea. Daughter of Aretas, king of the Nabataeans."

Salema picked at the dried grass beside her.

"I'm Pninah. This is Salema. The sheep all have names as well, but I'll spare you having to memorize them."

That evening, the three shepherds sat around a small fire, waiting for water to boil.

"She never asked us whose side we support," Pninah said. Fire licked around the edges of the pot before her. The flickering light held her attention.

"Everybody around here supports Hyrcanus," Salema said.

Woodsmoke curled upwards and then re-formed itself into a straight vertical column.

Onias reached out and adjusted the pot. Smoke swirled again, and its scent passed briefly over Pninah before straightening again.

"Too many gentiles," Onias said. "The army. The woman down there with her guard. Her Idumean husband. The fortresses that keep changing sides."

"The mercenaries are foreigners?" Salema asked.

Onias nodded. "Foreigners hired by Jews to fight Jews."

✎

A few weeks later, Av passed into Elul, the last month of summer. Pninah and Salema harvested the two pomegranate trees near the farm. Pninah took two baskets of the ripe fruits, one balanced on each hip, down to the Nabataean camp. She walked alone and unafraid into the camp and gave the fruit to the few women there. The Nabataean and few Jewish men kept their distance, honouring her new friendship with Cypros.

"Any news from Jerusalem?" Pninah asked.

Cypros smiled, holding one of the pomegranates in her hand.

Pninah waited.

The Nabataean woman's smile disappeared.

"Some inside support my husband and Hyrcanus," Cypros finally said. "They opened the city gates one night and let us in."

"Then the siege is over," Pninah exclaimed.

Cypros smiled again and made a gesture with her free hand to lower Pninah's volume or enthusiasm or both.

"Aristobulus retreated into the Temple and the Citadel," Cypros said. "It's a very defensible position. Our men are now inside the city but not inside the Temple."

"I used to live at its base," Pninah said.

"Not in the valley."

"Yes. In the valley."

The expression on Cypros's face was inscrutable. She was beautiful to look at. Curls of black hair escaped from beneath her cream-coloured head covering. Her eyes held a faraway look that was neither cruel nor kind. Pninah could not read anything in the expression at all.

"Will you go for Sukkot?" Cypros asked.

"How?" Pninah asked.

"You can camp outside the city in your tree-branch shelters like you Jews do each year. You can't get into the Temple, but you could gather outside. The Galileans will be there, I am sure. I have never been, but my husband goes every year, along with most of Idumea. I thought a Jew would still want to go."

"How?" Pninah asked again. "We're shepherds."

Cypros squinted at her. She started to shake her head, then stopped and smiled yet again. "Oh, the sheep," she said. "So how do other shepherds go to the festivals?"

"They don't."

Cypros looked down at the pomegranate in her hand, then back at Pninah. "Does that make shepherds not Jews then?"

Pninah laughed. "You're not Jewish at all, are you?"

"I'm Idumean," Cypros said. "Idumeans are Jews."

"When it suits you, you're Idumean."

Cypros regarded Pninah with only the barest hint of a smile at her eyes if not her mouth.

"You're in a camp full of Nabataeans," Pninah said. "You talk with a Nabataean accent. You probably don't even know the Shema."

Cypros relaxed.

"My uncle is King Aretas of Nabataea. My husband is the governor of Idumea."

"We talked about that already," Pninah replied. "And I'm from the Tyropoeon Valley." She had brought a gift of pomegranates—that should be enough without needing to justify where she had once lived. "They don't teach us how to talk to kings and queens in the valley."

Cypros's nearly immobile face suddenly broke out into a proper smile—not one of her planned smiles but a genuine grin. "That's why I like you." She looked out again towards Jericho. "I wasn't always a princess or governess. I was once a shepherd girl like you." She put her pomegranate back in the basket with the others. "Only I led my sheep away from water instead of towards it."

# 31

## 65 BCE

"YOU'RE NOT GOING to Jerusalem," the Nabataean captain said.

In the moment, in her anger, Cypros could not remember the man's name. It was morning, three days after the end of the Sukkot Festival. The first Jews from Jericho to brave Jerusalem's troubles had come back from Sukkot reporting terrible things about the city. Nabataeans and other gentiles polluted the land inside and out. Unclean animals—camels—were everywhere. The sons of Salome Alexandra continued their dispute and Jerusalem suffered the consequences. None of the pilgrims had been able to get inside the Temple compound where Aristobulus and his supporters remained resolute. Their reports spread through intermediaries from Jericho to the Nabataean encampment at the base of the foothills.

"We should be back home in Raqmu by now," Cypros

said to the severe-looking man before her. *What was his name?* She could not think when so unexpectedly thwarted. "Or back in Ashkelon," she added to the Jewish captain who was watching this exchange.

The Jewish captain nodded but did not interfere.

"The governor was very clear that you were not to go up to Jerusalem," the Nabataean said.

Qaaid. She finally remembered. Her head cleared.

"If I decide to go on my own, would you dare to stop me?"

Qaaid smiled. "You know none of my men will touch you. Nor I suspect, will your Jewish overseers."

Cypros ignored the insult. "Then I'm going." She reached out her hand for the camel, but Qaaid moved the reins away from her.

"We won't touch you. But we will touch the camels. The camels stay here. The horses as well, I presume." Qaaid looked to his Jewish counterpart for support, who continued to stare at the ground.

"I need to be at the siege," Cypros said. "It's taking too long." She turned to the Jewish captain and snapped her fingers at him to get him to look up. "Hyrcanus should have presided over Passover, but we did not even leave Raqmu before Passover. At least he should have presided over Sukkot. Instead, nobody celebrated Sukkot."

The Jewish captain finally met her eyes and smiled at her. He put his hands out at his sides, palms up. "Your husband's instructions were clear," he said.

"If the governor wants to consult you," Qaaid said, "he knows where to find you." She saw the smile behind the thick beard. It showed in his eyes.

❦

Two days later, the fall rains started. Two days after that, the camp flooded, just like the younger shepherdess said it would.

"I told you to move the camp when we first arrived," Cypros said to Qaaid. She stood ankle deep in cold water at the entrance of her tent. The other women were inside, behind her. "You ignored me then. I'm going for a walk. When I get back, I want the camp moved to that spot"—she pointed to an elevated plateau a short walk to the south—"with everything dried out and back to how it should have been from the beginning."

Qaaid started to form a half-smile that did not look like the sort of response she was hoping for. She stepped forwards and startled the man with her proximity. She did not touch him, but she alarmed him. He took a step back. "Show some basic competence," she said.

The man looked around at his own men watching this.

"Even the shepherdesses up the hill knew this area would flood."

"Now, governess—" he started.

She took another step forwards, making him splash and stumble as he kept distance between them. "Perhaps you should be reassigned as a pit hauler," Cypros said. "You can't plan. You can't take counsel. And you're slow to react when you're finally standing ankle deep in your own problem."

She turned then and walked back into the tent, closing the flap behind her. The women were wide-eyed, staring at her. She paused for a moment, not long enough for the Nabataean man to recover his dignity, and then re-emerged again, walking quickly from the tent and almost straight into him.

"Move," she shouted at him. "Speak! Give orders! Make a plan! Show some semblance of basic ability or you're not going to retire as a leader of pit haulers—you're going to carry the pit loads yourself. Do I have to lead your men for you?" She nearly screamed the last sentence at the man, and her spittle flecked the front of his tunic.

The man was at a complete loss for words.

Cypros did not wait for him to recover himself. She kept walking, weaving between waterlogged tents, making for the slope where the shepherdesses would be. She sensed men separating from the crowd to follow her, and she let them follow until they were away from Qaaid. Then she turned. Kaiden led this group of three men, her usual Nabataean minders. They stopped when she did.

"Not today," she said.

She raised a hand when Kaiden started to speak.

"Not today. Moabite raiders are not going to sweep across the plains after a rainstorm to attack a sheep farm. Aristobulus is not going to escape the siege and abduct me. Help Qaaid get this camp back in order. I want a peaceful evening tonight. Not waterlogged chaos."

Kaiden nodded. He did not look happy about the direction, but he gestured to the other two and they turned around.

Resuming her sloshing progress towards the hill, Cypros felt for the first time in days the potential for peace within. Escaping the children in Raqmu had not solved anything. Spending barely more than a month in the Jericho camp left her impatient with the gossip of the women and angry at the men. She wanted to go back to Ashkelon where being governess meant something. She would spend today with the shepherdesses. For them, freedom and self-direction were as natural as air.

*I should have been a shepherd's daughter.* She smiled despite the cold. She wrapped her cloak about her tighter. *Queen of sheep.*

But no. She would be queen of more than sheep. She remembered the desert. She remembered the pillars of distant smoke, those last physical markers of her mother and father, brother and sisters. She remembered the dead, the powdery drifts of fine sand, the deep gullies of sharp-edged rock, the dried wastes and dull senses as she had laboured to redeem her father's defeat. That had been Aretas's take on those events. She had had her own more intimate need for revenge, a closer evil to purge.

She would be queen one day of more than sheep.

Her feet stayed underwater until she reached the first hill. As she began her ascent, she cast an eye about until she found a hint of white where the flocks were in motion. They were moving away from her, but she would catch up eventually. By the time she did, her feet would be dry.

She thought about how Kaiden and the other men usually followed her under the guise of guarding her safety. Though many might have desired her in their thoughts, none dared interfere with her physically.

None of her relatives accompanied her on these walks, today or any other day either. The Nabataean women had no interest in Jewish shepherdesses. The Jews in turn would not have welcomed Nabataeans. Her marriage to Antipater and acceptance at the Temple, however facile, bought her singular access.

As she walked, her feet slipped inside her sandals. The leather was smooth and wet as if oiled. She struggled to find footholds where the slope would cooperate with her footwear. She crested one hill, sighted the flock's location, and then descended that slope to climb the next. Part way up the second hill, she placed one foot higher than she should have and threw her weight forwards just as that foot slipped inside the sandal. Rather than fall into the hill, she drove the unfaithful foot down as though demanding that it find traction within the leather. The sandal gripped the ground firmly. Her foot inside the sandal did not. Her movement twisted the ankle, and she fell awkwardly, with a sudden spark of pain that shot up to her knee. She rolled sideways, grasping her ankle with a choked cry, and then lay back, looking up at a clear bright sky. Pain lingered in the bone, numbing her foot as her ankle swelled. Water from the wet ground began to soak through her clothing.

She cursed the slippery, worn leather, cursed this extended stay on the Jericho Plain, the nights and days of rain, and now this injury when she was on her own. She lay there for some time despite the damp, trying to decide what to do. Her return to the camp would only complicate the work she had set them on. Qaaid would mock her behind his beard. It was just a sprain.

She rolled over onto her knees and told herself not to test the ankle on a slope. She crawled up to the ridge on hands and knees. At its peak, she spotted the sheep again. They were at the crest of the next rise and drifting beyond it. She could tell, though, that they were not marching much farther. They had found the day's feeding grounds and were drifting now in various directions. There was no sign of Pninah or Salema.

Cypros sat on her hill and tried to ignore the pain and the cold. She saw that the swelling was obvious—a bad sprain. She stood up on it and let out a weak whimper that surprised and shamed her. She steeled her face and put her weight down on it again, but it would not submit to her. She sat down again and slid down the slope, letting her cloak bear the friction and gather the stains. At the bottom, she resumed her crawl across the flat section and then back up the far slope, dragging her ruined cloak behind her.

When she finally got to the top of the next hill, the sheep were close by. They noticed her but paid no heed. There was still no sign of Pninah or Salema. Cypros stood up, balancing on one foot, and surveyed the land. She finally saw the two. Both were on the ground. Something was wrong.

Cypros looked back the way she had come. She could only see the edge of the Nabataean camp from this angle, and they were too far away for her to signal for help. She hopped forwards a few steps, then gave up her dignity and traversed the thin grass and stone on hands and knees. When she got to the pair, Salema did a double take seeing Cypros crawling. "She had a seizure," Salema said.

"I twisted my ankle," Cypros said. "How long ago was the seizure?"

"It lasted a long time," Salema said. "She's sleeping now. She'll sleep for a while; then she'll be okay. She's always okay eventually. This one will be the same. It's only a muscle sickness. It always goes away."

Cypros crawled up beside Pninah, shuffled her forwards, and then lifted and settled Pninah's head on her lap. "Did she hurt herself?"

"No. I think she knew it was coming. She said something I didn't understand. Then she sat down, and it happened. Sometimes she knows before it happens. I kept her head away from the rocks."

Cypros brushed the hair away from Pninah's face. The eyelids fluttered, but the woman stayed asleep.

"What about your ankle?" Salema asked.

"It hurts like Adonai cursed it," Cypros said with more passion than she intended. She looked up to see Salema's startled expression: eyes wide and the beginning of that nervous smile. Cypros smiled back, and the girl burst out laughing, covered her mouth, then shook her head.

"I'm sorry," Salema said. "I shouldn't," but Cypros waved her quiet.

"If my father heard you say the Lord's name that way—" Salema said without finishing the thought.

"We'll keep it as our little secret," Cypros said. She had no use for the old man, but she had come to respect Salema's love for her father. She was not sure about Pninah's relation to the family. It was clear, though, that Salema adored her father and Pninah respected him.

Cypros ran her palm across Pninah's forehead, brushing invisible hairs smooth, cupping the cheek in a way she remembered doing with her own children when they were younger.

When they were younger.

Salome was only three, and Cypros could not remember the last time she had touched her daughter or any of the children in this way. Antipater used to touch her this way after they had made love. For some reason, it had irritated her in a certain season, some years after the wedding. She had reacted sharply towards him a few times, and then he had never touched her that way again. She felt something surge within her, a wave of heat and water at her eyes as she remembered the giving and receiving of this expression of tenderness, remembering it only as she extended it to Pninah while her ankle throbbed. Where had it gone? Where had the instinct to touch in this way gone? And why had she chased it from her husband's hand?

Her chest hurt. Her throat constricted. When Salema reached out to put a hand on her shoulder, she knew it was compassion for her ankle that motivated the girl.

"It's not that bad," Cypros said.

"How will you get back to your camp?"

"We'll worry about that later."

She had witnessed one of Pninah's seizures before: the bulging eyes and twisted face, her lips in a terrible grimace that was no human expression at all, except perhaps a kind of terror. The woman claimed to never remember anything, neither fear nor possession. The only parts that lingered were the physical pain and exhaustion and sometimes shame. She was always weak for the rest of the day, though she would be able to walk again before long.

Cypros continued to hold Pninah's head in her lap, caressing her face and whispering in Nabataean. Salema got up to check on the sheep. She would call or whistle to bring back those that had strayed too far.

Holding Pninah, Cypros wondered if certain friends always shared a tender intimacy like this or if sisters would.

She tried to remember her sisters, slain on the desert road, but she could not. These shepherd girls had replaced those faded memories.

She wanted to get up then and walk this mood off, but the head in her lap had not stirred. Her hand continued to stroke Pninah's quiet face. Cypros squeezed her eyes closed, then opened them and felt no different. Her ankle throbbed, reminding her that she would be walking nothing off this day or probably the next.

Eventually, Pninah awoke. She sat up with a wan smile.

Salema returned, and once she was sure that Pninah was okay, she went off to get her father.

"How long have you been here?" Pninah asked.

"Long enough to love you," Cypros said. "And to think about others I love, though poorly."

Pninah rubbed her neck and twisted her head to each side, stretching out the muscles there. "Is the siege over yet?"

Cypros laughed quietly. "No. But our camp flooded, just like your sister said it would."

Pninah looked at Cypros with a quizzical expression.

Cypros shrugged. "Salema. I think of her as your sister."

"Sister is good. I never had a sister. She is like a sister to me. Onias is like a father to me as well. More than my actual father."

"What about your mother?"

"You can be my mother if you like," Pninah said. Her crooked post-seizure smile resurfaced. "I never really knew my mother. I don't think anybody did."

"I'm not going to marry Onias," Cypros said sternly.

Pninah burst out with a laugh. It took a lot of energy from her to laugh when she was like this, and when she spoke again, it was barely a whisper. "I didn't mean it that way. You can be my friend then."

Cypros put her hand on Pninah's. "Friends is good. We are strange friends, though: a Nabataean governor's wife and a shepherdess from Jericho."

# 32

## 65-64 BCE

AS WINTER BEGAN to soften, Cypros returned to the hills to look for the sheep and their shepherd-esses. The season was still cool. It occasionally rained. More would come. There were some days, however, when the air felt mild like that of the Ashkelon seashore.

Kaiden and the other two Nabataeans followed her as usual. She had barely found the girls when strangers appeared.

"I see people," Salema said, pointing north, towards the Jericho-Jerusalem road.

A crowd made its way towards Onias's farm.

"What do they want?" Pninah asked.

The Nabataean men stirred and stood and conferred among themselves.

"We should go back," Pninah said.

"I'll come with you," Cypros replied.

"No, go back to your camp. It seems like a lot of people just for a visit."

"Which is why I'll come with you."

Salema called to the sheep as Cypros and Pninah began the trek back to the farm.

Kaiden caught up to Cypros and spoke to her in Nabataean.

"Stay back," Cypros said in the common Aramaic. "They're Jews. They're not going to want you around. Keep back."

The crowd turned out to be some of the Jerusalemites who had opened the gates and let Hyrcanus, Antipater, and the Nabataeans into the city. This group was looking for Onias. They paid Salema and Pninah little attention, though Cypros and her guard did momentarily distract them.

"You did it before," one of the Jerusalemites protested, turning his attention back to Onias. He was a big-bearded man with eyes that looked too large for his head and eyebrows to match.

"I did no such thing," Onias said.

"During the drought," the big-eyed man said.

An argument ensued about how alike the drought was to a siege. The crowd argued one view while Onias protested the opposite. Salema ushered the sheep into their pen. The speeches comparing droughts to sieges continued. Cypros pulled Pninah and Salema away.

"What are they talking about?" Cypros asked.

"My father is a holy man," Salema said.

Cypros looked at the girl with eyebrows raised.

"He's from Jerusalem," the girl said, her chin tilted up. "My mother and my brothers died there from an illness.

After that, he became a shepherd. But Jerusalem remembers him. He's an important holy man."

"What is this drought business?"

"There was a drought, early in the reign of Salome Alexandra. It was very bad. My father prayed in the Temple for the city—a special prayer to God. Everyone knew he did it. The drought ended that day—right as he finished praying. It started raining and rained for a week. The seasons went back to normal again. Everyone knows he did it. That's what happens when he prays."

Cypros stared at the girl as though she had just sprouted feathers. "Your father?" Cypros said. All she could think of were his missing teeth.

"Now they want him to pray to end the siege."

"I got that part."

"But he thinks Hyrcanus and Aristobulus are both crazy—a shame to their mother's memory. Neither one of them deserves the throne."

Cypros felt both surprise and a stirring of anger. She said nothing while the girl stared at her.

Cypros looked at Pninah. "What do you think?" Cypros asked.

"My parents served the Sadducees," Pninah whispered. She cast a side-eye towards the clearly Pharisaic crowd. "I left those beliefs in Jerusalem. Here, I believe in the Pharisees' way. Onias is teaching me to pray and to read. I don't know anything about Aristobulus and Hyrcanus."

"But Hyrcanus supports the Pharisees," Cypros protested.

The two before her looked back at the house where Onias stood in his doorway, arguing with his visitors. Both of them ignored Cypros. When the big-eyed man placed a hand on Onias's shoulder and pulled him into the yard, Salema yelped and stepped forwards. Onias waved her back.

Pninah wrapped her arms around the girl from behind. Cypros stood still and silent, unsure what to do. She looked over at her guards, who were ready for orders. The three were well-armed. The crowd numbered about twenty, but it was hard to tell if any were trained fighters or not. To run back to the Nabataean camp for reinforcements would take too long.

"I'll go with you," Onias said. He was waving his hands up and down as though clearing a cloud of smoke. "But I don't believe in your mission. I'll pray as Adonai directs me to me pray, and if I pray Balaam's prayer, you will respect Adonai's wish."

The crowd let out a shout of victory, and more than half of them turned as though to march back to Jerusalem that very moment.

"The Temple awaits," the big-eyed man said when Onias turned back to his house.

Onias gave the big-eyed man a long stare. "I have a daughter and guests to bid farewell to and proper walking clothes to change into. You can give an old man a few breaths to prepare."

The big-eyed man opened his mouth, paused, then nodded. The crowd did not back off into the outer yard, nor did they seat themselves. They simply stood where they were and waited.

Onias came over to his daughter and ignored the other two women. He shook his head and gave Salema a small smile. He reached out a rough-knuckled hand and laid it alongside her cheek. It was a gesture that made Cypros's throat catch. The old man leaned forwards and planted a soft kiss on the girl's forehead. Then he drew Pninah to him and gave her the same gesture and the same kiss.

When he finally spoke, he spoke to Pninah. "You look weak, child," he said. "I need you to be strong. She's yours to look after while I'm gone."

"I'll keep her safe," Pninah said. In this, Cypros heard the echo of Hanne's promise to care for her own children.

"I have no business with Nabataeans," Onias said to Cypros, "regardless of how you might think you're serving Eretz-Israel. But while you are here, please have your men keep watch over this farm. It's a safe country, but Moab is only a day's ride away."

Cypros was still adjusting her view of this old man. In addition, Pninah's uncertain loyalty to Hyrcanus stirred her thoughts in one direction, and the old man's gesture as he had touched Salema's and Pninah's faces affected her emotions in another. Suddenly she could clearly see the faces of her own children.

*I should have asked him about the dead Moabite on the road.*

Too many conflicting thoughts swirled inside her. She nodded in response to his request.

The old man turned away. He went into the house, taking Salema with him. After a short while, he returned alone and went off with the strangers from Jerusalem.

It was some time before Salema emerged from the house. When she did, her eyes were wet. She reported nothing about her private conversation.

Once the others were gone, the three Nabataeans approached.

"We'll go back to the camp," she said. "You two"—she pointed to Kaiden's companions—"stay here. Over there." She indicated a spot overlooking the farm. "I don't want anyone disturbing this place while her father is away. We'll send replacements for you before dark."

⁓

One week after Onias's departure, Cypros awoke in the pre-dawn darkness with a vivid dream still on her mind. She had dreamed of yellow-legged trungas, the birds so often seen along the Ashkelon shoreline energetically stepping through shallow water, plucking morsels from the mud. Their dark and formal attire contrasted comically with their bobbing heads, flashing white bottoms, and delicate twitching stride. She lay awake in the dark thinking about the birds and understood the omen. If she saw trungas today, the siege was over. Onias had done his work.

There was no reason to expect trungas on the Jericho Plain. She considered a trip to the Jordan River, but such an outing was also unlikely to yield trungas, and it would unwisely put al-Qaum to the test. She should pray and wait. The trungas would come.

She got up before dawn and made her way east from the camp. Despite herself, she walked in the direction of the Jordan. It was a long walk from the camp to the river, and she would not get there on foot. The direction of her prayers, however, indicated not just the direction of the rising sun but her instinct to make the dream come true.

She knelt and prayed. The light of dawn pressed against her eyelids, but she did not open them. The heat of the morning sun pressed the top of her head, but still she bowed and prayed.

Finally, she heard Kaiden stirring on his watch, likely unsettled by her extended worship. Or simply ready for his morning meal.

Still, she prayed. Only when she was truly finished did she rise and stand. Then she opened her eyes.

The sun made her squint. Mist rose in the far distance, in the direction of the Jordan. She strained to hear the unmelodic call of the trungas, but the Jordan was too far away. Its banks here were too steep for shorebirds.

She looked back towards the camp, ignoring Kaiden. Finally, she looked up high, and that is when she saw them. The great black birds of the desert rode high overhead. They were a strange sight this early in the morning. They were not trungas. They were vultures, twenty times the size of a trunga. She had never seen seven vultures in flight before, but seven flew together this day, heading south-west. Vultures, not trungas.

"Is everything alright?" Kaiden asked as she passed by him on her way back to the camp.

"Can't you send someone to find out where Onias is?" Pninah asked Cypros.

The three were in the hills beyond the farm. The sheep were scattered around them. Kaiden and two other warriors sat together one hill over.

"He's my father," Salema said. "Just ask anyone where Onias is. They'll know. He's Onias."

"I did send someone," Cypros answered. "They detained him. It's the only thing that makes sense."

"Who?" Pninah asked. "Who detained him?"

"Hyrcanus. Or my husband. Only one of them would have the authority."

"I'll go," Pninah said, standing.

"No," Cypros said. "Your job is to look after Salema."

Salema looked up at that, a frown on her face, mouth opening to speak.

"I'll send someone else," Cypros finished before the girl could protest. "Someone more reliable. I'll send Kaiden."

That was a stretch. But he would do it. For her. Even if Qaaid protested.

"Send him now," Pninah said.

"Tomorrow will give him time to prepare."

"Then send him back to the camp now to prepare."

"Pninah." Cypros shook her head. "Impatient Pninah."

Pninah stared back at her with thin lips pressed together.

"Fine. I'll send him back, and he can even start today and finish tomorrow." Cypros stood and signalled for the Nabataean men to approach.

She looked at the two shepherdesses as the men made their way over. "Qaaid won't be happy," she said.

Pninah's expression did not change. "I don't care about Qaaid," she said.

◈

South of Jerusalem, in southern Idumea, and on the desert routes between Petra and Gaza—south-east even of Gaza, on the routes into Egypt—there were places of both burning and feasting. The great black birds avoided the places of smoke and fire. Fortunately, not all bandits saw the need for flames. When they left their victims exposed before the sun, the birds feasted.

The strange concentration of desert men and camels in the great city with its Temple of sacrifices and fire had created an exodus of men, women, and children. Most fled south with their livestock and possessions.

The concentration of desert men and camels north of Idumea had emptied Idumean and Nabataean territories of their usual guard. A boom season for bandits had developed in the south. The results, when the men could restrain themselves from setting everything on fire, created a bountiful harvest for the great scavenging birds.

The squawking and posturing of vultures at their business was a raucous affair. Even the noisy trungas on the shores of the Great Sea did not make this much commotion. If the great black birds had anything among them like the Festival of Sukkot, this was it. The southern desert had once again become a glorious place for both bandits and birds.

❧

Kaiden had travelled alone to Jerusalem to inquire about Onias. Qaaid would not let anyone else go with him. He did permit the man a camel, if only to ensure his speedy return.

Kaiden left alone, but he did not return alone. He came back with Onias and twelve other men, all Jews.

The Jews walked. Onias rode. He did not ride a camel or a horse. He rode reclining, on a frame carried by the Jewish men who took turns bearing his weight during the long walk through the canyon to the farm. Kaiden led the way, directing them straight to the small farm.

Onias was silent. He did not rise from his bed to welcome the farm or to look for the girls. He lay still, wrapped, spiced, dead.

⋖

Salema ran from the hills when she saw the men returning. Cypros followed behind. Pninah stalled. She did not want to know.

She called the sheep and led them down the slope, back to the farm. It was early, but she could not linger in the hills too long. Something was wrong.

She heard Salema scream and saw her faint from a distance, but still Pninah did not abandon the sheep. She hurried them along. She mixed up some of their names, but they seemed to understand her urgency. By the time she got the sheep back to the farm and into their pen, Salema was awake. The girl wept loudly, finished the last few steps, and then stretched out across the wrapped body of her father. Onias had come home.

A dozen men stood about. They were Jewish men, not Nabataeans. Kaiden stood nearby looking dejected. The other three Nabataeans who had been guarding the women moved alongside him. They tried to talk with him in Nabataean, but the tired man did not respond.

"How?" Pninah asked.

The men said nothing and would not meet her gaze.

She turned to Kaiden.

Kaiden pointed to the oldest of the Jews, a man with only grey hair in his beard and none on his head.

"They stoned him," the man said. His voice was quiet and hoarse.

"Stoned him?" Cypros interrupted. "Who stoned him?"

"They made him pray," the old man continued. "He prayed as he said he would. He prayed that God would not regard either brother kindly, that both brothers would quit their contest and be done with Hasmonean madness."

"They became a mob," another of the Jews said. "They stoned him for resisting them."

❧

Black and white beaks clicked as the great black birds ate. Red ran below yellow-rimmed eyes of darker, duller black. The season of bounty wound down.

The siege of the great city continued, but its flow of refugees dried up. So did the air. It did not rain that winter as often or as much as usual. The cold weather was colder than usual. The drier air more cruel.

The birds, in whatever bird way they had among them, communicated portents of gloom. When they ate, they did so more aggressively than they had in the fall.

Good times come to an end, even for birds.

# 33

## 64 BCE

THE REST OF that spring was a season of sorrow in the foothills south and west of Jericho. The girls talked less than before. They took the sheep out each day and brought them back each night. There were no sounds or signs of joy in that grey season.

Late in the spring, Cypros came with treats. Rather than the simple breads and dried foods stored at the farm and in the Nabataean camp, she brought specialty items from Jericho. There were richer sweet breads with cream and pickled olives and smoked fish.

It rained the following day. As usual on rainy days, the sheep were taken out but brought in early. Cypros did not appear.

A boy came by later. He was from Jericho, the son of a merchant who had sometimes traded with Onias. He came to the door, dripping, carrying a package wrapped in a waxed cloth to keep its contents dry.

"Come in," Pninah said.

The boy entered the small farmhouse and presented his father's gift. It was a small block of cheese, cured dates and olives, a jar of spiced wine, and another of olive oil.

He shrugged and smiled when Pninah thanked him for his gift. His eyes strayed off in Salema's direction, then returned to Pninah. Salema helped unpack the merchant's presents, but otherwise she did not speak or interact with the boy.

"Have you heard the news about the Passover?" the boy asked.

"That it happened?" Pninah asked. "Presumably with Aristobulus still in charge since it's his people inside the Temple."

"No, not really." The boy squirmed. He glanced at Salema again, but the girl chose to ignore him. The boy sighed.

"Those rebels with Aristobulus got what they deserved," he said. He tapped on the table. "They sent a message over the walls asking to buy animals they could use for the Passover sacrifices. Hyrcanus's people agreed but demanded a huge price. A crazy price. Ten times the normal price." He glanced quickly at Salema.

"The people inside the Temple agreed," he continued. "Sadducees always have lots of money, so it didn't matter. They were going to eat most of the sacrifices anyway. They must be getting thin inside the Temple by now." He giggled when he said this. The sound was not an innocent child's giggle. It was an adolescent boy's giggle that bore something cruel within its tone.

"So Aristobulus's men paid the money by lowering it over the walls in sacks. Sacks and sacks of money. They dropped it in the bridge area. Do you know the Zion Bridge?"

Pninah nodded.

"Antipater's people collected the sacks and went back to their side of the valley. You know the valley, right?"

Pninah nodded again.

"So they collected the money." The boy looked towards where Salema had been, but the girl had gone into the back room. The boy scowled. "Anyway, they collected the money, but then Hyrcanus's men refused to provide any animals. But they kept the money anyway." He said this last bit with a grin directed at Pninah.

"That will teach them, right?" he said. "They stole the throne. Now they're stuck in the Temple and lost all their money. No animals, no sacrifices, no Passover. Serves them right. I'll bet they're getting awfully hungry by now."

Salema came back into the room and busied herself at a side table.

"I heard that when the time for evening sacrifices came and it was obvious that there was no fire and no sacrifices in the Temple, Hyrcanus's people were cheering. No Passover for anyone this year." The boy was all grins. "Those people in the Temple got what they deserved."

"They were lied to," Salema said. She turned from her chores, a knife in her hand, and stared at the merchant's boy.

"They got what they deserved," the boy repeated.

"They were lied to," she said again. "Tricked by the same people that murdered my father."

She did not stop staring at the boy. Pninah considered taking the knife from her, but Salema had not brandished it. She just held it. And stared at the boy.

"I heard about that," the boy said. "About your father." He did not meet Salema's gaze.

"Thank you for the gifts," Pninah said. "Please thank your father for us."

The boy nodded.

"Was there something else?" Pninah asked.

The boy shook his head. When he left in the rain, the house became quiet again. A short while later, Salema picked up the small block of cheese, left the house, and hurled the cheese across the field.

A week after Passover ended, the wind began to blow. Its intensity signalled something new. An early spring sun appeared, and though the cold vanished, it was not a relief. The wind blew and the sun glared and not a single cloud appeared. All rains stopped. At night, the air hardly cooled at all. The wind that blew remained overheated, day and night. If Av were a lion, that merciless month was advancing with a loud and early roar.

When the spring rains did finally start again, it was as if only to confirm the season and then announce its cancellation. The rain evaporated as soon as it hit the ground. Nothing soaked into the soil. Plants withered and died.

The girls went looking for early figs in trees to the south and found them shrivelled and white. Most had already fallen from the trees. The rest would soon. There was nothing to harvest.

Cypros came up the slope a week later. Pninah saw her searching. She and Salema were with the sheep in a gully where the green struggled to hold on. The Nabataean sat down with the girls on a stubbly slope.

"The wheat outside Jericho stopped growing," she said. "Is that normal?"

Salema shrugged. Pninah did not know anything about growing wheat.

Two weeks later, Cypros concluded the matter. "They tried to save what was on the stalks," she said. "The farmers from Jericho found the stalks empty. There were only hulls where heads of grain should have been."

In the month of Tammuz, the wind continued to blow, and the sun blazed hotter yet. Grapes died across the country. The following month, olives fell from the trees. They were dry, surrendering only half the quantity of oil their pressers expected. Cypros brought each of these reports up to the farm as they became available. No one else came to the farm.

"Do you think the drought is because of the Passover fraud?" Cypros asked.

"How about the murder of my father?" Salema countered.

Cypros nodded.

"Either way," Salema said, "your siege is destroying our country. The people who back your husband have gone mad, and now God has cursed us. Because of you."

Cypros left the hills that day shaking inside. The young girl's anger was not just an orphan's emotion. The girl's anger had iron in it. It spoke the truth—a truth Cypros could not accept.

In the morning, she went out to pray to al-Qaum. Her prayers that day were shortened by the relentless sun that threatened to consume her as she knelt on the Jericho Plain.

The next day she made an earlier start and prayed for a sign from al-Qaum—something to show her the way ahead.

Instead of an angel of mercy from God, or an omen of relief from al-Qaum, a Nabataean rider came from Damascus. He was on his way, alone, to Raqmu. Only he rode this route. His fellow messengers were dead. This was al-Qaum's omen: a rider.

"The Romans have taken Damascus," the man said.

Damascus. The place of her birth. The last home of her family. *Her* home.

"We were beaten by the Romans because our entire army is encamped outside Jerusalem instead of protecting our own country," she raged at Kaiden.

She went back inside her tent and paced. The other women avoided her. She had no one to properly talk to, no one who would understand, no one to finally wrap up this cursed, drawn-out siege that was almost a year on and still had no forecasted end in sight. She wanted to go straight to Jerusalem and demand an explanation for the past year of men idling and accomplishing nothing, but it was too far to walk. Qaaid would not let her take a camel. Kaiden was polite, but he did not have answers. She would have gone there alone, but not without a camel.

Av came next to the Jericho Plain as it did everywhere else cursed by God. The drought continued. The summer fig crops failed. The pomegranates shrivelled and dropped from the trees too early. The course of the Jewish curse did not ease. Slow death threatened the entire country.

She thought of the girls in the hills. In their time both had been orphaned. She thought about the sheep and wondered how they would survive if the fall rains did not come and revive the stream and the grass. The girls had struggled through the spring shearing and had money again, but money was of no use if there was nothing left to buy.

The drought must also be affecting Idumea and Nabataea. Famine was an indiscriminate enemy.

The year proved to be a hard one for the desert's great black birds as well. Carcasses found in arid places were thin and dried and offered little sustenance. Then things changed.

By chance, the birds travelled north later in the year and witnessed the emptying of the long-besieged city. First a vast army of men on horses and men on foot left travelling south, far to the west of the Salt Sea. They appeared to be bound for Idumea, travelling on the road that led to Ashkelon and its environs. There was something about this force that did not draw the birds. It looked like a group on its way to a winter refuge, though it was early in the season for an army's retirement.

A second force left Jerusalem at the same time. This group rode camels followed by a large contingent of foot soldiers. The camel riders and foot soldiers headed east, into the canyons and on to the Jericho road. There was something about this group that drew the birds' attention. The birds held high circling positions overhead and watched. And waited.

Only a long morning and part of an afternoon passed, and then a third force exited Jerusalem's gates. This was a large group of horsemen. They came out of the city gates with the kind of speed and energy that invigorated the birds' blood. This was the posture they looked for from men. This was the flow of beast and man and equipment that signalled feasting to come. This third group did not follow the Idumeans but took to the Jericho road. The canyon walls echoed with horse hooves pounding on stone.

If birds could laugh, the vultures would have laughed. Men and horses were not dry and fleshless. Men and horses were a good and welcome respite from the desert's desultory fare.

When Antipater appeared unannounced at the Jericho camp, Cypros approached him cautiously. She looked behind him and saw the rest of the cavalry as it came into view. There had been no advance riders. "What happened?" she asked.

"Go home," Antipater said as he stepped off of his kneeling camel. "To Petra, I mean. Why are you still here?"

He stunk of camel and human sweat. She had not seen him for a long time, and on some nights, she had even yearned for him. Now, his appearance and his stink repulsed her.

"Why are you here?" she asked, stepping back. "Is it over?"

Antipater scowled and walked into the tent that she shared with the other women. He unbuckled his sword and cast his eyes about until he found a flagon and drained it.

"There's a Roman garrison at Damascus now," he said.

"I know," she said, standing in the tent's entrance. "They are in Damascus because my uncle's army has been busy doing nothing at Jerusalem."

Antipater looked about the tent as though expecting to see the children. The layout and signs of women in the place seemed to confuse him. "Aristobulus sent a message. And a bribe. To the Romans."

"How does someone inside a siege send a message and a bribe outside the city, all the way to Damascus?"

Antipater shrugged. "We don't know. We found out later. We sent our own men and money."

"You bribed the Romans?"

Antipater nodded. "We tried."

"You gave money to the men who conquered the town where I was born?" she shouted at him. "You rewarded them for destroying the homes and lives of my people?"

"We sent them goodwill gestures with regards to events at Jerusalem, nothing more."

"Then why are you here?"

"Because he accepted both gifts, ours and Aristobulus's. But he honoured only Aristobulus's. Pompey ordered us out of Jerusalem. The Idumeans were sent south. The fortress mercenaries were turned back over to Aristobulus. For Nabataeans, the Romans were particularly clear: if they caused any trouble on their exit from Judea, they would, how did he put it, 'be declared enemies of Rome.' I came with the Nabataeans to escort Hyrcanus and see if you were still here."

Cypros looked back out the entrance and saw Jerusalem's

haggard ex-king approach. He was sitting uncomfortably on another nearby camel without any Jewish attendants.

"They took Damascus," she sneered, redirecting her gaze back to her husband, "but we're not enemies yet?"

⚜

Events in the canyon drew the focus of the birds overhead. The riders on horses caught up to the foot soldiers just before they left the canyons to enter the plain. The riders did not slow down as they approached the men on foot but rode straight into them, hooves adding to the carnage of spear and javelin. There was no parley, no discussion, no standoff for posturing such as the birds had observed in the past. The men on horses charged and the men on foot fled. To the dismay of the birds, none of the horses fell. Only foot soldiers.

War spilled onto the plain. Resting camels and their riders roused. Their shouts added to the chaotic chorus that called to the hills and the plain, to the river and the far Jericho city.

The pace of slaughter accelerated as horsemen continued their assault. They finished off the foot soldiers and then turned towards the camp. The camel riders did not come to the aid of their brothers. They fled. Beasts and their riders were caught by a hail of arrows and javelins and spears.

The business of the birds was to mark bodies and coordinate a descent when the valley cleared. There was no immediate clearing of this valley, and it turned out that there was no need to mark bodies. Carnage ruled. Thousands fell. The pitiless sun would not set. Blood ran like the river, into the river, beyond the river before the horsemen finally returned to the western side of the valley.

Individual horsemen stopped on occasion to loot a body or to end its life, then loot it. After such pauses, they continued west. They entered the canyon road and returned to the city from which they had come.

Only then did the birds begin their descent. There were five hundred or a thousand bodies for every bird, and yet they descended on only a few victims. They shared their meals as they always did. They postured and snapped at one another in their usual style of fellowship. Feasting, even among the birds, had its formalities.

# 34

## 64 BCE

IT WAS EARLY for an end to pasturing, but there was little grass. Wandering the fields was not helping the shepherdesses or the sheep. In the middle of the afternoon, Pninah and Salema started back to the farm when riders suddenly appeared from the direction of the canyon trail. They watched the large group as it entered the plain and turned in a great arc towards the Nabataean camp.

"Camels," Salema said. It was about all she had said the entire day.

Pninah nodded and watched.

"A lot of camels."

"Maybe the siege is over," Pninah said.

There were thousands of beasts and their riders flooding into the valley. At the head was a group of guards distinguished by its mix of horses and camels together.

"That must be Hyrcanus," Pninah said. "But where are the rest of the Jews?"

The Idumean horsemen were missing. Only a small guard accompanied the former king.

"And why is he here?" Salema asked. "If they won, he should be in Jerusalem. Maybe they lost."

"I don't think it's possible to lose a siege if you're the attacker," Pninah said. "You wait long enough and the people inside run out of food."

"Unless they come out and attack."

"If Aristobulus had that kind of strength, he would have done it at the beginning. Before he ran out of food. Nobody wins a siege from inside the city."

Salema whistled and made a peculiar clicking sound with her tongue that the sheep responded to. When she started walking again, they followed. At the pen, she stood aside, and they filed into the stone enclosure.

"All home again," she said as she closed the gate.

"Foot soldiers," Pninah said, pointing. She watched the men appear on the plain, and Salema followed her gaze. Neither of them said anything when horsemen appeared behind the foot soldiers. It explained why the men were running. And dying.

"They came out and attacked," Salema said. "Aristobulus had the strength after all."

"It doesn't make any sense," Pninah said. "Where are the Idumeans? Where are the mercenaries from the other fortresses?"

The two watched as slaughter made its way across the plain. By the time the Jerusalem army got to Cypros's camp, it had been abandoned. The horsemen ran down the tents and then gave chase to the fleeing camel riders.

Hours later, as evening began to dim, the horsemen returned. They did not return in flight. They returned at a slow pace. Some stopped and dismounted. They conducted activities on the ground that the two shepherdesses could not identify from their distant post.

A short while later, riders from the Jewish army approached the farm.

"Oh no." Pninah reopened the sheep-pen gate and led Salema inside. The walls came up to chest height. The men on horseback would see them over the walls.

The company rode into the yard and gathered in front of the pen. Hungry eyes took in the two shepherdesses.

"What do we have here?" one of the men said. "Two lovely chickens and no rooster to bother us."

"I am the daughter of Onias, Jerusalem's holy man. He was murdered for the sake of your stupid war," Salema shouted at the soldiers, startling Pninah as much as the men. "Get off this land or the curses of this entire year will continue for years to come. God will roast this nation for its crimes. Go, or the Angel of Death will come and drag you off screaming. Onias himself will haunt you."

The men did not say anything at first, and then a couple of the older men moved to the front of the group with solemn looks on their faces.

"Your father was a good man," one of the older soldiers said. "I met him once, many years ago. Before your brothers and mother passed. We were trapped inside the Temple grounds when your father was murdered. That was the work of Hyrcanus's men, not our king, Aristobulus."

Salema tilted forwards as though to speak again, then settled back on her heels and kept her mouth closed.

"May Adonai bless this family," the man continued. "The Temple is once again free, and we will sacrifice there in your father's honour. The Nabataeans are gone. They won't bother you again. Aristobulus is still our king and high priest, and he had a home, in better times, not far from here." He pointed in the general direction of the abandoned royal residences.

The man looked at Pninah then with an expression that suggested that he was trying to place her. He studied her closely and frowned. After a moment, he signalled his companions. Together they rode away, joining the larger force returning to Jerusalem.

By the time darkness fell, the plain was empty but for the dead and the desert birds. The birds were far enough away that they could not be heard from the small farm. If any victims lived and called out on that field, they also were too far away and not heard. The land between the farm and Jericho had become a graveyard.

"That avenges my father's death," Salema said.

"I don't think the Nabataeans stoned him either," Pninah said.

"God will deal with those who did. The Nabataeans had no business in Jerusalem to begin with."

❧

The following day, the Nabataean retreat was on the move again before dawn. They continued southwards along the foot of the Moab Mountains. Cypros sat on her camel weakly, tired and overwhelmed by the sudden turn of events. Their dead lay on the Jericho Plain behind, and she did not know how many they were. The last she had seen of Antipater was his turn back into that unexpected storm. He had gone to defend the last of the Nabataeans trying to cross the river.

She thought of Pninah and Salema. *Goodbye, my friends,* she murmured. She lurched with the camel's gait in the semi-darkness. She was just one of many on this road, returning to Raqmu.

At some point, they passed the place where they had found the dead Moabite. She gave no thought to the place or its failed omens when they passed it.

Cypros arrived at Raqmu with the others, weak and beaten by the journey. They had skipped two of the way stations. The camels moaned with vigour, voicing camel protests to Raqmu's red cliffs.

When Cypros stepped down onto the sand, she did so with no joy and no energy. Her children judged her mood rightly and held back. Hanne took her by the arm to a bath. After the bath, Cypros slipped between familiar covers and slept like the recent dead.

Antipater arrived at the camp with Hyrcanus three days later. They came with an army of desert men shocked by the unexpected assault, by Roman warnings to cause no harm on their retreat, and by the sheer brutality of their march. The seriously injured numbered several thousand, much fewer in number than their dead. Of the sixty thousand that had marched, six thousand remained on the Jericho Plain, food for the scavengers of that place.

There were no words in Aramaic or Nabataean for the sorrow that rose throughout Raqmu.

Antipater's brother, Phalion, was among those left behind.

"I saw him fall," Antipater told Cypros. He had been caught on the western side of the Jordan, killed as he had entered the water.

No one had collected Phalion's body. It had floated while others had fallen on solid ground. He would be carried to the Salt Sea, the sea that some people called the Dead. There, his body would not sink until the flesh fell away from its bones. Then the bones would slide beneath the salt, lost forever to his people.

There was a season of mourning at Raqmu in the weeks that followed, but very few burials. Those who had survived grieved in whatever their custom. Yet the mourners' expressions of grief varied drastically from person to person, regardless of whether they hailed from the city or the desert. Some were loud. Some were quiet. Some mourned with an immobility that mimicked death itself. Some flashed with anger and spirit and, given a chance, would have ridden back to Jerusalem to reap their revenge, whatever Rome's threats.

A month after Antipater's return, Cypros walked Raqmu's canyons with her uncle. They were on a trail beyond the Siq.

"Your scheme promised to net me twelve cities," Aretas said.

Cypros nodded and kept her head down.

"Twelve cities," her uncle repeated. "With only a few

months of effort. To be completed by your husband's festival of flatbread, not the last one but the one before."

Cypros did not point out that the Nabataean army had not even been assembled yet by that first Passover. Events might have wrapped up sooner, without Roman interference, if they had been handled on her original timeline. She thought of Qaaid's resistance to her trip to Jerusalem but kept quiet on that point. He had followed her husband's direction.

"Instead, you've cost me more than a year of trading," he continued. "Six thousand good men dead. And Damascus lost." He stopped his pacing and looked at her. "It's your birth city, you know." He stooped and leaned in and peered at her with black eyes. "You might think of yourself as a Jew now, but you were born in Damascus. You do remember that."

Cypros nodded.

"It's now Roman. Your childhood room now is probably the room of a Roman whore. Or a soldier's lair from which he ventures forth to terrorize your old neighbours and childhood friends."

Cypros kept her head down until his fingers touched her chin and lifted her face to his. "Where is my snake in the desert?" he asked. "You were to make something of your husband's position, not to turn yourself into a sheep. My sister and I had a plan for you. We married you to a Jew—that Jew—for a reason. I heard you became a shepherdess in the year you were away. What happened to my snake?"

Cypros lifted her chin higher, away from his hand. "What are six thousand men in exchange for thirteen cities?" she asked.

Aretas leaned back, taking her in, his gaze moving from eye to eye. His lips stayed firmly together.

"The Roman General Pompey," she said, "is en route to Damascus." She did not add that without a Nabataean army to defend it, the city had fallen without the general or his main forces even being there for the assault. A mere auxiliary force had taken the city.

"What of it?"

Cypros took a chance and started walking. He followed and caught up with her.

"What about Pompey?" he asked.

"Send another delegation," Cypros said. "Rome trades with Nabataea. Without Nabataea, there is no spice for the empire."

Her uncle kept pace beside her.

"Stores in Rome have already been reduced by this year of trade interruption and now drought," she continued. "Pompey will not want to be the author of a full trade collapse."

Aretas gestured for her to continue.

"A full trade collapse would affect the temples, the palaces, even the households of the senate. You could cause that trade collapse. If Pompey displeases you, direct your remaining supplies to Egypt. The consequences would hurt Rome for years to come. It would be remembered for a lifetime—with Pompey to blame."

Aretas frowned. "What else?" he asked.

"Provide a better gift as an alternative, a reward to counterbalance the threat. Don't make him feel forced. Seduce him." Cypros looked up the canyon at a project already planned. The rock face was not yet carved, but drainage systems around it were under excavation. She stopped walking, forcing her uncle to stop and notice what she was looking at. "You'll have to leave off some of your grander plans to pay for it. Hyrcanus has no money. Obodas can complete your plans, or his son after him. Your bribe will need to be rich."

"We are to pay for this? Pay for Jewish problems?"

"We're Nabataeans. We store water in the desert. We carve cities from stone. We plan."

"What do I get for my gold and my people's blood?"

"Make it an issue of law," she said, looking back at her uncle. "It is in Rome's interests to put Hyrcanus in the Temple as high priest where he belongs. He is the rightful heir to that position and a more stable partner for Rome."

"More stable than his brother?"

"The Romans freed Aristobulus from his temple-prison with a word. That should have been enough for him." Cypros's face twisted with anger and then stiffened and stilled. "Aristobulus killed six thousand Nabataeans who obeyed Rome's decree. We left Jerusalem in peace as Pompey ordered. We sent the Idumeans home as well, which left us unprotected. That makes Aristobulus duplicitous against his brother and us both. But he also defied Rome. His actions cost Nabataea six thousand desert men who will not lead caravans this year—or any other year. Even with peace, the trade across the desert will be restricted for years to come by the loss of those men. Aristobulus caused this. He defied Rome's solution to the siege. As a result, prices will go up."

"Why will they go up?"

"Because you'll make them go up." Rage flared within her. She worked to control her tone, to not shout at the man. She needed to drive her uncle forwards but not away.

She wanted to hit him. "If Rome wants stability, they need a stable man in Jerusalem, a man allied with Nabataea."

"Hyrcanus."

Cypros smiled. "I said to put him back in the Temple where he belongs. Give the throne to Antipater. He lost a brother in this contest. He risked Idumea for it. And he's married to your niece."

"You think that with my help, my bribe, you can get your husband on Jerusalem's throne?"

"On it. Beside it. In charge of it. One of those."

"You still haven't told me what I get out of this."

"You planned with your sister to put me in the seat of governess of Idumea," she said, "to protect your interests at the Gaza port. That was a small plan."

Her uncle did not respond to the barb. They kept walking.

"That was a Gaza-focused plan," she said. "I belong at the court of Jerusalem where I can do good for both of our countries. A Nabataean should have influence everywhere. Look at this place." She gestured at the work around them. "We build for eternity. Eretz-Israel has other ports. Think about more than just the deserts. Think about Eretz-Israel and Nabataea as one power governed by two allied kings."

# 35
## 64-63 BCE

CYPROS PACED AND brooded. The retreat from Jerusalem was a failure. The murder of six thousand Nabataeans was a national tragedy. But they had mourned now for over a month.

*Let the bereaved mourn longer if need be. But those who rule need to think and act.*

She had talked with Antipater. She had talked with Aretas. Husband and uncle had talked with each other.

Neither husband nor uncle had shared the content of the meeting between men.

Two nights later, she turned and pressed herself against Antipater in the dark. She did not need light in the tent to know she had his attention. "Have you broached the Damascus plan with Hyrcanus?" she asked.

His body against her grew tense and he turned away.

"Leave the running of nations to the men who lead them," he said.

She lay there, dismissed, for only a moment. Then she got up and walked outside the tent. She walked outside Raqmu's tent city and into the darkness of night, letting her guard scramble itself alert.

She did not worship al-Qaum at night very often.

The moon floated overhead, lighting the desert such that her disgruntled guards did not need torches.

She bowed and prayed until she had nothing more to say or beg. Afterwards, she did not immediately stand but knelt in the same place, contemplating what to do next. As a girl, flight had always been the next thing to do. Surreptitious collection of water and flight. Revenge had been a protracted but precise affair. With household conflicts in the Ashkelon palace, particularly with Efrat, her actions were likewise clear and specific. She had known what to do and been bold with her choices. Her choices had borne quick results.

Creating the bond with Hyrcanus had taken longer. Her Nabataean heritage and Antipater's Idumean blood had been obstacles to overcome, but they had won over the high priest. They had maintained their relationship with the man when he had become king. Remaining loyal to him after he had given up the throne was a calculation that had borne results they had been able to use to their own ends.

But here, in the desert, defeated by a Roman decree and Aristobulus's treachery, she could not incite action. The men would not allow her into their council. She could persuade her husband and uncle in private, but neither man gave her access to Hyrcanus. Territories needed engaged rulers.

Hyrcanus ruled nothing now and bore no visible signs of wanting to do anything further about it. For all anyone knew, his life would be forfeit if he returned to Eretz-Israel now. He moped about Raqmu like a boy deprived of sweets.

Aretas led, but he focused his leadership on trade routes and the revival of contacts and contracts. He led what was in front of him with no regard for the greater prize of Eretz-Israel.

It was like he was the one who had forgotten Damascus.

Antipater seemed content to let Idumea continue to manage itself. Aristobulus could hand over the palace to a more loyal supporter at any time, and they would not find out at Raqmu for weeks.

Cypros picked up her mat, rolled it up, and then walked farther into the desert. She gave only a passing thought to the likely dismay of her guards. There were animals in the dark. Predators were a soldier's concern, not hers. She walked and brooded and let those with pole weapons and bows worry and watch.

Two more nights passed. She returned after prayers one night to find Antipater was still not back from another meeting with Aretas. Hanne had settled the children. Cypros talked to the nurse but took little interest in what the woman had to say.

Antipater finally returned long after the partial moon had begun its drifting journey across the sky. He gestured to her and left the tent. She followed him outside, and he immediately set to walking.

She did not feel warm towards him. She felt cold and distant. Her mood made her glad for the darkness.

*I'm tired of trying to explain what you can't understand.*

He had become small to her. Her mother had thought strategically. She had orchestrated this marriage for a reason. But there had been no way for her to know that the boy she had picked would turn out to be so indecisive.

*What really happened outside Jerusalem? You dedicated more than a year to a siege and got nowhere. It should have taken you two months at most to breach the walls.*

There were other questions that she wanted to ask but could not. The stupidity of the last year could not be queried.

Antipater reached out and took her arm, then her hand. He moved her hand to his upper arm where she should hold on to him while he walked stoically beside her.

*You're going to show me how to share warmth and devotion now?*

"Neither Hyrcanus nor Aretas will travel to Damascus to meet with Pompey," Antipater finally said.

Her attention sharpened. This was not about warmth.

"'It's beneath the dignity of kings to negotiate with an envoy,'" he quoted. "They think of Pompey as just an envoy."

"Isn't he?" Cypros sensed that he may have stiffened at this, but her hand on his arm was light, and she did not look at him.

"So they're sending me," he said.

Finally. This was her plan in action. She did not ask for details about the discussions with Hyrcanus. The fact that he had refused to join this mission was enough. He had been briefed. He had approved the plan, if not his part in it.

He would be useless in a negotiation anyway.

"When do you leave?" Cypros asked.

"Tomorrow morning."

"The rain will start again tomorrow."

Antipater stopped pacing and looked at her.

"You're not happy with me," Cypros said.

"I'm not happy with the weather."

&s;

Antipater departed for Damascus to meet with the Romans. Nearly two months passed. Kislev, wet and cool, slid into Tevet. New snow began to appear on the peaks of the highest mountains.

"When Antipater returns from Damascus, I want the tent cleared," Cypros told Hanne. "Morning, afternoon, or night. I need to be alone with him."

"Yes, of course," Hanne agreed as she tidied stray blankets and hung rain cloaks from interior tent cords to dry.

Several more days passed. Cypros had expected Antipater and his men to return days before, but still he did not come. Cypros paced and waited.

When Antipater finally arrived, it was in another rainstorm. The camels moaned and blew wet air. Men talked through the downpour.

By the time Antipater entered the tent, the children were gone and only Cypros remained. He stopped and looked around in surprise. She approached him with a smile, slipped past him, and closed the tent flap, looping the canvas cords closed against the wind.

"You're wet," she said by way of explanation, removing his outer cloak. Antipater's face relaxed, and he stood quietly as she removed the rest of his clothing and led him to a mat before the fire. A pot was boiling there. She poured the boiling water into a larger basin of unheated water and then took a small jar and poured an aromatic balm into the water. She swirled the water about with her hand, dipped a cloth into the mix, and then began to wash the grime of travel from Antipater's face, his head, neck, shoulders.

He took her hand when she got to his chest and caught her eye. She looked at him, smiled with her mouth closed, and shook her head. "Lie back," she said. When she was done with him, when he was clean, she took him to their chamber within the tent. Candles burned there, shedding a dim and flickering light.

"Now," she said.

Afterwards, they lay as they had years before, untroubled by the busyness of a palace around them, untroubled by children or servants. All exterior sounds were drowned out by the ceaseless rhythm of rain. It might have just been the two of them at Raqmu.

"Tell me," she said. "What happened?"

Antipater groaned.

"That bad?" she asked.

"No. Not bad. Not good." He rolled over as though to bury his face in the blankets and go to sleep, then rolled back and onto one elbow. "The timelines of empires grate on me," he admitted. "I like Idumea. I can get things done in a short amount of time. I can go anywhere in a long day. And they're all Jews. Idumean Jews. Uncomplicated."

"Pompey is complicated?"

"Pompey, Rome, the Seleucids he conquered and keeps around him as advisors, Jerusalem."

"Jerusalem?"

"Nicodemus was there. Aristobulus had the same idea.

Or maybe they found out we were going and needed to head us off."

"Did he bring additional . . . gifts?"

"Of course. To match our own from the looks of it. The Romans are getting rich, accepting presents and not making decisions. Who decided that that Rome was the judge of Jewish conflicts?"

"Apparently, we did," Cypros said. "When Aristobulus solicited Pompey's involvement to begin with."

"Well." Antipater sat up and looked at the curtain dividers before him. He stared at them as though he could see through them to some far-off place. "They've taken Macedonia and the Seleucid lands. The Parthians are on the run. Fleeing to places west of Rome. Even Spain, I hear. I guess Rome's sword makes them who they are."

"How did the negotiations go?"

"Negotiations." Antipater said the word as though considering not her question but the word itself. "A lot of talking. A lot of explaining our position: Hyrcanus's superior age and claim, Queen Salome's will, Maccabean precedent, and so on." Antipater snorted. "Nicodemus talked up Aristobulus's case: a lot about character and aptitude for leadership. I don't fully disagree with him. Aristobulus is probably the better leader."

"Antipater," Cypros said sharply.

"When they murdered Onias outside Jerusalem, Hyrcanus could have stopped it. But he was drunk. The Passover theft was not his idea—Malichos thought that up. But Hyrcanus went along with it quickly enough and was not even drinking at the time. I don't know if Malichos distributed the money or just kept it for himself."

Cypros sucked air in through her teeth. "The Passover theft was by Malichos? For his own treasury?"

"I don't know. I suspect so." Antipater turned, still sitting, elbows transferred to his knees. He found Cypros's eyes in the dim candlelight. "I genuinely don't know."

"So, then what?" Cypros asked. "Nicodemus won you over, and you gave up the mission in favour of Aristobulus?"

"No, no of course not," Antipater grumbled, looking back at the curtain as his eyes narrowed and mouth grew firm. "We reached an impasse. We managed to make Pompey curious to meet both brothers and see them in a room together and nothing more. We go back to Damascus again at the beginning of spring. With Hyrcanus this time."

"I'll go with you."

"No, you won't."

She moved closer to him. He responded. She put a hand on his chest when he leaned towards her.

"Yes, I will," she said. She kept her hand on his chest until he met her eye. She had more to say but restrained herself. She waited. She made him wait.

Finally, he nodded, and the candles flickered as they moved together again in the semi-darkness.

On a hillside overlooking the rain-streaked Plain of Jericho, Pninah and Salema sat huddled beneath an oiled sheepskin. The sheep around them continued to graze. The two shepherdesses had not spoken for some time. Each held a corner of the skin to keep it in place as they peered out at their charges while water ran over the rim, pooling at their bare feet.

"We'll have to shear the sheep alone again this spring," Salema said.

Pninah nodded.

"Do you think you can?" Salema asked. "Remember how to do it I mean."

Pninah nodded again. "I'll do my best."

A gust lifted their temporary shelter, and the two adjusted their grips and pulled the covering back in place. Salema adjusted her position to sit on the back edge of the skin and pin it behind them. Water droplets glistened on both of their faces.

"What about selling?" Pninah asked. "Do you think Ezra will come again this year?"

"He'll come. That's his business. He needs us the same way we need him."

Without Onias, one of them would have to walk to Jericho alone again while the other looked after the sheep. It would be another long day, there and back, carrying supplies and hoping for no trouble on the way. Salema still knew nothing about cities. *It will have to be me again,* Pninah thought. *I better not get sick on the way.*

The wind lifted their shelter again and they shuffled about, clutching at edges and recovering themselves.

"Don't you wish sometimes you could control at least one thing?" Salema asked. "Like make the wind stop."

Pninah put a hand on Salema's. "I gave up trying to control anything in my life years ago," she said. Salema squeezed her hand back but did not say anything.

The wind continued to blow.

The rain continued to fall.

The sheep continued to graze.

❧

As spring came upon them, Antipater left Raqmu once more to see the Romans. This time he took a much larger company, including Hyrcanus.

Cypros rode with them, not in a wagon with children but on a camel with the men. She brought one Nabataean maid along to assist her, but otherwise she was the only woman in the company. With her husband present, she did not need an escort of cousins.

When the shine of the Salt Sea appeared before them, she thought of the shepherdesses in the foothills.

*Could I explain any of this to you? Pompey? Schemes, foreign empires, plans to reclaim a throne?*

She shook her head.

*Would I even want to try?*

She smiled to herself. It was a sad smile. Shepherdesses did not know anything about how empires were started. Her Nabataean maid was probably just as simple.

# 36

## 63 BCE

AS BEFORE, THE caravan from Raqmu travelled along the eastern shore of the Salt Sea. As they approached its northern tip, Cypros watched Antipater closely. He engaged only with the men to his right. What remained of his brother perhaps still floated somewhere to his left, waiting for bones to finally separate and sink. He did not look west until they were long past the sea.

Cypros looked west often. She saw nothing but bright water and the far mountains that extended north into the shepherdesses' foothills. The caravan was too far from the place where the Jordan entered the sea to expect a view of anything disturbing. She had a mind to send someone to check whether the bodies on that plain had been properly buried, but it was not her caravan. She dared not broach the topic with Antipater.

Past the sea, they continued northwards on the eastern

side of the Jordan Valley, hugging the shadow of the Moab Mountains. In this way, they avoided any chance of encounter with Aristobulus's delegation.

She shared a tent at night with her maid. Antipater was not happy to have her or the maid along. They set up extra precautions for the women's tent, arranged special privacy measures for the women's bath, and allowed for more frequent stops. Cypros thought most of these efforts were unnecessary, but Antipater maintained a begrudging air of formality that would have amused her if not for the circumstances of the trip.

They travelled with the camels for two weeks. Antipater mostly rode at the head with Hyrcanus. He only came to visit her a few times over those two weeks. Each visit was at night. He would send the maid out of the tent but would not himself stay long. Their conversations were brief. He accepted her presence, took what pleasure he could from her, but was otherwise distant. She wondered how much influence she could wield in her birth city if this was their only preparation.

The sight of Damascus with its high gates and broad walls should have filled her with pleasure, but things had changed. The Romans had held the city for a year now and had already begun to leave their mark. Simply dealing with Roman soldiers and banners at the gates was enough to dampen her enthusiasm. The straight, wide thoroughfares were as she remembered them. The tall palms were where they always had been. Some things had not changed.

"I was born here," she said in a low voice to the maid. The young woman did not answer. Cypros had announced this fact many times already on this trip. Though Cypros registered the maid's silence, she knew she would probably announce it again.

Roman dignitaries had been expecting the caravan and led them to a complex that Cypros did not recognize. The outer courtyard could have accommodated the camels for several nights at least, but once the animals were unloaded, they were taken away. A housemaster introduced them to three cooks and then assigned each of them servants to show them to their respective rooms. Whoever lived here normally was nowhere to be seen.

Cypros found herself in a room with her Nabataean maid.

"No," she said after the door closed and she understood the arrangements. "Not even for one night."

She opened the door and looked down the hall where other Nabataeans and Jews were settling. The maid tried to stop her, but Cypros shrugged her off and went walking. Nabataeans and Jews alike stepped aside, alarmed at her striding down the hallway they shared. They were on the second floor here. She went down to the ground floor where the richer rooms would be.

"Who is in here?" she asked one of the startled servants standing outside a strong-looking door. The middle-aged man responded to her Nabataean in kind.

"The Jewish king," he said. "The guard is still inside."

Cypros was startled herself until she realized that the man meant Hyrcanus.

"Where is the Idumean leader?" she asked.

"The Jewish leader. Not the king?"

"Yes. The governor."

"Oh, you're his wife."

"Yes."

The man turned and gestured for her to follow. A few steps farther down the hall, the man turned and ceremoniously presented another closed door. "His guard is also inside."

Cypros reached for the door.

"Oh, no," the man said, putting a hand on the door.

Cypros stopped and looked at the man, trying to read him.

"He asked not to be disturbed," the man said.

"I'm sure he did."

Cypros pushed the door open, entered, and closed it behind her. Inside were two guards, as startled by her presence as her husband was. A slave woman finished pouring a jar into the small bath. Antipater was naked, about to get into the bath.

"Now go," Cypros said to the slave. She turned to the guards. "You as well. Stay outside the door if you must, but out of this room."

With the room cleared, she turned and found Antipater already in his bath. He was scooping hot water over himself with cupped hands.

"Pass me that cup, will you?" he asked.

She threw it at him and it bounced off his knuckles and clunked its way across the floor.

Antipater sighed and scooped more water onto his face.

Cypros walked up to the tub, and when she got there she struck him across one cheek. He flinched and jerked his head back and into the tub's stone rim.

"Hey," he protested and stood.

She struck out at him again, hitting him in the chest

before he could react, and then stepped away when he reached for her. She had his blood up, but not enough. He started forwards, stepping over the edge, and as he was in that awkward pose, she struck out again, knocking him backwards. He lost his balance and nearly fell over the tub's opposite edge.

She stunk from the camel and the day's travel. She wanted to make peace and share the bath or claim it for herself, but now was not the time.

Antipater braced himself and stepped out, eyes on her, anger in his face. He came at her then and she got one open-handed smack across his forehead before he caught her and flung her at the bed. She scrambled out from under him as he tried to get on top of her, smacking him again on the top of the head.

"Woman," he growled and caught her by an ankle as she tried to escape off the far side. He dragged her towards him, and she let him do so. He shifted his grip to her knee, but before he could pull her closer, she kicked with the other foot, driving it into his stomach. She did not hold back. He gasped and buckled over, and her reaction was so fast it surprised even her. She did not escape—she followed him. As he sucked in air, she threw herself at him, wrapped her arms and chest around his head and neck, and hauled him back down onto the bed. He was still trying to breathe when he caught her by one wrist and opened his eyes again. Rage burned there, and then the blade pressed against his throat and everything grew very quiet and still in the room. She straddled his chest, one hand at his throat, the other in his hair.

"You were going to leave me with the maid on the second floor?"

He lay silent beneath her except for his laboured breathing.

"Perhaps you had plans for your own bath maid?"

"Maybe just teach you a lesson." His voice was hoarse. "Women don't belong on this kind of trip."

She pressed a bit harder. As the blade's flat face sank in, flesh folded around either side. He knew its double-edged sharpness. Even if he had not known before, he could feel it now.

"Maybe it's you and Hyrcanus that don't belong here," she said. "This is my city. This is al-Qaum's city. You and Hyrcanus and your god had a year of merrymaking at Jerusalem with nothing to show for it but the murder of an innocent holy man and a Passover fraud. Then the both of you exited the city like schoolboys scolded by their tutor." She leaned in close to his face, maintaining the pressure on the blade. She knew her breath stank. "Your cowardice and inability to see ahead cost your brother his life."

She said it on purpose. There was no impulsiveness in her, no slip of the tongue. She pressed a bit more with the blade to be sure he remembered it was there and stared into his eyes and breathed on him and dared him to contradict her.

"You are going up against Pompey," she said. "He has taken Greece, Asia, the pirates in the sea, Syria, now Damascus. Before all that, he conquered countries north and west of Rome. Even Romans fear him. All the world fears Rome and Rome fears Pompey. You bribed him once and failed. You're going to try to bribe him again, with nothing but defeat to recommend you." She laughed in his face. She watched him flinch at her words and her breath. Water from his chest soaked through her clothes to her skin.

"What do you recommend?" he asked. He looked calm. Angry, but calm. His eyes flicked down once as though to try to see the knife or remind her that it was still at his throat. After a pause, he gently laid a hand on her knife-hand wrist and held it there, as though to keep her grip steady. Otherwise, he remained very still. And calm.

"I recommend that you get dressed. You get my maid moved down to the main floor, in an adjacent room. Then go for a walk and soak up a little of the atmosphere of this city you've never been to. When you come back, arrange for a private dinner in this room for you and me. We have plans to discuss."

"Hyrcanus and I have a dinner arranged with several of the leading Pharisees from Jerusalem."

"You tell Hyrcanus to meet with his Pharisees on his own. He can join us afterwards. The three of us will meet with his Pharisees all together in the morning."

"I can't tell a king—"

"You can tell *that man* anything you want, and you know it. His guards here are my people. His security is the security my uncle gives him. If we tell him to shut up or to meet with Jerusalemites on his own or to meet us or to not meet us, he will do exactly what we tell him." She leaned in close to his face again.

"Antipater." She never called him by name. Today she did. "Antipater, get this into your mind. We are not here to survive this negotiation. We are not here to get things back to normal. We are here to win something new, and that man will do what he's told or we'll abandon him and take Jerusalem ourselves. You can tell that man anything you damn well please. And you'd better be pleased to tell him what I tell you to tell him."

Antipater let go of her wrist. "I'd like to keep my hair and not lose it in patches," he said.

She let go of his hair and then backed off with the blade. She did not put it away, but she moved it away from his neck. His sombre tone told her all she needed to know.

She got off him.

"You'll be in the bath now, I presume," he said.

"Have one prepared for the maid as well," Cypros said. "On the ground floor."

She began undressing while he got dressed. "Then go for your walk."

# 37

## 63 BCE

CYPROS HAD ONLY ever seen Damascus's old agora from the outside. Children did not enter these pillared halls. The only thing Cypros remembered about it from her childhood was that her father had insisted that it was not an agora at all—even though everyone called it that.

The Romans had taken it over since their arrival the year before. Pompey held court each day at one end of the vast chamber, receiving delegations from Apamea, Cilicia, Chalcis, and even Egypt. No one knew why Egypt was meeting with the Romans at Damascus, but the agora, whatever its architectural status, had become an international crossroads.

The agora itself was a massive rectangle framed by great passageways. The passageways were lined by a double row of tall, Corinthian pillars that supported the stone and timber roof. Beyond this frame, on three sides, were many smaller connecting buildings that provided rooms for dining, private meetings, waiting areas for incoming delegations, guard assembly stations and the like. Only the front of the agora was free of surrounding buildings. From the front, the double row of pillars, the wide shaded passageways, and glimpses of the interior of the agora were all on public display.

The interior of the agora, however, was its heart. This was a vast, open space, two steps down from the surrounding pillared walkway. In various seasons it had served as a sheltered marketplace, a court, a collection of jewellers' shops, and even for a brief period as a place for al-Qaum worship.

Now, it was Pompey's room. The layout now was closest to that of a court. Pompey with his advisors and generals sat like judges at one end—judges who had meals brought to them and entertained themselves at times with private conversations or distractions while visiting delegations waited. In fact, behind Pompey was a collection of other Romans who seemed to have no part in these proceedings other than to occupy the space and quietly mingle amongst themselves.

Cypros moved between two pillars in one of the side hallways that looked down on the central court area. She paused, then moved again, looking for a place to see and hear better. Women were not usually a part of the proceedings in this place, but a latticework of wooden screens had been set up along this one side as an exception. Damascus had never been conquered by Romans before. All the rules were different now. Also, it seemed that Pompey liked women. There were rumours that he recruited new admirers from these public onlookers. Guards circulated in this women's viewing area, ensuring civility and peace. It was understood that the guards also offered private invitations to select women—exclusive receptions with the visiting general.

A Jewish woman stood near the screen, watching and listening to the opening remarks. Cypros approached her from behind and then stood a few steps to one side. She could see and hear better here. She did not recognize the other woman at first.

Before Pompey and his leading men stood Aristobulus with Nicodemus and the rest of his retinue. To Aristobulus's left were Hyrcanus, Antipater, and their joint Nabataean-Jewish delegation. Another group occupied Aristobulus's right, which Cypros at first took to be part of Aristobulus's party—making their representation twice the size of Hyrcanus's. It soon became clear, however, that they were a third party.

"Who are they?" she asked the woman with her at the screen. "The ones on the right?"

"Galileans," the woman said. "As well as Judeans and a few Itureans."

Cypros recognized the voice. "Shamirah?"

Aristobulus's wife turned and smiled.

"It seems that we are here not just to watch our husbands compete with each other," Shamirah said, "but also to watch them both compete against independent-minded Jews who don't want either of them on the throne."

"Do they have another king in mind?"

"They would take the Romans over a Hasmonean. But what they really want is for the high priest and the Sanhedrin to lead the country and for the Hasmonean line of kings to be abolished so they can get on with the rest of their lives."

The Independent Party had the floor. Their spokesperson was starting an impassioned speech that seemed like the beginning of a long tirade that would wind up saying exactly what Shamirah had just summarized.

"Your husband slaughtered six thousand of my people," Cypros whispered, "against the wishes of the Romans and any semblance of royal decency."

Shamirah laughed. It was not a loud laugh, and it was certainly neither jovial nor cruel. There was something wry and sad about the laugh. It conceded to Cypros's point.

"He took the throne from Hyrcanus by force," Shamirah said, her eyes focused past the screen. "He's named after the uncle that starved his own mother to death in order to claim that throne. If he keeps on the way he's going, my husband is going to get us killed or thrown into prison. Sometimes I think he's mad."

She turned and caught Cypros's eye again. "Idumea runs itself perfectly fine while your husband is away. But with Aristobulus present, Jerusalem is a tangle of betrayals, upheavals, muddled taxes, chaotically unclear protocols, jealousies, hatreds, changing priorities, and absolutely no clear future direction. Murdering Nabataeans was an afterthought. He could do it, so he did. I can assure you that he thought nothing about it the next day."

The words were brutal, but the voice speaking was resigned. Even kind, with a tinge of sadness.

"Your Hyrcanus is no better," Shamirah continued. "He might not be ambitious enough to initiate the next disaster, but he'll go along with whatever those around him want. The Pharisees can be as ruthless as the Sadducees. Take the crucifixions of the Ashtaroth priestesses. Execution would have been enough. He didn't have to torture them for days on end. Or the stoning of Onias. The Passover fraud. Passivity before violent allies or violence from the throne itself, take your pick. Salome's sons are both a disgrace."

Cypros opened her mouth to speak but found she had nothing to say. Salema's scornful remarks came to mind. The shepherd girl and the rebel king's queen appeared to think the same way.

"I'd take the side of the Galileans given the opportunity," Shamirah said. "How about you?"

"I'd put my husband on the throne."

Shamirah shifted her position, turning partially towards Cypros. She appeared to no longer be following the Independent Party's speech. "How would that work?" she asked. "He's Idumean. An Edomite with a new name."

"Idumeans are Jews."

"Well, not—" she started, but then she stopped herself.

"They converted two generations back," Cypros said.

It was Shamirah's turn to open her mouth but then not speak. She turned back to the screen and the speeches beyond it.

"Eretz-Israel run like Idumea," she said. "That would be an improvement."

A guard came and spoke quietly to Shamirah. Then he left.

"What was that about?" Cypros asked.

"I have a private reception with Pompey later this evening," Shamirah said.

"What kind of reception?"

"I wasn't sure before. But now I am."

❧

The next morning, Cypros met with not just Antipater but Hyrcanus and seven of the Sanhedrin from Jerusalem. They met in Cypros and Antipater's private room. It was a strange and unprecedented gathering. She had not needed to get rough with Antipater to force the meeting. She had explained it to him calmly the night before, and he had submitted to her direction.

"Aristobulus is going to bring up the bribes today," she said to the assembled men. "He's going to complain that he already paid Gabinius twenty-two thousand pounds of gold to secure his throne."

"That much?" Hyrcanus blurted out.

"And he paid Scaurus a second payment of about thirty thousand." The men of the Sanhedrin grew noticeably pale.

"The gift he brought this time is even richer," she said. "According to Shamirah—"

"Shamirah?"

Cypros could not tell if the would-be king was trying to assert himself by constantly interrupting or if he was merely leaning on his long-standing relationship with the Antipater household. "Yes, Shamirah," she said. "Your sister-in-law and I have been watching the proceedings, and she likes to talk. She let me know that their current payment to Pompey is valued at nearly forty thousand pounds. Of gold." She let that sink in. "It's only appropriate. If Pompey's men were paid twenty and thirty, Pompey should get forty."

"What do you recommend we do about this?" Antipater asked. It was a staged question.

"Don't offer any further bribes."

"Romans like to get paid," one the older members of

the Sanhedrin said. "No different than the Seleucids generations ago."

"Proceedings won't wrap up today," Cypros said. "Let them play out. In addition to complaining about payments already provided, Aristobulus will bring some of his younger men into court today. His aim is to counter the claims of the Galileans. He will try to show that the youth of Judea are behind him and that the Galileans are rebels that don't represent the nation. It won't play out the way he expects. I'm speaking with some of the women from the Galilean and Iturean contingent right after this. We have more in common than they currently know."

In Pompey's courtroom, Aristobulus and Nicodemus appeared to have forgotten their roles with respect to each other, as well as the nature of their judge. Nicodemus was not deferential to his chosen king, Aristobulus, and neither of them appeared to take Pompey very seriously. Pompey's small bulbous nose, small eyes, and tiny mouth gave him a harmless appearance. Perhaps that contributed to their chosen posture. Cypros admitted to herself that she would have found him believable as a wine steward but not a conquering general. Man against man, going by appearances alone, any ordinary Nabataean could have taken the Roman down a dozen times in one of their ceremonial games. In an alley or a desert wasteland, the man looked like the sort who would cower and whimper at unexpected noises. How Shamirah could go to him in private was not something Cypros cared to imagine.

In the agora, Pompey seemed to be focused on personal

comfort and amusement. Hard men surrounded him. The Romans were intimidating. Just not their general.

Aristobulus's and Nicodemus's parallel speeches waxed on about bribery, ethics, and fair dealing. They interspersed this content with remarks about Hyrcanus's lack of fitness for rule and other non-specific slanders. Why Nicodemus was talking at all was a mystery to Cypros. As the morning went on, Pompey's expression began to sour.

As the day dragged on, Aristobulus and Nicodemus continued to lecture the general and gradually Aristobulus's followers began to also talk among themselves. Occasionally one of them raised his voice to be heard over his peers. They seemed to be hosting their own hearing, presenting only their own arguments to themselves, with no one outside of their group following their additional lines of rhetoric. The lack of decorum was remarkable.

Whether Jerusalem's younger men were entering the spirit of the free-for-all that Aristobulus and Nicodemus were demonstrating or were merely bored did not ultimately matter. They wore purple, which Cyprus knew was an affront to Roman sensibilities. They had not merely combed their hair for this appearance but had oiled and mounded it up with waxes and cleverly placed clips as though they were embarking on a Dionysian festival procession. They wore jewellery and ornaments better suited to women—not in keeping with Jewish or Roman expectations for this kind of gathering. Everything about their approach was irreverent and perhaps in another context, intimidating. But it was not intimidating here. Bold chaos did not seem to rattle Rome.

Aristobulus's supporters stood in sharp contrast to the

modest clothing and manners of both the Jewish-Nabataean group and the Galilean-Iturean party.

"What about the Galileans?" Shamirah asked.

Cypros nodded at the group across the room. "They're coming around. They have no money for bribes anyway." She hesitated then. She wanted to speak further, but familiarity with Aristobulus's wife was still new. Nabataean aggressiveness overcame Idumean caution. "Your husband's supporters look like buffoons."

"Getting someone to posture as a buffoon is much easier when they already are buffoons. I did not even have to speak to them directly. When my husband's passions overrun him, it takes very little to give him new direction."

"How much longer will it take?" Cypros asked.

"Two days. He's got no patience for ceremony. He's already coming undone with all the formalities here. Your side and the Galileans will do best to just let Aristobulus and Nicodemus dominate the floor and ruin themselves in public."

Shamirah turned towards her. Cypros was reluctant to leave off watching the Aristobulus spectacle, but Shamirah had stopped speaking. When Cypros's eyes met Shamirah's, the temporary queen continued. "Pompey is not what he looks like. He's a conquering general and won't put up with the likes of my husband for long."

Cypros nodded.

"If things go the way I think they will, I need your assurances that you, your husband, Hyrcanus, even the Galileans, will remember me and my children."

"They know," Cypros said. "We will remember your loyalty to Queen Salome's wishes for Eretz-Israel."

～

Over the course of the next two days, the independent demands of the Galileans began to align with the reasonable and orderly proposals of Hyrcanus's party. With Hyrcanus backed by the neighbouring Nabataeans, the entire province of Idumea, and even prominent members of Jerusalem's Sanhedrin, Aristobulus with his pompous supporters and his chaotic, slanderous, and accusatory speeches began to look surrounded.

To everyone's surprise, however, at the end of the final day, Pompey announced that he would not come to an immediate decision. He intended instead to visit Petra. He wanted to see the fabled city of rock and meet with Aretas. He would decide on the Judean question in the summer or fall.

Shamirah nodded at this pronouncement.

"As you said," Cypros murmured. She was aware that Pompey was not travelling to Raqmu for merely a casual visit. Pompey had begun to assume that control of Eretz-Israel would come as a gift, one brother or the other vowing subservience to Rome and handing over even larger bribes for the privilege. Whichever brother came out on top, the Galileans would get at least part of what they wished for: they preferred Roman rule to Hasmonean.

According to Shamirah, Pompey's visit to Nabataea was now his immediate priority. It would be an invitation for the desert people to also bow their knee.

"He's the most successful military leader in Roman history," Shamirah said. "He told me that himself."

Cypros shook her head and pursed her lips.

"People already describe him as Rome's Alexander." Shamirah stopped speaking.

In the silence, Cypros felt compelled to look at her.

"'Pompey the Great' is what they're calling him," Shamirah said.

Later that evening, a hastily arranged meeting was held again in Antipater and Cypros's private room. Three Galileans and an Iturean were present this time along with Hyrcanus and his Sanhedrin allies.

"We've gotten nowhere," the Iturean said. "You or us. He's put off his decision, and now we have to wait another half-year or longer."

There was no proper protocol in this cramped assembly. All eyes turned to Cypros. She was the only one that each man had, at some point over the past week, personally spoken to. She was the only one with private access to Shamirah.

"Do nothing," Cypros said. "Aristobulus will leave tonight. He's taking all his armed men with him along with new recruits from the Jews in Damascus. They are all armed men and known in the city."

That caused a stir. She raised her hands and then lowered them, calling for silence.

"Just do nothing. This will not sit well with Pompey. He can be patient in a courtroom because he likes watching people make fools of themselves. He'll even provoke foolishness. It amuses him when he sees it in others. Insolence with armed men on the march, however, he will not abide."

"Where is Aristobulus going?" Hyrcanus asked.

"Alexandrium. He'll start with travelling westwards,

but it's a misdirection. He's going south to Alexandrium. Shamirah will let Pompey know."

"How can she get messages directly to Pompey?" one of the Galileans asked.

"I'm from Damascus," Cypros said. "I know the servant network here. Channels of communication have been arranged."

There was silence among the group of men in the small room. They watched her with questions in their eyes. Her eyes went around the room, meeting each man's gaze as though she were one of them. None looked away. None asked the question they all wanted an answer to.

"This has all played out as you said it would," the Iturean finally said.

Cypros looked at her husband. His eyes narrowed, but his mouth did not open.

"I want dinner, wine, and a bath," Hyrcanus said. "Not in that order. All at once would be preferred."

The men exited the small room, Antipater with them. They closed the door behind them.

Left alone, Cypros walked over to the empty stone bath and leaned against it. She rolled her hands into fists, then shook them out and wiped them against her robe. She looked towards the window and thought about Hanne, then Pninah and Salema.

She wanted her friends with her. But these young people could not be her friends. She wanted them anyway. Regardless of appearances or rank, they were who she wanted.

Shamirah came to her mind. An image of the woman in Pompey's bed made her shudder. She had no proof of it, but the woman somehow had access to the general and he listened to her.

According to status and roles, Shamirah was more suited to be her friend. But she did not want to know Shamirah when this was over. She wanted to know Hanne and the shepherdesses of the Jericho foothills.

# 38
## 63 BCE

WHEN POMPEY AND the Roman army left Damascus in pursuit of Aristobulus, Hyrcanus and Antipater rode with him. Cypros lingered in Damascus. As she rose the morning after Antipater's departure, she remembered her last conversation with him.

"I'll catch up with you at Alexandrium," she had said.

"You're confident that Aristobulus will dig in there?" Antipater asked.

"He tells his wife what she needs to know. Shamirah told me."

"Alright. I'll leave you fifty men and your maid."

"Appoint Kaiden as head of the fifty."

Antipater paused. "Why Kaiden?"

"I trust him to do what I tell him to do and not follow his own lead."

Antipater nodded. "The Jewish guards won't like it. A Nabataean in charge."

"Then leave me only Nabataeans."

"You're still Idumea's Governess. I'll leave Kaiden in charge. Will you bring Shamirah with you as well?"

"No, Aristobulus ordered her to round up others to join him at Alexandrium. She should at least pretend to follow his orders."

"Fine," Antipater said. "Follow a week behind us. No more. I don't want to be chasing around the country looking for you."

That was last night. Today was a day to tour Damascus. She had childhood places to revisit now that the bulk of the Romans were gone.

❧

As spring came, a properly modest sun and early blooms in the Jericho hills confirmed a new promise of peace. The punishment of the nation eased. The Maccabean brothers seemed to have set their grievances aside, although rumours abounded regarding Hyrcanus's whereabouts. Some said that the former king had abandoned Eretz-Israel and gone to live with gentiles. Others said he was dead, killed on the Jericho Plain, a murder that Aristobulus would not admit to. These and other theories made their way to the small farm overlooking the plain. They came by way of rare travellers who stopped for the respite of conversation and fresh water. There was no other source of news for the two shepherdesses.

Those who stopped by the farm never failed to carefully look Pninah and Salema over. The men had questions in their eyes that went unasked. So far, no one had caused trouble. Each had eventually moved on.

The two began to leave the farm early and stay out late. No one chased sheep across the hills just for conversation and a moment's rest.

They left at dawn most mornings, this one included. It was a lazy day and they did not travel far. One of the sheep had a bandaged leg from a tangle with a thornbush.

"I see someone," Pninah said, pointing with one hand back towards the farm.

Salema came up beside her. "A cart and donkey," Salema said.

"It looks like Ezra."

"Can't be him. It's too early for shearing. He knows that."

The pair stood still and watched. The flock spread out around them. The man at the farm began waving frantically at them. Behind his cart and donkey were two horses.

"A dust storm," Pninah said, pointing farther north, up the valley. The storm was low to the ground, and light flashed within it like lightning chasing across the ground instead of the sky.

"He's waving at us," Salema said. "I think it is Ezra."

The girl began to walk back to the farm, calling for the sheep to follow without consulting Pninah.

Pninah ran to catch up with her. "The pasture is still poor near the house," she said.

"It's Ezra," the girl said. "Something's wrong."

They made their way back to the farm, calling the sheep, hurrying along those reluctant to leave off the new grass.

When they got back to the farm, they ignored Ezra for

the first while. They ushered the sheep into their pen and closed the gate before giving him their attention.

"Good," Ezra said when they finished. Then he said something else in a language that Pninah did not understand, and two other men appeared from around the side of the house. They were strong men, not overly large but muscular, wearing armour on their chests and dressed in tan and red. They had swords at their sides. The red of their tunics matched the red on the horses' saddles and bridles.

The two strangers spoke to Ezra, again in the unknown language. Ezra kept checking in on Pninah as they talked, and he glanced at Salema as well before continuing with the soldiers.

After a few rounds between the men, the soldiers counted out a sum of money to Ezra, a small sum, and then the strangers went to the sheep pen.

"You can't go in there," Pninah said, but Ezra stepped in front of her and smiled.

"They're Romans, girl," the trader said. "They'll go wherever they like."

Salema had not moved since they had finished with the sheep and come up to Ezra. Her face wore a stunned, uncomprehending expression. Pninah went over to her and put an arm around her, pulling the girl in to her chest.

The soldiers looped a noose around each sheep's head and then connected the nooses to a final long rope. They led the sheep from the stall, and as they did so, Ezra turned to Pninah and whispered, "Don't say anything. They're Romans."

Pninah knew that with a call, she could get the sheep moving her way. As it was, they came out of the pen tangling their ropes and complaining to one another. Pninah felt a tear tracking down her face, and she wiped it away. She returned her arm to Salema, holding the girl to her, wanting to protect her from this brazen daylight theft. The Romans mounted their horses, and then one of the two spoke to Ezra again, still in that unknown language.

The two men talked back and forth, and then the Romans rode away. The sheep at first resisted, and then as their nooses snugged up, they were pulled down the slope towards the approaching storm of men, animals, and equipment that was the invading Roman army.

"What was that?" Pninah hissed at Ezra when the Romans were gone. She spoke as though somehow Salema, in her arms, would not be able to hear. "What just happened here?"

"The Romans have bought your flock," he said.

"We did not agree to sell our flock," Pninah said.

"They're Romans. You don't agree. They tell, and you submit."

"What do they want with our sheep?"

Ezra smiled, nearly laughed. "Look," he said, pointing at the ground cloud now flashing with armour and weaponry and the red of uniforms and rolled up banners. "Armies need to eat."

Ezra walked over to his donkey and unhitched the animal from the cart.

"What are you doing?" Pninah asked.

"I'm hungry," Ezra said. "I want something to eat as well. Make us something. I need to water my donkey. Later, we'll go down to the Roman camp around the time of the evening meal, and you'll get paid for your flock."

Pninah was dumbfounded. "Then what was. . .?" Her voice trailed off as she pointed to the place Ezra had been when he had received the coins from the Roman soldier.

Ezra laughed. "That was for me. You had a larger flock here than they had money for. I worked out a good deal for you." He smiled. "It's what I do. They may be Romans, but they understand how to barter. At least with someone careful at it."

The trader took a fistful of the reins near his donkey's mouth, a strangely controlling grip, and began to walk down the road in the direction the Romans had taken. There was a stream some distance that way. The man had no desire to carry water. He would lead the donkey to it.

"Get something out for a nice midday meal," he shouted over his shoulder. "We have something to celebrate."

Salema broke from Pninah and rushed silently into the house. Pninah watched her disappear into the shadows. She looked back to see Ezra still walking away, his strange grip still near the donkey's mouth. She could hear Salema already hard at work inside, emptying bins, pulling the bread down from the cooling shelf, splashing water into a jug. It was as though all her shock had evaporated. She thought only to provide the required hospitality.

They did not even know for what price the flock had been sold and how they would find the right people to collect payment from in that distant horde.

Pninah walked over to the house and looked in. The girl was not preparing a meal but emptying their stores into a strapped bag. "What are you doing?" Pninah asked.

Salema did not answer but took another similar bag to their beds and stuffed their blankets and a sheepskin into it. She tried to fit another into the bag, but it would not fit. She grabbed their two cloaks and threw one at Pninah.

"What are you doing?" Pninah asked again.

"Hurry," Salema said. "Before he comes back."

Pninah put a hand on Salema's arm to stop her frantic haste, but before she could get the girl to stop, Salema struck her arm hard. "I can't explain now. Just take your cloak and take the food bag. I'll take the other bag and the water jug. We go now. Run. I'll explain later."

Pninah rubbed her arm. The girl's tone and manner were alarming and sounded older than her years. Everything about her brooked no disagreement. Pninah believed that if she protested, the girl would grab her by the hair and drag her out of the house. As it was, she followed under her own power. Salema glanced to confirm that the old trader was still on his way to the creek and not looking back.

"Let's go," she said and began to half run across the farm in the opposite direction. They did not go over the top of the first hill. They skirted it, putting the swelling of the land between them and the house. In this way they continued, sticking as close to the low ground as they could. They weaved back and forth among the hills, always away from the farm, never giving a sign as to which route they might have taken.

"What's happening?" Pninah finally cried. She was exhausted, and the food bag was heavy. The girl's urgency had driven Pninah on without further argument, but she needed to drink and eat. "I'll be sick soon," she finally said. "I have to rest."

Salema stopped and looked at Pninah. "Okay. For a little while."

"What's happening?" Pninah asked again.

Salema sat down on the grass. Her face was pale despite all their running. She looked like someone who had cried herself dry, though Pninah was sure no tears had yet been shed.

"What's happening?" she asked again.

"The trader sold us to the Romans," Salema said.

"What?"

"I can speak Greek. My father taught me. The trader doesn't know who my father really was. He thinks we're ignorant sheep farmers."

"They talked Greek? The Romans and Ezra?"

Salema nodded. "The money was Ezra's commission. He showed them the farm. And us."

"Us?"

"The Romans like women and girls," Salema said. "They asked if I had a little brother as well. I don't know why. They hoped there were more of us. 'Two will have to do.' That's what one of them said."

"Do for what?"

Salema frowned at Pninah. "You don't know?"

Pninah thought of Anna in the Temple, saying something similar about Rachel. The words were different, but the tone was the same. Pninah did not trust her voice and instead shook her head in answer.

"It's in the Torah," Salema said. "There are lots of stories of—"

"I understand," Pninah said. "I just didn't . . . understand. Didn't make the connection."

Salema nodded. "I've had more time to think about it."

Pninah tried to remember what she knew about Ezra,

good or bad. She could not remember anything useful. He came around at the end of the shearing season to buy what they had to sell. She never remembered Onias offering a single opinion about the man. He had been someone that served a function in the countryside. That was all.

*Sold us,* Salema had said. Pninah looked at her, intending to ask the girl to confirm her wording, and then she saw that Salema was crying. Pninah leaned forwards and knelt, holding Salema while they both cried.

After a while, Pninah moved back and held Salema at arm's length, her hands on the girl's shoulders. The girl looked up and met her eyes.

"You understood what they were saying and said nothing. Kept even your ability to understand their language a secret."

Salema nodded. "When you took me and held me against you, that made it easier. I didn't have to control my face. I put every effort into listening and deciding what to do next."

"You're unbelievable," Pninah said. "You saved our lives."

"I think so."

"You got us food and blankets so we don't have to go back to the house where Ezra can find us."

"And money."

"And money?"

"I got it first in case we had to run too soon. It's at the bottom of your bag—it's what we have left from last year's fleece. It's not much, but it's some."

Pninah pulled the girl back into her arms and held her close. She looked at the slope of hills around her and realized that she was somewhat lost. "Do you know where we are?" she asked.

"Yes. We're going south, towards Qumran. We should keep going—he has a donkey. If he gets lucky and finds us, we'll have a hard time getting away from him."

"I wish we had one of those soldiers' swords," Pninah said.

Salema laughed. Not a belly laugh. Not a joyful laugh. Just a short laugh. "I have the small knife we use to cut fruit. It's in your bag as well. It's the second thing I grabbed, but it's at the bottom, so if we need it, just dump your bag out to get it."

# 39
## 63 BCE

THE SPRING SUNLIGHT in Cypros's childhood city made everything seem like the Jews' description of God's original garden. The ancient walls were a collage of subtle colour shifts: grey and white stones dusted with hints of red and puffs of powdery yellows and spots of brightness where green took root. The whitened street stones smoothed by a thousand steps likewise told an ageless tale of nations and languages passing through. Damascus was a crossroads.

Beauty here, however, was not just in the stones. The dominant yellow flowers of the region, both wild and cultivated, were accented by drifts of silk-petaled poppies. Red dominated. Even the dust motes that hung in the evening light were magical.

On the day they were to leave Damascus, the camels

were returned to them. Cypros did not inquire where they had been or who had cared for them.

The caravan took more than a week to work its way south to the Sea of Galilee, along its eastern shore, and across the Jordan River, where they arrived at a town called Bet Yerah and spent the night. A few days later they arrived at Alexandrium.

The Romans were gone.

Antipater waited with a small guard, impatient to be off.

"Where is everyone?" Cypros asked. She had yet to see the full Roman army. She had expected tens of thousands to be assembled on the plain and was keen to see the spectacle. The remnants of cookfires dotted the landscape, attesting to the recent Roman passage, but none of the men, animals, or equipment were in sight.

"Gone south," Antipater said. He was standing before a Jewish tent. Nabataeans had started to dismantle it as soon as she had arrived.

"Aristobulus wasn't here?"

Antipater helped her off the kneeling camel. "He was."

She stepped back, stretching one leg to ease the tension in her back. She looked up at her husband, indicating for him to continue.

"He was surprised that we found him so soon. He thinks Pompey has an augur who tracks him by the movements of birds."

"That's not how it works," Cypros said. She was glad to be back on the ground. She wanted to stretch more. A queasiness crept up on her. She did not want to expose either weakness before her husband or the men around her. "What happened?" she asked. "If he was here, why is everyone gone?"

"He came down and negotiated with Pompey. Then he went back to the fortress each night."

Cypros looked up at the cliff fortress that loomed over the plain.

"Why was he allowed to go back?"

Antipater shrugged. He looked over at the Nabataeans loading his camel. "He went back and forth to and from the fortress for several days. Pompey wanted to strike a deal, a bribe, to obtain assurance that Aristobulus's sudden departure from Damascus wasn't the start of a new rebellion."

"Rebellion? From Rome? We're not subjects yet."

"Yet." Antipater let the word hang between them.

It was hot. Antipater's men finished their work and then waited for the governor's attention. She wanted to rest. To sit down. To ease whatever was suddenly troubling her head and stomach.

"You let Aristobulus go back and forth to his fortress and somehow expected that to wear him out?" she asked. "After climbing the stairway every day for a week, he was supposed to get tired of it all and sign over Jerusalem to Hyrcanus and Pompey? Just give up? Defeated by a staircase?"

"Cypros."

"Why has everyone gone south? What happened?"

"It was pretty clear that Pompey wasn't going away. And I think Aristobulus expected reinforcements to come that never arrived."

"Shamirah did her part," Cypros said. "So what happened? Where is everybody?"

"Aristobulus just left. We think he's gone to Jerusalem,

so that's where everyone is headed. It looks like we're in for another Jerusalem siege now."

"He left? You let him leave? With all of his men?"

"They went out the back door."

"The back door?" Cypros looked up at the mountain fortress again.

"Or the front door, depending on which side you're coming from."

"You didn't put anyone on the plateau above the fortress?"

"No."

"You didn't tell Pompey that there was a plateau above the fortress? That it's faster to get to Jerusalem from the upper side of Alexandrium than it is from down here?"

"No."

"And I gather that Aristobulus had spare horses up top waiting."

"It appears so. We couldn't follow him from here. You're not getting horses or camels up those stairs. We have to go to Jericho and up through the canyon."

Cypros breathed in deeply and let it out slowly. "Pompey must think you're a fool."

"He may think that of Hyrcanus. I was not present for the meetings between Pompey and Hyrcanus. For the most part, Pompey conducted this work on his own. He had his mind on Petra. When Aristobulus left, Pompey flew into a rage, and I was called in to explain things."

"And he let you stay behind and wait for me?"

Antipater nodded. "They only left earlier this afternoon. I told him we'd catch up by tomorrow."

He started to walk over to his waiting camel, then

stopped, and turned back towards her. His hands moved about, adjusted the neckline of his tunic, rubbed one arm and then the other. He looked towards the rest of his company again, then back to her.

"Go," Cypros said. "I'm not travelling any farther today. I'm going to look at this fortress. I'll meet you at Jerusalem."

~

For the next four days, Cypros felt ill and stayed in her tent. Cramps and nausea consumed her. Dizziness came and went. The maid went in and out bringing water and a weak vegetable broth and carrying out her waste. Cypros drifted off to sleep easily and awoke slowly. She lay continually weak and heavy with sweat.

When asleep, she dreamed about Pninah and Salema. When awake, she tried to focus on Shamirah but decided that the woman would not be a friend to her in this illness. The temporary queen would abandon her, judging her to be a weak ally.

The illness made her think about family. She went through each of her cousins at Raqmu. At a time like this, they would leave her to the servants. They would go off laughing to tents some distance away in case what she had could be passed on. The desert was a hard place. It bred hard men. It created women who strove for laughter and turned away from avoidable sorrow. Or at least that was true of her relatives.

Jews were different. Jews seemed to be drawn to suffering. They distributed their pain as though it were a burden that could be shared.

She awoke at one point and misidentified her maid as

Hanne. She wondered if the women closest to her would always be slaves or servants. But Hanne was neither. She was a servant, but not a captive one. She was a Jew. A northern Jew. One of the Galileans. Hanne could leave Ashkelon at any time. Hanne chose to stay with Cypros and the children.

Cypros thought again about Pninah and Salema. They were a little over a day away. She would go there. They would care for her.

The Nabataeans and Jews were both glad to break camp. They left the Alexandrium fortress unexplored. Climbing the narrow cliff path now seemed pointless. Aristobulus was not there.

*My friends are in the Jericho hills. Not here. Not anywhere else.*

Her camel lurched to its feet and they set off. It was morning. She wondered how far the shepherdesses would have gone with the sheep in this early season. It was too early for shearing. The sheep would be fat with wool. She looked forward to seeing them again.

As the sun floated high overhead and heat filled the air, Cypros rode with her escort up to the old Onias farm. It was empty. The sheep were nowhere to be seen. The pen's gate stood open. The water troughs were dry. Fresh grass and weeds were starting to grow inside. The trampling and nibbling of the sheep should have allowed no such thing.

Cypros made her way over to the farmhouse. She had never been inside before. She found evidence inside of recent violence. Baskets were upended against the far wall along with both mattresses. The mattresses had been opened and straw littered the room. The bucket she recognized as their household water bucket was smashed, and the stone bowl she had seen from outside the house was cracked as though struck but without intent to completely demolish it. The crack, though incomplete, had ruined the bowl. There was no bedding.

She went out of the house and scanned the hillside again, but she could not see the sheep anywhere. She went back inside and found a black stain on one of the mattresses, which she took to be old blood. Outside, she scanned the hills once more, then looked across the valley at the Moabite mountains.

Moabites.

It was the only thing that made sense. Perhaps thieves from Jericho, but most likely Moabites.

*I left them here, alone.*

Onias had been killed because of her siege. Aristobulus's army had come through here because of her siege.

Maybe it had been Aristobulus's men.

She felt heat flood back into her face. She returned to the intimacy of the house. Once inside, tears broke through and tracked down her cheeks. Her eyes cast around looking for a sign, but a sign indicating what, she could not say. Pain boiled within, something deeper than the sickness she was climbing out of, something akin to childbirth, but not the birth of a living child. This was the pain of a stillbirth—raw and unrelenting and merciless inside her. Her nose ran. Her throat hurt. She wiped her face and tried to dry her eyes, but the pain in her stomach and chest rose up and sweat poured from her. When two short sobs burst forth, they surprised her.

The Nabataeans sat on their camels out in the yard and said nothing. Her maid waited for instructions. The Jewish horsemen waited some distance away. None had heard her outburst within the house.

*I'm sorry, my friends. I'm sorry.*

She could not say anything out loud. When she left the house for the last time, her face was dry. The camel groaned as she climbed back on it, the beast rising on knobby-kneed legs.

She was about to give orders when she realized men were missing. "Where's Kaiden?" A new hoarse quality had entered her voice, but she kept it steady.

They pointed uphill, behind her. Kaiden and three others were traversing the crest of the next hill.

Cypros quietly cleared her throat. She did not dare to speak again. Not yet. She looked around her, at the farm, the distant creek, the plain where she had camped the previous year. She saw a dabb lizard sunning itself on a rock of nearly the same dull grey colour. Her stomach was improving, but she was not hungry. She remembered craving dabb in previous years. From the corner of her eye, she could still see the cracked stone bowl in Onias's old house. Pain rose up again and gripped her throat from inside. She fought to control the water in her eyes and the trembling of her hands.

*Dabb is no substitute for friends.*

The thought made her nauseous. That this was her poetry, her expression of pain, her counterpoint to illustrate friendships lost, should have made her ashamed. She was aware that shame had little to do with her life. She felt something different than shame. She felt loss and hurt and anger—but she was also aware of an inability to properly grieve. Other responses were her trade tools. Action purged shame and smothered grief.

*I bury.*

But that was also not true. The Jews buried—and mourned. She did not bury. She had been at her best when she had left nine unburied in the desert, food for the birds.

No, that was not true either. She had been at her best when Antipater and Hyrcanus and Aretas had given up on Jerusalem and left their own people unburied on the Jericho Plain—when *she* had resurrected the vision for the conquest of Jerusalem. *She* had sent her husband to meet with Romans. *She* had sent her husband back, with Hyrcanus, to meet with Pompey a second time—and had gone with him this time to make sure they achieved their aim. She would not let the goal be buried.

She had not been at Alexandrium, and Aristobulus had escaped. The fault was hers for sentimentally lingering at Damascus. Jerusalem was her duty. No. Not her duty. Her art. Its conquest was al-Qaum's gift. His to her. Hers to him.

Kaiden rode up then and waited until she focused and nodded for him to speak. "There is no sign of them or the sheep," he said.

"They're gone," Cypros said. Her voice was cold and steady. No pain gripped her throat. The smoothness of her speech surprised her.

*This is what I was made for.*

"The Moabites," she said. "Or Aristobulus's men."

She said it with a flat tone that so surprised her she had to pause and picture what that interpretation implied.

She remembered herself in the desert. Neither Pninah nor Salema would have been able to defend themselves. Savagery against them would have been repeated. They both would have either died horribly or been taken as slaves. Emotion rose again, but only a little. Soon it would not rise at all. All she had to do was keep suppressing it, keep overrunning it with hard truths, keep burying it with cold facts, and like the dead babies at Ashkelon, they would go away. The Jewish practice of not naming children that did not survive was wisdom after all. Buried, without names, without graves to mark or mourn over, they went away. The hurt eased. The Jews shared pain, but not pointless pain. Sometimes they just cut the pain off and consciously forgot it.

*When there is nothing to learn, there is no point remembering.*

"Jerusalem," she said and pointed. Kaiden led the way. The company moved out.

Tension returned to her throat like a fist squeezing her windpipe. She did not look back at the farm. She rode the route that Onias had last travelled. Onias was something else she refused to think about.

# 40

## 63 BCE

PASSING ALONGSIDE THE western edge of the Dead Sea shore, Pninah stared at the white pillars that stood above the blue water. Some of the pillars drew up into ragged points. Others were topped by irregular caps, like a strange type of abrasive mushroom. In most cases, both types of pillars stood only a hand's width out of the water. A few stood twice that tall. They supported nothing.

"It's like there were docks here," Pninah said, pointing at the white formations. "The deck boards are gone, but the piers remain."

"It's just salt," Salema said. Her voice was sullen, her eyes hooded.

Pninah looked ahead. Qumran loomed in the distance, the outer walls gleaming white in the midday sun as though they too were made of salt.

When they came to the barred gate, there was no one

around. Men worked in the distance. Those farthest south laboured under what looked like a date palm grove, and those closer in worked in the water. They seemed to be raking the sea itself, moving water back and forth in long terraces that cut into the shoreline.

Pninah gestured, tired of trying to draw Salema into a conversation. They made their way towards the saltwater workers. When they arrived, the men stayed out in the water. The closest were only ankle-deep, drifts of salt covering their feet. The men looked at the two women, but none smiled and none spoke. Their eyes were not immodest but simply indifferent.

"The Romans have come to Jericho and the plain," she said.

"Tell them," one of the workers said, pointing down the shoreline to the date palm grove and the few buildings there. The men returned to their ceaseless saltwater hoeing or raking; she could not tell which, nor for what purpose.

She and Salema walked on, following a path in the hard rock even though there was little vegetation about and no reason to choose one route over another. Countless feet over countless centuries had worn a common trail in the soft stone, and they followed that route for no conscious reason.

At the grove, Pninah approached a man who backed away from her as though she were diseased and not merely sweat covered and tired. She gave him the same report about the Romans.

The man stood looking at her for some time. He did not gaze at her the way men in Jerusalem or travellers visiting the isolated farm had. These men merely looked, as though at an inscription they had yet to comprehend.

"Manoach," he finally called, waving to get the attention of a man standing below one of the palms. Only now did Pninah notice that the men were all dressed the same. They wore white robes that brushed the ground. Everything here, it seemed, was the colour of salt.

A tall man separated himself from the others and approached. White streaked his hair and beard, and lines creased his face and neck, but he was not old. He seemed strong and healthy. He looked to Pninah like a man who had spent too many years, perhaps decades, in this Qumran sun. She judged that he had seen and done and endured more than most. There was a kindness in his eyes that Pninah had concluded long ago was only found in those who had overcome great sorrow. Anna had that look. Anna was not sun darkened, and her hands were not heavy and grooved like this man's, but her eyes and face were the same. They reminded her of Onias.

The Qumran priest came and stood before them, looked at Salema, then at Pninah, and nodded. He had not said anything yet, but Pninah felt like he had asked her to speak.

"The Romans have come," she said for a third time. "They're in the plain between Jericho and the mountains now. I don't know if they are coming this way or if they're going to take the Jerusalem Road."

Manoach continued to hold her eyes, and then, after a while, he nodded as though she should continue.

"They took our farm," she said. "They stole our sheep. They were going to take us as slaves, but we escaped."

A hint of an expression flickered in his eyes and moved his mouth the slightest degree, but he still said nothing. He looked over at his companion, who shrugged.

"We don't have any family," Pninah continued. "Mine died years ago, and her father took me in. The Pharisees at Jerusalem, during the siege, murdered him. Stoned him."

Manoach turned his attention to Salema, and though he did not touch her, she seemed to sense his attention and lifted her head and eyes to him. "Onias," she said. "My father was Onias."

This time there was an expression: a squinting of his eyes, a flattening of his mouth. "Stay here," he said.

He went back to the other white-robed men and spoke to a couple of them, and then two of them set off towards the white-walled compound. Manoach stayed among the palms, talking to others there, circulating as he passed on news of the Romans or their visitors or other matters altogether. Occasionally he looked back at the women as though to make sure they were staying put, and then he continued his discourse with his fellow white-robed work-ers. None of the men followed his gaze to inspect either Pninah or Salema.

The two men who had gone running to the compound eventually returned, carrying several baskets and water skins.

Manoach brought the runners and their goods in front of Pninah and Salema. He stayed several body lengths away from them and reached out a hand. "Open your bags," he said. "Show me what you have."

Pninah unslung her pack, as did Salema. Pninah stepped as though to hand her pack to the priest, but he put up his hand and waved her back.

"No, there," he said. "Open your bags there."

Pninah did so uncertainly and began removing the food

items, spreading them out on the sand. She did not expose the money or the knife.

"Now you," Manoach said to Salema.

She complied, spreading out the blankets, the one sheepskin, and the water jar.

Manoach studied the items laid out, and once satisfied, he nodded.

He began sorting items from the baskets, transferring some things into one basket and others into its opposite. When he had the new mix he wanted, he lifted the one basket and brought it over and set it in front of Pninah along with three full water skins. Then he went back to his previous place and crouched down.

"You need what's in the basket," he said. "Bread. Cured meat. It will carry you far and supplement your nuts and fruits. The dates are from this grove, last year's harvest and well dried." He gestured for Pninah to begin reloading.

"The water jar is too heavy," he said to Salema. "Take one skin. Your protector can carry the other two. Leave the jar here. You're too young for such a heavy load." He looked at Pninah after he said this, and while her ears heard a rebuke, there was nothing in his face to suggest such. His face seemed to be regarding her kindly and wishing her strength.

"I can carry what remains," Pninah said.

The man nodded. "Rest over there," Manoach said, pointing to a shady place a bit farther south. "You cannot come into the compound, nor these buildings nor the tents outside the compound. You cannot touch or interact with any of the men here. We are all servants in this place, and we have taken vows. You cannot stay here, but you can rest over there. Stay the night if you wish, but you cannot stay here longer."

"Where can we go?" Pninah asked.

"Do you know how to pray?" Manoach asked.

"We say the Shema every morning and night," Pninah said, and his expression gratified her. He was pleased. It was not the duty of a woman to say the Shema every morning and night, but it was allowed. "And her father taught us to say other prayers."

"Good. Say them all—especially the thanksgiving ones. And then go south. There is a settlement at Ein Gedi that might take you in, but I would advise that you keep going south. If you make it as far as the Petra-Beersheba Road, then you should turn towards the Great Sea, to the west, and go to Beersheba. Do you have people anywhere?"

"No," Pninah said.

"Then stay in Beersheba, unless you find a village along the way that makes you welcome."

"What's special about Beersheba?" Pninah asked.

Manoach smiled, his first full expression of any kind. "It's where Abraham dug a great well and later Isaac dug another," Manoach said. "It's a special place for someone who knows how to say the Shema."

"Is it still in Eretz-Israel?"

Manoach frowned. "I don't know. I've been here a long time. It's Idumean or Nabataean now. Sometimes, perhaps both. Today, I don't know who it acknowledges as master. Regardless, it is still Beersheba. All of Eretz-Israel lies north of it, and the Negev desert lies to the south. If you stay here the night, then leave before dawn. The sun between here and Ein Gedi is without mercy. There is little shade. It will take you more than one day to get to Ein Gedi, so find shade in the hottest part of the day and travel early and late."

"What if the Romans come this way?" Pninah asked.

"Staying here won't help you. We don't have weapons. We are not like those of Jerusalem." He said this last bit looking at Salema, then turned his attention back to Pninah. "If the Romans do come south, then just hide. You cannot outrun them, but two such as you could find a place among the rocks. Climb into a hollow and just wait for them to pass. You can do that."

# 41

## 63 BCE

THE PROGRESS OF Cypros's joint Nabataean-Jewish guard through the canyon to Jerusalem was slowed and swelled by a congestion of traffic that followed in the Roman wake. Boys on donkeys and men leading mule-drawn wagons were crowded round about by men, women, even full families on foot come to participate in the spectacle of Rome's conquest of Jerusalem. There were celebrants in this crowd and theatrical mourners, angry fathers, and loud boys. It seemed to Cypros that all the women here—mothers and grandmothers alike—were drunk. Some were haggard with drink, some serene, some laughing as riotously as the donkey-riding boys, and some sullen and plodding in the heat. This was not a pilgrimage to one of Jerusalem's holy festivals. This was something feral, something poisoned, something akin to the feasts of the desert's great black birds. This was the mob that had stoned Onias. Or one like it.

Riding high above the slow crowd, above even the few on horseback, Cypros understood that all human populations were never far from this kind of greedy madness for change, for spectacle, for violent resolution regardless of potential outcomes. The world was not wise. The world left good people like Pninah and Salema naked and ruined in the Jericho foothills and moved on, like vultures in search of new spoils.

*It's all entertainment. Even the lives of others are just entertainment.*

The world needed to be commanded, its baser impulses reined in. It needed to be ruled.

Cypros considered what she might find when she came to Jerusalem and concluded that Roman rule might be the answer after all. There was something amoral about the Roman Republic. It had a reputation for demanding only the stability of Rome. All else was secondary. It absorbed its enemies' gods as though they could be co-opted with bribes. Al-Qaum, properly positioned, might gain a temple on Capitoline Hill—an honour for al-Qaum in exchange for the submission of Nabataea. Her desert people would be elevated by acceptance into the Roman family. Her Nabataea would also be lowered by bowing to Rome. Both outcomes would be simultaneously true. Above either of these truths, however, would be the promise of Roman law—a check on the madness of mobs.

From what she understood, Rome could endure many things, but there were two things it would not stand for, regardless of the cost. Defeat was the first, disorder the second. Rome had lost many battles over the centuries, but it would never accept defeat. It kept coming back. It ruthlessly wore its enemies down regardless of the cost in money or lives or prestige. It might emerge from a war in rags, but it would emerge.

Likewise, they disavowed disorder. If there was an unforgivable crime in the Roman world, it was disorder. Corruption, injustice, even economic failure were permitted. But if any of these led to disorder, to dissatisfaction with Rome's rule, to even a hint of insurrection, death was not an excessive remedy.

This crowd walked the road from Jericho to Jerusalem to witness Rome's work, but Rome would not respect this crowd. The western republic had business to conduct in Eretz-Israel's capital.

Cypros had every reason to believe that Rome's business in Jerusalem would change Eretz-Israel's fate forever. The process of that business was as much a war machine as the stone launchers they hauled along with them. Onlookers were simply insects observing a plow horse's labour. If they got in the way, they would be stepped on. Rome would not even notice.

At Jerusalem, Cypros made a quick decision and directed her caravan away from the crowds and towards Phalion's residence. It was in the Upper City, within the city's walls. Having been betrayed once by the keepers of the city's gates, Aristobulus's force had gone straight to the Citadel-Temple complex to await the Romans. The rest of the city had been left open for occupation.

Antipater's brother, Phalion, was dead on the Jericho Plain or washed down to the Salt Sea. His family had been slipped out of Eretz-Israel to Alexandria, Egypt. Cypros decided to occupy the Phalion family residence.

The Nabataean-Jewish caravan descended on the residence not simply like a throng of dusty adventurers looking for lodging but with the arrogant air of invaders come to claim a conquest. Cypros recognized some of the servants and sent them to prepare a bath for her. Others she directed to find and fetch Antipater wherever in the city he might be found.

"Go talk to people," she said to Kaiden. "Find out what you can. I want the basics sorted out before Antipater comes."

"I'm Nabataean," he said.

She stared at him.

"This is Jerusalem," he added.

Cypros stared at him a moment longer, then signalled to one of the heads of the house servants. "What is your name?" she asked.

"They call me ben Aviel," the man said.

"I don't care who your father was. What is your name?"

"Also Aviel."

"Go with this man." She gestured towards Kaiden. "He has questions for Jewish ears. Make sure he gets answers."

The man nodded. The unlikely pair exited the courtyard together on foot.

Another servant approached, and Cypros waved her over. "The bath."

"It is ready," the woman said.

"Then take me to it."

❧

Antipater came late in the day. "I can't stay long," he said. "We have another conference with Pompey when it gets dark."

With a gesture, Cypros directed him to sit opposite her. They were in the private room that had once belonged to Phalion and his wife. Antipater knew nothing of her visit to the shepherdesses' farm, and so he asked nothing about it. He looked tired and distracted.

"I don't want this siege taking up another year of our lives," she said.

Antipater sighed. "That's all very well—" he started.

"Fill up the canyon. You can't conduct a war over a destroyed bridge or from the bottom of the valley. The Tyropoeon Valley needs to become a flat thoroughfare. Then Rome can march right up to the gates and climb over them or smash them down."

"Cypros," he started.

"They have elephants, don't they?"

"Yes, but—"

"Then just get it done. By midsummer at the latest. I want to be back in Ashkelon by early fall."

"Cypros."

She arched an eyebrow at him and waited. Her debrief with Kaiden had been thorough. Aviel had participated and been an additional source of good information.

"We tried that already," Antipater said. "Pompey launched rocks at the Temple while his men tried to fill in the valley, but Aristobulus's archers and slingers kept picking the Roman labourers off. We tried using Jewish labourers, and they killed Jews just as happily as Romans. The valley is deep, but it's not very wide. They can reach us."

She stared at him and did not speak.

"Listen," he continued. "Pompey is probably as ambitious and impatient as you are, but he's not keen on losing hundreds of men every day. They fall into the valley. Nobody can drag them out without risking their own lives, which means they're starting to stink already. That stink reflects on Pompey."

She stared at him longer and still did not speak.

"You're not being reasonable, Cypros." He frowned and rubbed his flat forehead with the heels of both hands, then looked at her again. "Sieges can take months. Even years. That's how these things work. Aristobulus has already been besieged here once—he's made whatever preparations are required to withstand a longer siege this time. He might be impulsive, but he does learn."

She continued to just stare at him.

"Listen, the valley is a good idea. But sending men to die while hauling stones and dirt would lead to a revolt within the legions. Rome doesn't do revolts. They'll starve Aristobulus out happily enough. Don't worry—they'll get the job done. We'll get what we want in the end, but we need to keep the legions happy while we're at it."

"With no credit to us whatsoever," Cypros said.

It was Antipater's turn to stare.

"We either create something that makes Rome happy and successful, that saves face," she said, "or we stand back and let them grind out an eventual win entirely to the credit of Rome's stubborn determination. Where is our leverage then?"

Antipater looked around the room as though to confirm that there were no other witnesses to this conversation.

"Well," he said. His voice was quieter now. His eyes bore a hungry look. "What do you suggest?"

"Pompey wants the valley filled in. With the valley filled in, he can assault the walls at will."

"Yes, but—"

"And you agree that the valley can be filled in. You're okay with that plan, if we could make it happen."

"Well, sure. In fact, it would make a grand statement. It would make better use of Jerusalem's space. The valley is an eyesore, a lair for bandits, right under the shadow of the Temple itself. If someone could get rid of it, what a mark that would be for a new kingship."

For a moment, Cypros thought of Pninah. The shepherdess had spoken fondly of the valley. She had talked about how its tree-shaded coolness had provided respite from the heated stones of the Upper and Lower City. She had spoken about the quiet down in the valley, even during the festival seasons, how the crowds could be seen crossing the Zion Bridge, but she had been sheltered down in the valley from the noise and bustle and chaos. The valley had been her sanctuary. "I'll take you there one day," had been her promise.

*You can't take me there now.* Cypros imagined explaining herself to her friend. *So I'm going to get rid of it. The Romans can have it. I'm going to make something new out of Jerusalem. For you. In memory of you.*

She realized that this imagined conversation was contrary to burying painful memories. Hurt welled up within. She quickly stuffed it back down. She needed to be about the business of resolution and not justification.

"You've got nothing," Antipater said. He looked like he was going to stand up.

"What is the law about war on the Sabbath?" Cypros asked.

He stopped and stared at her again. He settled himself. "Defensive only."

"How close can you get to the valley's edge without drawing slingers or arrows?"

Antipater stared at her for a moment before answering. "If we're motivated, we can get right up to it. We can raise shields to protect our men. But you can't work in the valley itself that way. Or even at its edge."

"But you can get fairly close to the valley, even during the hostilities, without getting struck."

Antipater thought about that for a moment. Then he spoke. "Maybe a few casualties, but fairly close. Why?"

"Pompey has elephants?"

"Yes."

"Plenty of horses? Mules? We can recruit others?"

"Yes."

"Men? Slaves, I mean. Soldiers as well."

"Of course."

"You can supply Idumeans and mercenaries from the loyal fortresses."

"Okay, Cypros—"

He stood up to continue his protest, but she waved him quiet and to sit down again. "For six days, you raze Jerusalem and the surrounding areas for stone, wood, rubble of any kind," she said. "Make your own rubble. Take down Aristobulus's old house. His entire block. Some of the old walls that don't make sense anymore. Use the Romans to level the areas you want to rebuild later according to your own designs."

"Cypros."

"When we get the boys back from Raqmu, I want you to use Herod to help think through new street layouts and districts."

He did not interrupt her but stared at her. His eyes suggested that he was beginning to think she was crazy and he looked like he was going to stand up again.

"You do that for six days. Make mountains as high as you can in front of the valley. The whole valley. I want the whole thing levelled. Sell it to Pompey. Not just one path for his army but the whole valley."

He continued to stare at her, but his expression grew calm. His shoulders relaxed.

"Then on the Sabbath, the Romans are to lay down arms. I don't want a single sword or shield or bow or even a sling in sight. Nowhere around. On the Sabbath, they fill in the valley. I want torches lit. As soon as three stars appear at dusk and mark the beginning of Sabbath, the labourers begin working. They can work through the night and into the day until Sabbath ends at the following dusk. Work in shifts. I want six days of mountain building and one day of dumping it into the valley."

She held his gaze as he processed her plan.

"Have you got it?" she asked.

He nodded.

"Aristobulus cannot initiate any fighting on the Sabbath, right?"

He nodded again.

"Then you do it again. Six days of demolition and hauling. One day of filling in the valley. And again. And again. Like a waterwheel. Like a shipbuilding operation. Methodical. Like the way Romans do things."

"Blessed of God," Antipater breathed out.

"You tell this to Pompey yourself," she said. "This does not get translated through or credited to Hyrcanus. This is your contribution. To Rome's glory."

# 42

## 63 BCE

CYPROS DID NOT return to the area around the Temple Mount until after the Romans had left Jerusalem. Horses, mules, men, equipment—even elephants—vacated the city. Then she called for Kaiden and arranged for a tour.

Antipater accompanied her. Kaiden led the convoy. Antipater merely provided supporting commentary.

Where the Tyropoeon Valley had been, a great scar lay, like a crescent moon cupping the walls of the Temple and Citadel complex. The ground was still rugged and uneven, but it was new ground now. Buildings could arise here. Large sections of the rest of the city had also been unevenly levelled. The walls and buildings that had overlooked the valley were now the valley's fill. Most Sadducean houses and neighbourhoods had been targeted, but not every-thing about the Roman occupation had been carefully calculated. Parts of the market were gone, as were other important buildings.

Stone launchers had scarred the Temple walls. Two sections were broken where the two breaches had occurred. Some of the pillars within the Temple were damaged, as was tile work throughout the complex.

"This all needs to be repaired before Sukkot," she said. "Most of it at least."

Antipater nodded.

"At Hyrcanus's expense."

Antipater opened his mouth, but when she stared at him, he closed it.

There were black stains within the Temple complex. The blood of men. Priests. She did not need to tell anyone to clean it. They had tried. The old grouting would have to come up along with the damaged tiles. There was no cleaning this kind of stain.

The Roman breach of the Temple had been more than an orderly military victory. The legions became their own mob for that one day. Pompey himself had succumbed to the spirit that had swept the Temple Mount. He had walked in the blood of priests to enter not only the Court of Gentiles but also the Court of Women, then that of Israel and then even farther into the Holy of Holies.

He had backtracked the next day. He had ordered repairs to commence, commanded the surviving priests to begin the work of cleansing the Temple of this gentile trampling, and left the Temple's treasury unmolested. But the damage had been done. He had violated the sanctuary. It was a miscalculation that Cypros would like to have prevented. She had not been there when it had happened.

The Jewish public would not openly turn on the Romans for this sacrilege; the legions were too powerful. But they would take the tales home with them to Jericho and Galilee and Iturea and even Idumea. Roman ruthlessness would be remembered more than Roman victory.

After the tour, Cypros went for a walk in an olive grove outside Jerusalem. She saw an old man there under one of the trees. He had a great cloth laid out on the ground and two young boys with him. The man grabbed one of the lower limbs of the tree and threw his weight into it, shaking the tree as best he could. A great deal of effort was expended, with little result. A few olives fell onto the cloth. There was some discussion with the boys, and then the old man gestured and one of the boys ran and got him the indicated long pole.

The old man worked the pole between a couple of branches, talking and gesturing as he did so. The boys followed the pole's course. The man then wiggled his end of the long pole, using a lower, heavier limb as a fulcrum, and shook the upper branches violently until olives rained down onto the cloth and the boys.

Cypros had not been able to hear the old man's words, but she heard his laugh. It sounded toothless. It sounded like the way she imagined Onias would have laughed. In her imagination, the old man became Onias and the two boys his daughters.

Emotion surfaced again within her, but this time she did not supress it. She had won. Jerusalem was hers, or as close to hers as it ever would be. The Romans would grant no one the kingship. Pompey had given Hyrcanus the high priesthood but not the throne. He had left the throne vacant.

Instead, he had given Antipater administrative power over Judea as well as the provinces of Idumea, Samaria, and most of Galilee and Iturea. It was not the kingship, but it was close. Antipater's area of control did not cover all of Eretz-Israel either. Pompey formed a new province out of parts of Galilee and Iturea and gave its administration to his delegate in Syria. Along the coast, cities such as Gaza, Joppa, Dora, and Strato's Tower were attached to this new province. Only Ashkelon was left to the Idumeans out of respect for Antipater.

Inland, Pompey had other innovations to inflict upon the land. Scythopolis was made independent of both Eretz-Israel and the new Syrian province. So were Hippos, Samaria City, and a few other places populated by people from the Independent Party. They would still owe Rome both loyalty and taxes, but they would be subject to neither Jerusalem nor Syria. Pompey had divided a nation to ensure its order.

Antipater was happy with what amounted to a reduced kingship. It was a kingship without a crown over a country missing many of its parts. But it was four times the size of the governorship of Idumea, and it controlled Jerusalem and the Sanhedrin.

If she squinted and imagined creatively, it was all she had hoped for, plus a blood strewn, broken Temple, thousands killed in the siege, thousands taken into slavery overseas, freshly razed neighbourhoods, a new arcing wasteland scarring the middle of the city where a valley once lay, and a newly imposed debt required to reimburse Rome for its invasion.

All because two brothers could not get along.

She wondered if that was true. She wondered if allowing Aristobulus to escape to Egypt might have created a different result. If she and Antipater had backed the younger brother, if Nabataea and Egypt had joined forces to push back Pompey's invasion, could they have succeeded? If they had, what would have come of it? Knowing the Romans, it would have taken at least ten years of fighting to create a wall that the Romans would not cross. Perhaps longer. The Gauls had been resisting Rome for a century or more now, had even sacked Rome itself once, but still the Romans would not relent. Gaul was still trying what Eretz-Israel had not.

Instead of going the way of Gaul, Eretz-Israel had turned on itself and handed the crown to Pompey. An Idumean and a Nabataean governed the country now, at the pleasure of a Roman general. Rome itself did not even know of the victory yet.

Cypros thought practically about where things stood. She had betrayed Eretz-Israel for Jerusalem. She had abandoned Raqmu for the same cause.

Two months before the Temple had fallen, she had sent Kaiden to Raqmu along with a large Jewish contingent. They had collected Cypros's children and Hyrcanus's family, along with Hanne, the tutor, and others of their retinue, and had brought them to Ashkelon. Her uncle was on his own now. Whether he believed that he had been betrayed or not, she did not know.

She watched the old olive farmer teach his boys how

to harvest trees that were hundreds of years old. Some were perhaps from the time of King David. Some had witnessed Solomon pass beneath their limbs. Hezekiah as well. Certainly the prophets: Isaiah, Jeremiah, Ezekiel, Daniel. Others.

The old man worked in a long line of noble men who grew olives and made oil and did good within Eretz-Israel. He and his boys would buckle before the taxes that were coming. But he would not break. A thousand years from now, his grove would persist. Men would still harvest these trees in the same way, for the same reason. Perhaps it would be all Rome then. Or perhaps there would be no Rome left, just like the diminished Babylonian Empire. Perhaps it would be all Nabataea then, with no memory of the Jewish Temple at all. Regardless, the olive grove would be there. Olive oil would still flow.

Cypros looked back at the remnants of the city. It would get rebuilt. Antipater would pull their boys into the rebuilding plans. Other people's livelihoods and homes would be her children's education. Then the boys would go the way of the old prophets and the Babylonians and everyone else. But the olive farmer's line and profession would persist. Whatever her sons built would eventually fall. The olive farmer's art would not.

Raqmu's stone city came to mind, and she knew that unlike most nations of the world, the Nabataean city would last forever. That city would outlast even Egypt's pyramids, for the city was the mountain itself.

*But what I have done won't last.*

Pninah and Salema sat heavy in her heart. She could not remember any other moment in her life that felt as simple and deep and pure as sitting in sunlight while the sheep grazed around her and her friends talked. There was no refreshment as clean as the spring water Salema drew. There was no sound more pleasant than the shepherdesses' chatter and bright smiles—smiles that could be heard in their voices.

Onias had been like the old olive-grove farmer. He should always be here. Not stoned before walls that were now half-destroyed, but with his girls in the hills outside Jericho. Calling the sheep by name. Saying his Jewish prayers at dawn and dusk the way she paid homage to al-Qaum. This land needed him.

She wiped her face. She was ashamed of herself. This served no purpose. It was like digging up those Ashkelon babies to give them names. It was like collecting the bones of Ashkelon's priestesses to apologize for the barbarity of crucifixion. She did not know anything about the Ashkelon temple. She did not know anything about her buried children. She did not know anything about the fate of the shepherdesses, stolen and missing from the land. She only knew that she had the tattered remains of Eretz-Israel in her grasp along with something resembling the Jewish throne. In trade, she had lost her friends, and her uncle now faced Scaurus and Roman legions.

She hoped Aretas had someone like her to counsel him and not someone like her to betray him.

"Al-Qaum's greatest curse is to give a man everything he wants," her father had once told her. "Al-Qaum's blessing, by contrast, is for caravans to face sandstorms, heat, and the unexpected drying of an oasis. Because if caravans get everything they want, they grow weak and slow and soft."

She remembered her father's lesson and understood it. But she could not act upon it. There had to be something more in this victory, in this disaster, but she did not know what it was.

That evening, in Phalion's home, she spoke to Antipater without looking at him.

"I'm going to Ashkelon tomorrow. I want someone sent to Alexandria to fetch Phalion's family."

Antipater did not answer her. Silence had become his sign of agreement.

# 43

## 63 BCE

A T EIN GEDI, Pninah climbed past a sharp-edged rock, out of the shade afforded by the proliferation of short palms and vines below. She hurried, hearing herself pant, feeling her heart race, trying to lose her pursuer. She stepped carefully past a narrow area where a fall would kill. This was a good path for the local ibex or goats, not people. At the end of this narrow section, the trail broke to the right, descending again, but she turned left, climbing upwards into the rocks until she found the entrance to a cave partially obscured by the straggly fronds of a palm growing against the mountainside. She slipped inside the cave. She stayed quiet, straining to hear footsteps over the pulse pounding in her ears. Eventually, they came—deliberate steps that moved confidently over rock.

Pninah closed her eyes when the footsteps approached the turning point, willing her pursuer to descend at the curve in the path. That person did not descend. There was a moment of silence, and then a scrape that seemed closer, then another step and small tumble of stones, and then confident feet making their way towards the cave.

The palm fronds parted, and Pninah screamed, and Salema screamed, and then they both fell to laughing. Salema tickled her prey, and Pninah tried to push back into the shallow cave, but the stone let her go no farther.

Salema stopped her torment, and the two sat there in the dim light, panting and smiling. Pninah's hair had come free, and she pushed it back, tucking it away in a barely adequate manner.

After a rest, the two came out of the cave and made their way back down to the trail. They took the descending path to the falling stream and the pools that lay there.

"It's beautiful here," Salema said, "but we can't live in caves in the winter."

They took each other's hand, helping one another down the final big drops.

Their welcome into Ein Gedi had been nearly complete. Only one thing kept them apart from the rest of the village: Pninah's seizures. They could have stayed with several families, including the one they now worked for, but instead, they kept themselves apart. So far, they had managed to conceal Pninah's condition. When the seizures had come, it had been when they were alone, in the evenings or at night.

"They say that the Romans have burned Jerusalem," Salema said, "and torn the walls down. But I don't believe that."

Pninah nodded.

"I think they probably did capture Aristobulus,"

Salema continued as they both began to strip to get into one of the smaller pools. "But they wouldn't have needed to burn anything."

"They took Damascus without destroying it," Pninah said. "I've heard the traders coming through confirm it."

"Do you think they'll leave?" Salema asked, sliding into the water. "Or are they now the ones in charge?"

"They'll go," Pninah said. "The Seleucids never stayed. They just wanted our taxes."

Salema submerged herself. She was under for quite some time, and by the time she resurfaced, Pninah had made her way into the water with her.

"I don't see why they were allowed to come into Eretz-Israel to begin with," Pninah said. "If they leave, we could go north again, pass through the canyon, and I could show you Jerusalem." She had said this without thinking, then realized her error and quickly looked at the girl. "Or we could stay here." The girl's face had darkened. "We'll stay here. We might see Ezra again if we went north."

"We might." A vein grew in Salema's forehead and her lips twisted. Pninah put a hand on the girl's arm.

"The farm," Pninah said.

Salema nodded. "I can't see the farm again. Not yet."

Pninah nodded in return. "We'll stay here. If for some reason we have to leave, we'll go south. Find the road to Beersheba like the Qumran priest said. See what is there. We can go anywhere we want."

"And stay far away from the Romans."

"And girl-selling wool traders riding donkeys," Pninah said and was rewarded with a laugh. Then Salema slipped back under the water again, coming up glistening and shivering but smiling.

"What's for dinner?" Salema asked as they re-dressed.

Pninah smiled and did not reply. There was nothing for dinner. Their stay at Ein Gedi had been safe from harm but not easy. They worked keeping house for a woman who had been ill for some time. They tended to the woman's children and looked after the affairs of the house, including cooking, but the work earned them no wages, merely meals. Recently, the woman's relatives had come up from the city Arad in the southern mountains to visit. The relatives were now looking after the woman and her family and would remain for another few weeks. Pninah and Salema's services were no longer needed, and they were being very careful with the few coins they had remaining.

They had lived in three caves so far at Ein Gedi. The first one they had vacated because of scorpions. The second because of a snake. It had been just one snake but a large enough one to put Salema off the location. Their third cave was higher above the settlement, but it satisfied them. In the winter, though, it would be too cold. They needed something better within a month or two at most.

Finished with bathing, they walked back up the narrow ibex trail, climbing the edge of the cliffs until they came to their small cave overlooking Ein Gedi and the Salt Sea.

"Tomorrow, we'll try the market again," Pninah said. "We can at least try. The baker looked like he would have hired us today."

"They were having quite an argument," Salema said with humour in her voice. "I wonder what he did to make his wife so angry."

"Whatever it was, it cost us his attention, but maybe tomorrow he can focus on us. His place is disorganized, some of the baskets are broken, and the whole place just needs to be cleaned. They are too busy by themselves. We can help them, even if just for a few days."

"Do you hear something?" Salema asked.

"Just the wind. Maybe thunder far away."

"There's no thunder this time of year," Salema said. "It's something else."

"I wish there were pastureland here for sheep," Pninah said.

"You liked our farm."

"I'd never been a shepherdess before." She immediately regretted saying this.

*Why do I keep bringing up the farm and making her sad?*

But Salema did not grow sad. Her attention was focused, her head cocked to one side as she listened. "I definitely hear something."

Pninah could hear it now as well, and the comparison to thunder, very distant long rolling thunder, was apt. It could be a storm. Or an army.

The first Roman to appear from behind a screen of palms caused both Pninah and Salema to flinch. They were well above the settlement, visible to any who cared to study the cliffs but not noticeable with all the buildings between the mountain and the Salt Sea to catch the wandering eye. The man they saw was red shirted and wore shining, solid armour. He rode proud, spine straight and shoulders back, and behind him marched a great rectangle of men similarly clad in red and silver, their armour chain mail instead of plate but otherwise matching the leading rider. The rectangle of men passed slowly but inexorably. Some of the men within the formation rode stately horses while the rest were on foot, swords and spears shining, banners furled and unfurled, olive skin and brown skin and pale skin intermixed within the throng. Then came the trumpets, and then more rectangles of men marching, and then more again. It appeared as if the entire Roman army was on the move.

Pninah lifted her eyes to the Moab Mountains across the Salt Sea and realized for the first time that she could faintly see the eastern shore there. Cypros, the Nabataean woman, would have travelled that route. The Romans chose the western shore.

"They're going to Raqmu," Pninah said.

Salema nodded but did not reply.

The army did not stop. The small settlement of Ein Gedi was of no concern to this vast formation of men and equipment. Another rectangle of soldiers passed, and then a different formation appeared, one of slaves carrying loads, lines of them shouldering great poles the length of six men or more, others dragging vast logs, wheels attached at one end, ropes strapped over the naked shoulders of those tasked with this burden. Slaves farther behind carried tools: great picks and hammers so large they must take two or more men to wield. Others wore yokes from which swung buckets that were clearly heavy. From the ground, it would have been impossible to see the burden that weighed these buckets down. But from their elevated view, Pninah could see that some contained iron balls. Others were filled with great spikes, and others yet bore curled up chains. These men looked beaten, not freshly claimed for this life of terror, but old hands at misery and torment. Their bodies bore old scars and filth that was the work of more than a march from Jerusalem to Ein Gedi.

Another group then passed, also slaves, chained about their necks, new bandages on wounds that for some still bled, loaded with packs that were tied to them. These looked like new slaves, men not yet inured to a life without hope, men who might fight or run given a chance. Their loads were bound to them. They were not trusted to hold on to anything. Some carried these loads on their backs, and others dragged them, pressed onwards by the Romans patrolling their flanks with whips, some short and cruelly tied up with bits of bone and stone, others smooth and long enough to reach the farthest recesses of the crowd to touch just one prisoner with the bite of Roman discipline.

"Those are Jews," Salema said.

"No," Pninah said. "Mercenaries. Men who worked for Aristobulus. Traitors to Hyrcanus, given to the Romans as their punishment."

"You don't know that," Salema said.

Pninah pointed towards a man near the front. "The tattoos on him," she said. "I've seen mercenaries around the Citadel with those markings. Those are not the markings of a Jew."

Salema nodded then.

There was nothing either of them could say when they saw what came next.

Women walked in the next group. They bore lighter loads than the veteran slaves and new prisoners. They were not as supremely turned out as the shining Roman soldiers, but their dress was not as dishevelled as the other slaves' either. Their tunics were simple but shorter than usual.

Their hair and skin looked clean. They carried their wrists crossed delicately in front of them and wore black cuffs that stood in stark contrast to the smooth skin visible there. The chains that passed from cuff to cuff were lighter than those that bound the men, but even from their mountain lookout, Pninah could see that they would do the job. The women were as much captives as the men. These walked without obvious distress or tears. These, like the first wave of slaves, were used to their lot. They did not carry loads beyond their personal packs, which were identical, as though some shop in Rome had specifically designed and manufactured such a captive's kit.

"That is what Ezra tried to sell us into," Salema said.

Pninah's heart rate did not slow down after the women passed, for what came next were creatures that had not been seen in Eretz-Israel since the days of the Seleucids' last great siege of Jerusalem: elephants. Five of the great creatures followed the women, their grand tusks draped with iron bars and poles affixed with knots of rope for the long march. Their tall backs were mounded with cases on iron brackets that were worked into leather harnesses that encircled each animal's great girth. The siege beasts were awe-inspiring transporters, and their march along the Salt Sea was a sight Pninah would never forget. It seemed like an entire village could have been mounded on top of one of these creatures. They plodded along at such a slow but relentless pace that Pninah wondered how the Romans would stop them when they made camp at the end of the day. When the elephants reached the stream that crossed the shoreline road, this final company came to a halt, and the elephants spread out and stood for some time drawing water up from the small pools to be found there.

After the elephants came more soldiers, both cavalry and foot. Then followed wagons pulled by great horses. The men who populated this unit did not look like slaves at all but like soldiers without armour or weapons. Perhaps they were cooks and camp makers.

"He's a doctor," Salema said, pointing at a man who rode alone in a cart pulled by a pair of donkeys.

"How do you know?" Pninah asked, but the girl did not answer.

The Roman army continued to pass for the rest of the late afternoon. On and on they came. Later that night, from their cliffside dwelling, the girls could see the invaders' fires beyond the immediate greenery of the Ein Gedi oasis. The Romans had made camp near another stream and rare patch of green beauty in this land that was otherwise rock and heat and salt water.

The next day, when the Romans had gone, Pninah and Salema walked south to see what could be found in the remains of the Roman camp. Of the tens of thousands that had camped there overnight, only three remained: a woman, dead; a man, one of the prisoners, also dead; and one of the longer-tenured slaves. This last man was not dead, but he had a large wound on one leg and great purple veins that ran from his leg up under his tunic. The veins around his neck were also raised and purple. Sweat poured from the man's forehead and neck, and his eyes were rolled back in his head. Only his rapid, shallow breathing betrayed that he was still alive. Others from Ein Gedi had also come to see what remained of the Roman camp, but no one approached the living man or the bodies of the other two.

The residents of Ein Gedi returned to the main settlement disappointed. No treasures had been left behind. They talked about the elephants for the next few days and the great destruction that the beasts had made. The animals had eaten everything around the Roman camp. They had even pulled down trees and stripped them of leaves and the finer branches.

"They're going to find the harvest in the Arabah and around Petra a little less rewarding," Ein Gedi's baker said to Pninah. "And yes, I can use your help."

# 44

## 63 BCE

A FEW WEEKS PASSED before Antipater followed Cypros back to Ashkelon. He had been away from the coast for three years. He came back no longer just the governor but something resembling a king. He came with kingly gifts for his wife, including an elaborate gold necklace strung with emeralds and pearls.

That night, the late fall air was unseasonably warm, cooled by a breeze from the nearby ocean. Cypros and Antipater retired to their colonnade of stone benches around the raised fire platform. Cypros kept a light shawl at hand, occasionally pulling it over her legs and torso for warmth and then removing it again, undecided about the night air.

"Pompey has finally left for Rome," Antipater said. "He's taken Aristobulus with him, along with the children. Royal captives for his collection."

"Shamirah?"

"Not Shamirah. She seems to have negotiated her freedom effectively."

"What do you know about Scaurus?" Cypros asked.

"Marcus Aemilius Scaurus," Antipater said. "The Romans do like their names."

"He won't get anywhere at Raqmu," she said.

Antipater frowned. His gaze did not move from the flicker of flames along the raised fire platform.

"Raqmu is impregnable," she said.

Antipater nodded but continued to stare and frown.

"The Romans cannot get into Raqmu," she said again.

Antipater let out a deep sigh and sat back into his cushions, stretching his legs. He looked out towards the ocean. "I haven't seen the ocean in almost three years," he said. "I can hear it and smell it, but I haven't seen it in a very long time."

"I was there with the children this morning. It's cold already. The saltwater pools are still there, waiting for spring. About Raqmu."

"They can't get into Petra," he admitted. "None of their siege equipment can knock a mountain down. As long as Aretas defends the Siq, which is rather easy to do when an army can only go a few men wide through it, Petra is safe. If Scaurus decides to send elephants through single file, all the Nabataeans have to do is figure out how to kill one and it will block up the whole channel. Aretas might starve to death in there or die of thirst, but the Romans won't get in."

"They won't starve or go thirsty," Cypros said. "Aretas has years' worth of grain and other goods stored up inside. They'll live well, waiting out the Romans. And the Romans will have effectively killed trade from the east for all the world. They can't traverse the Great Desert alone. Only Nabataeans know the way."

"Your uncle might not starve, but Petra's water supply runs through the Siq. It will be an easy matter for Scaurus to cut that supply off and use it for his purposes."

"You weren't listening to Herod's silly lectures about Raqmu's construction," Cypros chided. "They have years' worth of water inside as well. In cisterns, in aqueducts, behind two dams, in a lake even. They already grow vegetables there, and I'm sure that some of the trees are large enough to bear fruit by now. Aretas will do just fine. And it only takes a few men to escape over the cliffs and cut off the aqueduct line to the Siq, and Scaurus will find himself in the middle of the Arabah with no water. I've personally seen how that story ends. Unless you're Nabataean, the desert is a ruthless opponent. Ask the murderers of my family. Ask the Seleucids who went east into the Great Desert to escape their final war with us."

"Us?" Antipater said. "You're Nabataean again?"

Cypros pulled the shawl back over her legs. "Where is the necklace from?"

"Scaurus," Antipater said. "A pledge of friendship. He's a collector. He's amassed quite a collection of gems and seems to prefer them engraved. These were not engraved, merely mounted."

Cypros got up and walked over to the fire, then walked away from the fire and out into the darkness as though leaving for the ocean. After a moment, she returned and sat down on Antipater's cushion, leaning into him, and putting her hand alongside his face. She held out her other hand,

and when Antipater reached for her, she dropped something into his palm.

Antipater looked at her in surprise, then held the gift up to the firelight to see more clearly. A bejewelled necklace.

"Scaurus conquered Damascus," Cypros said. "The jewels probably came from a noble family in that city, friends of my parents. He would give you my family's treasures, stolen when they looted my childhood city. And you call that a gift of friendship? I expect you to go to Raqmu and do what you can to resolve things with your Roman friend. For my uncle. For my kin."

She walked away from the fire then, her shawl held in one hand, trailing behind her. She did not look back. She had not seen Antipater for weeks, and this was his welcome. Her ears listened closely, but he did not move from his stone seat. She knew, without looking, that he would stay many hours by the fire, brooding and thinking. Eventually, he would do the right thing. She had only to push him relentlessly and walk away. On this topic, his mind would do the rest.

# 45

## 63 BCE

For Pninah, waking from a seizure was not like waking from sleep. There was first only pressure and light, as though her awareness was rising from below water, the world soundless, sights indeterminant, waves pressing on all sides, into her eyes and the soft hollow of her throat.

This time, she felt the pressure of awareness in three places: the back of her head as it rested on small sharp stones, her left hand held in another's, and her right wrist held in a restraint. Sight conveyed only light and vague shapes. After a few moments, she registered sound, vague sound, like underwater murmurs, and with that came pain in her head, followed by an awareness of pain throughout her body. Her muscles, no longer seizing, throbbed with an ache that would last the rest of the day and longer.

Thinking of the rest of the day brought a consciousness

of place to her. She was not at the farm. She was not in Jerusalem. She was at Ein Gedi. She was at the baker's. She was outside the baker's shop.

Awareness of place brought awareness of her situation. This was the first time she had seized in public at Ein Gedi. Her secret was out. She could now distinguish voices. Concern and alarm intermingled. Salema was talking, protesting some point, and others were speaking. They spoke of her open but unseeing eyes, and so she closed them and willed her body to rest, but the hands holding her hand and wrist were relentless with their squeezes, caresses, and taps. They sought to bring her around when she wanted to leave.

*I am sorry to have done this to you.* It was a message for Salema.

Smell then came to her. That and taste were always the last to return. The smell of bread, of dust, even of the Salt Sea—all of it came to her like it was new. Her sense of smell was always at its best at this point in the recovery, and then it would fade and become regular again.

"How many times before?" someone asked Salema. A male voice. The baker.

Salema confessed its regularity, and there was a new wave of voices in the crowd: concern and alarm were joined by indignation. Pninah waited for it, and soon the word she dreaded most appeared. Salema protested, but the people at Ein Gedi had no permanent teacher or priest among them, and none knew anything about Anna or her judgments.

"Get rid of her," the baker said. With her eyes closed, Pninah sensed that he was playing to the crowd. "Get her up and gone from this place."

A swoon came at this point, during which Pninah heard

nothing and saw nothing, though she could still converse with herself like someone struggling silently, bound, underwater. Then hearing and sight returned a second time, and when they did, she could see and hear clearly again. Recovery was often like this, in two stages. She sat up. She sensed that it was Salema behind her, propping her up by pressing into her back and holding her shoulders and chest. No one held on to Pninah's hands or wrists anymore. No one wanted to hold down a demon. Her hands lay limp in her lap, and her lap was dry. That was a mercy.

She tried to move, but her limbs were loose, like a child's cloth doll. Firmness would come soon. She would not be strong for a day or more, but she would be able to stand soon. Salema understood.

Salema tucked her chin over Pninah's shoulder, supporting Pninah's head by letting it rest against hers. When Pninah straightened her head, supporting it on her own strength, Salema relaxed her embrace.

Pninah looked around and saw the villagers of Ein Gedi gathered. They kept their distance. They conversed among themselves with sideways glances at the demon-woman and her child, the two sitting in the dust before the baker's shop.

The baker came and crouched down before the pair, looking into Pninah's eyes. "You can see me now?" he asked.

She nodded. She knew not to try talking yet. They would become certain that she had a demon if she attempted her post-seizure, mumbled, slack throated speech.

"What did I ever do to you that you would bring this evil into my family's home?" he said, holding her gaze intently. He looked genuinely hurt, and then his expression changed to match the snarl that entered his voice. "You need to get out of here this afternoon. Now. Don't go back to your cave. Now we know why you both, two witches in our midst, preferred to live in caves. Get out of this place. Now."

The baker stood and walked away. The rest of the village distanced themselves from the pair but lingered, watching them closely. None came to offer water, brush the dust from Pninah's hair and clothes, or help Salema with her burden.

After a time, Pninah moved her arms and then her legs. There was great pain there, but she ignored it, braving mobility. Salema helped her stand up.

Pninah ignored the faces and voices around her. She had long ago ceased to look for pity or kindness. Someone had held her wrist, but that someone was gone, and she remembered the grip as one of restraint, not tenderness. Looking at the ground, she saw no feet coming to her side but Salema's. She did not look to faces for what could not be found in feet. To search otherwise was foolishness.

The pair walked away from the baker's house and ovens. "We can't go north," Pninah whispered.

"No," Salema said quietly. "We'll find the Qumran priest's road to Beersheba."

They did not say anything else as they passed south through the village. They walked along the shoreline, and when they came to the destruction that had been the Romans' camp, they passed through to its far side. Screened then by a tall boulder, Salema motioned for Pninah to rest in the shade.

Pninah sank down and leaned back against the stone, grateful to close her eyes. "Wait," she said, raising her hand slowly, but Salema was already gone. Pninah was alone.

There was no smell of decay here. The great black birds

of the desert had come and cleaned all three of the bodies left behind by the Romans. There had been talk within the village of jackals or even hyenas and whether the corpses would draw such beasts down from the upper lands or up from the Arabah, but none had come. Enough birds had passed through that the carcasses were clean and did not pollute the air.

She slept then for a while with her head tilted over onto one shoulder. She dreamed that she was just another body to be cleaned. Her murder and consumption would be an act of mercy for one otherwise forced to endure her illness. She saw her bones lifted by the largest birds and carried out to the sea, where flesh would float but bones would sink. In this way, in her dream, the land was cleansed. She was a burden to no one now—no one even had to bury her.

When Pninah awoke, Salema was crouched before her, watching her closely. Her expression asked, "How do you feel?" even though she said nothing out loud.

"Better," Pninah said.

"Liar," Salema answered.

A wry smile crossed Pninah's lips. She looked around and saw supplies from the cave, their two packs, the water skins filled and dripping.

"I took the back way," Salema said. "No one saw me." She picked up the knife and held it, thumbing its blade. "Do you think I could turn back a lion with this if we encounter one?" she asked.

"No," Pninah said.

Salema nodded. "Then I hope we don't encounter one."

The girl helped the woman stand, and then the two began to walk slowly south, bare feet on rock. Pninah looked at the haze over the water, then turned her attention inland where water still stained the rock in cracks from the previous day's rain. Winter approached, and with it there would be more rain.

*At least Av has passed. We won't die of thirst.*

They walked slowly for two days, sleeping out in the open, grateful for the lack of rain. After the two days, they ran out of sea to their left, and only the Arabah Valley lay before them with mountains to their right. Across the valley to the left, they could see the Moab Mountains as well. They paused and ate the last of their provisions, a few almonds and crumbs of stale bread that they carefully swept up from the bottoms of their packs. Salema found one last dried date that had somehow become wedged in a crease in her bag. She carefully bit half of it with a broad smile and then handed the other half to Pninah.

Afterwards, Pninah pointed, and the two shouldered their packs and continued south, looking for the road. They had full water skins, so they could allow themselves the comfort of conversation and quench their thirst when needed. At about midday, in mid-sentence, Salema suddenly jumped and screamed and hopped on one foot as a scorpion scuttled over the rock and disappeared between two large stones.

"Just a scare?" Pninah asked, but Salema's face said otherwise. The girl backed off from the scorpion's lair and then sat down, her face pale and distorted with pain, the one foot already starting to swell.

Pninah dropped her pack and knelt with the girl, taking her foot in her hand. She found the red point that the swelling was emanating from. There was no stinger in the wound.

"It's clean," Pninah said.

Salema nodded, looking only at her foot, trying to hold herself calm as a tear escaped and ran down her cheek.

Pninah helped her back to her feet and found them a new place to rest farther away from the scorpion's hideaway, although there was no practical danger now. The creature was gone.

Pninah opened her water skin and made the girl drink a little, but what she needed was time.

"It's getting numb," Salema whispered.

"How's the pain?"

"The same. The surface is numb. The pain is inside. So intense."

Pninah nodded.

Perhaps an hour passed, maybe less, Pninah had no way to tell the time, and then Salema's breathing began to change. The girl began to pant as though she had been running.

"Slow down," Pninah said.

"I can't breathe right," Salema said. "Like there are too many blankets. There's not enough air."

Pninah had felt this way before in the heat of Av, but the air now was cool, too cool. It would be cold tonight. There was no explanation for Salema's distress in the weather. She tried to remember what she knew about scorpion stings. She had no training about this and had never seen anyone stung.

A short while later, Salema suddenly sat up and vomited. A stream of water and half-digested nuts showered the rocks around them.

"My girl," Pninah said quietly, and she wrapped her arms around the girl, but Salema pushed her away. "I need to breathe," Salema said and stood up, hobbling with only the heel of her injured foot touching the ground even though the sting was on its upper side, not its toes or underside.

"We need to walk," Salema said.

"You have to rest," Pninah replied.

"Walk," Salema said. "We have to get to the road."

Five more times before dark, Salema's dry stomach retched up nothing but a thin stream of drool. The girl began to sweat and complain of the cold even though night had not yet fallen.

"You feel nauseous," Pninah said, as much a statement as a question.

The girl nodded and continued to hobble along, accepting Pninah's assistance, each with one arm around the other.

"If I have a seizure now, we're finished," Pninah said. It was an attempt at humour, and Salema snorted, something like an agreement.

"I need to sit," Salema said.

After a while, shivering more than the temperature justified, her foot severely swollen, she threw up once more, her insides finding some last trace to deposit on the rocks, and then she stood again.

"A bit farther," she whispered.

That night, the two wrapped thin blankets about themselves and shivered. Salema whimpered in her sleep, and Pninah barely slept at all. She wanted a donkey to put the girl on or a fire to give them warmth. There was nothing here in this place to burn, and she had never learned to build a fire without coals to start with. At one point in the night, she wanted to turn over, her hip and shoulder aching from the unpadded stone, but she did not want to disturb

Salema, who, despite her quick shallow breathing, seemed to finally be asleep.

Throughout the night, Pninah heard noises that she had never heard before, sounds of the night she had not even heard that first night sleeping alone in the Jerusalem to Jericho canyon. Grief and anger had driven her through that night. This night was different. Caring for another was different. She ignored the ache in her bones and tightened her embrace around the girl and felt the child ease back into her for whatever warmth they could share between them.

# 46

## 63 BCE

FOR THE FLOATING black spies of the high blue skies over the Zin Valley, west of the Arabah, the woman and the girl were an anomaly. This pair of humans did not walk like humans walked, purposefully targeting pools and streams, aiming for the well-defined paths. These two wandered as though they had no idea where they were going. And they did so as though they were one being, each with an arm around the other.

One day the girl dropped her pack, and it was left behind. The next day, a water skin. The woman and the girl often fell, the smaller one dragging the larger down. Once, they both tumbled over a small cliff only a few feet tall, staggering off it sightlessly and crashing into the desert below as though they had both fallen from a great mountain. The smaller one rolled and rolled on the ground, clutching her foot, and then throwing up precious water while the larger lay still for quite some time, long enough to give the birds hope. Then there was movement, and the woman sat up. The great birds soared past, continuing to explore what else might be found in the great expanse of the Zin and Arabah wilderness of stone and sand.

There was an army of men to the west of the red canyon that at first showed promise. This army ate abundantly, but they burned their waste indiscriminately. The smell of that camp overshadowed everything else carried by the wind. The feathered cleaners of the desert preferred armies that moved, not human pairs making their doomed but still-living way through the landscape. They liked armies that camped and set fires even less, as they left no place for birds to descend and forage amongst their leavings.

Pninah felt the dry weight of encrusted grime. She wanted to run her hands over her face to clean herself, but they were as dirty as her face must be. Like Salema's was. When it rained, they did not take the opportunity to clean themselves but huddled in the shelter of a boulder or a thin thorn bush. These shelters were no shelters at all. Water ran over and through their clothes. The two were like mute cattle in a field, able to do nothing but endure. When the rain relented, they could not preen on the desert's flat rocks like lizards, soaking up the sun, for what sunlight came through the haze was not enough to warm or to dry them. They had to walk to find warmth as they searched endlessly for the Petra-Beersheba Road.

They had no food. The rain gave them an abundance of water but no food.

"If it were Av, we'd be dead," Salema said, her voice cracked as though parched.

Halfway down the length of what they judged to be the Zin Valley, they finally found the road. It ran into the mountains to their right, the imposing cliffs that separated the Zin from the Negev, and also to their left, through a gap in those lesser heights and presumably into the Arabah. There were no markers to confirm either direction's destination.

Pninah pointed to the left. "That way looks easier," she said. "But it probably leads to Raqmu and the Romans."

Salema looked to the right and said, "I can't climb those mountains."

The distance was too far to see clearly, but the mountains were imposing, nearly as forbidding as those that overshadowed Ein Gedi.

Pninah made the choice for them, leading them on the right-hand path. The slave women trailing the Roman army and the woman's body at the Roman camp had communicated a clear message: though the mountains to the right seemed unclimbable, to go to the Romans was no choice at all.

As they walked, Pninah forced herself to look up, to keep scanning the valley around for signs of travellers on the road, to be the leader of this company of two. What she would do upon spying them she did not know. This did not seem like a route for families or benign traders. This was a path for bandits and other forms of violent men. The Romans might pass this way when they finished with Raqmu, perhaps travelling next to the Great Sea or Egypt.

There was no one else on the road.

"Maybe the Romans have scared off all trade," Pninah said.

Salema continued to silently limp beside her. Though they had not eaten for several days, the girl was still frequently nauseous. She rarely vomited now, but the swelling in her foot remained the same, and she shivered almost continually, even more so in the night. Pninah did not know whether this was from the scorpion's sting or simply from the weather, their lack of fire and shelter and food, and their always-wet clothing and blankets.

Up ahead, Pninah thought she saw a new branch in the road, a slight change in the land that was not merely an illusion brought on by running water or blowing sand. Her interest sharpened as they approached, and it eventually became clear that the way into the Zin Mountains had an offshoot to the left that led farther up the Zin Valley.

They stood at the crossroads for some time, uncertain which route to take. "The left path either goes to Egypt or goes a long way around these cliffs," Pninah said.

"Neither of us can climb that route ahead," Salema said, though they were still too far away to know for certain how steep that path might be.

"We'll go this way then," Pninah said. She chose the longer route or the route that would lead them away from their destination—she did not know which. She just started walking.

More mountains appeared ahead, and after some time, Pninah began to worry that they were not only off course but heading towards an equally punishing climb. She wanted to say so, but her worries were only speculation. Hunger clouded her mind. Clouds overhead smothered the light and brought afternoon gloom. Then she heard a rumble. She thought at first it was thunder, then realized that it was the sound of approaching men and hooves.

"Get off the road," she said and pushed Salema towards the nearest line of rubble. They quickly made their barefoot way across the small stones at the roadside edge and huddled down with their dust- and mud-stained blankets pulled around them, trying to disappear into rocks that were not much larger than their crouching bodies. The riders were on camels, riding to a Roman reception at Raqmu—or riding to somewhere else. They wore Nabataean headgear and long swords. Their clothing was the colour of the desert itself, like that of raiders seeking to blend into the landscape. Their style was the opposite of the Roman army's red and silver spectacle. These men carried no banners, but Pninah imagined bloodshot eyes above their mouth coverings and fists that might trail handfuls of entrails as their flag.

Crouched, silently watching, she feared that the men or the camels would pick up their scent. The filth that clung to her and Salema would betray them in this place without witnesses.

The armed company rode on and away. She put her hand on Salema's shoulder, keeping them hidden for a while longer, waiting and watching as the riders faded into the distance. At the place where she judged the fork in the road to be, the camel riders turned to the right, heading towards the Arabah.

She signalled for them to stand again, and they made their way back to the road.

Late in the day, the valley began to curve to the right, heading back towards the setting sun. The Zin Valley seemed to make a large turn here. Though she could not see around its cliffs, the turn suggested that they were not bound for Egypt after all. They would re-enter Eretz-Israel from its southern border.

Before dark fell, they moved off the road and found a flat place among several large boulders where they could sleep. There were three openings that led in and out of this sheltered nook. It was not a good place to defend themselves if a lion or hyena found them, but it was the best she could find. They curled up together on an accumulation of sand. The softness was a relief after nights of bruising bare rock. They pulled still damp blankets over themselves and pressed up against each other, using a piece of floodwater wood from some long-ago time as a pillow. It was the best place they had found in several days.

Pninah's hunger had abated. A kind of lethargy had taken its place. Below the starless night sky, she could feel her legs pulsing long after they had lain down. Salema shivered against her, and there was a scratching sound of some desert creature, something small, beginning its nocturnal activities. Eventually, sleep came, and though they both frequently woke in the night, they slept later than intended and began the next day's journey after the sun was already high.

At about mid-morning, they came to a place that filled Pninah with a new dread. The valley route had indeed turned around and was headed back north now, into Eretz-Israel, but the following valley passage was wider and smoother than their previous path. The route rose steadily upwards, but floods from previous years' rains had washed the way clear. If bandits came upon them in this place, there would be nowhere to hide.

There was nowhere else to go. Climbing the long gradual slope would be its own trial.

*I cannot worry about everything.*

She did not point out the problem to Salema. The two plodded along slowly.

As feared, she eventually heard riders in the distance, coming from Eretz-Israel again. It seemed that no travellers in the Zin Valley would come from Raqmu or the Arabah while the Romans were there. As the new company approached, Pninah could make out the squeak of wagons, but she could not see them, shielded as they were by what Pninah guessed were hundreds of riders. This company rode horses, not camels.

Pninah's heart sank as they approached. She and Salema moved well off the road, but there was nowhere to run to, nothing to hide behind. She prayed that the dirt encrusting them, the filth in their hair and on their hands, and the stench that rolled off them would be their shield. They might look old and worthless. They surely advertised their impoverished state. They might even appear diseased or possessed.

A seizure at this point would be just the thing.

Then she realized that the raiders might leave her and take Salema for their sport. She could not have a seizure here. She moved closer to the girl, putting her arm around her. They both kept their heads down.

The horses came on, and then a few camels, and then two wagons, one larger and one smaller. The company did not slow down, and she did not look up beyond the animals' hooves and legs to mark their passage. When they were well past and thundering down the Zin Valley road, she looked up. She took in the size of the group they had escaped, and as she did so, there was a shout in the company. A lone man on a camel slowed and broke away from the group, turning out into the desert, turning around, and then coming back towards them. There were other calls in the company, and the whole party seemed to slow down. The one camel rider came back towards her. He wore Nabataean clothing.

Pninah felt her heart race, and she clutched Salema. She wanted to say something reassuring, but she could think of nothing to say. The sound of her voice in this place might spark further trouble, just as her looking up at the back of the company had caused this one man to sense her and break away and return.

She breathed out slowly, aware that her breath was as foul as the rest of her. Her clothing was stiff and stank, and her body would surely offer nothing to attract a raider, however lecherous in this empty wilderness, draped as she was in this odour and dried mud. She felt dizzy, and as the man came to a stop before them, dismounted, and walked up to them, she kept her eyes down. Heat and a faint trembling washed over her—not a seizure. Fear. She and Salema might not attract the sport of lecherous men in their current state, but they could still attract a sword, the cruelty of death or injury or even torture. Men sometimes tormented animals for the pleasure of hearing them scream. How much more so a human? Particularly ones presenting an image as disgusting as she and Salema currently projected.

She wondered how quickly she could empty her pack

and get to the knife. She wondered how many she could cut before death claimed her.

The Nabataean crouched before them, bending to get a better looked at their downcast faces.

The rest of the company had stopped and turned back and were approaching. Pninah imagined the men developing a feral interest. She now understood that her and Salema's stink and poverty and hunger would be no deterrent to these men who lived on blood in a place without children or temples or homes. They should expect as much mercy from this lot as they might find in a lion's den, as much respect as their bodies might receive from the argumentative beaks of the desert's great black carrion birds.

*Just one man will be enough. If I die but kill one, that will be enough.*

A tremor ran through her, but the cowardice was gone. Salema was her daughter now. Or sister. She would give her life defending the girl.

She let one shoulder droop lower so she could get the pack off quicker.

The man crouched until his eyes could meet hers, and she looked up at him with a fierce expression and let the pack drop at her feet.

Then she saw the edge of a smile on one side of his mouth. Not a cruel smile. He nodded as though satisfied with a discovery that pleased him.

"The shepherdesses," the man said with his thickly Nabataean voice. "From the Jericho hills."

Pninah squinted in surprise. The man looked clean and well rested. His expression was that of happiness and not cruelty.

"Salema," he said. "And Pninah. Why are you here? What happened to you?" He looked from girl to woman and said nothing else, waiting for an answer.

"The Romans," Salema whispered. "They took our farm. They tried to take us, but we got away."

Pninah recognized him. One of Cypros's guards. Kaiden.

The larger company approached, and Kaiden stood up.

"Why have we stopped for these two?" a man asked. He was a Jewish man, wearing the clothing of some kind of royal official, riding a horse as did the rest of his countrymen.

"They're Jews," Kaiden said, and then he explained who they were. To Pninah's shock, the official-looking man got down from his horse and approached them. He put a hand on each of them, first their shoulders and then their faces, lifting their eyes to his. He looked from the girl to the woman.

"The Romans did this?" he asked, looking at Pninah.

"The wilderness did this," Pninah said. "The Romans never came within a hundred cubits of us." Pninah glanced at Salema, then back at the Jewish official. "And she was stung by a scorpion."

The man knelt and took Salema's foot in his hands, forcing her to balance on one foot and lean into Pninah for support.

"How long ago?" the man asked.

"Four days," Pninah said. "I think it was four days."

He released Pninah's foot and stood back up, signalling one of the other riders to him. "How long since you've eaten?" he asked.

"I don't remember," Pninah said. "I think the day after

the scorpion. We have water," she offered, holding up their one skin.

The man smiled and looked kindly at her. He turned to an approaching Jew and said, "What we wrapped up from this morning. And some watered wine." Then he turned back to Pninah and Salema.

"Do you know who I am?" he asked.

Pninah shook her head.

"I am Antipater, the husband of Cypros. You spent a year teaching my wife how to shepherd sheep when she should have been at Petra."

"She wanted to be near you," Salema said abruptly in her high child's voice.

She had clearly surprised Antipater, and he started to smile, but before he could speak again, the girl continued. "She wanted to see your victory over Aristobulus the Usurper."

To Pninah's relief, after a pause, the man finished forming his smile and then let it linger in his eyes as he spoke again. "That's right," he said. "You're Onias's daughter." He turned to Kaiden. "You left out the most important detail."

A Jewish man with a delicate white scar on the bridge of his nose approached and offered Pninah and Salema two small linen-wrapped packages. Upon opening them, they discovered honeyed goat-curd cheese pressed into leavened bread and rebaked so that the topping was browned and dry. They had been prepared earlier in the day. Pninah felt tears fall as she bit into hers, and when she looked at Salema, the girl was a wild child, like one born among animals in a pen, filthy and thin and ravenous as she consumed the offering.

Antipater had drifted off, but the man with the thin scar

remained, and when they had finished their bread, this new man offered them dried figs and cups of watered wine. They ate sitting along the roadside, without ceremony, without any thanks but their tears.

Antipater returned. "No more," he said. "Does the sting make you sick?" he asked Salema.

She nodded.

"Okay. Let your stomachs get used to this. You're out of danger now. There will be more. Just give yourselves time."

He motioned to Kaiden. "There is no point in you going back to Petra with me to negotiate with the Romans," he said. "The Romans may not appreciate that you slipped through their lines to begin with. I want you to go with Johanan and Shelomoh." Antipater motioned to the named Jews. "This is Johanan," Antipater said to the girls, pointing at one of the men. "And Shelomoh," he said, pointing to the man with the thin white scar.

"You three, take the smaller wagon. Empty its current contents into the bigger one and load up the spare horses. Leave four bedrolls for padding and take these two in the wagon. I don't see them being able to ride horses for some time to come."

He turned back to Pninah. "Have you ever ridden a horse?"

Pninah shook her head.

"See?" he said to his men. "So take them in the wagon. I want you to go to the inn this side of Beersheba. It has a good reputation. Get these two the best room they have," he said. Antipater motioned to another man who began to count coins from a bag. "And baths. They don't share the bath. Make them draw separate baths. Hot. New clothes. Good beds. Hot meals with meat and good broth."

"She needs green vegetables to help with her seizures," Salema said. Pninah was barely absorbing these proceedings, and Salema's interruption startled her. Pninah forced herself to sit still, saying nothing. Her stomach rumbled indelicately.

"Greens," Antipater agreed. He nodded at Shelomoh, who seemed to be the one taking mental notes. "Make sure she gets good greens with the meat and broth."

He nodded at the money man to count out a few more coins.

"Clothes. Cloaks. Sandals. And a doctor. For both of them."

Shelomoh nodded.

"How are you going to remember all of this?" Antipater asked.

"I'll treat them like my own family," Shelomoh replied.

Antipater nodded. "When they've recovered enough to travel again, take them to Ashkelon. Speak to Hanne, and she'll find them a place and get my wife."

Antipater turned back to Pninah and Salema, and it seemed that he wanted to say something else to them, then instead he turned back to Shelomoh and Johanan. "See that no harm comes to them. I want the best doctor in Beersheba to look at them. There is not to be a trace of a stain on their reputation. These are friends and guests of my family, and I don't want to hear even the slightest disrespect among the gossips. When you deal with the innkeeper and his wife, make sure they know that these two are precious to me, and

I will personally visit them on my way back to Idumea. I will reward goodness or evil as their hospitality deserves."

The two men nodded. Others were already emptying the small wagon, and before long, Shelomoh was helping Salema up into the back, and then Pninah climbed up alongside her. The small wagon lurched as it began to travel, and then the six of them—the two in the wagon, Kaiden on his camel, the wagon driver at the front, and the two Jews on horseback—set off up the Zin Valley road.

Pninah lay facing Salema. They could not change out of their still-damp clothes, but they were wrapped now in warm blankets. Tears hung in Salema's eyes, and they made Pninah's own begin to water again. After a few minutes of silently watching one another, Salema rolled over and then moved backwards, tucking herself into the curve of Pninah's warmth. They rode for the rest of the morning and into the afternoon, lulled asleep by the rumble of the cart. They were untroubled by the jolt of their transport when it encountered stones or ruts in the road. The voices of the men conversing with one another entered their dreams like incantations that blocked out all sources of evil.

# 47

## 63 BCE

THEY STOPPED LATER in the day, and Shelomoh heated water over a fire for Pninah and Salema to wash their hands and faces. The wagon driver and Johanan worked together to cook a quick meal.

Pninah felt the stiffness and grime in her clothes. They were finally dry, but there was no way to clean them, nowhere to bathe, and they had nothing to change into. She accepted the small meal of roasted vegetables, glad at least for clean hands, and then as the men packed up the horses, she crawled back up into the wagon with Salema.

"Do you need to sleep again?" she asked Salema.

The girl shook her head, and together they made comfortable seats out of the supplies they had, wrapping two blankets around themselves for comfort beyond just the warmth. The wagon set out again, and it was nearly dark when Johanan called a halt for the day.

Pninah walked about the small camp as darkness fell, staying well away from the men. Then she found her way over to Salema and lay down beside her. The girl pulled a blanket over them and was quickly asleep. It took Pninah much longer as her mind raced.

Shelomoh took the first watch in the starlit dark. She watched him as he shifted, stood, and occasionally walked around. Later in the night, she awoke to the sound of the watch changing, but she did not register which man was now up. She listened for where Shelomoh settled himself and thought she could hear his even breathing later in the dark.

The next day they set out again after a warm tea and light meal of two-day-old bread with stewed dates and figs pressed into the soft insides. Close to Beersheba, Johanan separated from the group and went on ahead at a quicker pace. When they arrived at the inn, Shelomoh went inside to speak to the proprietors, then returned with Johanan. When ready, a thin angular woman with white hair came out of the inn accompanied by two servants or slaves—Pninah was unsure which. The two were women, one middle-aged and one younger, about Pninah's age.

The tall woman motioned to Pninah and Salema. "Come, come," she said. She carried on with single syllables and clicks of her tongue as she helped her guests down from the wagon and led them into the inn. She took them straight into a bathing room, closing the doors behind them. The servants helped undress their two guests. Water was already boiling in several large pots in an adjacent room. The servants hauled and poured the pots' steaming contents into two tubs already partly filled. The older servant helped

Pninah into one bath while the younger servant helped Salema into the other.

Gentle hands guided Pninah back against the steam-warmed stone, her hair dangling over the edge of the stone tub. Her attendant poured hot water over her hair and set to work with aromatic soaps, letting the run-off drain away along grooves in the floor to some place outside.

"Sit up," Pninah's attendant said kindly. It was the first time she had spoken, and to Pninah's ear, her accent sounded Egyptian. She felt uncomfortable being cared for in this way, by strangers, perhaps even by a gentile, but she sat up, and the woman began to scrub at her neck and back with a soft cloth. Filth came away, and the water in the bath darkened. She lifted her arms when directed, and the woman's hands were efficient, delivering almost a massage as she cleaned and rinsed, cleaned and rinsed.

The proprietor's wife was fussing with other boiling pots in the side room that seemed to be open to the air above, mixing the contents between pots and barking instructions at her staff. Occasionally she asked Pninah and Salema questions but did not wait for answers. This did not seem to be a matter of rudeness but rather of habit, as though the woman could only function with conversation, even if she only conversed with the air.

The two servants offered occasional soft-spoken instructions and little else.

When the water reached a state of particular murk, the serving women reached into the tanks and, after some vigorous pulling, removed a plug from each one. The water drained out into a pipe that also emptied somewhere outside.

"Lift," the proprietor's wife said, holding a bucket near the head of the tub.

Pninah hesitated, not understanding what was being asked of her. Then it became clear that the woman wanted to rinse the tub, but Pninah did not know how to stand up modestly. She finally crouched in the tub, trying to cover herself. The woman poured her bucket into the tub. The older servant used her hands to move the last of the heavier dirt down and out the drain. Operation complete, the woman reinserted the plug and, with many trips back and forth to the adjacent warming room, refilled the tubs with clean, warm water.

Then they repeated the previous procedure: the soaping, the cleaning, the rinsing, and finally the redraining of the tub. Pninah sat still, her knees drawn up to her chest, her arms wrapped around them. The tall angular woman came and stood over Pninah, looking down at her, holding a large blanket.

"You're a bit too big, my dear, for me to pick up," the woman said. "You'll have to stand on your own."

Pninah got up hastily, embarrassed, and the woman quickly wrapped her up in a heavy blanket.

"You dry yourself off, and we'll get another one for your room." She then turned her attention to Salema, who was similarly being wrapped in her own oversized towel. Once the blanket was in place, Salema stood still, and the woman got down on her knees and inspected Salema's sting site.

"Does it still cause you pain?" the woman asked.

Salema nodded. "But not as much as before. It feels numb now."

The woman nodded and stood. "The doctor is on his

way. He'll give you something for the pain. The sting will go away on its own, but it will take many days yet."

She led her guests down a short hallway and opened the door to a room with two small beds. Though it was still early in the evening, two lamps were already burning.

"Your clothes are not fit to clean," the woman said. "The governor has made sure you are well provided for. New clothes will be ready for you in the morning." She scooped up a folded blanket and held it open in front of Pninah, beckoning her to come closer. Pninah stepped into her embrace, and the woman closed the blanket around her.

"Drop the wet one," the woman said. Pninah did so, and the proprietor's wife finished wrapping her up. When Pninah took a step away, the woman scooped up the wet blanket and handed it to one of the serving women. She did the same for Salema, handling this task personally, and when they were both dry and wrapped up, she shooed the servants away and started to leave herself, pausing at the door.

"It is late, but we have a nice lentil stew," she said. "The bread is from this morning. The wine is not watered down."

After a pause, Pninah realized that there had been a question in there somewhere. "That would be nice," she said, hoping she was saying the right thing.

The woman nodded and left the room, closing the door behind her.

After the woman was gone, Pninah, seated now on her bed, looked across the room at Salema with wide eyes. The girl stared back at her.

"What just happened?" Salema asked.

Pninah nodded.

"I've never seen a room like this in my life before," Salema continued, looking around at their accommodations. "And this bed. I've never seen one like it. Have you felt it?" She had her hand on the mattress, feeling its cushion while her eyes darted from the exotic copper lamps to the intricate, geometric carvings that framed their small door, from the colourful mosaic on the floor to the light that still filtered in through high, deep windows. "What did she mean by 'it's late'? It's still light outside."

Pninah shrugged. "I could eat some proper stew. The soldiers burned most of what they cooked."

Salema laughed and lay down on her bed.

"Did she mean that the doctor was coming today or tomorrow? After all, it's pretty late."

Pninah laughed and wanted to throw something at the girl, but she did not know what was safe to throw, and suddenly she was very, very tired. She lay down on her bed, marvelling at the mattress. She pulled her blanket close about her.

Before falling asleep, she felt the bed move, the young girl pressing in beside her, and soon the sound of their breathing synchronized. Both slept more deeply together than they had in months.

❧

The door opened a while later, and the proprietor's wife entered, for once not talking to others or herself. She saw the sleeping figures and frowned. She set a tray with steaming bowls down on a small table and left quietly, giving orders throughout the inn for silence.

When the doctor came, the proprietor told him to return in the morning.

❧

When the group left Beersheba, the morning air was clean and cool as though it had recently rained. The night's dew resisted absorption into the dry ground this one morning and chose instead to hang in the air to cool travellers as they started on their way.

Shelomoh took her arm as he helped Pninah up into the wagon. She found a comfortable seat against one low wall with Salema opposite her. She hoped nothing showed on her face, but for the rest of the day, she felt his handprints on her arm as though he was still holding her. No man had touched her since Gavriel.

❧

When they arrived in Ashkelon a few days later, Cypros was expecting them.

"The innkeeper sent a runner," Shelomoh explained to the girls. "Don't worry. They'll find a way to put it on Antipater's bill." He smiled as he spoke, as though this were somehow a secret between them, though the conversation was not private.

In total, they had spent four nights in the care of Shelomoh, Kaiden, and the other two men—one on the road to Beersheba, two at Beersheba being treated like royalty, and one en route from Beersheba to Ashkelon.

Ashkelon reminded Pninah of Jerusalem and Jericho. It was clear that important people lived here. The governor's compound only added to that impression, and Salema was particularly awestruck.

"I don't believe this place," Salema whispered to Pninah the next day.

"You should go down to the ocean," Pninah said with a smile.

Salema nodded. The girl was older than Cypros's children. At twelve years of age, she was only a few months older than Phasael and considered a woman now by many, though her body was only just beginning to change. This day, she did not look like a woman yet. She had the bright face of a child going to visit the Great Sea for the first time.

"Hanne is going to take us," Salema said.

"Don't go in the water," Pninah said. "It's not the time of year yet for swimming."

Salema made a face, then said, "You're not going to come?"

"I've been. At Joppa. You go have fun."

The girl ran off, a child again, if only for today.

Salema ran with Cypros's youngest, Salome, though the girl was only five years old. Nearly six. As they ran together, laughing with young-girl voices, it occurred to Pninah that this might be the first time that Salema had been just a girl. Not a shepherdess, a cook, a cleaner, a worker on her father's farm, but a girl with a friend.

Hanne went along to oversee the children, but most did not need her care. Perhaps only Salome did.

"I like Hanne," Pninah said to Cypros.

Her host nodded without saying anything.

"Why is Antipater going to Raqmu?" Pninah asked. "He can't possibly take on the Romans with the men he had with him. I saw the Romans. There are thousands of them. Tens of thousands. Elephants even."

Cypros smiled. "Elephants won't be much use at Raqmu."

"Their soldiers are not like ours."

"He's not going to fight," Cypros said, taking Pninah's hand and walking with her back into the palace. They made their way to an interior courtyard of low stone benches surrounding a fat olive tree that grew up within its centre. She gestured to Pninah, and the two sat facing the tree. "Scaurus is leading the Roman siege, and he trusts my husband. King Aretas is essentially my father—uncle, to be precise. He also trusts my husband. Antipater is there to broker a peace."

"He's going to get Aretas to surrender?"

Cypros laughed out loud. "No, certainly not. Peace. Not surrender. The Romans are fine in the winter months outside Raqmu, but when spring comes and then summer, the god of the desert will consume them. They'll starve, thirst, and bake alive in their armour. There are too many of them for that stretch of land with no access to the oases beyond the Siq." She smiled, but it was not a kind smile. "Al-Qaum cannot be defeated by the armies of Rome. The Seleucids learned that decades ago."

"Who is al-Qaum?"

Cypros looked quickly at Pninah and then smiled a smaller smile. She waved the question away and turned her attention back to the olive tree.

"Antipater will broker a peace—a tribute payment, a nod towards improved trade relations—something of that sort. Then the Romans will leave. My husband will come home, and his influence in Jerusalem, Nabataea, and even Rome will only be improved."

She gestured towards the gnarled trunk before them. "We are like that tree. The world may change around us, but we only thicken and improve. Olive trees live forever," she said. "Did you know that?"

*You are nothing now like our bored visitor among the sheep.* Pninah did not say so out loud.

"What plans do you have?" Cypros asked.

Pninah shook her head. "None. Look after her. I didn't think we would survive the desert. I didn't even know for sure that we were on the Beersheba Road."

"Her foot is fine now," Cypros said. "A few more days, and there will be no sign that she was ever stung."

Pninah felt water come to her eyes, and she leaned forwards, elbows on her knees, staring at the olive tree's exposed roots. "I thought I had killed her."

Cypros put a hand on Pninah's back. "You don't have a scorpion sting and no power to control one."

"It was my seizure that drove us out of Ein Gedi. We could have stayed there, safely, but for me."

"In a cave? Over the winter?"

"It's my seizures that made us live in a cave," Pninah said, her voice barely above a whisper but with a raw edge in its tone.

"I suppose you stoned her father as well. And arranged for Ezra's betrayal. And you brought the Romans here too."

The last bit gave Pninah pause. She looked up at Cypros. "Your husband," she said and then did not finish the thought.

"Yes. My husband. In fact, it was I who invited them

to Eretz-Israel. But that's a story for another day. Jerusalem, though, is ruined as a result. All of it."

"It was already ruined," Pninah said. "I left Jerusalem on purpose." She kept her eyes on the gnarled tree before them. "We knifed our own people in the streets. Crucified them outside the walls. Spied on each other. Lied to each other and about each other. Stole from one another. Abused people who couldn't defend themselves. Made them work long days in a field and then stole their money at the end of the day. Spent money meant for food on prostitutes. Women from Greece and Egypt and Africa and probably even Rome work in Jerusalem, wearing clothes as fine as yours, but they have no husbands and no children."

She looked at Cypros. "Three times men came for me in that city."

She looked back at the tree. "Twice I escaped on my own, and another time fellow labourers helped. I lost the right to work in one place because of such a man, and I went hungry more times than I can remember."

She turned to look at Cypros again and caught an expression that was more than just sympathy. There was something deeper than sympathy or even pity in the woman's eyes. There was recognition and empathy that did not make sense.

"The only difference between the Zin Valley and Jerusalem," Pninah continued, "is I could bathe as often as I needed to in Jerusalem. Otherwise, they are the same—scorpions and lions stalk you in the desert, and people stalk you in the city. And I don't know which is worse."

Cypros looked like she wanted to say something. The

expression on her face was one of naked recognition. She opened her mouth, but nothing came out.

"I'm glad it's been torn down," Pninah said. "Now it's as ruined as it tried to make me."

Pninah stopped talking and looked away from Cypros, past the olive tree, and beyond the courtyard to the smooth mosaics and columns beyond. She felt heat in her face. She was exposed now, no longer the sweet shepherdess of the Jericho hills. She could be foul not just with unwashed sweat and grime but also with carried sins, hates, and the stench of despair that did not belong in a beautiful place like this. She thought of Shelomoh then, and she wanted to cry.

Cypros's hand had not left her back. Pninah did not realize this until the hand moved, rubbed her back, and then stroked her hair.

"You're not in Jerusalem anymore," Cypros said. "But I want to take you there again."

Pninah looked at her and saw once more the strange acceptance and emotion on the Nabataean woman's face.

"I want to see it again, through your eyes," Cypros said. "Will you go with me?"

"To Jerusalem?" Pninah asked. "While your husband is away?"

Cypros laughed. "Well, he won't be pleased with it when he finds out. But he's not here to say no. And I am the governess of this region, so if I order transport for Jerusalem, we will go to Jerusalem. And we'll stay in the finest inns on the way there."

Pninah laughed, then grew quiet again. "Salema shouldn't go. Not yet. Her first view of the city should not be the aftermath of the Romans. Her father was murdered there."

"I'll arrange it. She can stay here with Hanne and the children."

"Good. She should be a child again for a few more months."

# 48

## 63 BCE

J ERUSALEM HAD NOT been destroyed. Rather, sections of it had simply been erased. What Pninah had expected to see from stories of conquests past was the rubble of broken walls, burnt beams, and collapsed roofs. Instead, the outer walls of Jerusalem were either perfectly intact or completely missing. Likewise, houses were either unharmed or gone. Whole sections of the city had been wiped clean, as though God's own arm had made a sweep of it. She could barely distinguish streets from old housing blocks—they were both blank spaces. The upper market was gone. Roman efficiency was in evidence all around.

Pninah got down from the cart and walked on ahead. She was still unused to her sandals, but walking into Jerusalem's new landscape, she did not notice the strange footwear. She could barely understand what she saw before her.

She kept walking, forgetting her host, walking until

she came to the edge of the Tyropoeon Valley, which was no valley at all anymore. She turned, eyes wide, face pale, and found Cypros behind her, and their horse and driver and escort farther back.

Without a word, Pninah turned and walked farther, past where the Zion Bridge had been, where remnants of it remained. Workers were busy swarming the broken stonework. She could not tell whether they were finishing its demolition or repurposing it as an access ramp. She walked on, trying to find landmarks that she recognized, and then she stopped and pointed down.

"You found it?" Cypros asked.

Pninah nodded and was surprised as emotion welled up. "My favourite tree," she said. "It was right about here. Down there."

"I'm sure it was beautiful," Cypros said. "A valley in the middle of the city. But it also had a bad reputation, even for Jerusalem."

Pninah looked along the curving length of rubble that had once been her valley. She could not smell the forest any longer, nor the pollution that settled in low places. She smelled only stone dust. "Yes," she said finally. "I thought it was our place of refuge in the city. Then bad things happened to me there. Bad things had always happened there. I just chose not to see them before."

"Now it's gone."

Pninah nodded. "Now it's gone. Let's go see the Temple."

The Romans' great stone launchers had done crushing but isolated damage to the walls of the Temple. Their mission had been entry, not destruction. Pninah had heard from Hanne and others that Pompey had entered the Holy of Holies. Sadducean priests had been slaughtered alongside their sacrifices. Before the Temple had been broken into, stones misthrown over the wall had crushed many of the interior decorations and people and had even broken some pillars. Much restorative work had already been undertaken since the Romans had left. The Temple did not look as bad as it could have.

Inside the Temple, Pninah searched for Anna, and then when she found her, she discovered that she could not bear to talk to her. Pninah left almost right away, leaving Cypros and Anna to converse while she went back to the public areas.

Near the main entrance to the Temple, where the Zion Bridge had once stood, she watched the workmen preparing to lever a huge stone into position. The number of men involved in this work staggered her imagination. Pompey had taken nothing from the Temple treasury. The treasury would now pay for all this and more.

She thought of Gavriel then. She wondered if he was among the workers that were spread out as far as she could see, carrying, building, repairing. He would not be among the stoneworkers nor the woodworkers nor the engineers, but perhaps he served as a runner, passing between groups like a sparrow among eagles and lions.

She stared again at what had been the valley. She had a hard time remembering its depths clearly. It had curled around the Temple Mount the way she had curled around Salema in the desert. The valley had protected the Temple. Now an army could march right up to its walls. The ground was uneven but solid. The valley had been filled beyond need, for the army had only entered at two breaches. The

Romans must have a compulsion to be thorough for its own sake. She could think of no other reason for this complete remaking of the city.

Cypros found her as dusk approached.

"You said you had something to talk to me about after we visited the Temple," Pninah said.

Cypros led Pninah towards another view of the former valley and the remnants of the Zion Bridge. "Who owns that land?" she asked, pointing towards land to the left of where the bridge had once stood.

They were looking at flat waste where previously there had been only open air. "Down below?" Pninah asked. "Underneath the new fill? I don't know; I don't think anyone. It was just rocks and trees and the stream at the bottom. There were no houses in that part of the valley. Our house—my house—was a little farther on." She pointed in the general direction.

"So who owns it now? This section, I mean."

When Pninah didn't answer, Cypros turned and caught her eye. "Who?" she asked again.

"I don't know."

"This land didn't exist before the Romans," Cypros said "It's new land, and I'm not leaving Jerusalem until we own it."

"We?"

Cypros smiled. "Yes. We. I have a plan. If anyone asks, you had a house down there. Right down there, among the trees, forgotten by anyone who keeps records, like the Sadducees and their followers."

She turned away from the view and this time led Pninah back into the Temple.

"Did you know that the Sadducees' side lost twelve thousand men to the Romans?" Cypros asked casually. "Priests. City business leaders. Shop owners. Even mansion owners and their wives, their children all burned, beheaded, thrown from the walls, run through with spears.

"Others were taken away with Aristobulus and the rest of the captives to Rome. They will be paraded in Rome and then sold there."

Cypros said all this as they found their way to the rest of their company.

"The entire Sadducean apparatus has been dismantled. Not gone. But thoroughly scattered. They will spend years trying to recover themselves. They have no power anymore. The Pharisees will make the important decisions now, including what to do with this new land. With everything changing now, it is time for Idumea to claim its share. Starting with you and me."

Pninah had no idea what to say to this. She climbed up into the wagon with Cypros.

"You cannot be a labourer," Cypros continued as the wagon rolled along. "Seizures will keep striking you down. But you can be a landlord. You can live off the rent of those who are privileged to have the use of your buildings. You would care for them and their workers the way you cared for your sheep—you looked after the sheep, and they supplied you with wool. I think five. Do you think five?"

"Five? Five what?"

"Five buildings. Small, of course. Modest. Shops on the bottom, residences above and behind. Near the Temple to take advantage of its traffic. You and Salema can live in one. Perhaps Hanne as well."

"Hanne?"

"She cannot work for me forever. Perhaps a few years more. The three of you can live above one shop. The others you can rent out, presumably to the shop owners who will live above their shops. Perhaps one will need more space for their business, and they can also rent the shop below you. You'll have a servant as well. Someone to take care of you. To help with cooking and cleaning, but also to protect you if you have a seizure. Your own attendant."

"We can't live alone—three women together."

"Why not?"

"How would I pay for this?"

"With the rent. Five shops. Four apartments."

"Nine places?"

"Ten, including where you'll live. But yes, you'd collect rent from nine."

"Where will I get the money for this?"

"From me. You'll pay me back, of course. You'll pay a regular payment for the properties until the debts are settled. All you have to do is choose tenants wisely and collect their rent on time. When they know that it is me who they are ultimately renting from, they will give you no problems with collection. Still, choose wisely. If you care for them, they will care for you."

They rode in silence for what used to be several city blocks while Pninah tried to process this. "How, even if you could do this, would you do this?" It was bad wording, and she was embarrassed. She tried again. "Women don't own businesses and land. And who would you buy the land from?"

"Women do own businesses and land. Have you not

heard of the vineyard up in Galilee, the one that makes that wine, the one with the red seal beside the handle?"

Pninah shook her head.

Cypros looked at her, then looked away. "Well, never mind. It's not common, but they do. And in terms of how I'm going to buy the land, I'll buy it for nothing at all."

"What? How?"

Cypros's gaze focused ahead, as though she were tracking some prey the wagon was creeping up on. "My husband leads this country now. Hyrcanus is high priest, and he owes us. For six thousand dead Nabataeans, the death of my husband's brother, the Roman bribes paid by Idumea and Nabataea, the loss of Damascus, now the siege of Raqmu, two years of my life living in a tent—that man owes me. He's high priest again, thanks to me. But not king. Antipater leads the civilian administration. So, between Antipater and Hyrcanus, we can do whatever we want in Jerusalem. And both men will do what I tell them to do."

Pninah looked at her host in surprise.

Cypros patted Pninah's knee. "Don't worry. We've got some formalities with the Sanhedrin ahead of us, but we'll get it done. Actually, Antipater has a few formalities with the Sanhedrin. He'll get it done. Half the Sanhedrin were Sadducees anyway, and they're all gone for now. The Pharisees will do whatever my husband and Hyrcanus direct. It will just take a bit of time. Before we leave Jerusalem, we'll start on the arrangements for the builders. Have you ever designed a building for five businesses and five residences?"

"Why would you do this for me?"

Cypros seemed to be staring at something far off in front of them. Pninah did not follow her gaze.

"Why would you do this for me?" she asked again. She watched the woman's eyes. They looked heavy and sad.

When Cypros spoke again, she did so very slowly. "I too have walked through the desert and come out alive," she said. "It's not something I can explain. Let's just say that I need to do this for you."

She moved as if to wipe her face, then put her hands back down. "I've left my dead in the desert, unburied. And I've had my dead taken from me and buried where I cannot find them. My words have torn down walls. But I've never built them. I've never grown anything. I am not doing this for you." She kept staring ahead. "I need you to do this for me."

She turned towards Pninah then with inexplicably watery eyes. "Now, what about the buildings? What kind of shops do you want?"

It was Pninah's turn to not respond immediately. The cart below them creaked and rattled over stone streets. Cypros's emotion distracted her. She saw it but did not know what to make of it. Then a thought came to her. It came with the feeling she had first felt when she had planned to go for her knife, before discovering it was Kaiden who had found them in the desert. It was a feeling not of fear but of forward momentum. It was the feeling of choosing, regardless of what came next. It was fear after all. But a good fear.

"A pottery shop." She spoke with a low voice, as though thinking out loud. Then she saw Cypros's expression and held her gaze. "My mother made pottery."

"A shop or a workshop?"

"I want a shop in front and a workshop in the back. Both."

Cypros smiled. "Now you've got the idea." She gave a brief instruction to the driver, then turned back to Pninah. "Yes. That's bigger than modest; that's two businesses in one: workshop and storefront. I like it. Greedy." She smiled at Pninah, then scrunched up her lips and nose into an expression Pninah associated with playing with babies. Then the woman burst into laughter. "You are the owner," Cypros said. "I want Salema to be your helper until the right man comes along. When that time comes, you will be her family and supply the dowry. Agreed?"

Pninah nodded.

"Good. Hanne will be your steady partner. She'll stay with me a few years longer until Salome is a bit older, but she'll come to stay with you more and more. By the time Salema moves on to start her own life, Hanne will be ready to join you. But you'll hire your own attendant. Hanne is not to be your nurse; I want her to have her freedom. She will own a half-interest in the buildings when she joins you and will help you manage them. What else?"

"What else?"

"The next business. If you're going to design one, you might as well design them all. What do you want the next business next to the Temple to be?"

# A Note from the Author

*Bitter for Sweet* is of course the story of Herod the Great's mother, Cypros. Her battles against racial, sexist, cultural, religious, and other prejudices are not foreign to us today. The terms of the conflict have changed over two millennia, but the rough outline for these conflicts has not. From the little that history records of her, she was quite a woman.

This book is also a tale about my daughter, whose name is not Pninah but who, much like Pninah, suffers debilitating attacks of the muscle kind. For me, Pninah's part of this tale charts an internal geography, not a historical one. I have kept the setting, circumstances, and cultural responses to Pninah's condition as accurate to the era as possible. But the heart of her struggle is, for me, timeless and personal. I share this so that readers familiar with differing flavours of epilepsy, or those sensitive to depictions of medical conditions in literature in general, understand that status epilepticus is not just something interesting I found in research books. Writing about this topic was not an academic exercise. By sharing Pninah's story in the context of Cypros's, I wish to practise the truth that serious medical conditions do not define a person, but they should not be invisible either. They can appear in literature. And there are parts of any condition, visible or not, that may have effects under the skin as great or greater than those the eye can see. Literature is especially well equipped to expose those otherwise hidden parts of life.

Over twenty years ago, Mackenzie Emily Potter laid claim to some of the deepest places in my heart. Since then, she has taught me almost everything I know about the muscle kind, and many other things as well. I wish she were well enough to set herself up in life such that she, like Pninah, could make more of her own choices. Her condition, however, is much worse than Pninah's. This book is for her.

# A Review Request

If you enjoyed *Bitter for Sweet*, please consider taking a minute to leave a review wherever you buy books. Reviews help other readers find my work, and it would mean a great deal to me if you took a moment to tell others about your experience.

**To Experience More:**
If you would like to read my author's commentary on these books, ask me a question, sign up for my newsletter, or find out about upcoming publications, please visit my website at

darylpotter.com

May your differences constrain you as little as possible and not only be a task to overcome but something that gives your life meaning and beauty. And along the way, may you be blessed with people who love you while you grow.

Daryl Potter
May 27, 2021
Oakville, Ontario, Canada

# Acknowledgements

From the very start of this writing journey, I talked to my wife about the third book. *Keziah's Song* was deeply emotional for me and laid the foundation for the books to follow. *Blind Man's Labyrinth*, as its dedication suggests, was also very personal. But I've been planning *Bitter for Sweet* from the beginning. Cypros's story meant a lot to me, and the addition of Pninah was a surprise that grew out of the writing itself. Cypros was planned. Pninah was not.

Trilogies are traditional, and in a sense this book closes a loop in Jewish history: it charts the course from Seleucid control of Israel through independence (characterized by civil war) and finally back to foreign control—this time by Rome. In addition to closing a loop, this third book opens a new direction for the ones that follow.

The first eyes to help me polish *Bitter for Sweet* were from a writing group I attend regularly. Thyra Root, Frederick Faller, Renaldy Kalixte, E. J. LeBlanc, H. Halverstadt, Heather Peach, David Joutras, and Rebecca Storozuk all reviewed the first chapter and provided invaluable insight. Their input helped shape not only that chapter but also my later revisions throughout the rest of the novel.

Amelia Wiens came next, and her first pass of the entire

manuscript diagnosed a significant problem that I was able to correct in the subsequent rewrite. Her unflinching feedback was the corrective I needed, even though it cost me months of hard revision work.

Amelia also took on the final stylistic and copy edit of this novel, and S. Robin Larin once again did a fantastic job in the proofreader role. A big thank you to both for sticking with me as I work on this multivolume project.

Damonza was once again on duty for cover design and typesetting. They remain an essential component of my creative team, and I'm very happy with how this part of the project also came together to help create a final unified whole.

Flavius Josephus, the first century CE Jewish historian, continues to be my primary source for the basic historical outline of these books. Josephus proved problematic this time around, as his two histories have several contradictions that impact the period in question. As a result, an extra amount of supplemental research was required to sort through the archaeological and historical records and finalize a clean picture of the era.

In addition to Josephus and countless other resources, three books on the Herodian period were particularly helpful. The first of these was *The Many Faces of Herod the Great* by Adam Kolman Marshak. Following this book, *Herod the Great: Statesman, Visionary, Tyrant* by Norman Gelb helped clarify many of the complexities of the period, and *Herod's Judea: A Mediterranean State in the Classic World* by Samuel Rocca took previous simplifications and gave them nuance and complexity. History is not linear or straightforward, and these various viewpoints were immensely helpful to both the research and creative stages of this work.

Kenneth E. Bailey's *The Good Shepherd* was my introduction to ancient Middle Eastern shepherding practices. It served as a launching point for further investigations regarding details his book first brought to my attention.

Lastly, I would like to thank my wife and children. This project would not be possible without their support. Many dinner-table conversations revolve around storyline ideas, approaches to research, new discoveries, and the art of making ancient times relatable to a modern audience. Their perspectives change mine and so help shape the books that follow. For their listening ears, input, and encouragement, I am always impressed and grateful.

www.ingramcontent.com/pod-product-compliance
Lightning Source LLC
Chambersburg PA
CBHW050844210726
48290CB00004B/1082